THE POSTHUMOUS PAPERS OF SIDNEY FEIN

Robert Wexelblatt

ISBN: 978-1-938349-88-1
eISBN: 978-1-938349-89-8

Cover illustration: August Macke, "Portrait of Ludwig Deubner," 1902

Typewriter Underground material produced in collaboration with Marc Zegans.

Layout and Book Design by Mark Givens

First Pelekinesis Printing 2018

For information:
Pelekinesis, 112 Harvard Ave #65, Claremont, CA 91711 USA

Library of Congress Cataloging-in-Publication Data

Names: Wexelblatt, Robert, author.

Title: The posthumous papers of Sidney Fein / by Robert Wexelblatt.

Description: Claremont, CA : Pelekinesis, [2018]

Identifiers: LCCN 2018027141 | ISBN 9781938349881 (pbk)

Classification: LCC PS3573.E968 A6 2018 | DDC 814/.54--dc23

LC record available at https://lccn.loc.gov/2018027141

www.pelekinesis.com

THE POSTHUMOUS PAPERS OF SIDNEY FEIN

Robert Wexelblatt

PRAISE FOR ROBERT WEXELBLATT

"Read here and there, mostly anywhere and no matter in what order; you'll think you're in Wonderland."
  —Ricardo Nirenberg's review of *Petites Suites* in *Offcourse Literary Journal*

"Thought-provoking, entertaining, and eloquent, like so any of his stories in *Petites Suites*, you can't help but marvel at Wexelblatt's ability to move and enchant in just a few concise pages. This inspired and truly original story collection is an exquisite joy, offering the equivalent beauty and charm a fine symphony might accomplish."
  —Nicholas Litchfield's review of *Petites Suites* in *Colorado Review*

"Robert Wexelblatt's new collection displays formal mastery, lucid exposition, and a sure way of stimulating the reader's curiosity."
  —Sarah White's review of *Heiberg's Twitch* in *American Book Review*

"Wexelblatt's book is laden with wit, with wry observation, gentle sarcasm, and wicked ironies. It always has just enough laughter to keep its characters (and the reader) from spinning off into the abysses."
  —Fred Marchant's review of *Life in the Temperate Zone* in *Harvard Book Review*

"Wexelblatt constructs rich stories that make heavy subjects dance weightlessly before the reader's eyes."
  —Review of *The Decline of Our Neighborhood*, *Publishers Weekly*

"Extraordinary variety—of style and technique, as well as substance and geographical setting—is the salient feature of Robert Wexelbatt's collection of stories, *The Decline of Our Neighborhood.*"

> —Jay L. Halio's review of *The Decline of Our 1Neighborhood* in *Studies in Short Fiction*

"A writer of great wit and superb imagination, Wexelblatt's worlds are welcoming and all-encompassing."

> —Review of *The Decline of Our Neighborhood, Booklist*

". . . Wexelblatt's first collection of short fiction must be admired for its academic brilliance and sophisticated wit. . ."

> —Review of *Life in the Temperate Zone, Publishers Weekly*

"Wexelblatt should no more be let loose behind a typewriter than in front of a classroom. Students might begin to think."

> —Donald Wayne Viney's review of *Professors at Play, Midwest Quarterly*

". . . loaded with wit, bristling with irony, draped in erudition and studded with metaphysics."

> —Zofia Smardz's review of *The Decline of Our Neighborhood, New York Times Book Review*

"This book proves that professors have a sense of humor—or at least that some of us do. The best thing that you can do for the "professional doldrums" is to buy yourself this book."

> —Review of *Professors at Play, Massachusetts Faculty Development Consortium*

Contents

Acknowledgments

"How Serious Was Sidney Fein?" first appeared in *San Jose Studies*

"The Birth of the Author," "On Ontology," "Sidney Fein and Saul Mandelbaum," and "Fein Re-Reads Dostoyevsky" first appeared in *Denver Quarterly*

"Riddle" first appeared in *Palo Alto Review*

"Socrates, Hamlet, Language and Insincerity," "On *Euthyphro*," "The *Königsberg* of Sidney Fein," "Fein on Two Sonnets of Alexander Fernlicht" and "Three Short Pedagogical Pieces" first appeared in *RE:AL*

"On Emma and Anna" first appeared in *Sulphur River Review*

"On Being Alone," "On Villainy," and "Fein on Kafka's Sentences" first appeared in *North Dakota Quarterly*

"An Incident" first appeared as "Un Incident Dans La Rue" in *The Battered Suitcase*

"On Philippe Leconte Duparc" first appeared in *Northwest Review*

"A Keynote Address," and "On Mystery," first appeared in *Essays and Fictions*

"On Irreverence," "On Contracts," "On Meaninglessness," "On Fernlicht," "On Zeicher's *Essay in Ethics*," "On Systematic Error," and "On Heresy" first appeared in *White Whale Review*

"In Treviso" first appeared in *Blue Lake Review*

"On Cinderella" first appeared in *A Bad Penny Review*

"On Wonder" first appeared in *The Commonline Journal*

"On Idol Worship" first appeared in *The Montréal Review*

"Fein on Faulk" first appeared in *Palaver Journal*

"On Sidekicks" first appeared in *Adelaide Literary Magazine*

PREFACE

THIS is a book of suppositions. Sidney Fein himself is a supposition on the order of the first term in an algebra problem: suppose that x = 1. Suppose there was a defunct intellectual with a certain style of thought and an independent income who published a few books and produced one child, a daughter he named Maya Nunfi. Suppose that this daughter, now an adult, has red hair and hires me to edit her dead father's papers. Why would she do so? Suppose she came across a short, retrospective essay I had written about him. Does this retrospective essay actually exist? It does, but only by virtue of a prior supposition. Some years ago, in an ambiguous mood prompted by reading a willfully opaque book of critical theory, I invented—or, I might as well say, discovered—Sidney Fein, the father. Why then should I not invent the daughter as well, the editing job, the papers in need of editing?

Apart from the following facts, my knowledge of Sidney Fein's biography is admittedly spotty. He was born in 1942 in Philadelphia, Pennsylvania. His family's fortune came from the business of clothing women of modest means. He attended elementary school in Philadelphia but, when he was twelve, his family moved to New York City. His undergraduate degree is from Columbia University, where he concentrated in the study of languages and literature; his graduate work was done at the University of Pennsylvania, from which he received a doctorate in philosophy in 1964. Fein married in 1966. His daughter, Maya Nunfi Fein, was born the following year. He and his wife separated in 1974 and divorced shortly thereafter. Fein raised Maya on his own. Thanks to his inheritance, he had independent means and took occasional pick-up jobs teaching at various universities. Fein published three books: *Diptych on Terrestrial Representation* (1973), *Want, Desire, and Need* (1977), and *Aristocratic Democracy* (1983). He died in 1984 at the age of 42. In addition to his books, Fein produced a quantity of both verse and fiction, some of it published under pseudonyms. Since inventing him, I have learned more and more about Fein's work habits and methodology, his interests, style, taste, and penchants. He often surprised me. For example, the discovery that Fein wrote poems and stories was a completely unanticipated.

This is a book of accumulated suppositions and to me it seems strange that it should have any weight at all. What is lighter than a supposition? A daydream? A snowflake? Yet the detective builds his more or less sturdy house-of-cards out of just such weightless things. What begins with the levity of supposition may end in the heaviness of truth. I wrote the posthumous papers of Sidney Fein as an open-ended thought-experiment, which is to say as a big supposition made up of many little ones. Each piece is itself a supposition and through each I learned more about Fein. To me, however, the most significant fact about this mental traveling is that, without Fein, I would never have moved an inch. I am not Fein; in fact, to my astonishment, sometimes even Fein himself is not Fein.

Sidney Fein is not my pen-name nor a cardboard cutout behind which I am hiding. To me, he is real enough. To me, Fein might as well be an historical personage known to no one else. To me, the posthumous papers of Sidney Fein are authentic papers and genuinely posthumous. I hope this work is neither solipsistic nor ludicrous, not just a series of abysses over which the tightrope of such a peculiar authorship stretches.

There is no intention to deceive here, though even that would not be so bad. To deceive people into the truth was the achievement of Socrates, according to Søren Kierkegaard, the foremost master of pseudonymity. Can serious playfulness really lead one into the truth? Why not? Why shouldn't Sidney Fein, who is himself both a playful thinker and a serious one, a thought-experiment who coins experiments of his own—why shouldn't Sidney Fein see one or two truths?

Robert Wexelblatt

THE BIRTH OF THE AUTHOR

What a wonder is Art! When we become too
placid, it braces our drowsiness with the tonic of
chaos; when too disoriented, it alone can slake
our thirst for order.
                    Klaren Verheim

EDITOR'S INTRODUCTION

SIDNEY FEIN had a taste for the bracing wit, sparkle, impish-
ness, and neoclassicism of the French. The music of Satie,
Ravel, Poulenc, the cinema of the Truffaut, Godard, Rohmer, the
art of Henri Matisse and Marc Chagall who, upon being called a
Jewish painter, retorted that he was a French one—Fein is on record
as to the appeal of them all. As he confirms below, André Gide's *The
Counterfeiters* was one of Fein's favorite novels and he frequently
included it on syllabi for courses completely unrelated to modern
French literature. Nevertheless, Fein could also be acerbic about
the French, in particular their philosophy, for the sometimes hectic
Rationalism of which he had a deep distrust. Indeed, Fein's parodies
and burlesques of various French thinkers have given rise, in some
quarters, to the notion that he was not only under the influence
of Gallic post-structuralists but yearned to join in their dizzying
discours. This is true in a sense, but only in the sense of Augustine's
saying, which Fein was so fond of quoting: "These things are true
in a way because they are false in a way." What fascinated Fein was

a coterie of intellectuals so preoccupied by thinking that reflection gobbled up reality, a society in which the greater one's offense to common sense, the higher one's prestige.

These previously unpublished notes clarify his relationship to at least one of these French thinkers on at least one point. Roland Barthes' celebrated essay, "The Death of the Author," first published in 1968, clearly lies behind Fein's piece, or not so much behind as beside it, like a mirrored image.

Fein's notes may also be taken as a kind of story or as the record of a story, though whether they are themselves pure fiction must remain a matter for speculation. That is, whether he invented "Klaren Verheim" as a character around whom to weave certain ideas, as he suggests, or imposed the name on some actual acquaintance I cannot say.

Fein was fond of the saying that style is a fire that devours whatever it illuminates. In contemporary French thought, as he remarked in *Diptych on Terrestrial Representation*, "reflection comes close to fulfilling Flaubert's objective for his unwritten novel *La Spirale*, a book which was to be sustained on style alone, having neither plot nor characters." There is no doubt that Sidney Fein was drawn to the French. He read them avidly, without losing sight either of the playfulness of their work or its self-promotion, nor what he deemed their contradictory ambitions at once to penetrate the world and to escape from it, like Malebranche or Proust, into sealed, windowless, cork-lined rooms.

• • •

THE BIRTH OF KLAREN VERHEIM
unpublished notes by Sidney Fein

1. **The Motive.** How can one be certain of one's motives when the conscious ones are so difficult to reconstruct and the uncon-

scious inaccessible without a year or two on the couch? But I will try. Klaren Verheim came into what may be provisionally called existence out of a mixture of inventiveness and idleness. The two moods are not generally close companions, it's true; nevertheless, on the long July afternoon of Verheim's conception I sat at my desk inflated by the urge to invent yet overcome by lassitude and vacancy. Out of frustration I became at the same time *enceinte* and incapable of labor. The rather adolescent solution I found was a hoax the dubious morality and metaphysics of which did not occur to me. I did not think of what I was doing as a deception. In my inanity, I had been reading through an essay I had abandoned the winter before. It is odd, but this piece that had displeased me when I considered it my own work seemed much improved as soon as I thought of ascribing it to somebody else. The idea appealed to me and, in no more than a moment, the image of Klaren Verheim appeared before me, fully grown. This work, which was uncongenial to me, was precisely the sort of thing he would produce. More out of impulsiveness than premeditation, I affixed the name *Klaren Verheim* to the essay and mailed it that same afternoon without a cover letter. I sent it to a scholarly journal, putting my own address on the return envelope for use in the likely event of a rejection.[1]

2. **A Motive Below the Motive**. It is the rule that in middle age one's flexibility should be diminished. One day you discover you have lost the buoyant sense of your own potential. You begin to squint at the world and, even with glasses, know that you are seeing less of it. I was shuffling into middle age and I suspect this fact made for an unconscious motive in the careless, undeliberate invention of Klaren Verheim.

He is an author akin to me to be sure; I would not deny it. But

---

[1]. Editor's Note: Though I have been unable to trace this essay, the title of which Fein does not divulge, I have located eight stories and sixteen poems by Klaren Verheim published in various literary journals during the late 1970s and early 1980s. In addition, there is the set of aphorisms which appeared under the title "The Proverbs of Klaren Verheim" in 1984, the last year of Fein's life.

Verheim is unlike me in so many ways that perhaps I invented him to gain access to some of what I was missing. I would not be the first to engage in such desperate measures. Having meandered into a dead end that long July afternoon, I was probably groping for a way of dilating the scope of my increasingly sclerotic imagination. If Sidney had nothing to say, perhaps Klaren did. If there is any truth in this, then Verheim would be a host invented by his parasite.

What makes this dubious motive more plausible is that from the moment his name popped into my head (*Klaren Verheim* = true home of clarity?), I never thought of him as a mere pseudonym. At first, it's true, I considered Verheim a sort of literary character, like one of those beloved autobiographical heroes around whom youthful writers are so fond of weaving their first novels. Later that was to change as Verheim deviated further from me and became more and more himself. At first, after all, I knew little about him save externals: his name, his physical appearance, his age. Verheim's initial production was his only by ascription since the essay had been written before his birth. However, I want to stress that all Verheim's subsequent works could *only* have been written by him, never by Fein.

3. **The Reality of Verheim**. Owing to the need for our species' brains to go on growing postpartum, the period of human gestation persists for many months after we are born. It was no different with Verheim.

The essay I sent out because an afternoon was sultry and I was fallow, mailed off with indifference, as a sort of joke, was accepted. One day in September the postman rang my bell, perplexed. The letter was in his hand. This was my first moment of queasiness, Verheim's first growing pain. I took the letter and, with it, responsibility.

It astonished me that the editor of the journal should write to *Mr. Klaren Verheim*. Why? Did I suppose the editor would not be taken in? In fact, this editor was well ahead of me. To me, Verheim was still just a momentary weakness, a prank two months' old and nearly forgotten. In my absent-minded hubris, I believed myself better informed than the duped editor, whereas exactly the opposite was the case.

The letter of acceptance required an acknowledgment and a few facts for a contributor's note. I hesitated to sit down at my desk, staggered by what I was about to do. What had begun as an idle *jeu d'esprit* was now serious because there is a distinction between a heedless hoax and a deliberate lie. Affixing Verheim's name to my essay had seemed to me innocent; writing a letter as Verheim was not. To write such a letter would alter matters; indeed, the acceptance had already changed things. Someone in the world believed in the existence of Verheim, had written to him by name through the Postal Service. Should I write back as Verheim, then his existence would be confirmed. My stomach dropped.

I confess it was in a state of mild nausea yet not without a sort of what-the-hell glee that I wrote the letter, put down a few biographical details, devised a signature. Verheim was now loose in the world.

4. **Verheim's Work**. I thought that for Verheim to write would require considerable effort on my part. At idle moments during the autumn I concentrated on being Verheim and not being Fein. All I achieved was a crude impersonation of Verheim, a ventriloquist with his dummy. The bit of writing that emerged was fitful, dismal, not at all what I was after. I came near giving up on Verheim.

One November night I was pacing my study working on what Sherlock Holmes calls "a three-pipe problem" when Verheim (you will excuse the crudity of the language here) spoke to me. It was not a hallucination; the voice came from inside me but unexpectedly and unbidden. That I recognized it at once as Verheim's voice should not be too surprising. Remember, I already had a relatively clear conception of Verheim in an external sense. This voice suited him. I knew his age, physical appearance, how he had been educated, but what he said was a shock. He informed me that he had an idea for a series of connected poems and even delivered a few lines. The first of the "Mr. Ponderoff" poems was written that night; the other four over the following days.

Many things about these verses surprised me, starting with their being poems at all, for not only am I no poet but it never occurred to me that Verheim was either. Most remarkable, though, was that he should invent an alter-ego for himself, that wise widower and retired bank manager Mr. Ponderoff. For one vertiginous moment, I wondered whether Ponderoff would now likewise begin inventing authors. An infinite progression, Hindu in its multiplicity, opened before me, and I thought with horror of Whitman's famous self-affirmation: "I contain multitudes."

Fortunately for my sanity, nothing of the sort occurred. Verheim simply continued his work at long intervals, putting in an appearance only when he had a good idea but then insistently taking over. Though I had conceived of him as chiefly interested in writing discursive prose (*à la* Fein), he almost always preferred imaginative forms: novellas, stories, poems. Far more inventive than I, more drawn to the concrete, Verheim was also a sharper observer of human behavior and more capable of sustained narrative. The endings of his stories in particular seldom failed to surprise me. Even the botched and the half-finished ones offered entirely unexpected characters and situations.

5. **Verheim's Independence**. I soon became accustomed to carrying on Verheim's limited correspondence, adept at slipping into his style of dealing with editors, which was more informal than my own. There was one rather interesting exchange over a poem. The editor wanted three changes of diction and the whole poem rearranged from free verse into regular quatrains. Verheim wrote back that this was really a violation of his principles but he would give in on the quatrains. On the word choices, though, he would not be moved. The editor accepted the poem anyway, and with respect. There was also a letter from a creative writing instructor

telling Verheim that one of his short pieces had been adopted at his institution as a model in their fiction courses. Verheim wrote a humble and gracious reply, asking whether his story was supposed to be a good or bad example. The trickiest exchange was with a female editor who accepted a story with a somewhat overheated expression of admiration and then suggested a meeting. However, the next phase in Verheim's existence had to do with money rather than love.

Klaren Verheim's published work appears in the sort of journals whose payment usually consists of a couple of free issues at most. One day, however, there came an acceptance letter with a request for his Social Security number so that a check could be issued to him. My old queasiness returned and for two days I fretted about what to do. At last I thought I hit on a solution. Verheim wrote back begging that whatever payment was due him be forwarded directly to Amnesty International.

It didn't work. A week later we received a letter from the business manager of the journal. She was full of approbation for Verheim's generosity, wished more contributors would follow his example, and hoped he would carry through with his intention. Nevertheless, accounting procedures required that the check be issued to him, the author, and to do so they must have his Social Security number.

I had the sense of crossing some boundary as I loaned my own number to Verheim. To hand over a flawed essay was nothing; indeed, that first thoughtless act seemed to me to take place outside of normal time or in some kind of inconsequential literary space. My Social Security number was another matter. It meant that Verheim's status was becoming less putative and more official. When the check arrived, I was so eager to be rid of it that I had Verheim instantly endorse it over to Amnesty. In my hurry, I neglected to ask them not to pass his name on to every liberal organization on the planet. Soon mail poured in for Verheim, almost entirely glossy requests for cash to support orphans, whales, and Democrats.

It was at about the same time that Verheim offered me the affront of poaching on my terrain. I had become used to his literary activities by then and was guilty of supposing him limited to them. Therefore, I was amazed to hear his voice one day almost maliciously insisting on writing an essay about one of my own enthusiasms. This essay, which I have never had the heart to send to a publisher, turned out to be a blistering critique of Gide's novel *The Counterfeiters*, a book I deeply admire. All the same, I am compelled to acknowledge the justice of what Verheim has to say against Gide. For example, in considering the chapter from the third part of the novel called "Bernard and the Angel" he writes as follows:

> There is something the matter with the whole chapter. One problem, of course, is the break in tone from the rest of the book. E. M. Forster's remark that Gide has "introduced mysticism at the wrong point" seems apt as applied to this awkward reworking of the story of Jacob. But what might make an attentive reader still more suspicious is the following paragraph, surely the worst written in the whole novel:
>
>> Then the angel took Bernard into the poor quarters of the town, whose wretchedness Bernard had never suspected. Evening was falling. They wandered for a long time among tall, sordid houses, inhabited by disease, prostitution, shame, crime and hunger. It was only then that Bernard took the angel's hand, and the angel turned aside to weep.
>
> Suddenly Gide, or at least his putative novelist, turns into a sentimental sociologist. Ignorance of, and lack of genuine sympathy for, the poor are all too obvious from the heap of five abstract nouns and the fact that no human beings are mentioned. This is also the only paragraph in the entire book where we leave the milieu

of the upper middle class. When a novelist departs from realism, good prose, and his natural habitat all at the same time, things are apt to go awry. Why do it? All, it seems, to score an easy moral point…

It is a reflection of the metaphysical complexity of this Verheim business that what, from his standpoint and that of potential readers of this piece, is apparently an essay is, from my point of view, a work of fiction. Verheim's remark about the "putative novelist" is a source of anxiety.

6. **Fein's Deception, Verheim's Truth**. Verheim receives mail, is described in contributors' notes, donates his earnings to charitable organizations, faithfully keeps up his correspondence. He has a personal style, history, and bibliography. He is not a mere *nom de plume* behind whom Fein hides, on whom Fein fobs off work for which he does not want credit or blame. On the contrary, what is revealed in the work of Verheim is unknown to Fein until Verheim makes it manifest. Just as significantly, Verheim has readers for whom his existence is genuine. The question arises: are these readers deceived? Or could we say that, at least in some luminous cases, readers of Verheim's work become *un*deceived?

What should one call a lie that reveals the truth? Good storytelling? This is no trivial question, nor one limited to aesthetics. Just such a deception is the first principle of the Socratic Method, for example.

This reflection made me mindful of the greatest and most prolific of all inventors of pseudonymous authors. I mean Søren Kierkegaard, the Danish Socrates and Master of Irony. About a year after Verheim's birth I found myself paging through Kierkegaard's *Point of View* searching for a dimly recollected passage where he sets out to justify his use of pseudonyms. I found it on page 39, but was not entirely satisfied; for, like anyone seeking plenary justification, Kierkegaard begs too many questions.

... from the point of view of my whole activity as an author, integrally conceived, the aesthetic work is a deception, and herein is to be found the deeper significance of the use of pseudonyms. A deception, however, is a rather ugly thing. To this I would make answer: One must not let oneself be deceived by the word "deception". One can deceive a person for the truth's sake and (to recall old Socrates) one can deceive a person into the truth.

First Kierkegaard begs the question of his pseudonyms by relegating their works to the category "aesthetic," an inferior one from his point of view. To the "religious" works he had no compunction about affixing his proper name. For my money, though, there is no more profoundly illuminating religious work than *Fear and Trembling* by Johannes de silentio, nor do I think that book could have been written *without* Johannes, an author who is made sleepless by the story of Abraham, admires and is appalled by faith, but is above all honestly ignorant of its nature, as he is of Søren Kierkegaard and Regine Olsen. To be written, *Fear and Trembling* required not the invention of a name but a complete personality who could confide in us not only his feelings about Abraham and Isaac but also his theory of drama and his indignation at the Hegelians. Moreover, this book by Johannes is a great deal more engaging than any of the *Edifying Discourses* by Søren. Surely Kierkegaard felt this too. Why else would he have said that his whole reputation could stand on *Fear and Trembling* alone?

Kierkegaard also oversimplifies the issue of deception, the very question that drove me to consult him as an authority. He assumes it is a simple matter of the reader being misled—whether into truth or not is a separate matter. Evidently, for Kierkegaard himself there was none of the confusion, the ethical and metaphysical queasiness, Verheim has caused me. Johannes de silentio, Climacus, Victor Eremita, Judge William and the others are "really" Kierkegaard, or parts of him, while a reader, unaware of these equations, might believe somewhere there breathes a gaggle of bright fellows with peculiar names who can even get together for a banquet and fine talk.

Now, since there is no thinker I revere more than this one, not least of all on account of his unexcelled alertness, Kierkegaard must have had good reason for seeing the issue differently from me. The reason must be that there was on his part a deliberate, if half-hearted, effort to deceive others, to conceal himself from his fellow Danes, while for me there was nothing of the sort. In other words, Kierkegaard's aim with his pseudonyms was to *hide* his authorship, while I had only the wish to *extend* my own. If anybody has been deceived in my case (even into truth) surely it is myself. True enough, I wrote down all of Verheim's works; but, as I have already insisted in these notes, their true author was nevertheless Klaren Verheim.

Because there is no equation between Fein and Verheim, from another point of view no one at all has been deceived, not even me. The ethical queasiness I felt upon receiving that letter addressed to Verheim was quickly overcome precisely because I could find no deception. It was of no account to the editor of that journal whose name appeared on the essay. As for deceiving readers, well, Klaren Verheim did not come into the world to fool them but only to do them good.

My experience is that, except for certain vainglorious theorists, readers and authors are not to be compared to funicular cars, one rising up only at the price of the other's decline. On the contrary, readers and authors are roped together like mountain climbers, each egging the other on to greater exertions, providing a small margin of security, and, in a case of real sympathy, bearing each other out like friends.

EDITOR'S NOTE

Fein's notes break off here, with this telling phrase, one he certainly knew was applied in his diary by Kafka to Kierkegaard: "he bears me out like a friend." What is interesting is that Fein should go further, saying that a reader can be such a friend to an author. That is, he believes that just as a reader (Kafka) is able to derive consolation from an author (Kierkegaard) suffering lucidly through perplexities and torments like his own eighty years before, an author must believe in a reader who will someday grasp what he is living through, what he *means*, even if his provincial contemporaries cannot. All this goes to show what a deeply human and intimate matter the transaction between author and reader is for Fein. Reading and writing do not obliterate voices and souls; they are the means of extending them.

Given its title, content, and that little fillip about "certain vainglorious theorists," it seems pretty clear that Fein's notes for "The Birth of Klaren Verheim," which I found in his file for 1979, were intended to be at least in part a response to Roland Barthes. One way Fein establishes his own position is through his explicit and reiterated admiration for Kierkegaard, "that Individual," champion *par excellence* of the first-person indicative. In "The Death of the Author" Barthes, fed up with humanism, heaps contempt at every opportunity on the individual and inserts derisive quotation marks around the words *human person*. In contrast, Fein portrays Verheim as becoming, after his conception and birth, more and more an individual, more and more a *human person*, developing beyond his texts all of those human attributes denied by Barthes not only to the author, whom he openly despises, but even to the reader, whom he pretends to favor.[2]

---

2. No better example of this process can be offered than Verheim's story entitled "When I Was a Nazi," a memoir of his childhood in the early 1940s.

Those who want to classify Fein as a Franco-American thinker should be given pause not only by this indirect attack on Barthes' "Death of the Author" but by the exclusively French references of that essay. Barthes' makes his deconstruction of the author a virtually nationalistic undertaking. He appeals successively to Mallarmé and Valéry, followed by Proust and the Surrealists, finally battening on the contemporary linguists whom, like a terrorist casting about for bomb parts, he wishes to appropriate for his own ends:

> ... linguistics has recently provided the destruction of the Author with a valuable analytical tool by showing that the whole of the enunciation is an empty process, functioning perfectly without there being any need for it to be filled with the person of the interlocutors.[3]

That is, when you think you are having a conversation with your mother or a tête-à-tête with your lover, you are deceived; it is merely denatured language performing with and for itself. Against this vision of vacuity Fein's Verheim—wispily imaginary though he is— seems a creature of plenitude, with flesh, blood, soul.

For Fein, not only authors but any of us has the possibility of transcending politics, of extending his or her voice beyond local conditions and fields of power. Not so for Barthes. For him such an ambition is an offense at once political and metaphysical, the last lint ball left over from the *Ancien Régime*:

> The author is a modern figure, a product of our society insofar as... it discovered the prestige of the individual... It is logical that in literature it should be this positivism, the epitome and culmination of capitalist ideology, which has attached the greatest importance to the "person" of the author.

Barthes' guillotining of the author can be understood as another

---

3. Quotations from Barthes' "The Death of the Author" are from *Image, Music, Text*, tr. Stephen Heath, New York: Hill and Wang, 1977, 142-148.

attempt to complete the radical program of the French Revolution, the anti-humanistic one that detests much more than just oppression, capitalism, and cant. Indeed, Barthes could hardly have made his liberation anti-theology more explicit than he did in the fateful year 1968:

> In precisely this way literature (it would be better from now on to say *writing*), by refusing to assign a "secret," an ultimate meaning to the text (and to the world as text), liberates what may be called an anti-theological activity, an activity that is truly revolutionary since to refuse to fix meaning is, in the end, to refuse God and his hypostases—reason, science, law.

One can imagine Fein's mordant amusement eleven years later at the dizzying heights of freedom to which Barthes thinks our balloon will rise once we toss all this useless baggage overboard. Liberation is to be found only in an unreasonable, unscientific, lawless emptiness, a vacancy in which nothing can be said, where only what has already been said can rearrange itself: "… the book is only a tissue of signs, an imitation that is lost, infinitely deferred." Neologism is called in to replace the heroically repressive figure of the Author (author = authoritarian) with the hollow, non-threatening term "scriptor". A *scriptor* has no past, no feeling, no future, nothing to express, nothing to reveal. Who, Fein must have wondered, would suffer the travail of writing only to become a "scriptor"?

Verheim, on the other hand, exists precisely to become an author and on his own terms. He rebels at limitations, decides for himself what he shall write, even invents his own alter-ego, the sagacious Mr. Ponderoff. He will not settle for becoming that *reductio ad absurdum* posited by Barthes, a "scriptor" who is in effect nothing more than a dictionary. If Verheim stands for anything as a writer it is the opposite of Barthes' conception of what writing is and does:

> … writing is the destruction of every voice, of every point

of origin. Writing is that neutral, composite, oblique space where our subject slips away, the negative where all identity is lost, starting with the very identity of the body writing.

True, Verheim never had a body to lose; all the same, he acquires a voice and succeeds in making himself precisely a "point of origin". Nor is his identity lost through writing. Like Johannes de silentio's, it is born out of it, his subjectivity precipitated rather than dissolved by the act of choosing words. Barthes insists we must give up thinking of an author as a living being with an existence prior to the moment in which he writes. The author should be, in fact, like the putative one of *The Counterfeiters* and not André Gide: "... the modern scriptor is born simultaneously with the text." In easing Verheim into the world, Fein stands Barthes on his head, for the latter says "... the author enters his own death [when] writing begins," but this was exactly the point at which Verheim was born.

Finally, there is what Barthes offers as his one positive statement in an essay bursting with negativity. He is against authors, literature, individuals, reason, law, criticism, God, and meaning, but only, he flatteringly assures us, in the service of the reader; for "a text's unity lies not in its origin but in its destination." Well, a "unity" is a paltry thing as compared to a meaning, just as a scriptor looks pretty puny next to an author and writing glows less nobly than literature. Nevertheless, *à bas l'auteur* means *en haut le lecteur*. Surely we readers should be grateful to Monsieur Barthes for our promotion.

But what is this reader other than "the funicular car," as Fein puts it, whose rise is the concomitant of Barthes' debasing of the author, damning him for the sin of setting up as a "human person"? Surely this reader must be worth a great deal, must have a self worthy of being so exalted? If the reader is the "destination," then he must be a wonderful place. Not so.

... this destination cannot any longer be personal: the reader is without history, biography, psychology; he is simply that *someone* who holds together in a single field all the traces by which the written text is constituted.

Lacking so much, one has to wonder with what such a being could hold anything together.

Sidney Fein's vision of reading and writing is exactly the reverse of Barthes'. Barthes revels in the death of the author whose authority he judges on the model of a predestinating Calvinist God, the very God who haunted André Gide's youth and whom he tried to expunge from his novel *The Counterfeiters*. Barthes prescribes that this literary atheism will make of reading a null transaction in which all voices, all meaning and human confidences will be abolished, all communion will be revealed as illusory, all personality a discredited theology. Barthes divulges a deception behind which lies nothing but the spume of language against the shifting grid of politics.

For Sidney Fein, the invention of Klaren Verheim came to represent a deception that reveals a truth. One possible name for such a hoax is Literature.

ON ONTOLOGY

Beginning with an awareness of its own emptiness, each being seeks to have, to possess; it aims to fill itself and the better it succeeds the less of a being it is, the more of a having. Yet this is a crude, over-zealous fashion of putting things. More charitable is Augustine's way: "... whatever kind the being may be, the good which makes it a being cannot be destroyed without destroying the being itself."

-from "Emptiness and Fullness" in Want, Desire, and Need

EDITOR'S NOTE

Those familiar with the work of Sidney Fein will allow, I believe, that his originality lay in the handling of problems rather than in the unexpectedness of those he singled out, or that chose him. The sort of philosophical questions that engaged his best energies are perennial, durable, irresolvable, and childlike. The last quality he stressed himself in his final public statement, the commencement address he delivered in 1984 where he speaks approvingly of Cézanne praying "to see with the eye of the newlyborn." A dualist to his core, Fein was at his best when situated between opposites; for example the tension between emptiness and fullness in the epigraph above, or that between the individual and group (*Aristocratic Democracy*), or the contradiction between the Eleatic and Heraclitan views of life (*Diptych on Terrestrial Representation*). Fein's mind was nothing if not playful and he liked best to frolic in the energized fields between opposite poles.

Among his posthumous papers one naturally finds Fein's thinking less cooked than in his finished works. The most frequent pattern I have observed is Fein taking flight from some intriguing passage he had read, rather as a composer might write variations on someone else's theme. He was skilled at apprehending unsuspected aspects of old problems to which he sometimes devised novel solutions. But, just as often, Fein finds in some venerable conundrum inspiration for his sportiveness. There are among his papers numerous abandoned *jeux d'esprit*, parodies, and burlesques.

In his file for the year 1981 Fein included several sheets of notes, typed and stapled, with the words "Ontological Status" written in red ink at the head. This phrase should probably not be taken as a title but rather a casual memo of the contents. Fein's opinion of what he had recorded is suggested by the question mark he affixed at the end of the phrase and the fact that his notes went unrevised. Whatever his intentions for this work may have been, it was not completed. However, there is enough here to see the outlines of what that work might have been. Besides, the notes are interesting in themselves and offer an excellent illustration of the oblique way in which Fein tackled a problem.

ONTOLOGICAL STATUS?
unpublished notes by Sidney Fein

ONE of the more bizarre books into which I poked while writing *Want, Desire, and Need* was *Shulkhàn Arùkh*, or *The Set Table*, that vast, fantastic compound of inflexible Jewish law and acrobatic casuistry. The tome was compiled by Joseph Caro in the sixteenth century. Caro was Sephardic but his book must have been popular with certain Ashkenazic rabbis, for one of them not only adapted it for Eastern European Jews but even added a section that, with witty humility, he titled *The Table Cloth*.

Now it isn't surprising that I should be amused by Caro's archaic, pettifogging rules or still more by his athleticism in finessing the unavoidable contradictions that arise from them. After all, I'm a deracinated Jew; that is, a Jew in the sense that makes the definition of Jewishness such a trial to those who attempt it. Nor is it to be wondered at that I would note down a few passages as I read without troubling to ask myself why. I do this all the time, being one of those readers with a horror of underlining. Forbidden in childhood to mar a book, we take notes instead and seldom stop to ask why this or that passage seems worth copying. We inveterate note-takers are arrested by feeling alone, by interest, humor, pique; and, when such feelings are embodied in our notes, they can be retrieved simply by re-reading them. Anyway, one of the passages I copied out of Caro's book concerns the definition of nudity of which the author takes a most expansive view. In fact, it must have been Caro's elasticity that interested me. For him, nudity isn't just the nakedness of a body, or parts thereof, though no one could catalogue more comprehensively the range of corporeal bareness. In general, he finds any part of the body that is usually covered to be nude if uncovered—a shoulder, say, or an ankle. Thus, if a woman customarily wears gloves, then her fingernails, if uncovered, would be a case of indecency. Fingernails? Why not? Fetishism knows no bounds. Well, this is run-of-the-mill monotheistic Puritanism. What really interested me in the passage was the moment when Caro flips from objective to subjective by insisting that nudity in women is anything about them that attracts the attention of men, especially *Yiddisher Kopfs* like him who ought to be thinking of God and Torah all the time. That's why Caro includes in his catalogue of proscribed nudity "the voice of a singing woman." This phrase is what made the passage memorable. It struck me as amusing and so I wrote it down, perhaps with the notion of using it later to make some point about how ascetic men inevitably project their own hated sexuality onto women. Imagine a young woman singing innocently in a Sevillian garden. A susceptible member of the *minyan* passes the garden wall, overhears and breaks out all over in fantasies. Who's at fault? Caro is in no doubt. The sin belongs to the *chanteuse*. She is responsible for the unseemliness of the man's daydreams. To Caro, she is not merely their occasion but their source; for, in declaring her voice "nude," he makes her the agent of the Evil One as much as if she performed a striptease at the doors of the synagogue. What Caro passes off here as a conclusion is actually his starting point: women are ungodly temptresses, Circes and Sirens, at least the ones who accidentally show a bit of ankle, impudently permit a vagrant tress to escape, or can sing pleasingly.

Very well. There was nothing remarkable in my writing down the passage from Caro, but I was surprised by what emerged when Klaren Verheim got his hands on it. The fellow wrote a poem.

CARO'S TABLE

> Beneath the immaculate linen and
> those cotton socks two comely ankles swell.
> Is to think of them to be led astray?
> To contemplate how the bones flow so, to
> wonder what is bone, what flesh, stroking
> with one's mind the unrepeatably dear
> concavity between shin and calf, a
> triumph of trillions of contingencies;
> to caress even the curt yet tender words, the
> firm Teutonic nouns—ankle, thigh, throat,
> knee, brow, breast—into which a body can
> be butchered or beloved? Nudity,
> is vast, he warns, particularly woman's,
> albeit Solomon himself seems to
> crawl like some besotted beetle hopeless
> of the whole so seeking mastery of parts,

ON ONTOLOGY

anatomizing desire with
analogies—breasts like twin fawns, teeth
like shorn ewes—a pastoral, goatish lust
born of a mind that likewise conceived the
Temple cubit by cubit. Is her hair
naked, her contralto nude only because
their tones are beautiful to beguile
and divert, because all that is unclothed
even in imagination must distract
us from our joyless prayers and loveless
commandments, thwarting the profane
redemption of modest metaphor?
Even "the voice of a singing woman,"
the sage chides, is nudity, naked sound
that dissipates thoughts of his jealous
God whose table must be primly laid,
no ankles touched beneath its spotless cloth.

These verses are less of an attack on Caro than they appear at first, being made up of three interrogatives and only two declaratives, neither unambiguous. I almost have the sense of Verheim toying with *me* here, juggling with my penchants for both sensuality and asceticism. Still, his poem has some intrinsic interest. I rather like, for example, the picture of Solomon crawling like a beetle over the perfect body of the Shulamite. A woman lying down really is a sort of landscape. And the bit about "butchered or beloved" is a good condensation of the mental dismemberment characteristic of male lust. On the other hand, the allusion to *The Table Cloth* in the first and last lines is just the sort of over-clever literary trick I find irritating.

This isn't the first occasion on which Verheim has surprised me in such fashion. Last year he bowled me over by pouring out those Ponderoff poems, a shocking prank beside which "Caro's Table" is as nothing. "Caro's Table" is, like the singing woman, merely an occasion. It was the writing down of this poem that set me thinking about a rather elementary question that might be called the problem of ontological status.

I'll begin with a proposition I can see my way to giving provisional assent. The objective existence of persons not physically present to us, such as absent friends and historical figures, is real, but this objective existence can be apprehended only by methods that undercut its objectivity. Well, perhaps these methods don't entirely undermine objectivity; it's enough to say they loosen the ground under it. My notion here is that ontological status ("objective existence" being only one rung on the ladder) is ultimately guaranteed by subjective belief. It's not only possible to reduce ontological status to an opinion, you can hardly help doing so the moment you think about the matter. To put it another way, even historians can't tear themselves free from the chains in Plato's Cave.

Suppose, for instance, that a generation of schoolchildren is solemnly told that George Washington is a legendary character dreamt up by Parson Weems, that the real Father of the Country was Ben Franklin or Natty Bumppo. You might say that in such a case the teachers would simply be lying to their pupils. I don't deny it, but this is chiefly because I believed my own teachers. What is our knowledge of George Washington founded on after we've gone beyond faith in our teachers to all the documents, testimonials, books and paintings? Like the theater, faith requires a willing suspension of disbelief. You could argue that the sheer weight of the historical record should convince us of—or vanquish our disbelief in—Washington's objective existence in the past, and of the existence of the past itself. But what we are convinced of is fundamentally an opinion. We say it is the facts that we are convinced *of* and this is not untrue. But it is also the "facts" we are convinced *by*; and the end to which these facts are deployed is to substantiate an opinion. Take away this subjective belief and our apparently unassailable certainty about the past goes up in smoke. The process is circular because it is only our opinion that the facts *are* facts that makes them convincing in the first place. Perhaps when Plato distinguished between true opinion and real knowledge this was the sort of thing he had in mind. So at least where the status of a being is concerned (historical versus fictional, for instance) what we mean by real knowledge is an opinion about that status, an opinion we may believe for the best of reasons, but it is nonetheless an opinion. We confidently distinguish one book as history and another as fiction, even though we know very well how easily fiction and history are confused. A good example, in fact, is the Reverend Mason Locke Weems's *A History of the Life and Death, Virtues and Exploits, of General George Washington.*

Now what about Verheim and *his* ontological status? For that matter, what about Mr. Ponderoff? What of Sidney Fein? Bewildering? Vertiginous? Well, those poetic four days were certainly dizzy ones for me, taking dictation from Verheim uttering the words of Mr. Ponderoff, speaking from who knows where. Or maybe I do know. Ponderoff was born and, in a sense, dies in the words themselves, the words of those five poems, because all there is to know of Mr. P. has to be derived from those monologues of his. Ponderoff is like one of those insects encased in amber. Or he is like Athena leaping from the brow of Zeus—there he suddenly was, spectacles, grave voice, bald head and all. Ponderoff popped out with the sagacity of Athena but not her future.

Of the three of us, Ponderoff is the least real and the most completely known. These two coordinates are enough to place him in one circle of being, the lowest or highest as one wills. I, as the sole biologically existing being of the trio, belong in another circle with the billions of my species currently inhaling and exhaling all around me. While I am the most real (a term of convenience here which I'm not inclined to define), I'm also the least known, even to myself. As for Klaren Verheim, I feel that he comes in between, that he merits an ontological status all his own. While he is my invention, as Mr. Ponderoff is his, I've never been able to predict what Verheim will do, and it is just in this indeterminacy that Verheim resembles me. Though, according to the biography I supplied for him, Verheim was killed by a school bus in 1966, he may also have a future. It was, for instance, twelve years after his demise that Verheim wrote that unexpected memoir of his childhood.

Anyone reading this might wonder how I can claim not to know what my own pseudonym is going to do, at least anybody without experience of the tricks played by pseudonyms like Klaren Verheim. How can I insist I don't know what he will "do" when all he does is limited to linguistic acts entirely under my control? That's how it appears, that for Verheim to act I must act first. However, the actual state of affairs is just the opposite. After that first essay of mine to which I affixed his name, it was Verheim who initiated all his linguistic acts—the nasty essay on Gide for instance, all his fiction and poems. I don't write such things. This means that Verheim and I share a measure of choice. One might even say that Verheim has appropriated a portion of my free will, though he's done so without in the least diminishing it. On the contrary, Verheim's *raison d'être* is to widen the scope of my choices, sympathies, talents, and my authorship in general. Though his existence supplements mine it remains a kind of existence. "Caro's Table" is as good an example as any. Fein would have used that arresting passage from *The Set Table* as a prosaic citation whereas Verheim saw in it the occasion for a poem. *Tout simplement*, I am not a poet and Verheim is. Less fantastically put, the existence of Verheim permitted me to liberate another level of my response to Caro, to sex, to Jewish law, another stratum of my being which I could never have touched without him. Ontologically, we all resemble sedimentary rock.

Limited by our understanding of our own ontology, our sense of what is suitable to ourselves considered adjectivally (in my case "Feinian"), how much of our natures do we "objectively existing beings" suppress? How much must we fail to see of what is outside us because of the blinders worn on our insides, blinders not *affixed* to our natures but blinders that we stubbornly believe to *be* our natures?

In last Sunday's *Times,* I came across one of those theatrical ads that praise an actor with the X is Y formula. So-and-so *is* he-or-she. Zero Mostel *is* Tevya. Brando *is* Stanley Kowalski. The copula is intended to express both a relation and a judgment. The puff works best when both the actor and the character are famous. "Olivier is Hamlet," for instance, promises that Olivier's skills will bring Prince Hamlet to life on stage, but also that the great role perfectly fulfills Olivier's talents and so, of course, we'd better not miss the show.

If Olivier can be Hamlet, can Hamlet be Olivier? So says the Law of Identity, though we know this is neither intended nor true. Each performer's Hamlet is different, though, as we say, Hamlet himself never varies. This "Hamlet himself" is like Mr. Ponderoff, a creature of "words, words, words," to quote the Prince.

Good fictions have the power to confer life, initiate an ontology, convince us of the existence of characters, of whole worlds. Flaubert *is* Madame Bovary. Mary Shelley *is* Victor Frankenstein and what Tolstoy describes *is* Russia. Fructose Lysander *is* the author of the *Typewriter Novels,* beloved of *les écrivains de la Nouvelle Vague,* just as the story "Chlorine" defines Chlorine Danziger.[4] And it's instructive that in praising a novelist people will say they know the writer's characters better than the members of their own family. They confer this formulaic praise as if it were to be marveled at, but should we marvel? After all, everything about Raskolnikov and Elizabeth Bennet exists between the covers of their books, all we can ever know of their fates, thoughts, voices, habits, bodies. Or

---

4. For a biography of Lysander, the origin of his typewriter novels, and information about Danziger's life, see *Typewriter Underground First Fragments,* held in the Swizzle Felt Collection, New York City.

rather this intimate knowledge has its true existence in the imagination of readers sympathetically stimulated by the book. After all, reading too is a kind of performance, like Olivier's, and my Rodion or Lizzie need not look much like yours.

We have to admit then that a literary character is subject to a knowledge far more comprehensive than any we can attain of actual living beings, and also that this knowledge is not different in kind. Because we see characters as people we ask the same questions about them, feel for or against them the same as we would objectively existing persons. We often try to see people as characters though with much less likelihood of satisfaction because actual persons are hardly ever completely revealed even to themselves, let alone others. Literary characters and even the subjects of historians can be uncovered with Caro-like nudity. We living people have undetermined fates and, thanks to our large brains, something that is traditionally called free will. Calvinists, adhering more to aesthetics than theology, insist not that novels resemble life but that life really is a novel. Perhaps this answers some need in us, a yearning not only for an Author, but for the kind of ontological certainty art alone delivers. We want order because order suggests meaning; and we long for complete knowledge because gossip is one of our distinctively human capacities—and consolations.

A certain bibliophilic author imagines how an encyclopedic fiction of the most satisfying sort might challenge reality, the objective reality that so baffles us.

> Almost immediately, reality yielded … The truth is that it longed to yield… It is useless to answer that reality is also orderly. Perhaps it is, but in accordance with divine laws—I translate: inhuman laws—which we never quite grasp.[5]

---

[5] Editor's Note: Here Fein quotes from Borges's story "Tlön, Uqbar, Orbis Tertius," which can be found in *Labyrinths*, New York, New Directions, 1962, p. 17.

He cagily supposes we would eagerly grab at the artificial, the alternative of order and understanding, sacrificing the certain ontological status of our indeterminate world.

True, true, what is made by people is meant to be grasped by them. One needn't call in divine laws to observe that here in the humble human circle we are never quite grasped. Still, even good illusions are not good enough. Shortly before his death, Kafka put things this way: "There is no having, only being, only a being panting for its last breath, panting to be choked out."[6] To be choked out? But isn't panting two things not one, both a filling and an emptying?

To be? To have? Are they really exclusive? We certainly do plenty of grasping, and with both hands, though we ourselves are not grasped. Perhaps our sort of being is the vacuum nature abhors, the abyss over which she declines to leap. Who knows? Maybe all our grasping is just a way of shoring being up, distracting ourselves from its vacancy, an emptiness we try frantically to fill any way we can, but especially with fictions.

[6.] This is the thirty-second of the aphorisms published as "Reflections on Sin, Pain, Hope, and the True Way," in *The Great Wall of China*, translated by Willa and Edwin Muir, New York, Schocken, 1946, p. 286.

RIDDLE

VERY likely you know the story already. It's not obscure as parlor games go. A traveler wishes to get to a marvelous town he has heard of where everybody always tells the truth. But there's a hitch. Nearby lies a second town with quite a different reputation. Its citizens always lie. After traipsing all day through an empty countryside, our traveler arrives at a fork in the road. Clearly, one fork must go to the town of truth-tellers while the other leads to the den of liars. At this crossroads stands a beech tree and on a branch of the beech sits a boy. The boy must come from either the one town or the other; the traveler has seen no other settlements for miles and miles. What is the boy doing up in the beech? We can presume it is just to intercept tourists and pilgrims such as our traveler that the boy has stationed himself there. No doubt he has climbed up into the tree so as to look down the road. This way he will be able to spot anyone coming long before they can see him. This will give him time to prepare a reception. Indeed, the boy is prepared and, before our traveler can utter a word, lays down the rules of his peculiar game. He declares that he will answer one and only one question, and that with only a yes or a no.

The problem, of course, is to discover what question will enable our traveler to set his feet on the road to the complete truth.

• • •

It is impossible not to identify with this traveler, even if one is pained by his naïveté, his readiness to believe in fantastic tales, to abandon the duties of his life at home and set out on an absurd quest. This is in the nature of the narrative. Just try to identify with the boy, for instance. You can't do it. Not only is he there as an obstacle, an ambiguous obstacle, since he is also there as a guide, but he is inscrutable, infinitely less human than the traveler, whose ignorance, hope, and frustration find echoes in ourselves. All you can do is picture the smug face of that boy and perhaps the way his feet in their scuffed shoes dangle from the branch. The riddle doesn't merely put us in the traveler's place, though. The instant we make the tiniest of mental assents to the game, we *are* that traveler. We can see the dusty road, the sunny meadow off to our left, the line of pines at the edge of the cornfield to our right. It is late; we are perspiring from our exertions and annoyed by the boy. We may even have an impulse to clamber up that beech tree, seize him by the throat and demand, "Which way!"

A fork in the road. It is the most banal cliché of simplistic morality, but at the same time a sophisticated image that drags behind it tatters of Dante and Robert Frost. Forked roads are heavy with implication. And so the riddle has an ethical underpinning; truth is good, lying evil. But we travelers are not in temptation; we are idealists, seeking the unalloyed, completely dependable truth. Still, woe to us if we make the wrong choice. Salvation lies to one side, damnation to the other. We look sharply at the boy's face. Is he sporting the smile of an angel or the smirk of a demon? Are we certain we can tell one from the other?

• • •

There exists a solution; there has to. What's more it's there in advance. A boy in a beech tree wouldn't pose a riddle without knowing the answer already. Riddles are repetitions rather than variations, locks whose keys were manufactured simultaneously with themselves. The boy must have played his childish game often enough before. Still, it could also be more than a game. Perhaps the child has been sent to the crossroads by the authorities in one town or the other, stationed there as a regular sentinel. This gives rise to yet another association; for in this case the riddle is a test, the boy a sphinx, and the traveler, who is ourselves, turns into Oedipus, going on two legs at noon.

• • •

Imagine living in a town where everyone always lies. How could life proceed at all? Confusion would reign at every corner. You ask the time and are given a false answer. You ask somebody's name and receive the wrong one so that you mistake Hortense for Shirley, Chuck for Darren. Promises are worthless, including those of engineers and contractors. As a result, buildings, bridges, contraceptives and promissory notes—all would be flimsy, notional, worthless. On every hand the categorical imperative is flouted. The town's history, not to mention all the articles in its weekly newspaper and the earnest pleadings of its editorials, would be a tissue of falsehoods. Nothing is reliable except unreliability.

Yet there's something wrong here, something inconceivable from a human point of view. I don't mean the penchant for lying because that is certainly human through and through. No, it is the *predictability* of lying in this imaginary town that rings false and shows us that as we walked down that dusty road we were leaving the human circle. Every lie must have a veneer of truth to be fully functional; it must reflect a surrounding truthfulness. Even with known liars of the pathological sort—the boy who cried wolf, the oily used-car salesman—even with them there is still the poignancy of potential truth. That wolf may really descend snarling on the fold; that Buick may really be a steal. But in this town, no such possibility exists. Its citizens are under a compulsion to lie, to say absolutely nothing that is *not* a lie.

Riddles are formal problems whose terms are laid down in advance. They create a world outside of contingency. If he is from the town of liars, the boy has to lie to you whereas a genuine liar does not. This mechanical boy, this Pinocchio, is even more constrained since he has limited himself to a yes or no answer, like the simplest synapse of a binary computer.

Nevertheless, he arouses your curiosity, for you believe that the true way lies through him. And all of a sudden, given your sophistication, you make another literary association. You recall Kafka's parable "Before the Law" from *The Trial* and Joseph K.'s mournful conclusion: "It turns lying into a universal principle." So now you are K. and also the man from the country seeking the radiance of the Law. Suddenly this boy in his beech tree has achieved the stature of an infinite number of frightful doorkeepers.

But what if he comes from the other town, what then? He would be perched up there in the beech tree not to deceive but to examine you, to see to your worthiness. There he sits, lifted above the earth like a promise of paradise. A perfect town must be cautious, after all; so pure a barrel could easily be spoiled by one rotten apple. And yet, and yet. Is the heaven of truth-tellers any less inhuman or mechanistic than the inferno of liars?

Kant himself reduced his categorical imperative to absurdity. He was famously asked if, assuming he knew the fellow's whereabouts, he would tell an axe-wielding psychopath where to find his victim. Kant replied without hesitation that he would indeed reveal what he knew so as not to add the sin of lying to that of murder. Is such rigidity about the facts, such a rigorous principle of veracity either human or sensible? The town of truth-tellers would be as ridiculous as old Kant making us blush for the greatest of Königsbergers. Do you really like my new hair-do? Are you free for dinner next Sunday? Did you really read all of *Don Quixote*? How fresh are these nectarines? Never a fib, never a shading of the facts, not so much as a white lie to ease the crushing burden of social and economic life.

Within the riddle the predictability of the truth-tellers, the spell under which they labor, is the equal of the liars'. Both exist in a logical formula, not in the world. Imagine trying to live up to this inflexible ideal, this unbending standard of absolute fidelity to fact and feeling, with no give in it for our human imperfections. Wouldn't it be like sitting for hours on a plastic chair?

And so, prompted by this riddle, you may realize the complexity of our real condition, that as liars do not always lie, so honest people do not always tell the truth. Maybe you will even conclude that, though we do indeed reside on the isthmus of a middle state, this is not such a bad thing, that the perplexing, riven life of us mortals depends on our sometimes lying and sometimes telling the truth and that it is no easy matter to know when it's best to do which. One thing is certain, though. That child up in the tree, whether a liar or an honest boy, is not human.

Nevertheless, nevertheless, you still wish to vanish into the pure air of truth, to escape the confines and humidity, the snags and mendacity of our fallen world. Above all, you desire to find out whether the boy is a liar or a truth-teller. But shouldn't you be asking yourself whether it matters?

• • •

"Logic is a form of interior decoration," I once quipped. But even this glib remark is too generous. A decorator will bring in a new couch, new carpets, whereas logic adds nothing and teaches nothing. It is merely a re-arrangement of the old furniture. Of course, there are a bewildering number of possible arrangements; one can pile the chairs upon the tables, hang the rugs from the ceilings. Logic did not stop with Aristotle's *Organon*, cobbled together by Andronicus of Rhodes. Nowadays we have intuitionistic logic, also modal, multivalent, minimal, and combinatory logic, not to mention the special logics of concepts and relations.

Logic is supposed to prescribe the rules of thought and that is why you can only resolve this riddle with its help, by re-arranging the living room of what you already know. The answer is there waiting, somewhere between the end-tables. Logic has little to do with the messy way we actually think most of the time. Psychologically speaking, logic is untrue, though scientifically it is indispensable. And your problem is not of this world.

The boy in the beech tree is a logical entity or, to put it differently, his boyishness has been boiled down to a wish to exasperate, either a compulsion to deceive or an obligation to test. Moreover, his lightness should not be overlooked, his suspension. Though he might as well be on the ground, the boy is up in a tree, beyond the reach of anything but thought, the most weightless of human productions. And, of course, the heaviest.

So, think.

• • •

Have you found the solution yet? If so you will also have detected that the riddle conveys an unexpected moral; indeed, this moral amounts virtually to its solution.

It's simple, really. The traveler (Oedipus, Dante, Frost, the man from the country, me, you) points at random down one fork and asks, "Is this the way to the town where you live?" Should the boy answer yes, then that will be the way to the village of truth-tellers, if no, to the town full of liars. The trick is to formulate a question that either a liar or a truth-teller will have to answer in the same way. While in the province of human communications this would be impossible, in the world of logic, where tree-climbing lads are predictable, it is. Our capacity to solve riddles depends, so to speak, on dependability. But finding the question that solves the riddle is only a secondary move and, in that sense, a trivial one. To make this move we must first have made a more profound one, a movement of resignation, because to find out one thing we must give up hope of discovering something else which we should also like to know. In this case, to find your way to the town you yearn for you must surrender your wish to discover whether or not the boy's answer, the answer that guides you, is a lie.

And so, you picture yourself, well pleased with your cleverness, marching up the correct path, brushing aside a bumblebee, taking the high road to a place where for all you know the Platonic forms await. Nonetheless, you feel a little frustrated, a bit uncertain. Even as you triumph in this airless world of logic your victory is incomplete. Not everything has been disclosed to you and even on the way to purity you carry with you your maculate, unfinished self.

How pure, then, is any truth divorced from our needs, our points of view, our grievances? Even with our feet set firmly on the true path can we ever do better than muddle along?

EDITOR'S NOTE

Five years ago, Sidney Fein's daughter Maya made a portion of his papers available to scholars. When I began going through these papers I hardly expected to find much that was new. I was initially interested only in seeing if I could find any early sketches for the methodology now known as Feinian classification, but the only extant draft of *Diptych on Terrestrial Representation* shows little revision and I could discover no prior notes. Since the most distinctive feature of Fein's oeuvre is that he rarely dealt with the same topic twice, it is not surprising that each of his works should appear to have emerged all at once, self-contained, definitive, complete. Nothing leads up to or away from them. With Fein there is nothing one could call a program of research, not even much continuity to his thinking. Fein would be provoked by something he read, or he would suddenly devote himself to a problem, think it through, then, with startling rapidity, compose virtually finished statements, penetrated by his customary irony, and often in the form of a parody or burlesque. I could find nothing to deepen or extend our knowledge of his major books. I did find three essays that, according to a note, Fein decided at the last minute to exclude from *Want, Desire, and Need*, but all three were subsequently published in journals. As for *Aristocratic Democracy*, it was written, alas, on a computer.

On the other hand, I did come across a large number of fragments, outlines, and oddities among Fein's papers that are unclassifiable, even by Fein's method. Most are mere fragments, notions he seems to have given up on almost as soon as he thought of them. But by no means all. With the permission of his daughter I am trying to put the more complete of these items into publishable condition.

Fein's papers may not be classifiable but they are organized. He placed them in folders designated by year. I found these eight pages of untitled holograph folded up inside the green grade book he used in 1980, when he served as a visiting professor at Brandeis University.

"Riddle" may hold some interest for Fein scholars, particularly because of its elliptical and suggestively pejorative remarks about logic. Nevertheless, the plain style and sketchiness of the piece along with its presence in a grade book suggested to me that Fein did not intend to launch anything like a detailed critique of logic. I thought the piece might have been written for some pedagogical purpose, a lecture perhaps, or a plan for a provocative class. The frequent use of short declarative sentences and of the second-person pronoun would seem to substantiate such a hypothesis. As a teacher, Fein liked to engage his students' imaginations. Moreover, there was something written at one corner of the first page that made me think Fein was prompted by some specific situation. This clue was a female name, one I found also in the grade book.

I was able to trace this former student of Fein's. She has been most helpful but has asked me not to reveal her name. She remembers very well two conferences she had with Fein during the autumn of her terrible sophomore year. I will close with her account:

"As soon as I left for Europe that May, safely out of the way I guess he thought, my dad moved out of the house and the divorce case began. As it proceeded that Fall my parents became more and more vindictive, bitter, and vicious to one another. They seemed to me normal one minute and monstrous the next. To tell the truth, although I understand what was going on much better now,

I still haven't altogether recovered from the shock of those months, especially the awful pulling this way and that.

"The first call was from my mother. I say the first call but actually she was phoning two or three times a night. She said I had to testify for her, that I had to appear in court and tell the judge all these bad things about my father. She said it was her lawyer's idea. The next day my father called, just as insistent that I testify for him. His lawyer thought it would be valuable too. My dad's the methodical type. He had a whole list ready: didn't I remember this? Couldn't I recall that? It was just horrible. I couldn't eat or sleep let alone study.

"I'm not really sure why I went to Professor Fein. I didn't know him well or anything. I suppose it was wisdom actually. He really was a wise man and I loved his class. What made it so different from the rest was that you could never tell what was going to happen, I mean in what direction things were going to go.

"Anyway, I told him my problem. I guess I just poured out my heart to him. He asked whether my father's accusations against my mother were true and whether the things my mother said against my father were also. I told him I didn't really know for sure but I thought most of it was. 'Then what they say is in part untrue?' I remember him asking me. I said I couldn't really be sure but what was so terrible was the way they both just assumed I'd agree with everything they said. What should I do? If I testified for one, the other would be mad at me; and if I turned both down then they'd both be angry. I asked Professor Fein if he could find the right path for me. I remember him being very kind. He said he would like a little time to think over my problem and asked me to come back the next day.

"When I saw Professor Fein the following afternoon he told me that, in his opinion, the best thing for me to do was to tell both my parents how much I needed and loved them but to be very firm about not going to court. He added that I should also tell them, as I had him, that the divorce was making me lose sleep, that my work was suffering, and that I was having trouble eating. And that's pretty much what I did. At least they left me alone.

"I remember that before I left, Professor Fein looked at me with this funny smile he had and said that I should remember that it wasn't up to me to establish the truth of my parents' grievances. And then, maybe because he wanted to cheer me up, he told me some riddle with a boy in a tree. I couldn't solve it, but it made me laugh."

THREE SHORT
PEDAGOGICAL PIECES

Teaching Logic, or Barnabas' Ploy

AT the last minute, Professor Hugo van der Weg decided to return to Holland. Perhaps he was homesick, missed pitched roofs and legalized narcotics, meatballs and rice table. No one told me. Maybe no one knew.

Though I was deprived of the pleasure of meeting Professor v. d. W., his decamping was consequential for me. As Distinguished Visiting Professor (my pompous rating) I was obliged to teach only two courses per semester. My department chairman for the year was a decent fellow named William Pitt, like the prime ministers. He was one of those people who have the knack of turning high anxiety into a variety of charm and he telephoned at the end of August to beg me charmingly to take on another class, with no preparation and for no money, one of v. d. W.'s orphans.

"It's logic," he declared, as if he had said something that amounted to an argument.

"Pardon me?"

"The *course*. It's 210, Logic. Please? Pretty please?" He then proceeded breathlessly, as though convincing me were a matter of speaking a run-on sentence as rapidly as possible. "Look, I wouldn't dare to ask but it's a requirement for a lot of our students, though you shouldn't have more than twenty-five all together, so it wouldn't be fair just to cancel it and there's nobody else who can take it on—well, except for Harold Whitson but he's already agreed to do the

Flying Dutchman's Rationalism seminar so I can't possibly ask him."

"No, that wouldn't be fair."

I could almost hear him throwing his gaze heavenwards. "What can I do?"

Deans have it fairly easy; they can rely on bullying. But I think one of the criteria by which department chairmen are selected must be their ability to get people to sigh and say okay. So I sighed and said okay. But—Logic?

The class really was a requirement, as Pitt said, though in a respect he didn't mention. The Philosophy department, perhaps Pitt himself, had maneuvered things so that PH210 could fulfill the undergraduate math requirement. While this clever bit of academic politicking insured a healthy enrollment, lots of FTEs in the lingo of the trade, and looked good on the accounting sheet of the wisdom-lovers, it also guaranteed classes filled with the reluctant, resentful, and resigned. My impression was that the few philosophy majors, for whom the course was required, were likewise resigned, just more arrogantly.

It isn't remarkable that universities should place their faith in the study of logic, except that they really don't. What they do is require a course in it and allow the math-averse to make use of it. Who could object? Few faculty would have the gall to stand up in an open meeting to oppose the teaching of logic, even on the logical grounds that it is simply a dodge. More likely they'd support it, for isn't logic the fastidiously cultivated ground of rational discourse to which, on its grand or defensive occasions, the universities vow that they are devoted? Logic, somebody would be bound to remark, is the etiquette of thinking and obviously everybody needs to know the rules. At least, in the curiously exhibitionistic language of contemporary higher education, every student ought to be *exposed* to logic.

There is a time-honored trick for dealing with grossly oversubscribed classes. More than ninety students showed up for PH210 that first Tuesday. Assuming it was not intended to be used as a sweat shop or a holding pen for prisoners of war, the room was fit to accommodate less than forty. It's possible that a handful of these students actually wanted to take the course—I can't swear to the contrary—but you couldn't pick them out. So I began by trying to scare as many of them off as I could with a long reading list, some of which I made up on the spot. I promised to assign weekly homework exercises, three papers, and two essay exams. I endeavored to convey the assurance that all these opportunities to shine would be caustically graded. I followed up with an introductory lecture that was just shy of unintelligible. Speaking almost as rapidly as Pitt trying to inveigle a visiting professor, I laid out the scope of our subject, though I never actually claimed that I would attempt to cover even a quarter of it.

The word logic was never used by Aristotle, I told them; he favored *analytica*. The term was first employed by Zeno of Citium, a Stoic. I watched them write this scrap of trivia into their new notebooks. Aristotle is the first master of logic. Andronicus of Rhodes gathered Aristotle's writings on the subject into a book he called the *Organon*, as in organ or instrument of right thinking. Aristotelian, or classical, logic is where we must all begin. But since logic, like geometry, is a formal system derived from axioms, it is possible to formulate different logics just as there is a variety of geometries. No longer is logic restricted to Aristotle's bivalence. There is also, for instance, intuitionistic logic that leaves out the Principle of the Excluded Third, which is to say the idea that there is no alternative beyond being and non-being, so that contradictory principles can't both be denied, which is Aristotelian bedrock. In his classical logic every proposition is either true or its contrary is. But not in this form, where *not-not p* doesn't mean *p*. No, sir. More radical still is the minimalist logic of Johansson, which, in addition to excluding the excluded third, also leaves out the *ex-falsum sequitur quodlibet*. (This devastating phrase, which I did not bother to translate, led to some gratifying grimaces and I pressed on.) Now, modal logic is merely an expansion of classical logic. The statement that *p is necessary*, for instance, may be regarded as in a different mode from the assertion *p is possible*. Multivalent logic has numerous validity-functions, such as, in the case of trivalence, true, false, and something in between, so that here a proposition may be more or less true, albeit any negation remains simply false. Topological logic goes even beyond this (I threatened) since it has no determined number of values at all, only a hierarchy from, say, irrefutably true to damnably false. But wait; there's more. So far (I let drop with great nonchalance), I have touched only on the logics of concepts, concepts such as big, red, ugly, cool; but there is in addition the extensive field of the logic of relations in which we can frolic. Consider the statement *Rxy*, which is a way of saying that a relation—friendship, for example, or betrayal—exists between x and y. This means that R is a predicate of a pair of things, a fact which permits manipulation of relations in the same way that Aristotle manipulated concepts. For instance, negating *Rxy* yields *not-Rxy*, and the inversion of *Rxy* is *Ryx*.

By now notebooks were forsaken, eyes rolled, and looks of bitterness and surrender were being exchanged. In the time remaining, I persevered, relentlessly strewing forbidding twentieth-century names (Schrödinger, Russell, Frege) like so many nails on a highway. I distinguished formal logic from material logic in a muddled fashion and did my best further to perplex the class with baffling distinctions between mathematical logic, symbolic logic, and logistics.

Any questions?

Well, the only pertinent question left at the end of my excruciating monologue was whether any students at all would show up for the next class. Could calculus really be worse than this?

It's inviting to suppose ideas transcend the minds that wrestle with them, that ideas float on high and we stretch to grasp them. Yet ideas only live because minds conceived them. So, can any idea be higher than the mind? Well, maybe. The higher often depends on the lesser, though the dependence undermines the hierarchy. For example, the Idea of the Good certainly seems more exalted than the humble E. coli. Yet Plato's brain surely depended on his digestion and so on the bacteria in his gut. To abstract means to draw away from, often away from this world's realities. The loftiest abstract idea is apt to lie panting if it's deprived of the oxygen of imagination. I find it hard to understand a thinker's idea until I've imagined it, or imagined the thinker who thinks it. (What did the middle-class, middle-aged Macedonian Aristotle make of his trust-fund Athenian teacher? How did Epictetus feel when suddenly freed from his brutal master?) What the imagination conceives may sully the purity of the Idea; yet the mind needs to imagine if it is to stretch, to animate in order to grasp. In a classroom the airless-ness of the abstract can be lethal, retarding time and deadening souls. Not just good, but even bearable lectures require lots of *for instances*, little stories to open windows and quicken souls. Like the old woman pulling onions, we're all tied to this world.

Sixty-five students showed up at the second class, though none looked glad to be there. I felt real compunction and some ambiva-lence. I had evidently underestimated something, the aversion to calculus, my capacity to terrify, the students' willingness to work, perhaps even the sex appeal of multivalent logic. Or I had utterly misconstrued my duties.

I asked the students why they had come back.

Some admitted frankly to seeing no alternative, others that they needed the required credits and thought they stood a better chance of getting them from me than from mathematics. One surprised me by saying, with an air of regret, that he had read some of my work and had been looking forward to taking the class. Most, however, were silent and resentful of this Distinguished Incomprehensible Visiting Prof and his impertinent question. This pitiable sullenness made me repent of my selfish initial performance. I now wanted to throw open the aforementioned windows and reflected with shame that it is not up to the cook to decide how many people will be invited to dinner. So, I began to serve the first course all over again.

In the year 818, I began, a band of Norsemen attacked one of the monasteries on the Dingle Peninsula of Ireland, a common enough event at the time. What made this attack unusual was that the leader of these particular Vikings happened to be a Christian apostate, a man who had gained some education from the Benedictines in Gaul. The Norsemen slaughtered all but two of the monks, Brothers Albinus and Barnabas. Both were young, about your age in fact. The Viking chief had them dragged before him and, to their surprise, addressed them in good Latin. He offered a chance for one of them to have his life spared.

Why? Well, the apostate might well have been motivated by his apostasy, a resentment of his time with the Benedictines, an urge to mock the young Christians, or perhaps it was simply a love of intellectual games and a way of displaying his superiority, of showing off before his illiterate crew. In any case, what he proposed was nothing less than a debate to the death. Subject: the existence of the Christian God. The band of Vikings, he said, would decide the winner by vote and he himself undertook faithfully to translate the arguments for them. He pointed to Albinus and told him he was to argue the pro side, then, with malicious delight at the irony of forcing a monk to do so, he instructed Barnabas that he must argue the case against God. The winner was to live; the loser's throat would be cut on the spot.

Now poor Albinus, while one of the most devout, was not among the most gifted of the monks; moreover, he had been traumatized by the violence he had just witnessed, by the circle of uncouth Vikings around him, and by the monstrous idea that he could survive only if Brother Barnabas should die, as he surely must if he had to argue against God. Tottering under this load of woe, he fell to his knees and commenced to pray. Brother Barnabas, on the other hand, was a sharp-witted scribe and remarkably self-possessed. He stepped over to Albinus and raised him up.

The Viking chief ordered Albinus to get on with it, to state his arguments or be put to death at once. Barnabas patted his brother on the back and spoke to him encouragingly.

Albinus could scarcely think and was barely capable of speech. He managed to stammer only a few sentences. He said that if there were no God then when people died there would be no judgment and that was unfair. Also, he added, if there were no God then how could he be a monk?

As this pathetic speech was translated, the Vikings laughed. Some even said such a weakling deserved to be killed immediately and the chief was considering this when Barnabas, sensing the problem, insisted in a firm voice that the rules called for the debate to be completed and a formal vote. And so, the clever Brother Barnabas was commanded to give his arguments against the existence of God.

Barnabas spoke slowly and fluently. He declared that he would limit himself to three arguments, though he could easily adduce several more.

First, he grabbed up one of the Vikings' shields. Holding it aloft he said that the existence of this shield obviously proved that of a shield-maker, as swords do sword-smiths. Just so, he said, the existence of the cosmos and all of nature, the flow of time and the extension of space, required a prior cause and a creator, one that did not move or change and was not confined but infinite. Recalling his Aristotle, he said that this necessary Unmoved Mover was God. In short, if there is a shield-maker to make shields then there must be a God to make ash trees, ravens, Vikings, and Irish monks.

Next, he said that it has been argued that no God exists because the goodness and omnipotence of God are incompatible with—well, with events such as the destruction of this peaceful and holy monastery and the violent murder of his brothers. Evil events, in short. But the contrary is so. The very conception of evil requires one of good, likewise the freedom of the will to choose between the two. Only God could confer such freedom on us poor creatures, otherwise we should be bound by necessity like the hawk and the ox. The fact that we know we are free thus shows not only a divine presence but also that a spark of His divinity lives in us, in our immortal souls.

The apostate chieftain laughed and through his narrowed eyes reminded Barnabas that he was supposed to be arguing *against*, not *for*, the existence of God.

Barnabas replied with his third argument, that if there were no God then the chief would not have to struggle so mightily against Him.

This enraged the Viking apostate. But his men insisted on hearing the translation. Albinus had again dropped to his knees. You shall die a martyr, he whimpered admiringly to Barnabas. As for the scribe, he stood calmly, insisting on a faithful translation of all he had said, as agreed.

Compelled to be true to the rules he had himself laid down, the chief translated all that Barnabas had said. The men cheered and cast their lots in favor of Barnabas; for they admired his courage and his gift of language. Their chief objected angrily, pointing out that Barnabas had not only failed to prove God didn't exist but had actually argued for the opposite proposition. In the confusion, Barnabas raised his hand and meekly reminded the apostate of the terms of the game, which he outlined as follows.

Here I wrote on the board:

A vs. B

If A wins, B dies.

If B wins, A dies.

Barnabas observed that, as the men all agreed, *he* had won the debate. However, it was the proposition Albinus had been assigned to defend that had prevailed. Therefore, *both* monks had won and *neither* could be killed. *Impossible!* shouted the Viking chief. Barnabas, putting his palms together prayerfully, looked heavenward, and replied that with God all things are possible.

Here I stopped. I had used up the whole fifty minutes, yet I heard no squeaking desk arms, no gathered knapsacks, no slammed notebooks.

The students wanted to know what happened next. Did Barnabas save both his life and Albinus'? Was the Viking re-converted? Did all the Vikings become Christians on the spot?

Instead of answering, I said that the chief failed to grasp Barnabas' ploy and asked if they had. It's a question of logic, I said.

One young woman did see it. The Viking didn't say whether the better *arguer* would win or the more convincing proposition and so, by his rules, both monks could be spared. The others listened to her but were unsure and looked to me. They wanted an authoritative answer. I complimented the young woman and went on to observe that, as she had just pointed out, Barnabas had merely exploited the ambiguity that is always introduced into logic by semantics. And so, you see, I said, logic can be a matter of life and death. I smiled at the class then added gravely that there are always Vikings, always barbarians who want to demolish the temple of learning, yahoos who are impatient with reason and civilization, even those who are eager to vituperate and spurn the gift of knowledge, especially when it's forced on them.

The students and I left the room five minutes late but feeling not altogether displeased with one another.

The remainder of the semester was full of delight and, I hope, some profit.

Professorial Ethics, or Kant Up the Congo

MORALITY is proper constraint, among other things. The internalization of restriction is the prerequisite for adulthood and civilized life. This must be why so many people, even whole groups, are proud of their sense of guilt. I once explained to a Jesuit the difference between Jews and Catholics on this point. Over the millennia, I joked, Jews have evolved a gene for guilt whereas Catholics acquire it in the first month of life—after which there is no difference. Freud contends that saints are the guiltiest of us all because they have the most powerful sense of guilt. What he calls a powerful Superego heaps renunciation on renunciation, punishing any rebellious, naturally amoral impulse. Nietzsche railed against guilt and pity, calling them enemies of the Will to Power and marks of the slave. If life is immoral, merely a food chain, then the perfect saint must feel guilty simply for being alive and pity for the amino acids that keep him or her going. Guilt need have no relation to moral responsibility because guilt is a passion rather than self-punishment for any actual transgression. An underestimated behavioral consequence of having a keen sense of guilt is the desire to *avoid* guilt—a negative principle by which some conscientious people govern their lives. What a paralyzing conundrum it is for them, too; for, if one has a penchant for feeling guilty, and part of this feeling is the wish to avoid feeling guilty, then how does one proceed in life?

I'm a stickler about deadlines. I told my students that all papers will be docked one grade for each calendar day they are late. I asked them if two students who submitted papers two days late should be marked down equally.

Of course, they said. Equity is the most primitive of moral demands. *It's not fair* is usually a child's first ethical declaration.

What, I asked, if one student with a late paper is a slacker who skips classes, never hands in work on time, is disrespectful to me, offers no excuse, while another is among the best students in the class, never misses a lecture, has given me hours of pleasure discussing readings with me in my office, and tearfully offers the excuse that her printer broke down? What then? Should I treat them differently?

I asked my students to tell me the differences between the nice and the good. Each added a brick and, little by little, they erected a wall that separated the two.

The nice is softer than the good. We like nice people but don't always respect them, while with good people it's often the other way around. Nice people are more readily manipulated than good ones. Nice people make better roommates. Good people make you feel inferior. Nice people aren't always as nice as they appear to be. Good people are reliable because you know where they're coming from, but nice people tend to act, like, you know, situationally. When I write a song and somebody hears it and they go *that's nice* I'm furious; but if they say *hey, that's good* then I'm happy. Whenever somebody wants to fix me up they always say the blind date's very, very *nice*. Nobody really wants to be fixed up with somebody who's very, very *good*. Good people don't care what other people think of them; if they did, then they'd probably be nice.

I asked them if they preferred nice teachers or good ones.

This time nobody rushed to answer. Instead, they laughed.

I asked if they liked being called nice, if they wanted people to think of them as nice.

Wanting to be considered nice has a lot of operant conditioning behind it, one psych major said. A young woman agreed with him. Yeah, she said, niceness is the total suburban virtue. They were mostly suburban kids. They laughed.

What I asked myself was whether being nice is a way of avoiding guilt. Certainly, myself answered promptly, but it's not a reliable one. Niceness is a social virtue, and social virtues are close kin to vices. It's a capital error to confuse the social with the ethical. Even my students knew this, though, of course, they acted as if they didn't. They were nice kids.

About teachers, the students were happy to make a little list with me: Nice teachers give extensions and easy grades. Nice teachers let you out of class early. Nice teachers try to make their classes entertaining and never assign long, unreadable books. Nice teachers empathize with your problems and they'll always give you a break because of them. Nice teachers are never, *ever* sarcastic. Nice teachers want to be liked, even loved—they want to be given glowing evaluations by their students. In short, nice teachers can be *had*, but sometimes they're doing the having, especially if they're nice before the evaluations and not afterwards. Nice teachers are moral relativists. Incidentally, the students agreed that social life would be unmanageable on purely moral lines—that is, if conducted in accord with absolute morality. What? Nothing but duty and no lying? No way. Nice teachers want to be happy, one student added, but the good ones don't seem to care. Ah. No, someone corrected, nice teachers want to be *happy* but the good ones seem more *content*.

I asked if they thought nice teachers—nice people in general— could also be good.

Yes, said one student, but only if they're prepared to give up niceness. It's like when your parents say this hurts me more than it hurts you, isn't it?

Yes, I thought, it is. To be good means renunciation, often a sacrifice of more than the mere gratification of being complaisant. Captain Vere, Starry Vere, hangs Billy Budd. To be good he kills the nice. To Vere, duty is entirely depersonalized, as goodness is for Epictetus and Kant. An impressed man in time of war strikes and kills his superior officer. Case closed. Just the facts and the law. Should it matter that the impressed man is an angel and the superior officer a devil? This hurts me more than you, Billy. If Vere were not tragic, if he were not destroyed by his act, then he'd be a monster. A good person is one who follows duty "even to the thwarting of all his inclinations," says Kant with that Prussian rigor of his. There is no more masculine ethicist than Kant. Most men understand Vere; most women are outraged by him. Relationships, personalities, intentions, contexts and narratives are all irrelevant to Kant. He dismisses niceness as mere "inclination," an unworthy motive or at least not a moral one. Inclination is not just niceness; it is often selfishness. The student was right to say that nice people aren't always nice. Once begun, there is no end to the mutual manipulation of students offered special treatment and teachers after high evaluations, or worse—love. There's nothing compli-cated about this. A child can understand Kant's ethical system since the categorical imperative comes with the hardware. *It's not fair*. Billy and Claggart both act on inclination rather than duty. Billy likes being sweet, Claggart likes flogging men. They are allegorical opposites, pure good and pure evil, half-humans who anatomize Vere's completely human psyche and for that reason can pull him apart. Billy and Claggart are base and acid; they neutralize each other. Poor, human Vere understands all this and that is why he chooses to trim his course by the law that ends by crushing him between its gigantic stones. How does he survive it? But is Vere's fissured psyche an argument against Kantian duty, against the imperative of equity and restraint, against Law itself or just a confir-mation of his view that morality is like iodine—that it has to hurt to work? Not to those who prefer principles to feelings. And what if duty leads us to do something that is correct yet wrong, an act that is morally defensible but emotionally unbearable? Do we shrug or give up our scruples? If duty and inclination drift too far apart, you have the formula for tragedy, or at least a nervous breakdown. You have *la condition humaine* laid out by Melville in his last will and testament.

There is a passage in Conrad's *Heart of Darkness* that lodged in my mind when I first read this great story as an adolescent. It isn't one of those usually cited or explicated, and yet, for me, it became a sort of touchstone.

Marlow's steamer is well up the Congo, only fifty miles below the Inner Station and Kurtz, when he comes on an abandoned hut. Fuel has been left for him and a perplexing message: "Wood for you. Hurry up. Approach cautiously." Marlow enters the dilapidated hovel and, by the door, comes across a book.

> It was an extraordinary find. Its title was, *An Inquiry into some Points of Seamanship*, by a man named Towser, Towson—some such name—Master in His Majesty's Navy. The matter looked dreary enough, with illustrative diagrams and repulsive tables of figures, and the copy was sixty years old. I handled this amazing antiquity with the greatest possible tenderness, lest it should dissolve in my hands. Within, Towson or Towser was inquiring earnestly into the breaking strain of ships' chains and tackle, and other such matters. Not a very enthralling book; but at the first glance you could see there a singleness of intention, an honest concern for the right way of going to work, which made these humble pages, thought out so many years ago, luminous with another than a professional light. The simple old sailor, with his talk of chains and purchases, made me forget the jungle and the pilgrims in a delicious sensation of having come upon something unmistakably real.

The book belongs to the harlequin Russian, Kurtz's disciple and worshiper, madcap embodiment of the "pure flame" of adventure. Marlow returns it to him later.

> I gave him Towson's book. He made as though he would kiss me, but restrained himself. "The only book I had left, and I thought I had lost it," he said, looking at me ecstatically.

The book is a sort of talisman. In my memory of the story, the book belonged to Marlow, not the Russian. Towser or Towson on seamanship is an emblem of what distinguishes Marlow from those around him, saves him from the cruelty, hypocrisy, the exploitation and decay; it is a correlative of his character and what enables him to steer a true course not only up that snaking symbolic Congo, but even in the teeming whited sepulchre of Brussels. *An Inquiry into some Points of Seamanship.* So much is in there: duty, order, England, cleanliness, restraint, ethics, tradition, the sea, the whole romantic yet exacting world of sail but also of writing, integrity, character, reality itself. Conrad stresses the book's dullness only to set off its luminosity. Here are singleness of intention, honest concern for the demands of work, above all an ethical orientation that transcends any one profession.

We all have our meandering Congos to negotiate, even in academic life. We must grade our students, evaluate our colleagues, cope with cheating, lying, egoism, self-seeking, hypocrisy, self-importance, back-biting. Kant is a sort of Towson on ethical seamanship. His book on ethics is no more prepossessing but no less luminous. He tells us the right way of going to work, how to bear the strain of chains and gain purchases. Kant reminds us always to act so that the maxim of our act can become a universal law without contradiction and to treat all rational creatures as ends and never as means, certainly not as means to good evaluations. Kant is the West's first tragic philosopher. Unlike the pagan Greeks, for whom a good life is a happy one, he admits that being good hasn't a thing to do with being happy. He says that the object of life isn't to be nice, to be loved, liked, rich, or praised. He tells us something sorrowful but "unmistakably real": that happiness is not the goal of our lives, but rather to be worthy of happiness. It's as if Kant is saying that only the unhappy are worthy of being happy.

This hurts me more than it does you, Billy. I'm sorry your printer broke down.

The Limits of Relativism, or Anecdote of the Postmodernist

Professor M. was deeply convinced by her studies of recent French philosophy and its American epigones. What she was convinced of is the folly of believing in even the possibility of disinterested rational discourse. She had learned to call the outmoded Cartesian-Enlightenment-Liberal-Humanistic paradigm washed up, shown up, exploded once and for all, decentered and deconstructed. It was not only her professional but also her personal opinion that all these hyphenated traditions were a mask for what words really are. Nietzsche told her, Marx and Foucault told her, a considerable number of brilliant feminist critics and thinkers told her: disinterested discourse never existed, never would, and never could. Words are always about power. The more men spoke of rational debate, of principles of right and wrong, the more patriarchal they were. Indeed, Prof. M. once told a class that nothing was more patriarchal (and patronizing) than the claim to disinterested rationality, a so-called debate on the issues. Professor M. placed her faith in the heuristic mojo of the query the madman poses to the doctor in Chekhov's *Ward No. 6*: "But why do *you* say that?" The question, of course, is always rhetorical, never curious. As an intellectual of her time, place, and gender, as one who fell on certain socio-political coordinates and had read certain books and been educated in a certain way, Prof. M. was obliged to deny the objectivity of truth, to see reality as a cultural construct, like a TV program or an advertising campaign. Indeed, to hear Prof. M. lecture on advertising, the interests served by the writing of the U.S. Constitution, or the pretensions of science to disembodied truth could be an electrifying experience. An enlightening one too; for Prof. M. wielded a truly marvelous flashlight.

Prof. M. taught that we do not credit something because it is demonstrably true; it is true because we need to believe it. By her own principles, Prof. M. must have needed to believe what she said. If all beliefs are self-serving and self-interested, in thrall to our wishes and interests, reflections of our hearts' desires, prejudices, and allegiances, then so are hers.

I had been invited to spend a year at Prof. M.'s institution. It happened to be the year she was up for tenure. There were some problems and the most insuperable one, it turned out, was Professor Q. This surprised people.

Q. was a man of about sixty with a distinguished record of publications and the University's top teaching award to his credit. Not a bit crusty or hidebound, Q. was, on the contrary, rather youthful and spirited. He was known to cultivate the untenured, thought of as a good mentor without ulterior motives even with women, a generous and progressive man. He also had a name for integrity and an increasingly public distaste for recent developments in the humanities. On one occasion, I even saw him bridle at what he referred to as "politicization and undisciplined relativism." Still, he gave the new theorists their due; he even read their books. Q. knew a good flashlight when he saw one.

The story was that a debate broke out between M. and Q. at a department meeting. As an itinerant, I wasn't there but there were plenty who relished telling me about it. According to what they said, it began when the untenured Professor K. asked untenured Prof. M. if, as he had heard, she had declared at a private meeting of female faculty that the department had systematically discriminated against women in decisions on appointments, salary, tenure, and promotion. My sources agree that the blood rushed to Prof. M.'s face, for K. could be seen as a rival; however, she did not hesitate to admit that this was exactly what she had said.

It was at this point that Q. spoke up. He said he took such charges both seriously and personally, as he had participated in these decisions for a couple of decades. He asked Prof. M. for her evidence.

M. said the evidence was all around.

Q. asked what that meant.

M. refused to answer him, which made things much worse.

Q. asked again for her evidence, officiously seconded by Prof. K.

M. ignored K. but accused Q. of essentializing gender. Out of solidarity with M., Prof. L. made sisterly noises.

Q. said that, on the contrary, in the institutional decisions that she found unfair, apparently without evidence, gender was irrelevant, as the record would show should she care to examine it.

In other words, Q. frostily asserted what attorneys call the dispository nature of facts. Even worse, he declared that he and his colleagues had exercised disinterested judgment by applying objective standards to appraise individual achievements without regard to gender, race, or class.

To Prof. M., already angry and defensive, this could not go unchallenged. She stated that so-called disinterested judgments were not only impossible but undesirable. She declared that different people ought to be judged by different standards. This, since Q. obviously hadn't figured it out for himself, said Prof. M., was what was meant by diversity.

For example? Q. asked.

M. said that one good example was student evaluation data. To judge men and women by the same standard was clearly unfair, given the culture's long tradition of privileging patriarchal authority and decentering women which made students automatically perceive male faculty more positively than women.

Q. sighed and quoted from Blake's *Proverbs of Hell: One law for the lion and the ox is tyranny*. He then leaned back in his chair and remarked that it sort of looked to him as if it were Prof. M. who wanted to essentialize gender.

By now they were both worked up, my sources agree. One of them even said that, by then, *words were in the driver's seat.* This phrase reminded me of Kleist's essay about Mirabeau and the bayonet.[7]

M. came out with the formula of her deepest conviction. She said she was sick and tired of Q.'s patronizing liberal claptrap and that the controlling discourse of the University, as perfectly enunciated by him, was simply about the power of *people like him* over *people like her.*

Q.'s answer was more temperate than his tone. He said that it was precisely by seeking fair and objective standards that power was to be curbed.

M. repeated that she was disgusted and that someday people like Q. would find themselves tossed on the dust heap of history where they belonged.

Well, said Q., then you say it's all about power, decisions on things like appointments, tenure and salaries?

Of course, she said.

Q. wondered aloud what, if *she* had power, Prof. M. might do with it.

I hope you'll find out, she retorted.

Q. pointed out that if her agenda of privileging and valorizing and foregrounding the oppressed and victimized—beginning, it seems, with herself—could not be argued for on grounds of fairness and justice, but depended on who had more power, then, by her own reading of current relations, she lost.

At this point, M. warned everyone at the meeting that she would sue if she were denied tenure.

Q. observed that if she did so she would be obliged to appeal to the values that so disgusted her. She would need to make a case by adducing evidence.

---

7. The essay is titled "On the Gradual Fabrication of Thoughts While Speaking." It can be found in *An Abyss Deep Enough*, ed. By Philip B. Miller (New York: E.P. Dutton, 1982), 218-222.

Then the meeting broke up. I'm told there was a rush for the door.

And what happened? Prof. M.'s tenure application was turned down by her department. Q. voted against her. It was the first time he had ever voted against anybody. She did sue. The case was still in court when my year was up.

A flashlight is a tool for illuminating things other than itself.

Do patriarchal pretensions to fairness offend and repress the non-male, non-straight, and non-white or are they the best hope of the excluded? Is it better to deny their validity and attempt to overthrow liberal strictures than to make people live up to them through reason and shame?

Critique runs into trouble when it forgets that it is a secondary, essentially parasitic activity. Derrida's most brilliant and audacious exegesis of him does not replace Rousseau.

Radical relativism tends to smash up against the demands of both ethics and science, not because these are founded on unquestionable absolute truths but because they aspire to be. It's hardly a new story. Ordinary, moderate moral relativism respects the law, as Protagoras did. He was well-traveled and saw that laws are relative to time and place, but he recognized that the conception of Law itself is constant. The next generation of Sophists, men like Thrasymachus and Callicles, wanted to go further, holding that, if what is right is relative, then nothing is really right except what is to one's own advantage. They had good flashlights too and they turned them on the origin of the laws, finding in them only the interests either of the strong or the weak. This is the sort of insight that excited Prof. M. She cherished the idea of paradigm-shifting, was stimulated by disruption, wanted "new thresholds, new anatomies," in Hart Crane's phrase. This gave her both a purpose and a program of research. One tool isn't fit for every job, though. Many people find Marxist economic analysis indispensable but would nevertheless laugh at the notion of voting a communist into office. That is, a method of analysis is not an end, not even a program. For example, the assertion that all judgments are based on interests disregards the judge (perhaps Prof. Q. was such a one) whose paramount interest lies in achieving as much fairness, good will, and objectivity as he or she can manage.

The scientific method is a wonderful cultural product, and one thing it makes possible is that variously interested, differently constructed individuals may agree. This is to say that the scientific method burns away any interest other than the one in truth. I have noticed that female scientists, women who have struggled their whole lives against the expectations and prejudices of men, who have fallen in love with the ideal of an understanding of the world that is beyond question, are infuriated by the claim made by certain of Prof. M.'s colleagues that science is a masculinist, cold, even vicious and arbitrary, way of viewing the world. For such women, to dispense with evidence in favor of ideology is simply a regression into myth-making. Scientists do not mistake flashlights for ends-in-themselves. As one of them put it, she would eagerly eliminate her own prejudices if she only knew what they were.

Relativism is, up to a point, perfectly suited to democracy. The Sophists throve under Athens' democracy, while the aristocratic Plato, with his unquenchable taste for the absolute, scorned the "r" word and despised the rule of the many. His Republic is, above all, an anti-Athens. Relativism is hardly uncivilized; in fact, it is the consequence of one sort of cosmopolitanism. Relativism is not without clear standards either. It can judge in accord with personal interests but also by contingent laws and social contracts. Relativism provides a pragmatic, anti-idealistic, and non-elitist ethic to which all may adhere, even if most don't abide by it, so to speak. But I think to be authentically *law-abiding*, even for relativists, calls for a conception of law that is other than relativistic, as when in the *Crito* Socrates personifies the Laws of Athens in order to examine what he owes them, or when Vere hangs Billy Budd to uphold something of which the Mutiny Act and the Articles of War are mere shadows. In other words, the conception of Law itself sets a limit to relativism beyond which it loses its initial impetus towards tolerance and decency. Without this respect for Law, relativism's utility to democracy vanishes along with its goodness. Socrates easily wins his argument with the radical Sophists. Nietzsche notwithstanding, no good society can be built on the *Wille zur Macht*, only a monstrous one. Legalism with a Platonic aura, this is what I imagine animates the best, most far-seeing and humane of legal minds. The sort of relativism that subverts ethics altogether only lands you in the swamp, and you can't build much on a swamp.

I pity poor Prof. Q., who was led to violate his principles in order to save them. And I pity poor Prof. M. who discovered too late that, in practice, she depended on what she despised in theory.

Editor's Note

I found these three pieces among Sidney Fein's files for the years 1975, 1982 and 1983, respectively. I am responsible for the titles, as Fein gave them none, and for combining them. There are several short, occasional items of this sort among Fein's posthumous papers. Some, like these, may be read either as finished work or as abandoned fragments. These three items are not rough drafts but typescripts that have been worked over. Still, Fein did not publish them; he left no indication of what use he may have intended to make of them, or for what audience they may have been intended. This is not particularly surprising, as Fein often began work without such plans.

Sidney Fein never held a continuous academic appointment but, from time to time, accepted visiting professorships. While he could be acerbic about universities, and even wrote some stinging epigrams about its denizens, he also enjoyed and respected the institutions where he worked, and he loved teaching.

Fein's first stint as a visiting professor was in 1974. The invitation was owing to the critical reception of his first book, *Diptych on Terrestrial Representation*, published the previous year. The first piece, then, is clearly about the first time he taught logic or, indeed, any course. It conveys more than the intriguing story of Albinus and Barnabas. In it, Fein records the transformation of his attitude toward teaching itself. Initially, provoked by their unsatisfactory motives, he sought to drive students away. By the second class, however, he had redefined his role as a creator of motivation. Fein never confused teaching with entertaining, yet he came to see that, in a culture increasingly dominated by show business, a teacher had to demonstrate how absorbing scholarship can be. Fein came to refer to his pedagogy as "propaganda for thinking."

The second piece, as my title is meant to suggest, is about how Fein conducted himself as a teacher. One of his former students, who took an ethics course with Fein, reports that when they came to study Kant's *Foundations of the Metaphysics of Morals*, he told the class that this was his rule-book of professional ethics; that is, it governed his way of dealing with them. The Conrad passage is also revelatory. Fein loved Conrad, collected the complete Malay edition, and re-read one volume every summer.

Fein's reference to Kant as a masculine philosopher *par excellence* is intriguing, especially given the sexual politics of the third piece. What he appears to mean is that Kant rules out of ethical consideration those very concerns that most matter to women. I asked his ex-student about this. He thought about it for a minute then said that Fein had begun one class on Kant by asking the students their opinions of a certain situation. A young woman is going steady with a young man; that is, they've committed to an exclusive relationship. One day she gets a call from her high school boyfriend, who's in town on business. She hasn't seen him in four years. He asks her to meet him for a meal. Should she accept? Well, said the former student, all the men agreed at once that she shouldn't. To us, he laughed, it was a matter of principle. But the women all said they'd need to know a lot more. For instance, they wanted to know more about how exclusive this relationship was and whether it included plans to get engaged and how long it had been in effect. They needed to know the nature of the high school relationship, too. They even wanted to know what sort of restaurant the old squeeze had invited her to, also whether it was to be a lunch or a dinner, on a Friday night or a Saturday.

The final piece anticipates by nearly a decade the *Kulturkampf* that was to preoccupy American universities in the early 1990s and still does. In his published work, Fein displays a deeply ambivalent view of the influence of French postmodernism. His compassion for both Prof. Q. and Prof. M. may seem to leave his own position unresolved; however, Fein's analogy between critical theory and a flashlight suggests both his appreciation of writers like Barthes, Derrida, and Foucault and his belief in their limits, perhaps also his repugnance at the imperial designs of their American followers. One noteworthy detail is his placing these thinkers in the tradition of the late Sophists as radical relativists. A second is Fein's idea that a good legal mind must entertain not just the relativism of an ethics based on legislation and the absolutism of Law itself, but also human need. Perhaps his own preferred orientation to life and thought called for a rigorous, Kantian integrity tempered by a flexible and intelligent relativism.

A KEYNOTE ADDRESS

LADIES and gentlemen, I am going to begin with a confession. I have always been suspicious of academics who respect themselves. I admit I have said a pretty terrible thing, doing myself no honor and probably offending yours. I am anything but proud of saying such words, but I can't help it. Bear in mind that my suspiciousness is purely subjective, a feeling and not a conclusion, a sentiment in relation to certain of my colleagues that I regret and would rid myself of if I could. If I thought it proper to feel this suspicion I wouldn't have to call my statement a confession.

Confessions isolate because they disclose something disreputable and can lose you your place in the community. People confess a violation of the rules, a breach of decorum, an offense to taste, a crime of the heart. Confessing is showing oneself up. Nevertheless, to confess is also an effort to reintroduce oneself into the community out of which the confession reveals one deserves to be thrust. You, ladies and gentlemen, are such a community, an assembly of academics who do not deserve to be insulted. I hope that, even in the face of what I have said, you might be able to include me among your number, that, like Lord Jim, I might still be one of you. The difficulty is that I'm not repentant. The self-respect of academics troubles me, and I don't exempt myself. In so far as I too am an academic, I find it difficult to respect myself.

But why should I be suspicious of academics who are proud of their achievements, pleased with their degrees and titles, at home with their professional lives? I'm not altogether sure. It isn't just that so many of them tend to turn into administrators; nor do I think my suspicion can be put down to a self-hatred originating in my childhood or graduate training. It is, I grant, perverse to find suspect those of my colleagues who are most assured and confident, who can justly claim both virtue and social utility. All the same, even as a perverse and personal sentiment, my suspicion seems to me worth thinking about.

When it is hard to think something through, a good recourse for professors as for preachers is to adduce a text. So here's one. In Chapter Four of Part One of Dostoyevsky's *Notes from Underground* is found the narrator's account of a Petersburg intellectual with a toothache. The passage is notorious and unforgettable.

> I ask you, gentlemen, listen sometimes to the moans of an educated man of the nineteenth century suffering from toothache, on the second or third day of the attack, when he is beginning to moan, not as he moaned on the first day, that is, not simply because he has a toothache, not just as any coarse peasant, but as a man affected by progress and European civilization...

Remember it? Anyway, Dostoyevsky winds up with this less familiar statement:

> You laugh? Delighted. My jests, gentlemen, are of course in bad taste, jerky, involved, lacking in self-confidence. But of course that is because I do not respect myself. Can a man of perception ever really respect himself?

That is an arresting question, isn't it, maybe an improper one and doubtless in poor taste. Academics are above all people of perception; they too are deeply affected, if not by progress, then certainly by civilization which they can think themselves into believing they incarnate. The most eminent carry such a load of specialized knowledge that, to paraphrase a modern poet, within their fields they cannot be surprised. Surely this is by itself a sufficient motive for self-respect, even a *respectable* self-respect, if I can style it that way. And yet, it appears, not for me.

Would I prefer that professors should all be undergroundlings, miserable, isolated, victims of emotional self-abuse, like the alienated part-timers and exploited adjuncts who constitute a growing proletariat of the spirit? Hardly. Even the original Underground Man shouts "to hell with the Underground." The adjuncts and part-timers, I'm sure, agree. No, that isn't it at all.

Self-respect can be a worthy virtue, like self-reliance. It saves you from submitting to degradation; it gives you a platform from which to denounce injustice. Professors who respect themselves are certainly preferable to those who despise themselves, but the same is true of butchers and auto mechanics. It is only those who respect themselves *because* they are professors that trouble me. I feel the same about politicians. So, perhaps what I am saying is that certain professions ought to be more deeply penetrated by irony than others, that, for them, irony is the most accessible form of humility. Without this saving grace, academics tend to take themselves with immoderate seriousness. The wrong sort of self-respect leads to pomposity, arrogance, and that abstraction from reality writers of comedies from Aristophanes up readily ascribe to academic types.

The academics who provoke me are not without knowledge or insight, expertise or formidable lists of publications; what they lack is self-consciousness. They could use a bit more corrosive acid in their brains. In fact, "self-consciousness" may be a better translation of Dostoyevsky: can a *self-conscious* academic really respect him or herself? To this I am adding, with compunction, the uncertain and perhaps ethically misguided addendum: and *ought* they to respect themselves? It's obvious that self-consciousness can undermine a thoughtless self-respect—maybe even thoughtful and justified self-respect—by disclosing those nasty truths that are to be found only in the Underground. What is it I find suspicious if not the lack of self-consciousness which, reasoning backward from Dostoyevsky, I deduce from certain forms of self-respect? There are some academics who, should they be granted a moment of genuine self-consciousness, would simply blow up.

Wherein lies the dignity and self-respect proper to our profession? A good principle of human thought is that to understand north you should go south. Following this principle, let's look at a few academic jokes. Dostoyevsky's narrator tells jokes—jerky, involved ones—because he does not respect himself. What do academic jokes reveal about the respectability of our profession?

First joke, or rather an actual occurrence that is also a joke. A certain distinguished professor of linguistics was delivering a paper at a scholarly conference. Wishing to introduce a little levity at the end of his lengthy, highly technical lecture—a levity he never supposed might be leaden—he spoke of the double negative, explaining that vulgar usage was in conflict with logic, where a double negative signifies an affirmative. "It is curious," he wound up with a smile at his own wit, "that there exists no such thing in our language as a double affirmative that results in a negative." Suddenly, from the rear of the hall, an exasperated colleague shouted out, "Sure, sure."

What's amusing about this story in the first instance is its punch line. The linguist's point about double negatives is something everyone already knows and for him to bring it up for the sake of a cheap finale is banal, even insulting. That the facetious repetition of an affirmative functions as a negative is, however, something of which few people, probably even few linguists, will have thought. More importantly, this *particular* linguist hadn't thought of it. The joke works precisely because the joke is on him. He had intended to entertain his audience with his own unfunny joke and was anticipating a gratifying ovation. His effort at wit is so clumsy and pompous, the peripeteia so sudden, that the shout of "Sure, sure" must surely pierce him to the heart. And doesn't he deserve puncturing because, in my sense, he has respected himself too much? Not only does he look down his nose at the vulgarity of the double negative—though it was good enough for Shakespeare—he presumes his listeners will join with him. Nobody who says "I don't see no reason for it" is likely to be in attendance at a linguistics conference; they are beyond the pale. But vulgarity, common usage, the commonplace, real life leaps up at the back of the hall like a viper and bites him. The laughter he meant to provoke actually does break out, and at the right moment; but in that instant he has ceased to be the complacent purveyor of donnish wit and has turned into the butt of somebody else's joke, a much better one than his. On top of all this he is proved wrong—and, better yet, by a disagreement that takes the form of agreement. He has snatched annihilation from the jaws of approbation. If the right person slips on a banana peel—the blustering drill sergeant, the ruthless CEO, the head of the secret police, the tough grader—everybody breaks up.

Perhaps later that night in an airline seat paid for by university administrators who hoped to raise their own status through his lost triumph, our linguist began to reflect on his humiliation—on his life as an academic. I like to think that, five or six miles above the earth, he at last stumbled into the Underground with its subversive questions. If he can be defeated by two syllables, then what is he really? What value does his brilliant fifty-minute address have over against that commonplace, but diabolically clever riposte which was grasped in an instant by everyone and will be remembered far longer? Is there a purpose to linguistics other than to make careers for linguists? Has he forgotten what it is? Do his students ever guess at his motives, how much of the *Wille zur Macht* lies behind his long-windedness and intricate examination questions, the petty vanity at the root of his carefully toted-up list of scholarly articles; do they ever suspect what an ignoramus he actually is at times? And is it only "at times" that he is an ignoramus?

On the other hand, perhaps there was no redemptive existential crisis for this linguist either in the air or on land, no solvent against which his impregnable self-respect was not proof. Who knows? It's at least as likely that he began to think of the best way to work the crack about the double affirmative into his next lecture.

The second joke is my favorite of all academic jokes. It is actually a sort of parable and, like all good parables, short and gravid.

Professor X is running down Professor Z to Professor Y. Y objects. "I don't see how you can say those things about Z. The man knows everything." "That's right," X replies, "but that's *all* he knows."

The joke about the linguist is not ambiguous; this one is. The first story is comparatively superficial, perhaps because it's true; but this one seems to me to have the depth and concentration only fiction can achieve.

Who is the butt of this joke? Is it, as first appears, Professor Z, who only knows "everything"? Is Z one of those scholars who bestrides his field like a colossus and considers himself a good parent because, with only a little prompting, he is able to list all his children by their first names? Is Z a sort of idiot savant; that is, brilliant at polymer physics or comparative anthropology but an ignoramus when it comes to the price of eggs? Would his self-regard be demolished by a remark that sounds like praise but is really contempt?

Or is the butt of the joke the credulous and adoring Professor Y, so quick to extol his idol with the obviously excessive claim that he "knows everything"? Z might not respect himself but X does, and too much; he bows down before Z as if he were a god. There are academics who seek to dance around in the refulgence of some eminent authority in their field as though he were the golden calf, grounding their own self-respect on the adoration of another with whom they try to associate, planets to his sun. X's riposte, "but that's *all* he knows," is, in this view, immeasurably more devastating to Y than the more customary, "the hell he does."

Or is the butt of the joke Professor X? He sounds like one of those academics who ignore Socrates' advice to Meletus: not to run down others but to improve themselves. Professors of this sort, I think, abound because the Meletus-impulse is one of the nastier aspects of human nature exacerbated by academic life where status is at once relative, evanescent, and vital. The word "status," incidentally, has the same root as "state" and "stature"; all derive from *stare*, Latin for *to stand*. Where does one *stand*? To how many of us is this a perpetual anxiety? After all, why is X running down Z if not to increase his own comparative standing in the zero-sum game of academic status? And why does he wish to stand above Z if not in order to buttress his own self-respect which, for people like him, can only be found in the eyes of others? Well, perhaps X doesn't respect himself, but that is hardly in his favor, since he has made of his self-respect a motive for backbiting. Unable to deny the substantial achievements of Professor Z, he finds an ingenious way of diminishing them, by accusing Z of being a fool. "Z knows everything, but that's *all* he knows."

From yet another point of view even though the joke may explode X, Y, and Z, it might not be directed at any of them personally. In this interpretation, the real object of the joke is the rivalry of academic life, which in its worst form is devoted to professional jealousy and an equally petty adoration as well as to "knowing *everything*"—while ignoring everything *else*. Knowing without understanding, careerism without compass, data without wisdom, lots of head and scarcely any heart. Academics, the joke seems to say, may know everything but little good it does them, or us.

I wouldn't want you to think that I have no respect for our profession. On the contrary. What is most worthy of respect about the Academy is never knowledge, efficiency, or utility, let alone the self-regard or salaries of those who work in it. From Plato's time to ours, what is most respectable about academic life remains its idealism. The irony is that those who believe they have achieved this ideal, or are on the road to attaining it—or even that they will ever get there—may already have lost sight of it.

In April 1978, Sidney Fein was invited to deliver the keynote address at a conference to be called "Academe at the Crossroads: The Status of the American Professoriate." The conference, organized and funded by the Laterlake Foundation, was scheduled for a weekend in October. The Foundation was subsequently compelled to withdraw its support owing to embezzlement by its C.F.O. Cancellation letters were sent out at the beginning of September.

In reviewing Fein's file for 1978, I came across the above text which I take to be a draft of his undelivered address, composed sometime between April and August of that year. It is in the form of a typescript with handwritten corrections. Fein's habit was to write lectures and letters on a typewriter, then revise by hand and retype. Work he deemed less ephemeral, essays and his three books, he always began with a fountain pen. I cannot say if Fein had completed or would actually have given this address. Still, what Fein wrote is of interest.

Sidney Fein was an academic, though an intermittent, itinerant, untenured one. He held visiting appointments at six institutions, none for more than two years. Thanks to family wealth he did not need to rely on an academic salary and there were several years when he held no such position at all. He gave himself sabbaticals to complete his three books.

Among Fein's published works there are few discussions of academic matters. However, in *Want, Desire, and Need* (1977), he offers a characterization of university life that is echoed in this address, drafted the following year. There, Fein had lamented that "so much of academic life consists in listening to expressions of cynicism in a context of disingenuous idealism or of idealism in a context of low-down cynicism" (194). In this passage Fein is speaking of "the underside of those large educational institutions organized along the same lines as the Inca Empire." In his last book, *Aristocratic*

Democracy (1983), Fein takes up this point about hierarchy from a different angle. Here he mordantly sketches out what he calls "the ineluctable conflict between elitism and democracy, merit and equality" in American higher education, briefly outlines the levels of status among professors, researchers, staff, and administrators. He is hardest on the last: "… despite their obvious parasitism, administrators, enamored of the corporate model and eager to emulate it, have little difficulty in identifying the preeminent elite and proprietors of the educational establishment as themselves" (257).

Fein's judgment of academia appears harsh, but this is misleading. Sometimes he is just having fun. Fein was deeply grateful for the opportunity to teach and to the institutions that afforded him the chance of doing so. He had many academic friends, both respected colleagues and appreciative former students. It is worth recalling that, if Fein had really despised academic life, he was in a position to eschew it. Though the tone of the above address is derogatory and calculated to provoke an audience of professors, the jokes chosen to show academics only at their worst, I think his real point is in the closing statement about idealism. Fein certainly knew that the ideal of academic life is as unattainable as any other and that the purity of any ideal can be too exclusive, but, in admitting this, he does not relinquish the ideal as his standard of judgment.

Fein's attitude toward academia was that of a satirist, not a cynic. Satirists and cynics both tend to be disappointed idealists. The difference is that cynics pass directly from naive faith in their ideal to expecting the lowest common denominator, never stopping at reality. Cynics don't believe they can improve anything. Satirists, on the other hand, seeing how far reality falls below the ideal, cannot help reproaching it, deploring its failures out loud and mockingly. But their aim is improvement, not hopelessness.

Scattered among Fein's papers are several items relevant to this address, and they are all humorous or satirical. The self-importance of certain of his colleagues, the pomposity of academic processions, the pretentiousness of academic procedures all provoked him. He clearly relished academic jokes. I have found several among his papers, scribbled down without comment. Not all are at the expense of professors, though. For example, in his file for 1976, he recorded an amusing story about Robert Frost. Unfortunately, Fein does not give its provenance.

Frost used to teach a course each summer at the Breadloaf School for writers in Vermont. Fein's anecdote implies that the poet was not a gifted or particularly hard-working teacher, and that he neither wanted nor pretended to be. Fein writes:

> Frost would give the same one-question final exam year after year, the vapid, shopworn question, *What have you learned in this course?* A certain Mr. Smith, no doubt feeling exasperated and cheated of the grand experience he had imagined upon registering—three whole weeks at the feet of the Master!—wrote that he hadn't learned a damn thing and handed in his bluebook. The students had to return the following Monday to pick up their grades. Smith's bluebook had an "A-" on it. (N.B. This is already sufficient proof of Frost's wit.) Smith, who was not lacking in chutzpah, strode to the front of the room and demanded that Frost tell him why he hadn't received an A. Frost took the book, opened it, and pointing to what Smith had written in it, observed that he had spelled "damn" incorrectly.

Fein's disappointment with certain colleagues and his annoyance with the absurdities of academic life are also expressed in about a dozen epigrams scattered among his papers. They are waspish and caustic, recording a falling away from Fein's conception of an ideal. Here are a few samples:

On Professor X's Mind

"Henry James had a mind so fine
no idea could violate it."
We must let out Eliot's line
to suit X and thus restate it:
there is no idea so divine
X's mind can't desecrate it.

Tardif Professeur Blois

Professeur Blois is late to class,
as late as any French waiter.
His students do not cry "*Hélas!*"
Non! They wish that he were later.

Professor Assentator

So eager to be loved is he
his lowest grade's above a C;
gives little homework, yearns to be
his pupil's pal and chairman's chum,
though both know where he's coming from:
despised many, used by some.

Ad. Bldg.

It flashes like a helm hard by the dorms,
locus classicus of a thousand forms,
proof against student protests, unions, storms,
distinguished, as one gradually discerns,
from lesser piles with lesser concerns:
there no one teaches, and nobody learns.

ROBERT WEXELBLATT

Sidney Fein may have laughed at the Academy but rather as a loving parent does at the blunders and trespasses of a child. What he called his "suspicion of academics who respect themselves" is a distaste for complacency, self-glorification, and the willful ignorance of personal motives that lead some academics into bathos or worse. Because universities were to him marvelous places peopled by remarkable individuals heavy with achievement, exalted by potentiality, and dedicated to the worthiest of human aspirations—precisely for this reason universities were for Fein carpeted with banana peels.

SOCRATES, HAMLET, LANGUAGE AND INSINCERITY

THE claim of sincerity can be a proof of insincerity yet at the same time sincere in a deeper sense; that is, proof of a truthfulness more reliable than sincerity. So slippery is language that it is no small victory to get it to jibe with reality. Ironists are, I think, better at it than crafty rhetoricians or naive orators.

Good words matter because bad ones do. Just before he downs the hemlock Socrates says, "False words are not only evil in themselves, but they infect the soul with evil." That would serve well as his epitaph—or my epigraph.

Socrates at his trial and Hamlet in Act One assert themselves right off the bat by making nearly identical claims. Each is involved in an argument when he does so, Socrates explicitly, Hamlet implicitly—but this isn't especially noteworthy. What is remarkable is that these declarations should be undercut even as they are being stated and that, by canceling themselves, achieve the most accurate possible self-representation.

The opening of *The Apology* is often scanted in favor of more glamorous passages, such as the shaggy-dog story about Chaerephon and the Delphic Oracle or the Perry Masonish cross-examination of hapless Meletus. (Hapless? One must always remember that Plato declines to give us the case for the prosecution.) Anyway, it's no matter, since both these sections are brilliant elaborations of what is implicit in Socrates' opening sentence:

> How you have felt, O men of Athens, at hearing the *speeches* of my accusers, I cannot tell; but I know that their *persuasive* words almost made me forget *who I was:*—such was the effect of them; and yet they have hardly spoken a word of *truth*.

Socrates could have started almost anywhere. He might have begun by denying responsibility for the treasonable acts of Critias and Alcibiades, for instance, certain to have been raised by his accusers. He could have reminded the Assembly that nothing he is charged with—atheism, corrupting youth—is against the law. He might have invoked the Athenian respect for and delight in freedom of speech (they had four words for the concept). But he chooses instead to begin by speaking of language and how it can be used to create appearances, to replace *Is* with *Seem*. It is a significant choice because Socrates is stating the meaning of his life. If we isolate the words italicized above, the subtext is clearly that a persuasive speech is a lying one. Therefore Peitho is not to be trusted; the Goddess of the Rhetoricians pushes seductive appearances. Is the truth then *un*persuasive? Socrates says his accusers have used language to distort, to achieve a purpose, while he shall use words honestly, not to escape punishment, but to reveal reality. The portrait of Socrates just painted by Meletus, Lycon and Anytus as an enemy of the people is false. He repeats the very warning they have given to beware of his persuasiveness. The Assembly, he agrees, must be on its guard and judge only the veritable Socrates, the private servant of the State, the innocent Socrates who is a good man on a divine mission, the uncompromising moralist who never submitted to any injustice, neither of the democrats nor the of oligarchs. They should think carefully and not, for example, conclude that such a typical saying of his as that "Only the one who is wise should rule" is proof of monarchical sentiment, hearing only the "one" and not the "wise." Don't democracies need to be led by the wise?

Since he has nothing but words with which to defend himself, Socrates' attack on persuasion places him in an ironic position. Is it a mistake? Well, for him irony is the briar patch; nobody was ever more at home there than Socrates. Still, the situation is not simple. If he is persuasive then, by his own logic, he too may appear to be a liar. He could become that fool who has an ass for a lawyer. Thus, to *be* persuasive he must *appear* unpersuasive; to *appear* as he *is*, he must represent himself, so to speak, inarticulately, though in fact he is the most articulate of Athenians. Indeed, Socrates, the despiser of rhetoric, beats all the rhetoricians at their own game and, given how often this opening gambit has been imitated (think of Sam Ervin claiming to be "just a simple country lawyer"), he may also be called their teacher.

Socrates answers the warning of his accusers not to be "deceived by the force of [his] eloquence" by claiming incompetence as a speaker but then adds "… unless by the force of eloquence they mean the force of truth; for then I do indeed admit that I am eloquent." This is piling irony upon irony. Socrates claims sincerity but, as everybody knows, Socrates is famous for his irony. This is one of the reasons he is on trial. It is the essence of his pedagogical strategy to *know* yet to feign *ignorance*. The Socratic Method is also Socratic Irony; for if he is ignorant, he can put his little questions, suck his interlocutors in. After centuries in which traditional societies answered questions with appeals to tradition and authority, Socrates habitually questions both. To think for yourself is the only way to know yourself or, for that matter, to *have* a self. He is the first and the funniest of intellectual martyrs, and irony is his tool. Here he pleads unpersuasiveness the better to persuade. He even says that he shall "be using the same words in [his] defense which [he had] been in the habit of using, and which you may have heard in the agora." Socrates remains faithful to his Method to the end and so he is justified in appropriating the military virtue (*arête*) of sticking to one's post. How Nietzsche must have ranted at this; for, by likening himself to Achilles, Socrates forever altered the meaning of the word *virtue.*

In view of all this, is it claiming too much to say that Socrates' assertion of an *unrhetorical sincerity* is itself proof of *rhetorical insincerity* when the claim to speak badly is the ploy of an outstanding speaker? It may be a trick; nevertheless, Socrates is indeed speaking the truth of *who he is.* He is indeed no "*junior* orator." Orators lecture, but Socrates understood that, while all questions always have answers, almost all these answers are wrong. A man who doesn't have the truth in advance of his inquiry can hardly set up as a lecturer who answers questions; the questioner of answers has to be an ironist. Socrates did not get the better of golden-tongued Protagoras by speaking "a set oration duly ornamented with words and phrases" but by forcing the elder philosopher to submit to his cross-examination. In fact, Socrates didn't get the better of anyone by appearing to try to best them. Good *Eris*, not the bad; a mutual search for the truth, not a boxing match—that was his trade. Or perhaps it was his professional game. After all, good *eris* can look remarkably like the bad, a technique of humiliation. Socrates often mangles his opponents, but always to the *end* of the good. All good teachers know that the search for truth begins with demolition. In short, he has integrity but not sincerity, and the former is the superior virtue; it is the reality, not the mere appearance of steadfastness. Kant made much the same point in rejecting Rousseau's reliance on sentiment in ethics, calling sincerity the highest of virtues. Insincerity *can* be a kind of integrity. This is why Kierkegaard writes appreciatively of Socrates' cunning tactic of "deceiving people into the truth."

So, an assertion of sincerity might be a proof of insincerity. From such a complicated position one can reveal the truth only if it is offered with the proper irony, an irony that is acutely aware of itself. Socrates' contempt for *un*ironic rhetoric is both epistemological and ethical. He looks on the rhetorician, for whom language is merely a tool to attain some worldly aim, as the absolutist does the relativist.

The latter does not believe in *truth*, only in *truths*, all of which are partial, provisional, and self-interested. These days, the Sophists labor away on Madison Avenue, where the worlds of politics and commerce converge. You name it, we'll persuade people of it. Their skills are dazzling but their ironies lack the integrity of Socrates'. They certainly desire to deceive, but not into the truth. Socrates himself is proof that it requires greater mastery to reveal the truth than to conceal it. To *persuade* is easy enough; it needs only craftiness and a motive. To be a witness for the truth, however, demands talent, integrity, and—despite all the irony—a belief that there is something to believe.

A man may love his wife and yet wish her less near-sighted. Is Socrates' attack on rhetoric really a proof that he disliked Athenian democracy, or does it show that he knew where democracy's sore point lay? I see no reason to limit Socrates' mistrust of persuasiveness to politics; that is, to suppose he believed the common people could be easily misled by eloquent, resonant oratory. In fact, his appeal that they ignore the meretricious speeches of his accusers shows Socrates had at least some confidence in the Assembly's ability to discriminate *is* from *seems*. His defense is itself a lesson in his favorite topic, the distinction between appearance and truth, including the point that there is, in fact, something worthy of being called *the* truth. One need not believe literally in the story of the Delphic Oracle to acknowledge that "no one is wiser than Socrates."

Is democracy to be ruled by a plurality of appearances or can it, without surrendering its egalitarianism, find its way to the true path? Did Socrates *appear* an enemy of Athenian democracy as a way of really supporting (by improving) it? If the polis teaches man, as Pericles said, then can one exceptional man also teach the polis? Is he a bad citizen for not honoring Peitho, one of the "gods of the city"? Is Socrates guilty of treason and unheard-of arrogance, or of an idiosyncratic and highly ironic civic-mindedness?

The ironies are piled high in *The Apology*, one on top of another, like blocks. Socrates *seems* wise but is *really* ignorant (though he is *also* really wise). Socrates *seems* eloquent but is *really* blunt-spoken (though he is *also* really eloquent). Socrates *seems* to undermine the youth of Athens but *really* he improves them (he improves the youth *by undermining* them). Socrates *appears* to want to go on living but *really* he doesn't care (although he may *seem* to prefer life to death, he *really* prefers death to dishonor, like Achilles and Antigone). The Olympic champion *seems* valuable because he gives us the joy of victory while the philosopher *appears* to be an annoying pain in the ass; but *really* the athlete can provide us no more than the ephemeral, while the philosopher *really* offers the eternal. Meletus *seems* to speak sensibly but *really* his words are empty; Socrates *appears* to ask only little questions but *really* his questions are big ones. Adjectives, vituperation and political slogans—the language of his accusers—are shadows that appear to condemn, while Socrates' logic blows away his accusers' mist of modifiers. No, more—his logic turns the accuser's language against him: "You are a liar, Meletus, not believed even by yourself."

Only a perfect mirror reflects without distortion. But the more perfect this mirror the less we are aware that it is a mirror. Language, to Socrates, is what art is to Aristotle: imitation, not expression. Out of Socrates' contempt for appearances, all distorted reflections, comes the whole of Platonic epistemology. *Seems* can be denigrated only on the condition that there exists an absolute *Is*. Not hundreds of bridges but Bridgehood, not thousands of chairs but Chairness. Plato made of his teacher the founding father of epistemological elitism.

● ● ●

Prince Hamlet is put out that Polonius has arranged Claudius' election, but he is more furious that his mother has married his uncle and immediately after his father's death. Gertrude had appeared to love his father but now Hamlet suspects she did not. Or, if she did, she loved only in appearance, which is to say superficially. "Frailty, thy name is woman." If his mother is frail then all women—including Ophelia—are frail. His idealism is outraged and so he overgeneralizes. Disillusionment often breeds negative zealotry. Denmark is all shadows, Plato's Cave transmogrified into a national deathtrap. The love of women *is* not; at its very best it only *seems*. You cannot rely on it. Politics? Even worse. Uncle Claudius seems friendly and innocent but is really neither. Polonius, Laertes, Rosencrantz and Guildenstern, Osric—perhaps even Ophelia—are all other than they appear and therefore they abuse language, speaking as spies do. Hamlet demands of the world what he asks of the actors, a perfect mirror. For those around him (always excepting the indispensable Horatio) the precious common possession of language is subordinated to their own ends, or the ends of others.

It is no small point that Hamlet should be a stickler for good diction. What an irony that he wishes to be utterly what he seems—all of a piece, an *absolute* Hamlet—and yet must pretend, pretend to be mad, to have lost himself, that he must pretend to *prate*. Though he despises *seems* he cannot do without it as protective coloration. He despises extravagant language yet must counterfeit it. Nevertheless, the Prince has a talent for acting mad and a love of good playing. One even suspects at certain moments that things are so bad with him that he only pretends to pretend to be mad, that he crosses over the line. But mostly he doesn't; mostly he plays. He is obliged to confirm his mask of insanity with meaningless language and this he tries to do. Still, he cannot overcome his horror of *seeming*, of inflated diction, flattery, misplaced or artificial eloquence. So, Hamlet cannot help himself; language counts for so much with him that even Polonius sees there is a method to every apparently mad thing he says.

Hamlet proclaims his attitude toward language at his first appearance, in his self-defining third line.

Seems, madam? Nay, it *is*. I know not "seems."

To Hamlet, everything external is a potential deception; the Danish court is a whited sepulchre, half whorehouse, half pot-house. All its rituals are maimed. His own grief, however, is not feigned, like Gertrude's and everybody else's. It's no matter of black clothes, deep sighs, and official tears. And why?

> For they are actions that a man might play,
> But I have that within which passeth show ...

The "inky cloak" is no act. His punning and apparent insincerity conceal the deepest sincerity to be found at Elsinore. His mourning clothes are a mutable swaddling of an immutable soul. They *suit* him. So, it is ironic that to dig out the truth Hamlet has recourse to acting, both his own and the players'—ironic but also fitting. It is never acting to which Hamlet objects but *bad* acting, the sort that conceals rather than reveals. The same is true of his hypersensitivity to language, the player's instrument. Hamlet instructs the actors to:

> Suit the action to the word, the word to the action, with
> this special observance, that you o'erstep not the modesty
> of nature. For anything so overdone is from the purpose
> of playing, whose end, both at the first and now, was and
> is, to hold as 'twere, the mirror up to nature ...

That mirror must be perfectly polished. Words must imitate without overdoing. Hamlet loathes linguistic excess. "There is no waste in beauty." Laertes' bombast grates on him. Like his father's exasperating periphrases, Laertes' speech at Ophelia's grave drives Hamlet to mockery. He is provoked by Laertes' "treble woe," his call to heap earth on the grave high enough "To o'ertop old Pelion or the skyish head of blue Olympus." It's interesting that, just before he begins his burlesque of Laertes' pompous grief in a fun-house mirror, Hamlet should declare himself so emphatically: "This *is* I, Hamlet the Dane." In the center of all the Danish *seeming*, Hamlet intends to *be*, to be home, to be the chief mourner of Ophelia, to be his father's avenger, to be himself as whole-heartedly as his action-hero double Fortinbras is Fortinbras. To be, or not to be? To *seem* is a way of murdering the self. Yes, of course the famous question introduces an essay on death and suicide, but it applies also to appearances. Is he to be or to seem? To seem is not to be, not to be Hamlet the Sane Dane; to seem is to be a multiplicity of Hamlets, everybody's Hamlet.

"Nay, as thou'lt mouth, I'll rant as well as thou." Where language is concerned, Hamlet is gifted enough to outdo everyone's worst. He is Hamlet the Dane, his father's son, and if Laertes' father and sister have perished in his play, well, so it goes. Who can say for sure if he is being sincere or still mocking Laertes when he claims:

> I lov'd Ophelia. Forty thousand brothers
> Could not (with all their quantity of love)
> Make up my sum.

Might he still be playing at madness here, even after his sea-change, even though overwhelmed by the death of a woman he loved, drove mad, and killed? Is it with both insincerity and integrity that Hamlet speaks at Ophelia's grave? Claudius and Gertrude think his speech insane. Madness, mockery, sincerity, exaltation at his return—all are there, but so is Hamlet's characteristic finickiness about language. This is what Hamlet *is*.

He fights Laertes over who loved Ophelia more, but also over diction. Hamlet insists that language should accord with truth, no gaps to call into question truth itself, even the melancholy, intimate truth of a mourner.

The Prince is always confiding in us, not only through his soliloquies but also *via* Horatio, our stand-in, the friend anyone would wish to have. Despite this Hamlet is the most introspective and undramatic of heroes and maybe that is why he is the most interesting. He continuously reveals himself in "words, words, words," yet the heart of his mystery is never plucked out, not by a thousand books, a million articles. In the end language fails even him and we are left looking at the corpse of one who never is revealed. He has that *within* which passeth show. What is within him cannot be *played* ... even though *we* play him, over and over.

When Hamlet praises Horatio he is quick to insist that he intends no flattery:

> Nay, do not think I flatter;
> For what advancement may I hope from thee,
> That no revenue hath but thy good spirits
> To feed and clothe thee?
> Why should the poor be flatter'd?
> No, let the candied tongue lick absurd pomp,
> And crook the pregnant hinges of the knee
> Where thrift may follow fawning.

To flatter is an ignoble relativist's use of language, a means justified by an end, sophistry. Hamlet asserts his integrity not by claiming nobility but by denying that flattery would serve any useful purpose. This is honest humility. He claims nothing for himself.

The wisdom of our time: a speaker may be innocent but language itself never is. We live in a great age for the *unmasking* of language, the finding of what speakers do not expect or want to be found, did not intend. Signs can displace what they represent, what we desire to present.

An example. What is the real meaning of Socrates' praise of Spartan society? It is easy to take it at face value, especially for those too little sensitive to Socrates' irony, already convinced that he is *simply* an enemy of democracy. Is it not more likely that Socrates didn't praise Sparta because he thought so well of the place (it had laws against philosophers and boring food) but precisely because no Athenian would? To compare Sparta *favorably* to Athens on any point would be the most provocative form of social criticism.

Sparta is repugnant—that is the unspoken sentence that underlies all his praise and turns it into irony. Sparta is a terrible society—militarized, enslaved, backward—and yet, by its standards of civic and personal virtue, Athens falls short. See where you grasping Athenians have gone wrong? The war in which Socrates fought bravely against Sparta was unjust. He must have known that. Yet he is no political activist; he would not speak out, not even against the Thirty. He performs his duty but will assert no influence in the Assembly, which he pointedly calls "*your* Assembly." Democracy works by compromise. Therefore, a moral absolutist like him might manage to live a good life in a democracy but not one that is *both* good *and* political. Does realizing this make Socrates a bad citizen? Isn't it to defend himself against that imputation that he insists on his "service to the state," a service that would not have been possible in public office—and certainly not in Sparta?

Socrates criticizes Athens for its greed and love of show. Hamlet complains of Danish drunkenness and the corruption of the state. Still, both are patriots, but patriots with good noses, lovers who quarrel.

If we hold the mirror up to nature what it reflects ought to be the truth—*tropically*, as the Prince says of "The Mousetrap." In that play-within-the-play, the truth is revealed as a reflection which itself is not true but "an action that a man might play." The truth is what this action reflects, not the reflection itself. Thus, distortion of the mirror through language that holds up a tarnished mirror to what it represents makes the truth opaque; it turns *is* to *seem*.

But is there *a truth* at all? Does Hamlet, an undergraduate at thirty, find himself at last, the truth that *is* Hamlet? Is he too varied and indecisive ever to be a single Hamlet? Is the truth beyond all knowing? integrity an illusion? Or is the *rest*, that within which passeth show, is that only—silence?

•   •   •

"I cannot make Crito believe that I am the same Socrates who has been talking and conducting the argument; he fancies that I am the other Socrates whom he will soon see, a dead body."

Socrates in the *Phaedo*, about to die, still has to insist on his integrity, even to those that love him.

"Man is the measure of all things." Humanism drags relativism behind it. Relativism can be exhilarating, liberating. But some varieties can drive one to despair once one gets over the adolescent thrill of proving that the truth is merely that illusion one happens to believe. Can "good" language do any better than the inflated and distorted sort if there is no standard other than whatever dubious metanarrative one credits? And yet this relativistic formula is suspiciously imprecise. What might transpire underneath that breezy phrase "happens to believe"? Do we happen to believe *this* illusion and not *that* only because we fail to see it *is* an illusion? Is it just a matter of not knowing one's own biases—prejudices we would discard if we knew what they were, like good physicists? Marx and Freud carried on their life's work to be able to tell us what these biases are; contemporary Marxoids and Freudettes seem even more certain about the real meaning of that "happen to believe." It means we believe what is in our material interest to believe; we believe because we endured this sort of upbringing, belong to this ethnic group, that gender or class, have been steeped in this particular culture with a history of atrocious domination or unjust oppression; we believe what makes us feel both aggrieved and better. We ought to open ourselves to all repressed perspectives, attend to all marginalized voices. It will be liberating for us all. Sound pluralistic advice, of course, but doesn't it imply that we ought to pay attention to exactly those illusions we do *not* happen to believe? Why? In order that we should start to believe in them? Fat chance, once the magic of belief is banished. So, we do not believe; we "explore." We wander through a bewildering gallery of perspectives and dimensions where we meet with endless supplications and appeals. A terrible clamor fills our ears, all the permutations of a baffled *Wille zur Macht*. Overwhelmed, we try hopelessly to clamber above the noise but there is no escape, no promontory from which we can look down and make distinctions. In fact, there is no point higher than the podium from which the unmaskers and debunkers, the resentfully oppressed, the unjustly excluded, the defenders of their self-esteem, hold forth without irony, with only that measure of moral authority righteous relativists can claim.

There is no fulcrum with which to move the world. Thus, Nietzsche at the start of *Beyond Good and Evil*:

> What tempts us to look at all philosophers half suspiciously and half mockingly is not so much that we recognize again and again how innocent they are, how often and how easily they make mistakes and lose their way... but rather that they are not sufficiently candid, though they make a great virtuous noisy to-do as soon as the problem of truthfulness is even remotely touched upon. Every one of them pretends that he has discovered and reached his opinions through the self-development of cold, pure, divinely untroubled dialectic... whereas, at bottom, a preconceived dogma, a notion, an "institution," or mostly a heart's desire, made abstract and refined is defended by them with arguments sought after the fact.

For Nietzsche, the history of Western philosophy has invariably been governed, and, for him, invalidated, by the desires of the heart. Philosophy *seems* rational but is *really* mere rationalization. He may speak like a precocious child with a new toy, but what a toy it is—and what a child. The intensifying influence of French critical theory makes it appear that Nietzsche has finally won his point and so stuck us in a fun house where all the mirrors distort, and we must polish, not them, but our irony.

If the radical relativists are right, then Socrates is condemned again and Hamlet deluded. There can be no distinction between appearance and reality because reality is nothing but a persuasive appearance created by all those things catalogued by Nietzsche. The relativists allow only a single absolute, one objective truth, which is that there are no absolutes and no objectivity. Osric lacks Hamlet's rich nature and is nothing *but* "the glass of fashion and the mold of form." If we are like him, then each of us will sing only "the tune of the time," and wear only the "outward habit of encounter." We cannot fully *be* many things but only *seem* to be one, "a kind of yesty collection, which carries us through the most fann'd and winnowed opinions"—until, that is, like Socrates and Hamlet, we come to trial.

EDITOR'S NOTE

Sidney Fein was anything but a *steady* writer. His writing usually begins with a charge of energy and generally concludes when the vitality of the original conception is exhausted. Fein's oeuvre is neither one of construction nor deconstruction but the bringing to rest of intellectual—occasionally emotional—vectors, propulsions, dynamics. For Fein, an idea had a limited shelf-life, and he was never one to prod a corpse. This may be among the chief reasons why he seldom took up a subject twice and why his unpublished papers offer so many agitated, interrupted starts—and why there are so many of them.

A word about Fein's conclusions. Much of his work provides the sort of satisfaction to be gotten from good detective fiction. There is an appealing indirection or concatenation in the way he goes about things. He characteristically starts with an idea that is full of potential, leaves it to veer off in a new direction; then he will toss in yet more paragraphs that appear almost arbitrary only to wind up by drawing everything together in a way that seems surprising yet feels inevitable. Fein's prose shows how the inconsequential can have consequences. Sometimes, he announces the thesis of a work only when he is bidding it farewell.

Fein's unpublished papers include many items whose original impetus proved too weak to sustain. However, a few of his abandoned starts appear to have had a real momentum when he turned his back on them, and for these he might have entertained further plans. In my opinion, this incomplete, admittedly inchoate series of notes on Socrates and Hamlet is one.

I found the typescript of these observations stapled together in Fein's file for the year 1979. They might have turned out to be a good example of all his finest tendencies had Fein gotten around to working out the transitions and, above all, providing a proper conclusion and with it his thesis. As the thing stands, and depending on the reader's opinion of Fein, these observations may appear either tantalizing or incoherent. Still, Fein put the piece aside, Most likely to work on his last book, *Aristocratic Democracy*, to which one can see connections, just as there are hints here of the so-called Culture Wars that were to break out in the coming years. Unfortunately, Fein never got back to connecting the dots or clearly stating his point.

Though the origin of the notes for which I have chosen the loose rubric "Socrates, Hamlet, Language and Insincerity" is enigmatic it is not beyond speculation. Fein often said that Socrates' great contribution to Western thought (or, as he occasionally put it, Western *neurosis*) was the distinction (alternately, *wound*) between Appearance and Reality, a distinction he literally embodied, as when Plato called his teacher "a satyr concealing a god." In a broad sense, this distinction is Fein's theme in these notes, though whether it was the theme that directed him to Socrates or vice versa is hard to determine. From a narrower, more journalistic viewpoint, the essay is pretty clearly about some problems of language. I suspect Fein was piqued by the claims of certain contemporary theorists that reality, or truth, is a purely linguistic construct, created by discourses, by discourses referring to other discourses. Since Fein saw this radically perspectivist position as the latest form taken by traditional relativism, it is not surprising that writing about it would lead him back to Socrates whose arguments with the Sophists laid down what he deemed the opening salvos of a perennial debate. But why *Hamlet*? Simply because, according to a lecture he had delivered at Brandeis University in 1978, Fein thought of language as one of that play's central themes.

"Words, Words, Words" Fein titled that lecture, from Hamlet's answer to Polonius' question in Act II, scene ii: "What do you read, my lord?" In this lecture, Fein devotes a good deal of attention to Act V, scene ii, Hamlet's conversation with the foppish courtier Osric. The standard view of this scene is that Shakespeare was looking for comic relief and a way to slow down the rapid approach of the finale, Fein thought there was more to it. "In fact," he writes in his lecture notes, "Shakespeare speeds everything up in scene ii so that the catastrophe comes on the audience with the suddenness of a nightmare." Fein connects the Osric scene to all the others in the play where Hamlet expresses what, in this essay, he calls the Prince's "finickiness" about diction, his offended taste and its philosophical implications. There is, of course, social satire in the scene, and no doubt Shakespeare was prompted by actual Elizabethan models of the Osric type, but Fein looks deeper. In his lecture, Fein spoke of the way Hamlet teases Osric about his silly hat and the weather: "The Prince goes after Osric on temperature just as he had after Polonius on clouds, forcing him to contradict himself, rather as Socrates does Euthyphro and Meletus, albeit Socrates uses logic rather than a courtier's eagerness to fawn." Fein then cites this exchange:

> *Osric.* I thank your lordship; it is very hot.
> *Hamlet.* No, believe me, 'tis very cold; the wind is
> northerly.

Osric. It is indifferent cold, my lord, indeed.

Hamlet. But yet methinks it is very sultry and hot
for my complexion.

Osric. Exceedingly, my lord; it is very sultry, as
'twere—I cannot tell how.

What was Fein getting at in these notes on Socrates and Hamlet? At his hatred of ideology, for one thing. Fein, a great skeptic himself, could scarcely be objecting to the skepticism of the relativists. I think what he disliked about some of them was their sincerity, their lack of irony. For Fein, a skeptic *ought* to be an ironist, to be able to imagine that contradictories are both true. Just as importantly, Fein disliked misplaced debunking, the idea that interest always blots out belief or that a good argument is invalidated because its advocate wants it to be true. For Fein, *interest* does not undermine *belief* any more than *belief* can, of itself, validate *interest*. Fein tended to see interest in a broader sense than most contemporary ideologues, those he disparagingly calls "Marxoids and Freudettes." For example, he himself had a keen *interest* in human rights, logic, beauty, and he often asserts an ironic personal interest in the pursuit of disinterestedness.[8]

In an isolated note from his folder for 1978 Fein remarks on the danger to the oppressed of grounding their case on radical relativism. "The issue is not whether *Das Wille zur Macht* can't explain a good deal but whether it should be used to explain everything. When the powerless claim that the ascendancy of certain values is *purely* a matter of power politics, excluding any common ground on which to fight things out rationally, when they deny the point of arguing, they doom themselves to continued powerlessness or to a war in which truth will not be the last casualty."

Is Fein proposing Socrates and Hamlet as, in some sense, models for our own time? Why not? As he would say, you could do worse.

[8.] See *Diptych on Terrestrial Representation*, pp. 274-282 or *Want, Desire, and Need*, pp. 117-131

In the book Fein broke off these notes to complete, he struggles with the tension between elitism and the egalitarian spirit, discrimination in favor of excellence and unconditional openness to pluralism, a respect for the exceptional and the ethical obligations of tolerance, merit and equality. How, he asks there, can the highest standards of aesthetics or morality achieve their only political justification, the consent of the governed? Answer: at best, a little at a time. For Fein ideology is the enemy of what he saw as the perpetual task of good will. "Ideology," he writes acerbically, "is a short circuit, a premature ejaculation, the most lethal form of constipation."

Apropos, one of Fein's favorite aphorisms is attributed to Rabbi Tarfon. In common with many incisive Jewish sayings, it is perfectly poised between hope and despair. The rabbi's devout irony is, in fact, practically Feinian. "It is not required that you complete the task, but neither are you free to withdraw from it."

ON *EUTHYPHRO*

They say that, in his youth, Rabbi Israel studied eight
hundred books of the Kabbalah. But the first time he
saw the maggid of Mezritch face to face, he instantly
knew that he knew nothing at all.

I HAVE on my desk one of my daughter's textbooks, the
Mentor edition of *Great Dialogues of Plato* translated by W. H.
D. Rouse. It cost $4.95. It is a good book with helpful footnotes
and a minimum of scholarly obstruction. The editor has included
half a dozen dialogues: *Ion, Meno, Symposium, Republic, Apology,*
Crito, and *Phaedo*. With a little bit of searching I've dug out my
old high school text of Plato, a $.35 Pocket Library edition of the
Jowett translation, its edges yellow as the molars of a lifelong Latakia
smoker, its brittle pages as loose as if he never brushed. It includes
Symposium, ample selections from *Republic*, and of course the indispensable three-act tragedy of Socrates' trial and death.

Plato, however, left us a four-act play, or at least three acts with a
very curious prelude. The dialogue that both textbooks leave out is
the short, hilarious, perplexing *Euthyphro*. In the edition I have in
front of me this work is described as "a conversation on the nature
of piety," myopically in my opinion. *Euthyphro* is rarely taught to
undergraduates.

It's easy to see why *Euthyphro* gets dumped. Who wants to read a
conversation on the definition of piety, especially one that fails to
tell you what the definition of piety is? For that matter, who would
want to teach such a thing? While *Euthyphro* has the pedagogical
virtue of brevity (under 20 pages complete) it appears to be little

more than a circular argument that ends in bafflement. Worse, though Socrates and his young interlocutor are both facing capital cases and speak on the very porch of the King Archon, and though their topic is an undeniably lofty one, the tone of the dialogue is barely serious. Here Socrates' irony is transparently sarcastic and even the most sympathetic reader is bound to feel that he ought to pick on somebody his own size. There is no obvious connection between tying Euthyphro up in dialectic knots and the solemn proceedings to follow. So who needs to read this slight dialogue before the immortal *Apology*? If something has to go to make room for a couple more books from *The Republic* or every line of *Ion*, why not *Euthyphro*? And yet it seems to me this little conversation is full of significance and does not deserve to be overlooked, especially by students being introduced to Socrates. Plato placed it prior to his account of his teacher's trial for a reason and he has earned our trust. So, what is the reason?

If the purpose of *Euthyphro* were simply to make a sanctimonious post-adolescent Greek fundamentalist look like a moron, there was no need to connect it with the trial of Socrates. Of course, it might be that this conversation really took place on the eve of Socrates' trial and so Plato, in what are supposed to be his earliest and most journalistic dialogues, is only being a good reporter in recording it. But this ignores the fact that Plato wasn't there and that neither Socrates nor Euthyphro, the only ones who were, is likely to have dictated it to him from memory. Presumably, both had other things on their mind. Besides, the dialogue is too carefully constructed to be taken for reportage. So, why did Plato write—or fabricate—it, and how is it related to the rest of the story?

As a reporter, Plato has with justice been accused of hagiography, though in his case I think hagiography is clearly preferable to an uninspired if objective court record. That Plato revered Socrates is undeniable. In fact, it is an axiom. Therefore, it must follow that the dialogue makes Socrates look good and Euthyphro bad. Plato stresses the young man's arrogance, his hollow boast of certainty, his self-righteousness. The point must be to relish Socrates' brilliant demolition of Euthyphro's successive attempts to define piety which he claims to know all about and cites as his motive for the solemn act of laying a charge of murder against his own father. Grave also is the charge of *im*piety lodged against Socrates, of course.

In *Euthyphro*, Plato presents us with his purest, most succinct, and triumphant illustration of Socratic Irony and Method because Euthyphro is the perfect straight man for Socrates, the Platonic idea of a stooge. The very thing the old gadfly needs to be spurred on to do his best is somebody who thinks he knows and really doesn't. We could hardly find a better candidate than this young man who says of himself, "The best of Euthyphro, and that which distinguishes him, Socrates, from other men, is his exact knowledge of all these matters." These matters would be all the mysteries of theology and conundrums of ethics. He's plainly asking for it. So blind is Euthyphro that Socrates raises his irony to a higher power. He not only claims ignorance in his usual fashion but actually sets himself up as a pupil eager to be taught by this puffed-up, humorless puppy. He amuses himself by saying that if Euthyphro teaches him about piety then he will be able to beat the rap laid against him by Meletus et al. Euthyphro is so idiotically sure of himself that he misses even Socrates' broadest ironies, *e.g.,* "… I know that you are as much wiser than I am as you are younger."

So, for introducing Socrates, the dialogue is highly useful. It shows how Socrates' method and his irony depend on one another, since it is his assumed ignorance that enables Socrates to pose his devastating little questions: "I cannot do better than to be your disciple… And therefore, I adjure you to tell me the nature of piety and impiety, which you said that you know so well…" Euthyphro is astoundingly slow on the uptake, but Socrates' method requires somebody like him, and part of Plato's point seems to be that Euthyphro is not so exceptional. He becomes the template of all

Socrates' most distinguished fellow citizens—the poets, politicians, and artisans mentioned in *The Apology*—who are not so wise as Socrates because they claim to know something and don't, while he claims to know nothing and does.

So, *Euthyphro* serves as an epitome of what Socrates did for decades in the agora. "Here," Plato seems to say, "behold my master at work then decide for yourself if he was an impious subversive and corrupter of youth." Moreover, the content of the dialogue is chosen to emphasize the difficulty in charging him or anybody with impiety. In a particularly good instance of looking at trees rather than forests, it is on the definition of piety that most academic treatments of *Euthyphro* concentrate, each lecturer meticulously rehearsing the several definitions lobbed up by Euthyphro and the wicked smashes with which Socrates returns them. Piety's what I'm doing, what's dear to the gods, what the gods love, the portion of justice concerned with the care of the gods or with serving them, the knowledge of how to sacrifice and pray, and so on. I suspect students who undergo such lectures are apt to wind up like Euthyphro himself, with a spinning head and eager to flee the room: "Another time, Professor Optimus; for I am in a hurry, and must go now." Can these arguments about piety really be Plato's point?

Well, one might observe that Plato here *abstracts* the charge of impiety against Socrates as a way of ridiculing it. He turns the whole question into a semantic dispute whereas the actual charge against Socrates was probably political, something Plato takes pains to obscure. Socrates was accused of not believing in *the gods of the city*, which is to say the democracy of Athens. Admirers of his were deeply implicated in the three recent and bloody attempts to overthrow the popular government, including some close relatives of the aristocratic Plato. The effort by Plato to de-politicize his teacher's trial, to suppress its context and transform it into something timeless, to disparage the accusers and magnify the accused, has been a gigantic success. The hero he made of Socrates is indelible and endlessly fascinating. On the other hand, Plato has turned the trial of Socrates into a semi-intelligible blot on the escutcheon of the world's first democracy and *locus classicus* of free speech.

As Nietzsche saw it, with Plato's first dialogues the end of the drama coincides with the birth of formal philosophy. If Plato is not the "Socratic poet" Nietzsche called for I can't imagine who is. Western philosophizing flows out of the ironic ignorance of Socrates as a symphony does from the silence of the orchestra. Nietzsche's insight is just. In every sense Plato has written the last Greek tragedy.

Did Plato rearrange reality or make it up? Who knows for sure? We can say, though, that in these early dialogues, including *Euthyphro*, we are given much: a brilliant portrait of the man Kierkegaard called the first intellectual tragic hero; we see virtue (*arête*) converted from crude physical power to sophisticated moral integrity; we are instructed in the value of questioning answers relative to answering questions, learn why justice should be founded on reason and not faith, and bequeathed a durable illustration of the excellence of an examined life. What's more, Plato lays down for us the immensely generative distinction between appearance and reality by incarnating it in a physically ugly and mentally beautiful old man who preached and lived it, the "satyr who conceals a god." If this is art, then surely art is preferable to mere journalism.

And yet, and yet. I am dissatisfied with this received understanding of *Euthyphro*. It is provokingly orthodox; moreover, there is something incommensurable between this dialogue and those that follow.

Euthyphro is read deductively; that is, in accord with the axiom that reads *Plato adores Socrates*. This is not unreasonable, but it may be restrictive. Suppose for a moment that Plato's aim in writing *Euthyphro*, and making it a prologue to *Apology, Crito*, and *Phaedo*, was less simple, more contradictory, that his motive was even (who can say?) unconscious in part. Suppose that in it he filled the obvious gap in his account of Socrates' trial, the case for the prosecution. Suppose you knew nothing of Socrates other than this one dialogue. Then put the question: Is Socrates an improver of youth?

I think *Euthyphro* is ambivalent on this question. Yes, it is safe to insist that Socrates' questioning of Euthyphro, whom I imagine to be about the age of a college sophomore, shows his dogged pursuit of definitions, that his goal is to educate the young man maieutically, by provoking him to independent thought, and that he replaces blind faith at its most literal-minded with an open examination grounded in reason. Nevertheless, I believe an unbiased look at the text can also support the opposite view: that Socrates has no interest in defining piety, only in playing mind- and word-games; that he does not aim at educating Euthyphro, only at humiliating him; that while Socrates does indeed tear down traditional beliefs, he puts nothing in their place. In other words, *Euthyphro* can be seen as showing Socrates' method as completely negative. This second, subversive reading, I think, supports the substance of the two charges Socrates is about to answer.

Plato presents Euthyphro as obnoxiously cocksure, but he is also a young man with a serious ethical dilemma. He believes his father has wrongly caused the death of a man on Naxos and in a manner that suggests he values property (in this case a slave) more highly than human life. Not only does Socrates never address this problem, he dismisses it in a way that is unsympathetic and closer to unconsidered traditionalism than Euthyphro's reason for lodging the charge. Who, after all, really gets the better of this exchange?

> SOC. I suppose that the man whom your father murdered was one of your relatives; if he had been a stranger you would never have thought of prosecuting him.
>
> EUTH. I am amused, Socrates, at your making a distinction between one who is a relation and one who is not a relation; for surely the pollution is the same in either case ...

The social status of the man Euthyphro's father has done to death is interesting. Euthyphro, a democrat, is unconcerned that he was a common laborer. To Socrates, it apparently matters.

More to the point, Socrates never addresses the young man's problem, even though it is the classic conflict between family and justice, love and duty. He gives no consideration to Euthyphro's filial, civic, or moral duties. For example, Athenian law required every citizen to prosecute any crime of which he had knowledge, and Euthyphro's mention of "pollution" suggests that only a trial could clean his father up. Evidently, then, social justice is of little interest to Socrates. As for teaching, it is clear that Socrates has befuddled the young man but not that he has taught him anything. It could even be argued that, of the two, Euthyphro is the more enlightened, humane, as well as the more democratic, that it is he and not Socrates who acts on absolute moral values.

• • •

Axiom: Plato adored Socrates.
Corollary: All Plato's depictions of Socrates are adoring.

But does the corollary necessarily follow from the axiom? Wouldn't this be grossly to simplify human motives and relations? Isn't it overlooking the dark caves of literary inspiration? After all, X may adore and still resent Y, love Y dearly yet be capable of pointing out Y's shortcomings. Even while defending Y against all comers, X could still see how Y might provoke an attack. It seems to me that resentment is not only compatible with adoration but may even be conjured up by it. It is not unknown for disciples to bridle under the domination of their masters. Such feelings need not be conscious; in fact, for such a disciple as the youthful Plato, recalling in voluntary exile his martyred teacher, one would hardly expect them to be. Socrates had quite a stinger. I don't think it's too fanciful to suppose Plato himself may have felt it a few times, or at least sympathized with others who were being stung, even somebody as insufferable as Euthyphro.

In short, I think the picture of Socrates in *Euthyphro* is equivocal and the more one looks at the early dialogues the more clandestine criticism of Socrates one can find. For example, Socrates' humility in court can seem a lot like inverted arrogance, his claim of a divine mission like vainglory, his auto-obituary and suggestion of punishment-by-pension a kind of contemptuous self-glorification. His arguments in the *Crito* can seem strained, as if he were rationalizing a course of action already long decided. Xenophon, our only other source on the death of Socrates, considered that the old man was tired and sick and leapt at the chance of martyrdom; he saw the execution of Socrates as judicial suicide. Nevertheless, in all Plato's dialogues the dominant tone is reverential. The *Apology* more than makes up for whatever is questionable in *Euthyphro* as Plato shows his teacher eloquently triumphing over fear, public opinion, malice, and petty-mindedness, all without for a moment losing his calm or his wit. Nietzsche was certainly ambivalent about Socrates; yet the philosopher's self-defense inspired Nietzsche to say we do not study the *Apology* to understand Antiquity; we study Antiquity in order to understand the *Apology*.

Still, there remains this question: what is the effect on a young genius of being taught by an old one? Plato was inspired by Socrates, spurred to sublime achievements; his imagination was so dominated by his teacher's personality that well into old age he continued to make Socrates the hero of his dialogues. It is commonplace to say that Plato uses Socrates as a mouthpiece for his own ideas; but it no less true to say that Socrates laid out the course of Plato's life's work, determining both the form in which he wrote and the concepts he developed. Socrates' compelling personality could attract not only aristocratic idealists like Plato but also opportunists like Alcibiades, ascetics like Antisthenes, and hedonists like Aristippus. The simplest way to account for the many differences between Plato and Aristotle, especially in ethics, is to reflect that the latter never met

Socrates, though he certainly must have heard more than a little about him under the olive tree. In a city that worshipped physical beauty, Socrates was ugly; in a city mad for fashion, he went unshod and had only a single toga; in a city that adored wealth and status Socrates was penniless and plebeian. Socrates embodied for the idealistic Plato the distinction realistic Aristotle declined to accept, the cardinal one between form and matter.

It seems to me unreasonable to expect a mind as good as Plato's not to resist its own enthusiasms, its submission, not to be critical of or even to strike at the thing it loves, that convinces and vanquishes. Can one emulate a non-conformist by whole-heartedly conforming to him? Perhaps Plato's attitude toward Socrates is not so different from Nietzsche's. Nietzsche identified with Socrates ("I am the bad conscience of my age") and resisted him (scornfully saying his Idea of the Good "smells of the plebes"). He attacks Socrates as "decadent" yet praises him as "the one turning point ... of world history." He extols Socrates for having achieved a "triumph over human fear and weakness," and reveres him for putting his life on the line on behalf of all later philosophers, redeeming a lifetime of talk and proving "the dignity of his divine mission" by seeking death. Yet all this heartfelt admiration did not prevent Nietzsche from reviling Socrates for "perverting" morality or calling him "the buffoon who made others take him seriously." For such men to love Socrates is also to enter the lists with him. In an inconclusive fragment, Nietzsche wrote tellingly, "Socrates, to confess it frankly, is so close to me that almost always I fight against him." It's true. Socrates does *make* people take him seriously. But consider all that is buried in that verb, the hand-to-hand combat between student and teacher. Is it too much to claim that, even if he repressed it with all his broad-shouldered wrestler's might, Plato too felt at least a little as Nietzsche did?

Editor's Note

Sidney Fein's daughter Maya, who commissioned me to prepare the most suitable of his posthumous papers for publication, began her freshman year at Columbia University in September 1983. The above notes are in Fein's file for that year. The pages are untyped and clipped together, suggesting they were not revised. The passage I have placed as an epigraph is written on a separate sheet with the note, "for Euthyphro piece." I traced it to Volume One of Martin Buber's *Tales of the Hasidim*. At the bottom of the last page of the manuscript Fein drew a line under which he wrote: "Enough. Remember the way Mom would say *fresh*!" Thus, the article begins with Fein mentioning his daughter and closes with a memory of his mother's disapproval.

Fein wrote often about Socrates. He devotes several pages of his first book, *Diptych on Terrestrial Representation* (1973), to the historical significance of Socrates. Along with those of Plato and Aristotle, Socrates' politics are discussed in the opening chapter of his last book, *Aristocratic Democracy* (1983). The unfinished essay on language and insincerity focuses on Socrates as well as Hamlet. Like that piece, the present one has an academic origin. Fein's thoughts on *Euthyphro* were evidently suggested to him when he picked up one of his daughter's textbooks. The earlier piece is focused chiefly on Socrates' use of language and, while it makes much of his irony, there is no suggestion of the astounding thesis Fein propounds here. His decision to abandon this article with a reference to his mother calling him "fresh" suggests he gave it up because he worried the idea that Plato is ever less than whole-heartedly on Socrates' side might appear bizarre, unedifying, even perverse. His recourse to "unconscious motives" in the essay itself might be taken as a sign of his lack of conviction in the idea he is advancing. Though this is a speculative piece, Fein may have been on to something. Though it ends abruptly and lacks a satisfying resolution, what Fein has written is original and worthy of being read.

THE *KÖNIGSBERG* OF SIDNEY FEIN

THE "Königsberg" of Sidney Fein can be precisely dated. Fein produced it a year before completing *Diptych on Terrestrial Representation*, the book that established his reputation and turned his name into an adjective. Among his unpublished papers I found both a holograph version of "Königsberg" and a typescript at the end of which "SF December 10, 1972" appears in Fein's hand. The most striking difference between the two versions is that the holograph is written as prose while the typescript is arranged in 101 lines of approximately decasyllabic verse. Fein must have decided that what he had written wasn't an essay but a poem.

KÖNIGSBERG

From his bedroom window Kant would stare at
a sturdy Prussian tower. It thrust up,
a sound categorical tower, firm against the
scudding clouds, upright in the winds
on which he wrote an early tome.
Kant believed gazing at this tower focused
his mind on the gritty phenomenal, tuned
it in to the ether of the noumenal.
Psychologists would call Kant's tower a
specific stimulus; that is, what cheroots

were to Freud and rotting apples to Schiller,
the tower was to Kant; that is to say,
as tobacco smoke infuses Eros
and Thanatos, the odor of fermentation
Maria Stuart and the *Ode to Joy,*
so the *Critiques* aspire into air.
History teaches that nothing changes
and everything does, lessons learned, forgotten,
repeated. Nowadays easternmost Prussia
is westernmost Russia. The tower,
I suppose, is still there. I've never been
myself and so can't say for sure. The old
townhouses of Königsberg/Kaliningrad
are still German but not its citizens.
In the antique bottle there's new vodka.
Kant was not unfond of a good Moselle.
Tutoring, cards, and pool kept him in funds.
His life did not lack for tension though the
drama was invisibly interior. Kant
strove to save inner feeling from outward
mechanism, the absolute from the
relative, to clear a corner in doubt for faith.
In short, he wished to serve mankind by
reconciling the irreconcilable. He
managed it too, for about three weeks.
Kant lived buttoned up in routine, disliked
beer, so adored consistency he once
said he wouldn't lie even to a homicidal
psychopath. Famously precise, people
set their watches by his daily march to
the University which he loved and

never left. Teach to the student of middle
ability was his recommendation. The best
don't need you; the worst can't be helped.
Kant was even more regular than the
tower's clock, if indeed the tower had
a clock in it. Kant had no biography
to speak of but when he stared at that
tower he became original, a magisterial
synthetic a priori gem. He looked down on
folk like his pious unlettered mother until
Rousseau set him straight and made him our first
intellectual with a sour conscience
about it. Eight years of Pietistic
pounding drove the nail in but left him with
a life-long hatred of hymns. Still, privileges
must be redeemed, he felt. People are not
means but ends. The stewardess is the
flight attendant in embryo, a slave the
union man. The educated ought to advance
the rights of common folk. Toward the end of
his life, which began the year Newton died,
he lost both memory and sight and couldn't
even recall where the tower was let alone
the virtue got from staring at it. Routine
disintegrated into continental fame.
Kant held some revolutionary sentiments.
Mikhail Ivanovich was a rebel,
albeit a Russian one, thrice imprisoned
by the Tsar. He presided fecklessly
for a generation over Stalin's
icy inferno as his good wife froze

in the furnace. Königsberg has twisted
in the blood-stained century's howling winds.
Kant's Königsberg had a river with two
islands in it. So does Kaliningrad,
I presume, though I've never seen the place.
Four bridges linked the bigger island to
the mainland, the smaller had but two;
yet another united the two islands.
In Königsberg there were lots of ways to
cross the same river twice. Leonhard Euler,
who was a generation older than Kant
and believed in ether, showed that no
one could start at one point in Königsberg,
cross all seven of its bridges only
once, and return to where he began. This
is called the Euler Cycle. Perhaps one
sunny Sunday in May Kant set out to
prove Euler's point by walking back and forth
across the seven bridges. I can see it,
the whole town turning out to cheer the Herr
Professor on. Bratwurst on the river banks,
smacks on the Pregel. What a red-letter day that
would have been in old Königsberg where
for all I know Euler's puzzling bridges
and Kant's staunch tower may still be seen today.
Starry heavens may yet wheel on high, perhaps
the moral law still towers within, but
Königsberg has vanished like a something
that filled a nothing, like Euler's ether.

•   •   •

When Maya Nunfi Fein chose to offer me access to her father's literary remains it was with the understanding that I would see to the publication of those items having the most direct bearing on his three published books, the *Diptych, Want, Desire, and Need*, and *Aristocratic Democracy*. This is why, though I came across "Königsberg" early in my initial review of Fein's papers, I laid it aside to work on other items. The entirely unexpected discovery that, in the late 1970s, Fein had created a pseudonym, Klaren Verheim, took precedence over all other matters. "Königsberg" I regarded as little more than an oddity. Fein's papers include numerous parodies, bits of doggerel, burlesques, *jeux d'esprit*. It was easy to mistake "Königsberg" for one of them. Now that I have looked more closely at it, however, it is evident that this piece anticipates much in Fein's subsequent work and merits careful attention.

First, a word about the genre of "Königsberg." I am sure it was conceived as a poem. In the notes on the invention of Klaren Verheim, Fein expresses astonishment that his pseudonym should have produced verse: "… not only am I no poet, but it never occurred to me that Verheim was either." On the other hand, Fein actually did publish one poem under his own name, an untitled spoof on poetry that appeared in a defunct literary journal called *Lethe*. It too is made up of a-rhythmic decasyllabic lines. "People who write poems talk to themselves" is the way Fein begins his anti-poem, a line he subsequently shuffles no less than four times: "People who write themselves talk to poems… People write themselves who talk to poems… People who talk to themselves aren't poets…" then finally and revealingly, "People who write talk poems to themselves." Fein was a thinker in more or less perpetual dialogue with himself; consequently, he would be one of those who "talk poems to themselves." "Königsberg" is an instance. It began as a free-flowing rumination, Fein talking aimlessly to himself through the medium of that fountain pen he jokingly called his "one link to tradition." When it occurred to him that he had written a poem, he then typed it up, beginning a new line at roughly every tenth syllable. Though not a Romantic, Fein believed a poet was a particular type, more than somebody who turned out verses. In his own terms, Fein wrote a *poem* without being a *poet*.

So much for the genre of "Königsberg." The more challenging task is to determine its subject. Since Fein usually wrote about problems, one needs to decide what the problem or the problems were behind "Königsberg." The case calls for caution because these lines are steeped in Feinian irony. The title offers a clue to his intentions. Fein did not choose to call it, for instance, "Kant" or even "Kant in Königsberg." While he has many things to say about the German philosopher—and a few more about Euler and Kalinin—it is the *city* to which the title directs us, an emphasis reinforced in the poem's conclusion.

Fein was writing when the world was crudely divided between two ideologies. Ordinarily, the city of Berlin would have been used as the focus of this schism. If Fein chose Königsberg it is because here he is not interested in politics but philosophy or, more generally, the life of the mind. It was part of Fein's nature always to regard intellectualism with the greatest skepticism and to write of it mordantly, even though he was himself one of its distinguished exemplars. Königsberg serves as the symbol of a sort of existence to which Fein adopts a complicated range of attitudes, from open suspicion to bittersweet nostalgia. For example, one could see Fein's Königsberg as the home of an idealized intellectual life, a university town whose most celebrated citizen was Immanuel Kant and not the home port of the Soviet Baltic Fleet. The touching fantasy of Kant's Sunday promenade over the city's bridges to prove a mathematical point being turned into a municipal holiday might suggest the whole population's involvement in, and sympathy with, the life of the mind. Kant's fellow Königsbergers could be those "students of middle ability" to whom the professor addresses himself. He is also serving them by offering an object lesson, since there is obviously no need for Kant to traipse "back and forth" over all those bridges to prove to himself that Euler was right. But Fein undercuts this daydream in various ways, including making obvious that a daydream is all it is. In Königsberg, he cracks, "there are many ways to cross the same river twice," an ironic allusion to Heraclitus's famous saying that one "cannot step into the same river twice." Königsberg, home of the mind, is well supplied with bridges. This is almost to say that here nobody steps into life's river at all. Thought and reality are divorced by Kant who declared that we cannot ever know things as they are in themselves. The picture of Kant crossing back and forth over the seven bridges of Königsberg, walking the Euler Cycle is as absurd as it is nostalgic. It is a mere "exercise" in two senses. Yet, even if Fein means to joke about Königsberg's pretensions, the concluding lines are melancholy, even elegiac.

> ... Königsberg has vanished like a something
> that filled a nothing, like Euler's ether.

The Swiss-born mathematician Leonhard Euler despised a vacuum. He believed that an imaginary substance called *ether* fills all the space beyond the sphere of the moon and makes up the stars and planets, the "starry heavens above." Euler's role in Fein's poem may be the seed of Fein's later, lengthy deliberations on fullness and emptiness in *Want, Desire, and Need*. Fein sets the full, once-vital city of the mind—philosophy itself, perhaps—against an empty substance which is even lighter than hot air. He also suggests that a way of life can remain vigorous only so long as its values are credited but will evaporate when that faith is lost. Joy at being liberated from what is gone is replaced by a comfortless "nothing," especially if what has vanished is the earnest enlightenment of Kant and what replaces it is the cynical boot-licking of Kalinin. Kant and Kalinin—the two names are metonyms for high-minded thought and low-down politics. The lofty possibilities "Königsberg" once represented are gone, like ether—worse, like the false *theory* of ether. An emptiness has replaced that fullness, and in such a way as to make it appear that the fullness was never more than an illusion. This lost plenitude included the Enlightenment's confidence in reason and faith in human perfectibility, also its belief that history is progressive, to which the fate of Königsberg/Kaliningrad," twisting in the blood-stained century's howling winds," gives the lie.

The poem opens with Kant staring at his tower, aspiration fortified by effort. Though he does not mention it, Fein probably knew that Kant's tomb is in the tower adjoining the city's cathedral. What we focus on can bury us. So Kant is gone too. From the standpoint of eternity, which of us will not wind up "like Euler's ether"?

Also striking in "Königsberg" is the refrain that Fein has never been there. This is a personal admission and, as such, touching. It may signify that he never achieved a successfully integrated intellectual life, erected no system, that he even lacked a home along the lines of Kant's Königsberg, "which he loved and never left." Fein once called himself "a typical deracinated, rootless Jew." The opposite would be the life of a rooted German, as Kant was grounded in Königsberg. Here too Fein does not fail to suggest an irony. German militarism, "Easternmost Prussia," the state of which Kant was an employee, and "the winds of the century" have ended by removing Königsberg from the map and rendering the city un-German. At the Potsdam Conference in 1945, it was awarded to the U.S.S.R. and renamed by Stalin a year later, upon Kalinin's demise. Königsberg is "unchanged" only in the sense that a city struck by a neutron bomb would be. Moreover, those "revolutionary sentiments" of Kant added, if only in a tiny measure, to the spirit that led to the Russian Revolution and the victory of Kalinin, which is to say of Stalin, who also did not care for Jews. Kant, Kalinin, and Königsberg all begin the letter K, but that letter is the property of the quintessential Jew of the century, Franz Kafka, a writer beloved by Fein who is almost an unmentioned presence in this poem.

Let us return for a moment to the picture of Kant in his bedroom staring at the tower, the "specific stimulus" that focused his mind.

The tower is clearly phallic ("thrust up"), the very image of Kant's masculinist doctrines, in particular his ethics ("upright"). The tower is seen against the "scudding clouds." Kant did write an early work on meteorology, *The Theory of the Winds* (1756). Here Fein obliquely announces the theme of "ether," made explicit a few lines later in the phrase "ether of the noumenal." The tower is a "categorical" one. Kant's moral position, founded on the categorical imperative, his unprovable belief in synthetic *a priori* moral ideas, is all principle and law. His rigid absolutism removes from consideration both the context of moral dilemmas and the consequences of ethical choices. The hard overbears the soft. This is as contrary to feminist "relationality," "situationism," and "contextuality" as can be. For Kant, one is "upright" only if one is dutiful without inclining one way or the other. With the image of the non-Pisan tower Fein plays on the stiff verticality of Kant's ethics; but he simultaneously shows us something more human, namely the pathos of the thinker's dependence on the physical, for Kant needed the tower to concentrate his mind. Fein thus reminds us that Königsberg, for all that it may be a vanished city of the mind, was a real place, with actual bridges and townhouses which "may still be seen today." Kant, after all, may have had little biography to "speak of," but he was a living human being who preferred wine to beer and despised the eight years of "Pietistic pounding" at the religious school to which he was sent by his parents. Yet Kant was deeply enough touched by this Fundamentalist upbringing to become our first tragic philosopher. Unlike the pagan Greeks', Kant's ethics do not promise happiness as the reward of the good. On the contrary, Kant is like Shaw's Englishman who can only tell that he is being moral if he is uncomfortable. To Fein, Kant's ethics were related superficially to the Stoics' sense of duty and indifference to outcomes, but more profoundly to the Judeo-Christian penchant for guilt. Guilt would also be the sovereign concept of what might be called Fein's own moral position laid out in Chapter Seven of *Want, Desire, and Need*.

Above all, though, Fein's Königsberg is the place where contraries meet, where "easternmost Prussia" becomes "westernmost Russia." Fein makes this almost as explicit as a lecture in his presentation of Kant's philosophical position. He conceives Kant's life's work as a dialectical struggle to reconcile opposites, to hold together the wounds of the world with Band-Aids, an effort which, Fein dryly observes, succeeded for "about three weeks." It is on account of this struggle and its brief success that he praises Kant as "a sort of synthetic *a priori* gem." Fein seems to see Kant as the last thinker to attempt a unity of the analytic and emotive, to try honestly to circumscribe the whole. Though Hegel's ambition vastly exceeded Kant's in the construction of systems, there are Kierkegaard and Nietzsche to show not only how much Hegel left out but the futility of system-making itself. In fact, Kant was not so systematic. Like Fein, he was more humble and took up problems one at a time, and the problems that attracted him were dialectical. In epistemology, Kant synthesized the innate ideas of Rationalism with the Empiricists' reliance on sensory experience. In ethics he found a way to reconcile Hobbes's insistence on the normative virtue of law with Rousseau's assurance that goodness comes from nature rather than legislation. He also sought a way to counter the mounting evidence pouring in from the South Pacific for moral relativism. He endeavored to save inner life from outward mechanism, limiting science's competence even as he rescued it from Hume's skepticism. But, deeper than these "services" to mankind was Kant's solution to the crisis of how he, and all conscientious intellectuals, ought to live. Here the contraries that faced Kant were the Ivory Tower snobbishness he must have felt after he escaped the townies, the Pietists, and found his true home at the University, and the guilt triggered by Rousseau's attack on that intellectual life Kant most treasured. Reading Hume may have awakened Kant from an intellectual stupor, but it was Rousseau who shook him to his depths as a man, as a son of the working class. At the age of forty Kant wrote the following statement, one that would have meant much to Fein and to which he alludes in his poem.

I am myself by inclination a seeker after truth. I feel a consuming thirst for knowledge and a restless passion to advance it, as well as satisfaction in any forward step. There was a time when I thought that this alone could constitute the honor of mankind, and I despised the common man who knows nothing. Rousseau set me right. This blind prejudice vanished. I learned to respect human nature, and I should consider myself far more useless than the ordinary working-man if I did not believe that this view could give worth to all others to establish the rights of man.[9]

Kant's dilemma was that while he could not give up university life or his faith in reason to become an anti-intellectual, neither could he persist in despising the "common man," represented by Fein in the most telling way as Kant's pious, "unlettered" mother. The philosopher's "sour conscience" was bequeathed him even more by Rousseau than by the Pietists. This was a bad *social* conscience and, in the above confession, Kant reveals "revolutionary sentiments" in the freighted phrase "rights of man." In *Aristocratic Democracy* Fein would wrestle with the identical problem. He too believed that "privileges must be redeemed." The poem seems to suggest Fein's sympathy for Kant's solution of being an intellectual in the service of the common man, if only by the implied contrast to Euler, the detached rationalist, and Kalinin, whose dogmatic brand of sympathy for humanity led him to preside for decades over "Stalin's icy inferno."

Before ending these remarks, I want to return for a moment to Euler, who seems at first to appear in "Königsberg" only as a coda or an afterthought. Fein intended something serious by inserting him. What is it he says that Euler showed in his problem of the seven bridges? According to Fein, he proved that "no one could

9. Quoted in Ernst Cassirer, *Rousseau-Kant-Goethe*, Princeton, NJ: Princeton University Press, 1945, 1-2

start at one point in Königsberg… and return to where he began." The humorous conceit of Kant's Sunday promenade has a deeper meaning. In his life Kant crossed again and again over the river, not only the Pregel but the never-ending river of philosophical problems. Though he never left his native city, he ended up in quite a different place from where he began. So it is, Fein implies, for all thinkers, or at least for those like Kant and himself. They retrace their steps only to find themselves in unfamiliar neighborhoods. They cross the river over and over, but the river is always changing beneath their feet. Fein's own principle of not taking up the same question twice, making of every effort a new departure, is prefigured in this image. His style and mode of thinking are the constants of his work. They are the bridges, so to speak, while below him rushes an endless flow of problems. From time to time, one of these piqued his interest and he wrote about it.

"Two things," said Kant, "fill the mind with ever new and increasing admiration and awe… the starry heavens above and the moral law within." For the envoi of his non-poem Fein draws on the majesty of this statement, which describes the horizons of Kant's own vision. Where others would stress the nouns, however, Fein focuses on the verb *to fill*. Who and what are filled today, he asks. The heavens "*may yet wheel on high*," he says, and perhaps two centuries of imperial science and atrocious politics have spared us some tiny residue of what it means to be an upright human being, but he does not sound confident. Fein is uncertain not so much about the heavens or even his own duties, but the "admiration and awe" that filled Kant when he focused on nature and our souls. Planets and stars, bridges and towers—these may, like "Königsberg," outlast what they inspire. The Königsberg of Sidney Fein evaporates at the end like a literally ethereal dream-city. It dissolves in a sort of derisive longing for what Fein has imagined, what he may have hoped for or revered, but in which he lacks even a penny's worth of faith.

AN INCIDENT

AROUND noon last Wednesday, I was heading back to my office from the district court. Saint George Street was full of traffic, as usual. I was wearing suspenders and carrying a leather briefcase. I had on my unbuttoned overcoat, also a muffler, though no hat. I feel it gives me an advantage to show my hair, which is thick and still mostly black, because so many of my colleagues are going bald. Still, I could have done with a hat. A chilly, powerful wind was blowing through the city; people walking north leaned forward while those going south were swept down the sidewalk as if brushed by an invisible hand. Everybody lowered their chins and fastened their eyes a few feet ahead, intent on not falling. At the corner, a man in a quilted jacket was selling roasted chestnuts from a cart with little windows in it. He danced back and forth in the steam, stamping his feet and rubbing his arms.

Outside the Hochberg Building I caught sight of Dillon, a colleague. I had heard his wife was ill and thought I should ask after her; but, as I was moving north and Dillon south, he flew by and my greeting was blown back in my face. At each corner, eddies of wind blew bits of refuse and newsprint in miniature maelstroms. Particles of grit were driven into my cheeks. It was useless to smooth down my hair, though I could barely repress the impulse to do so. The saplings planted last year on Callowhill Street were bent halfway over while the flags on the Belvidere snapped furiously back and forth. People making their way to lunch swayed like a field of grain in a cyclone.

As I came around the corner of Filbert Street, the scene changed.

Half a block ahead traffic was stopped, horns blared, and the pedestrians on either side slowed, some moving tentatively toward the curb.

The sort of vehicle you associate with suburbs, a large station wagon, was pulled up in the middle of the street, blocking traffic. I was able to see right into the windshield and, so far as I could tell, only one person was inside.

It's just those crucial things we aren't sure of believing to which we give our deepest attention. Do my children love me? Does God exist? Am I a decent human being? If faith keeps us from asking such questions, then faith is inhuman. Grammatically speaking, it seems to me, the only correct attitude toward life is interrogatory.

What was there about a traffic jam on a blustery day that should turn me so philosophical? Was it merely a traffic jam? No. That's what I have faith in, I suppose, because it's just this imperfect, negative faith that provokes thinking and thinking makes me feel more alert and so more alive. The routine of daily life is something we really do believe in. We take it for granted. Yet who grants it but ourselves? Our habits, mores, expectations, upbringings, our media, even the evolutionary wisdom that prevents us from drawing attention to ourselves—all are on the side of order, of being able to predict what's going to happen next. We relish suspense so long as it is boxed up safely in some book or movie. Suspense is an aesthetic pleasure, not a moral one. Morally, suspense always resolves itself into the question of how rapidly predictability can be restored. That is the job of the detective hero.

So, when a late-model station wagon stops dead in the middle of a busy center-city street at midday, in midweek, when the engine continues to run so that it's not a mere matter of an empty gas tank, when a woman of thirty-five or forty, a matron dressed demurely in a pale blue blouse with brown, shoulder-length hair, sits behind the wheel of this vehicle with the doors locked and stares straight in front of her, oblivious of the horns behind her and the faces pressing in on either side, the catcalls and curses, you can't ignore it. Something is happening or is about to happen.

Something is happening that doesn't happen every day. And something must be done about the riddle, the dissonance resolved into a dominant major or, if needs be, minor. Summon the police, call an ambulance, phone the husband, the principal of her children's school. Action, notification, publicity. Quick, quick.

I walked up the sidewalk pushing forward against the wind, my hair blown back, grit striking my eyeballs like grapeshot. A small taut man in need of a shave leapt out of his taxi, beside himself with rage. I could see his mouth moving. He actually tried to push the station wagon. I saw his tight leather jacket getting tighter, his red face redder.

I continued making my way toward the car. I was now in the middle of the street. Naturally, I didn't think of myself as part of the crowd closing in on either side. The first siren was sounding faintly behind me. I saw her plainly now, staring straight ahead, not at me, but at the point in space I occupied, at my x and y coordinates. In every dimension but one her gaze and my body intersected.

The turbulent wind went on blowing noise, paper, motes. The buildings appeared to sway slightly, like old elms. What fascinated me was the woman's stillness. Here was the dead center of the city in the midst of a whirlwind of horns and shouts, deals and transactions, lawsuits and mergers. In the middle of the week, the middle of the day, in the middle of the whirlwind, that woman sat utterly still, fists clutching the wheel, eyes blank as a check on an exhausted account.

If she has failed, then what caused her failure, this woman somebody else married? Or is she just mad? I had a sudden idea: maybe this was a performance, not an incident but a happening, a one-woman show of protest, a commentary. A woman alone in a locked car, bunging everything up, on a busy, blustery day. It made me weigh contrasts: inside/outside, city/suburb, married/single, loving/indifferent, married/single, moving/still. As soon as you call something art it ceases to be entirely senseless. It might, for instance, become an intelligible declaration about senselessness. But whose? My own? I was thinking of all the things that placed me outside the station wagon and what put the woman inside. Where I stood everything was blowing around; where she was all was motionless. I think it must be that stillness that attracted and repelled me. Lack of motion always arrests us; it suggests either serenity or death.

I stopped ten feet from the car. Slowly, the woman removed her hands from the steering wheel. The crowd shuddered, surging in. She pulled her blouse over her head.

I think people who are reduced to stillness or hysteria by their lives, destroyed by living, have the advantage over me. Why? The most apathetic of audiences are not superior to me in detachment. For years I've felt as though I were living behind an infinitely long wall. Such a wall would have to be a round one, which is to say I'm in a prison yard. A person hemmed inside such a wall might think he's baffled and never suspect he's actually trapped. In this wall somewhere is a door, or just as likely hundreds, thousands of identical doors, which anybody would take for the same door. Whenever I stand before this door, or one of the thousands like it, I'm suffused with hope. I don't want to be but I am. Hope invades me. It doesn't matter what happened last time, the time before that; hope still hits the beaches undaunted. So, I run up to the door filled by this aggressive, alien hope, grab the knob and turn for all I'm worth. The door's locked. There is no lock. I stare dumbfounded, knowing how useless and painful it is to beat on the door. I wonder if it might be opened from the other side. That is the a hope inside hope, that there's someone on the other side whose case is the same as mine. Perhaps if we both were miraculously to arrive at the door at the same instant... ? But then I shrug, the way one does at romantic dreams. The door is both a possibility and a torment; to be tantalized is to be punished.

I drew closer to the station wagon. The woman was thrashing now, making herself naked in the car, tearing off her bra, her skirt, everything. Then the crowd closed in.

EDITOR'S NOTE

I found the text of "An Incident" in Fein's file for 1981. There is both a holograph version, extensively revised, and a clean typescript. The two are stapled together and the latter bears the date "February 13, 1981." Though Fein never published it, the existence of both a handwritten and a typed version suggests that he considered "An Incident" finished.

What Keats sensed when he first looked into Chapman's Homer I feel time and again while reading pages unseen since Fein filed them away. I ask myself if he abandoned them in a spirit of dejection, out of frustration, or perhaps with the intention of returning. What have I discovered? I have found that Fein published fiction under a pseudonym (Klaren Verheim) and that he wrote poetry; I have discovered complete and nearly finished essays which, in addition to their intrinsic merit, illuminate facets of Fein's published work. I have found scores of notes and fragments, personal and professional, which, while not suitable for publication, etch more deeply my understanding of Fein as man, thinker, and writer. I have become familiar with his working methods, his characteristic anxieties, tastes, and sorrows. "Nobility is no guarantee of happiness," Fein wrote in *Want, Desire, and Need*, "it is rather an attitude toward unhappiness." I have come to appreciate in Fein this kind of nobility, and I see it also in "An Incident."

To call "An Incident" a *text* is evasive. Is it fiction, memoir, fable? In fact, the genre of the piece is not easily fixed, and Fein did care about such matters, about conventions and forms, if only to violate the expectations they evoke. "An Incident" is certainly not an essay, but then neither is it quite a short story either. It is an anecdote penetrated by reflection. Its narrator is at once involved and detached, a man who simultaneously envelops and is torn open, for whom the incident is the occasion of picking scraps of truth from under the weight of his mundane life. Since, for reasons I will come to presently, I believe the spirit of Kierkegaard hovers over this work, I might as well call it a *dialectical lyric*.

"Before all, the critic must comprehend a work of art as a system of choices. I see no need to suppose these choices should have been arrived at consciously. In fact, I would almost say the supremacy of an artist is directly proportional to the number of crucial choices he or she makes without any deliberation at all." So wrote Fein in his first book, the *Diptych on Terrestrial Representation*.

Fein often writes of two things at once; a single remark may even express two moods. For example, this observation about critics and the unconscious inspiration of artists seems to me unemotional and melancholy at once, the former being the public attitude, a kind of *obiter dictum*; but the latter is personal and sad. While laying down the law for critics Fein pointedly explains why—notwithstanding his pseudonymous stories and poems—he never considered himself an artist. He thought himself too deliberate, too cerebral and self-conscious to qualify as an artist; nevertheless, he felt the need to make works of art. Make them he did, though he concealed them, disowned them, felt unworthy of them, denied that he made them. There is a forlorn earnestness that overwhelms the irony with which Fein wrote of his creative alter ego: "… all Verheim's works could *only* have been written by him, never by Fein."

I cannot say whether or not Fein considered "An Incident" a work of art, but it is certainly a system of choices.

The piece is divided into seven sections of varying length, the mystic number seven—seven sleepers, seven last words, seven days of the week, the sign of seven, seven-up, seven-eleven, twenty-four-seven. These sections alternate between telling the story of the desperate matron in the station wagon and a set of reflections whose relation to the tale is not obvious. This *discordia concors* is characteristic of Fein; I mean the juxtaposition of ideas and themes whose bearing on one another is a mystery whose solution provides some of the satisfaction of his best writing.

The first section might justly be called Capitalism and Its Discontents. The initial sentence situates the incident precisely in the center of a city on a Wednesday at noon, the middle of the middle of the working week. The sentence features the words *office* and *business*. There is a suggestion that the narrator, whose business has taken him to "the district court," might be a corporate lawyer, but also that what follows will have something to do with judgments, with verdicts.

The theme of business is reinforced in the second sentence when the street is described as *busy*. A strong wind blows through the city, and those with it at their back are swept along "by an invisible hand." This allusion to Adam Smith's famous simile for the providential workings of the free market was perhaps the sort of deliberate choice Fein disliked observing himself make, but there it is. In the very next sentence we read that people keep their eyes down, "intent on business and not falling." The expository paragraph winds up with a synecdoche for market activity, the chestnut-seller, an image that manages to be both warm ("roasted," "in the steam") and cold ("stamping his feet," "rubbing his arms"), as if the short-lived heat of commerce is easily dissipated by the surrounding cold. The battering wind of economic competition blows some forward, retards others. People must indeed "fasten their eyes a few feet ahead" to keep from "falling." The long view is perilous to pursue. People must concentrate on the immediate, the short-term, when any false step might lead to a collapse.

Why "Saint George Street"? The allusion is to the well-known legend of St. George, the archetype of the combatant against evil, slayer of dragons, protector of maidens. Perhaps Fein was mindful also of the historical St. George, a third-century Roman officer tortured and beheaded by Diocletian when he protested the persecution of his fellow Christians. Perhaps the narrator wants to be as steadfast as the saint, with the station wagon or perhaps the domain of Mammon as the dragon. The matron would be the maiden, a Feinian kind of irony. As a protector, he fails, of course, but, like the original martyr, is nonetheless tortured, and, in a sense, loses his head.

In any case, he is without a hat, without the protection that might constrain his thoughts, which are of the Feinian variety, self-conscious and subversive. What am I, the narrator seems to ask, beyond what encloses me? He expends words not on himself but his suspenders, leather briefcase, overcoat and muffler. The absence of a hat he puts down not so much to vanity as competitiveness, gaining an edge by a hair, an advantage that is not even sexual.

The narrator shows himself from the first to be ambivalent about his status, at odds with the world in which he feels suspended, muffled up, the affairs of which he carries around in a brief case. (His case too will be brief.) The gritty economic wind that propels some forward and holds others back he denotes as "chilly" and "powerful." He is hostile to it but also a little afraid. His advantages do not prevent his identifying with the street vendor doing business in a frigid world.

The next paragraph introduces two names: *Hochberg* is the name of a skyscraper, *Dillon* that of a colleague with whom the narrator would like but fails to make contact. The first name is obvious enough, *Hochberg* being German for lofty mountain. The sublime heights of this narrator's world are indeed man-made. *Dillon* might be inspired by one of the money-men of the day, Douglas Dillon, or perhaps Fein was thinking of Bob Dylan, quondam middle-class Zimmerman from Hibbing, reinventing himself in Affluent America by adopting the name of a suicidally alcoholic Welsh poet and declaring that, for authenticity's sake, he would invent his own

Depression. In any case, the narrator at least tells himself he wishes to express sympathy with this Dillon because he has a sick wife. Perhaps the sick wife's sickness is psychological; perhaps she is the woman in the station wagon, or one in a similar plight. Perhaps the solitary narrator is envious of Dillon for having a wife, even a sick one? The narrator tries to go through the motions but his greeting is "blown back in [his] face." This commercial wind allows of no intimacies.

Just as the paragraph began with the comparison of a building to a mountain, so it concludes with one between a crowd and a field of grain. In his first book Fein argues that there is a watershed in Western Culture and places it in the second half of the 18th century. As he sees it, *the human* is one of those concepts people define from its opposite. From the Greeks to Rousseau it was taken more or less for granted that what threatened humanity were the forces of nature—wild beasts, earthquakes, barbarians, and our own uncontrollable passions. He describes the serene Apollo on the pediment of the Temple of Zeus, arm outstretched, taming the centaurs. Reason and its products (urban life, detached philosophizing) were distinctively human and placed us outside of nature, behind the walls of civilization. Over the last two centuries, however, people have come to identify the human with the emotional, a true revolution. The cause Fein locates in applied science and its immediate consequences, industrialization and urbanization. Rousseau is as much an effect as a cause. As people moved into an artificial environment and the conditions of work were transformed by the machine, nature in the form of parks and sentiment became precious, the foundation of humanity and morality. As Rousseau set nature above civilization so he placed sincerity above integrity. In "An Incident," Fein's likening the artificial to the natural is at once ironic and nostalgic, as though the present (streets, office towers, the time-is-money economy) might be grasped by comparing it to the absent (mountains, fields of wheat, the to-everything-there-is-a-season economy).

With the literal turning of the corner of Filbert Street, Fein introduces the turn in the story.[10] Up till now the emphasis has been on
the movement of people, the relentless wind, the stamping of the
vendor. Now everything is brought to a halt: "traffic was stopped."
What has arrested everything save the unstoppable wind is "the
sort of vehicle you associate with suburbs." An interloper from the
suburbs threatens the city with gridlock. What are the suburbs to
Fein? His writings suggest several answers: hands at the city's throat;
bedroom villages haunted by boredom and menace; the source of
slow madness; places where niceness is raised to the level of a Nietzschean pathology. For example, four years earlier, in the "Suburban
Anthropology" chapter of *Want, Desire, and Need*, Fein wrote:

> In the country and the city, status is more important than
> in the suburbs. In those areas inequality is presumed
> as one of the conditions of life. In the former, status
> is founded on considerations of parentage, periods of
> residence and acreage owned; in the city, on money and
> power. However, in the suburbs, a fundamental equality
> can be taken for granted. To live in an affluent suburb
> at all requires a certain level of income, and the neigh-
> borhoods are too new to establish prestige based on an
> accounting of generations. For these reasons niceness
> is at a premium. Suburbanites want nice houses to live
> in, nice cars to drive, they want to rear nice kids who
> will attend nice schools staffed by nice teachers where
> they can make nice friends. Niceness creates what social
> hierarchy there is; niceness determines approval or disap-
> proval, whether one is in or out. Thus, *nice* is the great,
> insipid, stifling accolade of the suburbs whose adoles-
> cents longingly mimic the styles and tastes of the vicious,
> forbidden cities.

---

10. *Filbert Street* is the name of the thoroughfare on which the Fein family factory was
located, the locus of the career he rejected, and so might represent the "turn" of his
own life.

The "one person inside" the station wagon comes from nice suburbia which screens out the origin of its wealth and is the wellspring of commuters and kids without a clue about where the money comes from. The woman inside the station wagon is a single unreckonable individual, without counterpart, unless she is ill in the way Mrs. Dillon is, the way lots of marooned suburban wives are. She calls into question, she protests, she performs, she goes mad. Who knows why she stops? Still, she makes a bit of news. The exposition is complete, the incident circumscribed.

The second section offers the narrator's first reflection. There is no transition. This meditation is contrived to be both personal and collective, like Hamlet's soliloquy, where the speaker says *we* even if he means *I*. The unstable inner life of the narrator is revealed. His skepticism and a repressed will to protest tie him to the woman in the car. Here too the Kierkegaardian spirit of the piece is first manifested. Fein was a Kierkegaard fan. He often assigned *Fear and Trembling* and was fond of repeating to his students Unamuno's exclamation upon reading the Dane for the first time: "*Qué hombre!*"

The narrator begins by laying down a paradox, namely that faith is also doubt, meaning that the sort of faith he esteems settles nothing; it unsettles everything. Dogmatism repels him on the ground that it is inhuman to take up a declarative stance in the face of life. To our lawyer, as to the preternaturally alert Kierkegaard writing at white heat in the middle of his great crisis, "the only correct attitude toward life is the interrogatory." Certainty diminishes alertness, which is why Fein preferred *Fear and Trembling, Repetition* and even *The Attack Upon "Christendom"* to the *Edifying Discourses* and *Works of Love*. The narrator demonstrates this alertness when in the next paragraph he insists there is a significance to the incident, to the unexpected contingencies of life by which we should not pass like sleepwalkers. We should think about them not merely for the sake of plucking out their mysteries, but because the effort to pluck proves we are alive. So he refuses to dismiss the "incident" as trivial but, in a sort of secular version of the old devotional handbooks, makes of it an occasion of self-examination.

Fein never lets his balloons rise too high. To this lofty vision of alertness, he counterpoints an essayette on predictability, routine, the contentment induced by order and repetition. Of course people want more; we want suspense too, but we want it "contained in a box"—a television, for instance. Entertainment must be disruptive but is without real consequence. In calling suspense "a strictly aesthetic pleasure, not a moral one," the narrator refers directly to the first two of Kierkegaard's stages. Suspense belongs to the amoral aesthetic stage, routine to the ethical; and, since morality represents collective values, the group can always be counted on to favor the restoration of predictability—marriage, say, over seduction. But just as Kierkegaard's Abraham (father of faith and the archetypal individual) is a moral man who rises *above* morality, so the individual may also find her soul out of sympathy with routine, disgusted by it, may even see it as a temptation to be rejected for the sake of individuality, even when there is no real alternative to returning to it. After Abraham comes down from Moriah, even though he is transformed by the traumatic test, he resumes his life as a run-of-the-mill, sheep-herding patriarch. The station wagon will, in the end, be driven back to the suburbs.

Individuality is also stressed in the next paragraph where the person of the woman is given some substance ("a matron dressed demurely in a pale blue blouse"). Her breakdown, her revolt, is something not to be ignored. Fein reiterates "Something is happening" the way ancient Hebrew creates superlatives ("Holy, holy, holy is the Lord of Hosts"). The smooth flow of commerce and traffic is interrupted. Discontinuity stimulates alertness.

What is the appropriate response to this incident? What do people mostly do with discontinuity? We hasten to restore normality; musically, we want dissonance resolved. In his first book Fein has a passage on the power Beethoven derives from *delaying* this resolution, piling up false endings—toying with the listener, who knows a real one has to come in the end. The individual must either be reinserted into the group ("dominant major") or eliminated from its midst ("if needs be, minor"). Kierkegaard is right: if any respectable nomad had watched Abraham on Mount Moriah he would have seen a psychopath attempting infanticide. But our narrator is more discerning, more inward; he too wishes to be an individual, dancing undetectably, one who only appears to be a typical, respectable officer of the court.

Section Three: rising action, climax. As if he were studying a jury, the narrator notes the reactions of others to the woman in the station wagon, especially the taxi driver. The inaction of the narrator is juxtaposed to the furious motions of the cabby's mouth and muscles. Reflection contemplates action, curiosity coolly considers anger.

"Naturally, I didn't think of myself as part of the crowd." This is the only significant claim the narrator makes for himself. But who does not say it? It is natural that we consider ourselves simply selves, even if we are not, since we all begin "locked in our own bag of skin," as Kierkegaard has it. Socialization overlays childish isolation, the selfishness that is a feature of the aesthetic stage of existence. We learn our ethical obligation to reveal ourselves to the group, to pick up the phone when it rings, to confirm our fellow-feeling. Morality is supported by arithmetic; the "crowd" is superior to any one of us. "The greatest happiness for the greatest number" is the slogan of the greatest number and seems inarguable. So, it is the work of a lifetime to climb back inside one's skin, a risky, anti-social enterprise. The narrator is making a claim he seems to require for his self-respect. I am *in* the crowd but by no means *of* it. I am a busy man of affairs but still more a thinking being, a kind of philosopher. I am one of those individuals who both desire and fear to transcend the ethical conceived as group membership.

The climax is expressed without human interchange. The

encounter is an abstraction with "x and y coordinates," perhaps an allusion to the famous Cartesian Meditation about the unreliability of the senses. Any "incident" could be a mirage. Descartes pretends to doubt everything because a demon might have made it his business to deceive him. Yet, as Kierkegaard sternly and cheerfully points out, Descartes said he never doubted in matters of faith. Why not? Simply because scientific skepticism would make no difference there. For the scientist, it is only useful to doubt what can be confirmed or disproved. The narrator says that the woman stares "at the point in space I occupied, at my x and y coordinates." It was Descartes who invented those coordinates. Where one anticipates compassion there is only algebra. As we read later, intimacy is precisely what the narrator yearns for, probably always has. Quite simply, he is a lonely man.

Fein too was a lonely man. After the breakup of his marriage he clenched his fists and devoted himself to raising his daughter and to work. The price of becoming more and more an individual was to become more and more isolated. Maya grew up and Fein resumed his status as an ambivalent bachelor like his heroes, Kleist, Kierkegaard, and Kafka, a bachelors who did not believe in bachelorhood.

The lonesome lawyer renews his contrasts, opens wide the dualism of his thought. "The turbulent wind… the woman's stillness." This stillness "fascinates" him. In the next section, he will define fascination as a mixture of attraction and repulsion. To be *fascinated* by an incident is to take to it a half-hearted attitude. He notes her "fists on the wheel," as though to suggest the potential violence of her protest. Her eyes look to him as "blank as a check on an exhausted account." The allusion may be to Scott Fitzgerald's concept of emotional bankruptcy, drawing on resources that are no longer there. Is her passion spent? Is she a sprung spring? Is she an inspiration or a warning? Has the world already beaten her?

These questions are taken up in the next section, the fourth, through a rather fanciful attempt at exegesis. Fanciful, but also revealing. For example, the narrator indirectly complains about his bachelorhood by calling the matron "this woman somebody else married." She is a failure, he speculates. No, she is merely mad. Or no again, he has an idea: she is a performance artist making a point through a "happening." What point? The point he wishes to make himself against the world, the one Fein narrowly escaped, the factory on Filbert Street. He refers to the working day bitterly as "the Sabbath man was made for," inverting Jesus' clever reply to the Pharisees. Like an indulgent critic he spews out a series of contrasts which descends into self-mockery: "If you call something art it ceases to be entirely senseless. At worst, it becomes an intelligible declaration about senselessness." He sees that he is not so different from the crowd after all; he too is trying to impose order, even if it is an aesthetic rather than a moral one. He admits that it is his own life that lacks sense.

Facts fill the four short sentences of the next section. The narrator's reflections are checked when the woman pulls her blouse over her head. In the final section, the seventh, she will strip herself bare while "thrashing." But before his attention is commandeered by that catastrophe, the narrator turns on himself. His condition has been illuminated for him from the outside, so to speak. What confidence he has built up in his years as a rising urban professional, complete with suspenders and brief case, collapses under the weight of alienation revealed to him by this broken housewife. Not only will he not judge the woman as the crowd does; he feels inferior to her. She at least has been engaged with life; she has been "destroyed by living." To be so destroyed is respectable, the narrator thinks in his insularity. The wall that separates him from everyone is circular, so it must be infinite, an endless wall that keeps him in and everybody else out so that the scope of his life seems to him no more than "a prison yard." This yard is enormous—it could encompass vacations in Tasmania, trips to Samarkand. It is so vast a circle that one caught inside of it might "never suspect that he is trapped."

His romantic yearning for intimacy (perhaps the counterpart of the woman's—who knows?) is expressed by the symbol of a door. The wall that circumscribes his life has at least one door, but the only thing that gets through is false hope. He does not want to feel hope. Hope is the barbarian behind the great wall. He fears it but also longs for it. The door is worse than locked; it has no lock. A locked door suggests the possibility of being opened but a sealed one is a mockery. The narrator is precise about what he hopes for: "someone on the other side whose case is the same as mine." Fein must have been thinking again of Kierkegaard's *Fear and Trembling*:

> One might suppose the single individual could make himself understood to another individual who is in the same situation. Such a view would be unthinkable were it not that nowadays people try in so many ways to sneak their way into greatness. The one… simply cannot help the other… Partnership in these regions is quite unthinkable.[11]

Unthinkable? Hardly, for even Kierkegaard thought often of Regine Olsen, and who can say that it was not with a view toward partnership? The tormented bachelor Kafka wrote in his diary that he felt Kierkegaard bore him out like a friend. And there's another sort of partnership. But to be confirmed by a forebear is scarcely a solution to lonesomeness. Fein's point seems to be that, once a certain pitch of solitude is reached, hope becomes a punishment. A hope that is hopeless is a fitting punishment for one who spitefully punishes himself.

A respectable woman of a certain age stops her station wagon in heavy traffic, locks herself in, tears off her clothing. How might such an "incident" be reported? No doubt it would be simplified for radio and television, summed up in a few more or less prurient words about exhibitionism and nervous collapse. A high wind

---

11. *Fear and Trembling*, trans. Alastair Hannay, New York: Penguin, 1985, 99.

blusters through the city. The obstruction to traffic will be quickly dislodged, the transgression of predictability expunged, all will be comfortably classified, the poor woman seen to somewhere. Not much will have been lost, a half hour's business, someone else's wife or mother. Traffic and trafficking flow again. The world of contending egos, separate yet interchangeable, will pick up where it left off. But for the narrator, as for Fein, the incident lingers and chafes, like an insult suffered in childhood.

SIDNEY FEIN AND
SAUL MANDELBAUM

EDITOR'S NOTE

In reviewing Fein's papers, I have come across many items of a personal nature, unsuitable for publication. However, while they are personal, the following notes seem to me an exception. I found them in Fein's file for 1977, untyped and undated. I believe they are complete, at least in the sense that Fein did not intend to add anything to them.

Fein may have begun these notes as an essay on a literary question, as the opening suggests. However, he often starts with a curveball, misdirecting the reader as to his true subject. Whatever Fein's motives may have been, he has left us something unexpected and painful, intimate yet more than personal.

Saul Mandelbaum died in October 1976, a suicide. Mandelbaum was a writer. His publications include a novel, *Distant Light*, two collections of short fiction, a score of uncollected stories, and numerous reviews. He is not much read these days, nor was he notably successful during his lifetime. I myself had not read any of his work until prompted to do so by these notes. Mandelbaum's fiction may be minor, but, in my opinion, all of it is interesting.

Mandelbaum and Fein were elementary school classmates in Philadelphia. The friendship was interrupted and, so to speak, sealed off, when Fein's family moved to New York just short of his thirteenth birthday. Fein makes it clear that their adult relationship was slight; but he also reveals the depth of feeling left over from childhood, presumably on both sides. The two days Fein spent alone with Mandelbaum in the summer before his death are the occasion and the real subject of these notes. The pain Fein felt as he wrote is not superficial or obvious on the surface of his prose.

• • •

NOTES BY SIDNEY FEIN ON
SAUL MANDELBAUM

In 1956, T. S. Eliot delivered a lecture at the University of Minnesota. He later published it under the title "The Frontiers of Criticism," and it begins with one of those wonderful sentences that immediately strike you as templates. "The thesis of this paper," Eliot intoned, "is that there are limits, exceeding which in one direction literary criticism ceases to be literary and exceeding which in another it ceases to be criticism." This sentence is magisterial and so generative that by dint of it you could almost deliver the lecture to yourself. Eliot himself seems to have liked the tune so well that he introduces a variation on it in the coda of his lecture. He declares that the critic's job is "to help his readers to *understand and enjoy*." The italics are the lecturer's, a reminder to raise his voice, perhaps to stress that to *understand and enjoy* are frontiers and not mere bland infinitives. Like a flight instructor, Eliot lays out the obligation of a critic to maintain a steady horizon; like a funambulist, he warns against leaning too much either way. An excess of *enjoyment* lands you in the soup of "impressionism," he cautions, while concentrating too much on *understanding* leaves you stuck in the muck of mere "explanation."

You get the idea or, if not the idea, then at least the game.

Fiction too has its limits, horizons fore and aft, its frontiers. For instance, I would like to say that one boundary of fiction is fantasy and the other autobiography. I think this is a practical way of looking at the matter that works as well for readers as for writers, though what the reader and writer identify as fantasy and autobiography may be entirely different. Any reader unfamiliar with the facts of a writer's life may innocently mistake autobiography for fiction, while writers insufficiently disciplined by reality or simply overcome by longing may almost as innocently mistake their fantasies, delusions, and wish-fulfillment for legitimate fiction.

Now imagine a writer who errs *both* ways, I mean one who mixes up fantasy with autobiography. Perhaps such a writer would be mad in the sense that a mad scientist is; that is, quite capable of functioning in a professional capacity but to unheard-of and unwholesome ends. In one sense, such writing would miss being fiction both coming and going. In another sense, though, the two errors might cancel each other out, just as somebody heading simultaneously for opposite horizons wouldn't move a step. Here two wrongs can make a sort of right just as in logic two negatives make a kind of affirmative, and the result might actually turn into an authentic work of fiction.

• • •

There is something about the friends of our childhood—the enemies, too. They don't have to do anything at all to touch us. They hardly even need to *be*; a name will suffice. The children one grows up with are like characters in a favorite book, one that nobody else has read. Subsequent friendships mimic these early ones and often fall short of them in our heart of hearts. It doesn't matter that the folks you hang out with these days have seen the same movies as you, hold identical political opinions, get your jokes, call you three times a week and arrange a surprise party when you turn fifty. Just hearing the name of the boy I used to walk home from school with in fourth grade makes me feel an emotion for which I have no good word, a sort of excited sentimentality mixed with mourning, a sentiment *under* sentimentality, so to speak. What is it that gives these friends (or enemies) such power over our emotions? I guess there is affection for our little former selves and thus for the friends who knew us before we became big, compromised adults. Then too there is the bond of shared ordeals. Schoolmates are like army buddies; both can call on an irrational loyalty because both have been with us under fire.

But there is something more and this something is itself a sort of union of fantasy of autobiography. Thinking of these people we fantasize about resuming our youth, which is one part of reminiscing, and through them measure how far we have come, gone, risen, fallen. We make autobiographical judgments, especially, I think, moral ones. When you run into somebody you knew in the schoolyard the two of you instantly return there, to a real school-yard but also a fantastic one. I once observed two retirees who ran into each other on a golf course in Florida. The last time they had seen each other was in a Brooklyn public school. It was fascinating watching them change before my (and their) eyes, transformed into a pair of ten-year-olds. For them time and space had been twisted the way Cervantes could twist them.

This is more or less how I felt when I got the phone call from Mandelbaum last August. We'd been in touch just a few times over the years, mostly by letter. I wrote him a brief note when his first book came out. He wrote an even shorter one back. A couple years later he wrote again when he came across something of mine, I can't recall what. We met for lunch once in New York, a pleasant lunch since neither of us was living there at the time. We ate scallops at a three-star restaurant and, for a while, we were back in the old school cafeteria. That was around Thanksgiving. The following New Year's I received this odd little story from Mandelbaum along with a warm letter blaming the piece on our conversation.

• • •

Chopin's Ghost at the Henry H. Houston Elementary School

by Saul Mandelbaum

Each moment was like the last, the next, and each of these moments was crammed with so much normality that it was conceivable any one of them might last forever, that we could grow up, reproduce our kind, wither and die and it still wouldn't end. The square limestone building appeared to have been constructed with eternity in mind. Every classroom had its clock, each with long, curled hands as thin and aged as a great-aunt's. Death had not been perfected yet, was still in the development stage. The stairways were high and full of lively echoes. The school had nearly as many rules as Deuteronomy. The younger children were convinced that if they tried to go down the up stairway the stairs would not work. The office of the principal, Miss Vivienne S. Moratus, loomed by the entryway. There emanated from this sanctum the lavender scent of fierce women in blue suits, women who permitted no "j" to creep into their pronunciation of the word *education*. Nearby the kindergarten rooms with their toy desks and tiny chairs smelt of spoilt milk and the nausea of the homesick. The hallways were paved with granite, highly polished, treacherously slippery. Bright, boring pictures were tacked to bulletin boards. Though they called them *bulletin boards* none of the children yet knew what a *bulletin* might be. The lower panes of the eight-foot windows were pasted successively with maple leaves, brown cut-out turkeys, notebook-paper snowflakes, jagged green Christmas trees... the same through every childish generation, every corduroy-clad and pigtailed class.

Chopin's ghost was not yet visible; but, had it been, its confusion would have been obvious even to the littlest children, perhaps almost poignant to a few of the oldest ones. The Henry H. Houston Elementary School had its Romantics of course, but no salon, no eau de cologne, no émigrés, no geniuses; it was situated neither in France nor in Poland. Chopin's ghost was haunted by the school, by its dark cloakrooms and the crude murals in the cafeteria, by the exiguous auditorium and its noisy assemblies, the gymnasium with its scuffed white lines and metal folding chairs. But, most of all, Chopin's ghost was hounded by the music classes where pupils banged out simple tunes on plastic flutes, xylophones, and autoharps.

The school had a safety patrol, stairway monitors, inkwells. The playground was bounded by a low fieldstone wall topped with slabs of slate, equally bad for sitting on in warm weather or cold. Dodgeball was the favored boys' game, hopscotch the girls'. Chopin's ghost was not amused by these games and remained inside during recesses, avoiding the high windows. Most of the time, it loitered upstairs in Mrs. Roth's room with its little plaster busts of Beethoven, Schumann, himself, and Dvorak. "Beethoven turned his back on eternal principles," the ghost still believed, but recalled the generous and enthusiastic Schumann with deep gratitude— "Hats off, gentlemen, a genius!"—unaware of the tragedy that would overtake him and his hard-won bride. Dvorak was a mystery; the fellow looked like a peasant and, whatever music he wrote must have been honest, healthy, and perhaps a little coarse. So the ghost of Chopin speculated.

The first retention drill at the Henry H. Houston Elementary School occurred on October 10, 1953. The bells rang strangely— not continuously, as in a fire drill—but in short, piercing, wholly unmusical blares. This distinction was announced in advance without any political commentary on the morning of the tenth by the serious female teachers. They told the pupils that, in the event of a real attack, there would be little time and much flying glass, so that they must climb at once under the desks with the inkwells and crouch there until the same penetrating notes signaled the all-clear. The kindergarteners slipped easily under their desks, but some of the eighth graders found the prescribed position a tight fit.

In the music room, Chopin's ghost was not paying attention to

Mrs. Roth's instructions. Instead, it was musing seriously on the nature of music, recalling what, in life, it had written to Delfina Potocka:

> Music, rich, full of feeling, not soulless, is like a crystal on which the sun falls and brings forth from it a whole rainbow… he who has put his soul into the crystal is like one who has poured wine into it.

These reflections excited the ghost and fortified it almost to the point of visibility. The high ceiling of Mrs. Roth's room brightened with autumn sunlight; the windows opened onto a sky that could almost have been Polish. The ticking of the clock sounded like one of Maelzel's little metronomes, annoyingly counting out the seconds of his nation's exasperating oppression. For the first time, the black upright piano beckoned.

Carol-Ann Hauck, grade 4-A, was the first to see it. Though she was uncertain and distracted, she thought she saw it settle at the piano, adjusting the bench up several inches. Carol-Ann was not thinking of Chopin or ghosts, but of the bomb. "Let there be light," she remembered God had said. When the slow black hands clicked into ten o'clock, the bells shrieked three times, waited, then did it again, and so on through five clangorous repetitions, each more hysterical than the last as if marking the progress of a bomb unstoppably falling through the air toward the school. Chopin's ghost, which had been hesitating over the keys, jumped as if it had heard a bowl of Venetian glass shatter in the stillness of a Majorcan afternoon.

We all scrambled under our desks. Mrs. Roth marched up and down the rows making sure nobody talked. It is very dangerous to talk during a nuclear attack. When Chopin had recovered enough, he struck a C-minor chord, firmly if somewhat experimentally, perhaps as a protest against Russian oppression and American bells. Mrs. Roth spun around. We all peered out from beneath our desks. We could just make him out. In the stillness between the bells' clanging, he began a moody nocturne. With each note of the delicate melody, he grew more distinct. Already we were able to see that his frock coat was blue and the way his starched white collar stood up to meet his outlandishly long hair.

The room grew as silent as a salon full of rapturously attentive ghosts. We crouched even lower and Mrs. Roth stood still between the rows, her hand playing nervously with her scarf, her eyes wide behind her bifocals. Chopin's music poured out into the silence, sad, full of history, the suffering and woe of another continent, another century, nothing at all like the crudely optimistic noises of our flutes and xylophones and autoharps.

The all-clear began to sound just after the piece was done. Chopin's ghost, fading quickly, turned on the piano stool and regarded us with a look of melancholy triumph.

· · ·

It would be reckless to conclude much about the virtues and flaws of Mandelbaum's work from this *jeu d'esprit*, but I can't help reflecting that what he sent me is a fiction made up of equal parts fantasy and autobiography. All the furniture is right, the blaring bells, Mrs. Roth's scarf and bifocals, the granite floors, elocution and tailored suits, every mote and aroma of the school was, as they say about movies, historically accurate—but Chopin's ghost? Too little fiction or too much? I can't say. Chopin's ghost sure looks to me like pure fantasy but it might be part of the autobiography. I can't remember what was racing through my own half-formed mind as we ducked beneath our desks waiting for the windows to implode in a white-hot wind. How can I be sure what was haunting the mind of little Saul Mandelbaum, cowering next to me?

Now Mandelbaum has himself become a ghost, crushed, I believe, by a ruinous collision of autobiography and fantasy.

· · ·

For two weeks of his final summer Mandelbaum lived in a rented a cabin on a lake in Vermont. He phoned me from a bar two miles from this one-man writer's colony. He was up there all by himself. It was only later that I discovered his wife had left him in February.

"Sid, all writers go to hell, don't they? Well, it's literary as hell up here. There's this huge oil painting of Alexander Wolcott in the Rutland library. I swear it takes up two stories, like Ozymandias. The old owl looks as vainglorious as if Velasquez had been pleading to paint him; he's got a cape on and everything. I guess they appreciate critics in Vermont. For all I know, Vermont's lousy with critics. The guys up here look as if they'd just read the whole *Times* bestsellers list while somebody held a thirty-eight on them."

He was drunk. "Please come up. I've got the directions all written out." He needed company; he pretty much begged for mine.

Saul had made a mess of his life by putting it in order. In clearing the decks for his writing he had swept everything overboard. He had left himself nothing to do but write but then what was there to write about? And then failure had been heaped on him like the straws on the camel. He was not Bellow, Malamud, or Roth. The latter might have joked that they were the Hart, Schaffner, and Marx of American Jewish literature but, to Mandelbaum, they were Leonardo, Michelangelo, and Raphael. What was left for the likes of him, a latecomer with limited abilities? "I have bad mannerism," he joked with defeated pride.

One trouble the critics found with Mandelbaum's fiction is that it is cerebral without being serious. They failed to notice his childishness. When Saul stumbled on a new idea he'd toss it around, polish it up, then look for a factory window to throw it through. Does a juggler believe in his clubs? Mandelbaum's stories were routinely called "brilliant"; but the reviewers made "brilliant" sound like the worst thing a story could be. They made Saul seem an emotional stiff, like someone who had had a cardiectomy. "Well, I've never written with *all* of myself," he moaned, convinced by the critics,

"just the top slice of the neocortex, thin as Begelman's corned beef."
Saul thought that writing with *all of oneself* was the secret, and the
phrase became for him almost what the formula for Nylon was
for DuPont. In his own reviews Mandelbaum sounds like Philadelphia praising New York. By reading the notices *he* wrote you
can tell how hard he was on himself. Compared to his, anybody's
work was bigger, deeper, more stylish, vital, important, fascinating, edgy, humane, penetrating; everybody else was either full
promise or fulfilling one. Saul's reviews are all encomia; because
he couldn't bear his own work and had a generous, modest spirit,
he was absurdly lavish in praising others. Every intelligent novelist
in America wanted Mandelbaum to review his or her new book;
only the stupid ones volunteered to review his. He wasn't important
enough for the big shots and the small fry thought they could make
a name by roughing him up.

● ● ●

Up there on the Vermont lake, Mandelbaum had refined all the
d's—despondency, depression, despair. He was beyond being able
to conceal even one of them. His sentences fell off into stammers,
reconsidering themselves halfway through, or working themselves
down into a pit with heavy lists. Like Coleridge, his state of mind
was betrayed by his commas.

> A grief without a pang, void, dark, and drear,
> A stifled drowsy, unimpassioned grief,
> Which finds no natural outlet, no relief,
> In word, or sigh, or tear—

Whatever he might manage to write—though he wrote nothing—
could have been called *Dejection: An Ode*. An ode is not a natural
outlet for anything.

How had it happened, I asked. I meant the depression.

"You get there the way you get to California," he told me, "little by
little, with a desert near the end. Eventually you come to a place—

it's sandy, blank, and desolate—and it just hits you that there's no *reason* for going further. No *excuse*. Not just no good reason, Sid, no *excuse*. Other people could make far better use of all this air you're using up. Before you know it, you're thinking about the insurance and what the house'll bring. The world tells you over and over, always in refreshingly new and convincing ways, that what you produce isn't worth as much as a commercial for undrinkable beer, the teaser for a sit-com. For a while, for *years*, you defend yourself, you spit out the beer, you sneer at the sit-com. It's a way of life. A half-life. Then, one day, bingo! You just give in and agree."

I thought of Kafka's remark that in the battle between yourself and the world you should back the world.

Did he envy other writers, I asked.

"I guess I used to. Envy's a form of hope, you know—although not the *nicest* form, of course." He paused. "Whining's the sound you make just *before* it gets really bad."

•   •   •

Though a writer of stories may perform professional acts of imagination, that doesn't mean he isn't still an amateur. To imagine was almost an end in itself for Mandelbaum. It would have been so completely except that, as he said, "I need to make something out of what I imagine, need to find something in it." I suspected the hopelessness into which he had tumbled was going to be more grist for his mill.

We were sitting on a pair of old Adirondack chairs, out with the crickets and mosquitoes, drinking whiskey. We looked out at the lake which reflected the pale moonlight with smooth indifference.

"So," he said, "aren't you going to ask me what I'm working on? You know I came up here to work. Then I asked you to come. You ought to show an interest."

So I asked, "What are you working on?"

"Nothing. Well, I'm still working on my outline. Or thinking about it, anyway. It's going to be a novel about a man who wants to kill himself." He tendered me a brittle chuckle and a Jewish shrug. "What else?"

. . .

"Okay, here's what I've got, the bare bones," he began. "A man decides to kill himself. At first it's just a passing notion, a sort of daydream. That's common, I think, that daydream, and this guy's plenty common. Let's call him Robert Hall. Well, the idea keeps recurring to him. It's like a dissatisfied wife; he can't shake it. It's not just that his life now seems hollow, empty, pointless; it really *is*. Stale, flat, and unprofitable. Where he used to dream of ways in which things would get better for him, now he stops even trying to imagine solutions; and, because he's sure that escape's impossible, all he wants is a way out. Happiness? It isn't even a midnight fantasy, a wet dream. The urge gets heavier, weighs him down like a pair of concrete shoes. He really would like to be dead; the trouble is he has a horror of the act of killing himself. Hanging, drowning, bleeding out in the bathtub, leaping off buildings—no, he can't see himself doing any of them. And then he's terrified of *botching* the job. Not only would it be humiliating to screw up but he could be maimed in some terrible way. He pictures himself paralyzed and prays for a nice gallopingly terminal disease. But his doctor tells him he has the heart of a twenty-year-old and his cholesterol's ridiculously low for a beefeater. 'Good genes,' says the jolly internist, 'can't beat 'em.'"

"Go on."

"Okay. Every night Hall becomes a little more desperate. Finally, he decides to buy a gun but he knows nothing about firearms. He's not the hunting and fishing type. He drives to New Hampshire, finds a gun shop, picks out a pistol, fills in the form. Target practice, home and/or business protection. You need to give a socially responsible reason for desiring lethal force. He's excited holding the pistol. It's a lot heavier than he thought it would be. He carries the fancy box into his car and puts it on the passenger seat, his new copilot."

We sipped. I waited for him to go and he did.

"When you decide you want to be dead you naturally want to be dead right then, *at once*. I mean, *wanting* to be dead isn't the same as *deciding* to be. In Hall's case something odd happens. Now that he's got his gun, he's in no rush. He puts bullets in the gun the way he was shown at the shop. He's decided it would be best to put the barrel in his mouth—like Kleist and Hemingway—but, now that he's got his loaded gun, he's in no hurry. He hasn't changed his mind; he just wants to savor the relief of knowing he can off himself at any time. You understand? He feels a kind of provisional liberation. He can slip those concrete shoes on and off, like old loafers. He decides to give himself another week."

Through all this I was thinking: Hall goes to New Hampshire. That was only twenty miles away. He intends to imitate Kleist and Hemingway, writers of short stories. I hoped his novel was going to be a comedy, nicely poised between fantasy and autobiography, the second rescued by the first. Hall would be reconciled to Life and then Saul would give up fantasizing about putting barrels in mouths.

He finished his whiskey. "Well? What do you think?"

I told him it didn't sound much like a novel. "Just the one character?"

He laughed. "Oh, there's much more. I haven't worked it all out yet, but it'll go something like this. One night, Hall goes out for a ride, just to look around, get outside. He picks up a girl on the street, something he had never done before. She's very young, maybe still in her teens, a runaway. He takes her home, but he doesn't touch her. What he does is take care of her. He has serious talks with her. He gives her stuff to read, makes her listen to Mahler. Of course the girl's suspicious. What's she to think? He could be a pervert, but after a while she thinks he might be a do-gooder. She considers stealing from him, then running away, but she didn't like it much on the street. Also, he's nice to her. So she stays. After a week or so, she starts thinking he's a saint. He says wise and spiritual things to her. What I've got in mind is something like what Dostoyevsky would call *awakening her soul*. But Hall's fun, too. One afternoon, for instance, he takes her skydiving. How could she guess that all this goodness, this magnanimity is entirely due to his misery, what jumping out of a plane signifies to him? He tucks her in every night and reads her a Chekhov story. He's up when she wakes, making her pancakes or scrambled eggs. He tells her she has to go to college. He even makes her sort of want to, or at least *say* she wants to. Slowly, her guard comes down and she lets him know why she ran away and, to her surprise, he agrees it was the right thing to do. He stays with her all the time, except for one afternoon when he says he has to go out on business for a couple of hours. She doesn't know he's gone to his lawyer's to make out a new will."

This was, of course, the fantasy—the runaway daughter, a sex kitten redeemed by purity, disinterested love, and Hall's insurance policy. She will listen to *Das Lied von der Erde*, read Chekhov, and go to college. All because he blows his brains out."

* * *

Was planning a book about a suicide Mandelbaum's attempt to keep himself from having to use that New Hampshire pistol, was it a prelude to doing so, a way of telling me how close to the end of his tether he was? Robert Hall was a company that sold cheap suits, not the kind made by Hart, Schaffner, and Marx. Poor Mandelbaum. Would his Dostoyevskyan suicide story be fantasy or autobiography *avant le fait*? It hadn't yet occurred to me that it was both at once.

* * *

What I admire most about Mandelbaum's stories are their opening sentences. Perhaps this is because I find writing so difficult that any first sentence seems to me a little miracle, exploding into the world *ex nihilo*. When I read the news of his death, I pulled out my copy of his second collection and looked up the opening line of the last story. "Ever since my suicide attempt three friends have made a point of spending each Thursday night at my apartment." I noticed again what good use he had made of the stock phrase "to make a point of." Now I wonder which had been the fantasy—the suicide attempt or the longed-for Athos, Porthos, and Aramis who had made that compassionate point? Had I been unsuccessfully recruited as a musketeer?

Like his career, Mandelbaum's openings promised interesting things to come. "The sun had just touched the steppe when we climbed out of the Land Rovers, brushing the dust from our clothing in gestures that had become second nature." "It's easy for me to say what happened to my parents but impossible to describe them to you." "One Sunday morning at the end of July, just two days after my wife and I got back from our trip to Spain, our son Victor moved into the second-floor bathroom." "Who, what, where, when, how—apparently simple questions, and yet they are not really questions, only the breaths you draw in order to begin asking."

•   •   •

Suicides are generally unsympathetic. The living can muster only insincere sympathy for a sincerely negative judgment on what they intend to go on doing for as long as they possibly can. People prefer death to be free of moral sidebars. Leukemia, congestive heart failure—these are respectable ways of shuffling off. Even the most agonizing natural deaths don't bleed back into the works and days that preceded them the way suicide does—or murder, I suppose. Nothing's fair about this, of course, but Mandelbaum must have been beyond caring either about fairness or the stain on his reputation that would leach back into his adolescence, all the way down to our recesses in the schoolyard.

I remember a Unitarian minister who leaned over the widow of

Henry Whiteside and kept saying over and over again, "Cecilia, you have to think of it as an *accident*. It just wasn't Henry. You know Henry couldn't have been himself when he did that. Cecilia, you've got to think of it as an *accident*." An accident isn't quite as good as congestive heart failure but it is easier to swallow than the unanswerable reproach of deliberate self-murder. There is no fantasy about an accident, hardly even any autobiography. As Mandelbaum would say, there's nothing to be made out of it. If we knew that Shakespeare had committed suicide wouldn't we read *Hamlet* differently?

Life is always rushing to catch up with art. Mandelbaum starts off one of his earliest stories this way: "Evidently my neighbor is bent on dismembering himself and, to this end, he has employed several tools." Melancholy to think how such a fantasy can in retrospect reveal itself as prophetic autobiography.

True, he lasted out the summer. He didn't use the gun until October. But I failed him. I should have tried harder to convince him it's better just to go on waiting, like the rest of us.

ON VILLAINY

The noble type of man regards himself as a deter-
miner of values; he does not require to be approved of;
he passes the judgment: "What is injurious to me is
injurious in itself"; he knows that it is he himself who
confers honor on things; he is a creator of values...The
noble man honors in himself the powerful one, him
also who has power over himself, who knows how to
speak and how to keep silence, who takes pleasure in
subjecting himself to severity and hardness, and has
reverence for all that is severe and hard...

-Friedrich Nietzsche

EDITOR'S INTRODUCTION

It is not surprising that some of Fein's posthumous papers should
have a bearing on one another, especially those Fein probably did
not mean for the public but wrote for himself. This is the case with
the curious piece that appears below which concerns Fein's elementary school friend Saul Mandelbaum.

By the time Fein visited him in August 1976, Mandelbaum was
in psychological distress. He committed suicide two months later.
His wife had left him in February and he was drinking hard. Most
of all, Mandelbaum was convinced his work had failed.

Over the years, the two saw one another from time to time and
they exchanged a few letters about their work and other matters.
They could not be called close but neither did they entirely lose
touch. Both had unhappy marriages. Fein's dissolved in January

1974. Mandelbaum's was childless. When I found the following piece in Fein's folder for the year 1975 I thought it intriguing but less than comprehensible. Its occasion, as I eventually discovered, was Fein's first stint as a visiting professor the year before. He was appointed, on the strength of his first book, to teach a course in ethical philosophy but he also took on a section of logic. The meaning of these fragments only became clear to me when I happened on Mandelbaum's letter and his little story in a bunch of correspondence from the year 1974, mixed in with paid invoices, family letters, and bank statements. That summer, Fein had taken his semi-motherless daughter to Italy. The best place to begin is with Mandelbaum's letter sent in reply to a post card Fein had sent him from Venice.

August 21, 1974

Dear Sid,

Thanks for the post card. It's a fine thing to be thought of in the Old World and it's reassuring to see that Venice is still keeping its rotting head above the putrid water. The place looks as decadent as ever, still going for the title of longest decline without a fall. Aschenbach on the beach with his rouged cheeks thinking of the *Phaedrus*, Teutons and pigeons all over St. Mark's with its Italian fiddlers pumping out Strauss.

I appreciate your choosing a shot of the Grand Canal that includes the Palazzo Vendramin—speaking of Tods, or toads. Did you know Wagner actually went there for his *health*?

I trust you and Maya enjoyed your Henry James Memorial Grand Tour. I hope it cheered the both of you up. Very sorry to hear your marriage exploded. Yours is the third break-up I've heard about in the last three months alone. At least you're completely *au courant*. Do you think it's the Women's Lib stuff or just the headless chickens of the last decade coming home to roost? I can't claim Rosalind and

I are in the clear, though I do see her every morning at breakfast and, most nights, we sleep in the same bed.

My agent's pissed off, Rosalind's pissed off, I'm pissed off. We're in agreement though because we're all pissed off at me. I'm still staring at paper every day. I write down a word and sometimes a second—on a good day, a third. Fame is the spur?

So, you're going to take the Brandeis gig. Am I now obliged to call you Herr Doktor Professor for the next nine months? Am I resentful; am I jealous? I'm not sure. But I'm wondering if you agree with the poet's plea:

> 'Mongst all these stirs of discontented strife
> O, let me lead an academic life.

You mentioned that they want you to teach ethical phillerphobby. Good choice, I suppose, for such an upright guy. There are lots of answers to the same old questions. In physics and chemistry they're always asking new questions. At least I think so. This must be because there are answers for physicists and chemists, final ones, I mean. Maybe that's what guys like you and me didn't like about the sciences, the sheer precision of them. No essay questions.

Well, enough out of me. I'm enclosing a bit of *Kleinkunst*. Not only is it always nice to have a reader, especially an intelligent one, but I think it's apropos of your appointment and might interest you a little.

Comme Toujours,
SM

VILLAINY
by Saul Mandelbaum

"We sit here below, stuck in the narrow alleys of our virtue. It's unjust that we have to look up to him but that's how it is," said the doctor last night, carried away by indignation but also a sort of poetic resignation. *The narrow alleys of our virtue* really is almost a little poem by itself, isn't it? You can hear our valley in it, the hills pressing in on either side of the tight grid of houses, churches, lanes, and schools.

Virtue is supposed to be a good thing, so why did the doctor make it sound so disconsolate? And why should everyone have nodded when he said what he did? What did he really mean? Is there some kind of virtue under virtue then, a sort that monster, who lives above our town when he is not flying around the world, possesses and we lack?

His mansion was built more than a century back. The first owner of the mill erected it on the hill and it showed his relationship to our forebears. All that remains of the mill is a broken wall of red brick next to the railroad tracks, but the mansion on the hill still looms over us. When the doctor spoke of having to look up, it was a literal truth. The ancient respect for elevation persists and so, simply by purchasing the old manor, he took on the character of an aristocrat and became lordly. He is a tall, handsome man, with smooth black hair and a seigniorial bearing.

In evil, he is an artist and any artist is apt to be defined by something less than his finest work so long as people find in it a decisive gesture; in his case, an original contribution to the human repertoire of nastiness. For us, it is the episode of the valedictorian that is indelible, unforgivable, though any of us could adduce more ingenious, vile, elegant, or shameful incidents from his infamous career.

She had just turned eighteen. Her beauty was dark, like his, and her body precociously ripe; she moved in a way that struck us as both provocative and stern. Her intelligence was no less imposing than her looks. In her, spirit and body had conspired in some miraculous fashion to make her shine whichever way you looked at her, whatever she said. She was a diamond in our worn-out vein of coal. Her parents adored her so much that they hardly knew what to do with her and behaved toward her like peasants visited by a princess. Still, she was not in the least spoiled; her self-possession was inviolable. She treated her family with restrained affection, ignoring their deference. This could not have been easy. Her father got into the habit of walking a bit behind her in the street; he would even ask her opinion at the hardware store. No one would have blamed him had he puffed himself up for having sired such a daughter, but he was too humbled to boast of her, as if she really were a regal visitor with only an accidental connection to his family. It was more or less the same with her mother and sister. They regarded her with something like superstitious awe. Perhaps because her family declined the credit of her excellence, the whole town felt free to take pride in her, more content to be geese for having brought forth this swan.

From the moment she began to bloom we kept our eyes on her, but our gaze was furtive. We watched her intently throughout her high school years, anxious not to disturb a perfection that, despite her poise, we thought might prove fragile, looking on her as a gardener might a promising sapling, worried about frost, anticipating the fruit, finding relief in each spring's tender leaves. By sixteen she had the sort of beauty that makes you take a step backwards, as if it were a wind. Almost superstitiously, we never spoke of it.

In her next to last year she won the top prize at the Science Fair and was elected class president. We were amused by the way the boys fell over one another when she passed by. They had our sympathy; who wouldn't smile at their clumsiness? Adoration collected around her like a cloud she really seemed not to notice. She never abused her power to intimidate because to cow her peers required no act of will. She was like a child holding a grenade.

Graduation Day was a temperate one in June. Wispy clouds sailed over the athletic field. The grandstand faced south so we would have had to turn around to see the mansion up on the hill. The whole town was gathered behind the graduates who sat on rows of folding chairs on the football field, clad in dark blue robes that elevated the giggles and acne and lent them the dignity of a college of theologians, or a tragic chorus.

Her valedictorian's robe was immaculately white. Against it lay her long dark hair, too thick to be disturbed by the breeze. We were full of anticipation, but what could we be expecting? A speech we might not quite understand perhaps, yet one that would edify, raise us up, words that would dazzle our minds as her white gown did our eyes. She was the best we had. Naturally, we knew a commencement address is no occasion for originality, that we were there for a ritual, not a treatise. Nevertheless, we who had been observing her for years, we who were all in love with her in one fashion or another, who had numbered her perfections and sighed to think how far away her life was bound to carry her, awaited her speech almost as an apotheosis.

She began oddly, by telling a kind of fairy tale. Even if what occurred later had not happened we would still have remembered this story, if only for the sake of the melodious voice that related it. She seemed to be summing up her life among us, or telling us how we all were meant to live, offering a simple truth she had learned from us about living equably and decently, yet a truth she herself was to forsake. Some claimed later to have detected in this parable a cautionary tale and maybe they were right. The advice one gives to others may be good whether one follows it oneself or not; the truth one is on the point of betraying is nonetheless a truth, perhaps it is all the more precious.

"Once upon a time, a man and a woman were dragged before the king. The king looked on the young couple with pity; however, the evidence against them was convincing and the law clear. Not even the king could go above the law and so he delivered his verdict with a heavy heart, mitigating the sentence in the only way the law permitted. Not far from the castle was a chasm, wide and fearfully deep. The king ordered a rope stretched across it. The couple were condemned to walk across the rope, first the woman and then the man. In the unlikely event that one or both should manage to make it across, they would be pardoned. But that had never happened.

"Everything was done just as the law and the king dictated and all the people gathered to watch. The young woman climbed bravely onto the rope. Slowly, one step after the other, she crossed the gorge. The young man, who had scarcely taken a breath as he watched his love, shouted over: 'My dear, tell me how you managed to do it.' 'I don't know,' she called back. 'All I know is that whenever I felt myself toppling over to the left I leaned to the right, and whenever I started to fall to the right I leaned to the left.'"

The rest of her speech was more conventional. She laid out for her classmates the best of life's possibilities and thanked the town for its support.

That very afternoon she vanished, not on a fiery chariot and not into thin air. He must have kept his engine idling all through her address, the awarding of prizes, through the roll of sixty-five names, the minister's benediction, the cheers, hugs, snapshots—through all this he would have sat, patient as a spider.

We saw her embrace her parents, clutch her sister, wave to her friends; then suddenly she was running, the white robe streaming behind her as she fled over the grass, and, before anyone could think of stopping her, she leapt into his car.

FEIN ON VILLAINY

SAUL Mandelbaum teases the people he knows while with strangers he is formal, almost regimental. Both, I believe, are ways of holding off the world like a long-limbed boxer who stiff-arms an opponent's forehead. The courtesy and the teasing serve a self-protective purpose, but in such a way that he is never entirely cut off. Even in the fifth grade, he contrived to be both the shyest among us and the class clown.

I'm afraid his resolution to live by his writing—and Rosalind's paychecks—may be undermining him. Literature has not been good for him; it has made him literary. Now books are the semi-permeable membrane between him and the world. For him, Venice doesn't belong to the Italian Republic but Thomas Mann. Only a man far gone in literature could quote verses by the Elizabethan Bishop of Norwich at me—or expect me to pick up the reference. I had to look it up. The Bishop gave his poem an impressively prosaically title: "The Discontent of Men with Their Condition."

Literature has been bad for SM but he has not been bad for it. His work is always interesting and yet it isn't made to be successful. And, unfortunately, it's success he craves. Perhaps he knows this but can do nothing about it as he pushes words across the paper. That must be a terrible source of discontent.

SM is even less fitted to academic life than I am. He is one of those who believes literature is a wild animal and the universities are corrals. He wants more than the Bishop, who continues in this vein:

To know much, and to think for nothing, know
Nothing to have, yet think we have enow.

Genteel scholarly poverty might be enow for him, if he could stomach it, had the taste for it, or the discipline. But he doesn't. As a maker of narratives, he's contemptuous of philosophy and distrusts ideas. He would never agree with Keats' unexpected verdict that poetry "is not so fine a thing as philosophy—for the same reason an eagle is not so fine a thing as a truth." Saul would go for the eagles every time. He's an astute critic but dislikes seeing the suggestiveness of a story translated into the discursiveness of ideas. Thus, the mockery of "phillerphobby." To him, a story opens its palms to disclose two handfuls of possibilities whereas philosophy tightens its fist around just one.

Last year, I was busy preparing my first course and I hardly glanced at "Villainy." I noticed the stock, melodramatic characters, smiled at the ending, and took it personally. I thought of it as a not terribly interesting, rather ironic jibe at me for setting up to teach moral philosophy. I let my friend down, since what he wanted was an intelligent reading. But, now I've looked at it again, I see that what I took to be simple and even trite is neither.

• • •

I felt pleasure when my book was published. Was this pleasure the sensation of power? Perhaps the sense of power was even my chief sensation—but that's a thought one normally keeps to oneself, perhaps even from oneself.

There's quite a difference between saying that pleasure is the sensation of power and saying that the sensation of power is one sort of pleasure. It's the difference between the extremism of demanding everything of and for oneself and accepting a medium-sized basket with many eggs in it. *Das Wille zur Macht?* Well, Nietzsche had to sound extreme to hold our attention and he shouts louder and louder, more and more desperately: the weak should go to the wall, Christ is a big black spider, the Bible is unclean, Socrates was a buffoon, Kant a Tartuffe. Really, he's brilliantly theatrical. Though all his dramatic hollering suggests overcompensation, it's precisely as theater that the *Übermensch* is compelling, albeit that theater is in Bayreuth which even Nietzsche couldn't stomach in the end. (As SM reminds me, it was in Venice that Richard Wagner died.) Anyway, SM's story has started me thinking about Nietzsche, the "hard" one, though my stint as a professor last year made me realize that he is so various and inconsistent that everybody can have his or her very own Nietzsche, from the Foucauldians to the Feminists, from Existentialists to the Post-Structuralists, from the General Staff to the Propaganda Ministry.

SM believes his work has failed, that he's mediocre. He is too noble to extol mediocrity, to recast it as virtue and stamp everything superior as evil. But neither can he reconcile himself to his impotence. Perhaps something of this sort underlies his story.

•   •   •

The word *villain* derives from the Latin for farm servant. Villains were originally low-lifes. In England, even today, a villain is just a common criminal. In democratic America, however, villains are almost always upper-crust, deceitful gentlemen, often with pomaded hair and a thin mustache. Mandelbaum is playing with this cardboard American villain and that is what first misled me into taking his story too lightly and kept me from seeing it's set up to provoke a reader into questioning the story's assumptions—and so his as well. Is the town really virtuous or only pinched and predictable, like its grid of lanes? Is the sublime girl succumbing to a blackguard's blandishments or escaping from a suffocating watchfulness, the stress of expectancy and pride? Is the lord of the manor really exercising an outrageous and outdated *droit de seigneur* or does he passionately love the girl and/or she him? Could *they* be the couple crossing that chasm and not, as the narrator seems to presume, the decent people of the town, advised by a sinner to go on walking the straight and narrow between death and the devil?

What exactly is villainy? Who is the villain? Is it that "monster" on the hill making off with the girl, or is it the girl abandoning her town, her family, her class? Might it even be the village that's the villain, as etymology hints, villainous in its smug modesty and repressed resentment? Now I see that SM chose his title to maximize ambiguity and show me that storytellers set as much store by it as philosophers do consistency. "Villainy" ties itself up and then, if you re-read it, unties itself; it's a tale that's all *dénouement* so that you are left with a tangle of rope at your feet, ready to be stretched across life's chasms.

SM has written a Nietzschean story in more ways than one. Nietzsche considered that everybody from Moses and Socrates to Mill and Marx had gotten things backwards. (SM had a similar word for me: "Your whole syllabus is a botch.") From Nietzsche's point of view, it's the town full of "slave moralists" who are in the

wrong, traducing their more powerful betters with loaded labels—
"evil" and "villain."

> According to slave-morality …the "evil" man arouses
> fear; according to master-morality, it is precisely the
> "good" man who arouses fear and seeks to arouse it, while
> the bad man is the despicable being.

Good is bad, bad is good. Once upon a time, values were transvalued and need to be transvalued back. "At the commencement,"
he thunders, waving his arms, "the noble caste was always the
barbarian caste." But Nietzsche isn't aiming at only historical truth;
it is even more a psychological one, since what preceded civilization
must still lie beneath it, in us, there below our socialization: "… all
spontaneous motives, all new, future and stronger motives, are still
extant…" Well, if so, Saul's stage villain up on the hill might just
as well incarnate the frustrated motives of the old men and abashed
boys of the town, watching the dazzling girl walk by, like Susannah.
As for the females, wouldn't they be thrilled to see a young woman,
almost one of them, living dangerously on that tightrope, crossing
the abyss for the sake of a handsome, wealthy man complete with
a limousine and a mansion? It's almost like a woman's novel, isn't
it, like *Pride and Prejudice*, *Jane Eyre*, *Rebecca*. But the heroine is
anything but a plain Jane. In fact, the valedictorian, who fittingly
(here's SM being literary again) bids farewell to the town on her
graduation day, is beautiful and dark, exactly like the villain; she
is nubile to a fault and, like Lucifer, brighter than her classmates.
The town "takes pride" in her just because, like her family, they
sense she doesn't belong with them. She's a changeling, a princess
in disguise, a cygnet who doesn't even make the geese ashamed they
aren't swans. "One law for the lion and the ox is tyranny," wrote
Blake. Nietzsche turned that infernal proverb into a moral principle.
Aren't all Nietzsche's masters solitary predators? Aren't all his slaves
jumpy herds of prey with darting eyes and twitching ears?

Can the girl be a monster because she chooses to run off with a man the town considers one? That the townspeople want to think she's a victim proves nothing. For them it's the most comfortable hypothesis, but the story undermines this. For example, there is her "inviolable self-possession" which doesn't make it seem as though she could be easily seduced. Even the narrator has to allow that her fragility is merely a presumption, an unlikely one given her poise and achievements. She's no sentimental adolescent; the girl won the prize at the science fair. Her innocence is at once oblivious and powerful. She "cows" her peers without trying to do so. In one of the story's better images she is compared to "a child holding a grenade." But what if she knows all about grenades? What if she's perfectly aware of her potential for "villainy"; that is, what if the girl really knows her own strength? Is that strength good or evil—or beyond both?

• • •

I should say something about the doctor, the sole individual whose reflections we get to hear. He reminds me of Chekhov's doctors—intelligent, perceptive, humane, and ineffectual.

The physician's views have the authority of precedence. Those two opening sentences are crucial, not just because of SM's confessed difficulty in coming up with first sentences, but because it's the town *doctor* who's speaking—an educated man, a man of science, a man who has to make diagnoses. I suspect SM identifies with this doctor to some degree. Again, like Chekhov. From what I gather of his discontent, he too feels stuck in a cul-de-sac. The doctor might protest the injustice of things, the constriction of his situation; but, unlike the girl, he has resigned himself. His eloquence is static, fixed as the pinched landscape. Hierarchy, claims Nietzsche, is natural. "Life *is* appropriation," he says, a food chain, what other philosophers call "immoral." He has a point: even for vegetarians, not to exploit is to die.

The collective narrator (a Continental device, by the way, which I can't recall SM using before) questions the doctor's melancholy capitulation. If virtue is good, why should it be "disconsolate"? This fair question leads to an even better, more subversive one: "Is there some kind of virtue *under* virtue"—one the "monster" has and they lack? Virtue once signified power, military prowess. Achilles was virtuous in the original sense. It was Socrates who cleverly appropriated the word to moral uses, comparing himself to the hero of the *Iliad* and thereby supplanting him—insidiously, Nietzsche says. Thereafter to behave like Achilles was, in effect, to be a villain.

This narrator is not really at odds with the doctor, whose first word, after all, is *we*. He is a sort of specification of the town's consensus. The place conceives itself as part New England mill town, part feudal estate. What is left of the mill is a ruin, "a broken wall of red brick." The economic relations that once bound the lord of the manor to the town have dissolved. All that remains, the narrator says poignantly, is "the ancient respect for elevation." The story picks at this ambiguous above/below. The guilty couple must avoid tumbling into a chasm. The doctor complains of having "to look up" at the mansion and its proprietor, and the narrator later reminds us that this is "a literal truth," thereby provoking us to think of a truth that *isn't* literal. He saying "the *ancient* respect for elevation" resonates with his archaic word *seigniorial* to enlarge the story's associations, covering the terrain of both *Don Giovanni* and *The Marriage of Figaro* with sinister overtones: "In evil, he is an artist…"

An artist. Here, I think, is another hint of SM's oscillating identification; this time he sees himself as the "villain." As a writer better known for his reviews than his fiction, it is his misfortune to feel he too is "defined by something less than his finest work" and that his career is "infamous"—that is, *not* famous ("Fame is the spur?"). Poor Saul suffers from an unstable synthesis of abjection and aspiration. Perhaps this is so for all artists, at least the unsuccessful ones. When I read the town's verdict on the "monster," I think of the critics' dismissal of SM's labors. Maybe the splendid girl even symbolizes the fame he longs to wrest from the public. Or perhaps it's her escape from the middling to the heights that SM yearns to emulate? I doubt he himself could say. He is a fabulist who depends on unconscious inspiration and unmediated meanings. This makes him hostile to the "phillerphobbers" who pride themselves on having eliminated such things from their work where everything must appear to be rational, deliberate, and transparent—a boast Nietzsche has enormous fun mocking. How indignant would Aristotle be if he were told he thinks exactly like a Stagiran on the make, a middle-class kid irritated by the idealism of an Athenian aristocrat with a trust fund?

• • •

I find the meaning of the girl's tightrope story elusive. The temptation is to nail it down but it isn't solid enough and keeps floating away. The key elements are transgression, frustrated mercy, mandatory sentencing, an abyss and the equipoise that can safely pass over it. The castle suggests the mansion, the chasm the distance between it and the town. The condemned couple makes me think of the girl and the "spider" waiting for her; but the theme of balance seems to point in another direction, since moderation is hardly to be associated with the "monster" or the sort of life he carries on up at his mansion. In the story, though, it's only the female who makes it across; we aren't told her lover's fate. So perhaps the girl's story is a statement of intent, her valedictory promise that *she*, at least, will maintain her moral equilibrium amidst all "the possibilities of life" she is about to choose. On the other hand, the story is a confession of having done something illicit, so maybe it is also a cautionary tale, the moral being that it's best for oxen not to act like lions. The story may also be one of SM's many parables of the human condition—he is always summing up—an opinion subject to revision. A final possibility: this is Saul reminding me yet again that in "phillerphobby" contradictories exclude one another, while in fiction they don't.

I am quite taken with the blurry one-sentence paragraph that concludes SM's little tale. With those seven active verbs, it's like watching a tracking shot. Also, it's clever of SM to recapitulate the girl's biography, beginning with the family's embrace and ending with her leaping into the black car, all in sight of the townsfolk, the tragic chorus of elders and peers. This finale is satisfying in a way that philosophical writing seldom is, except for the most literary—Plato, Kierkegaard, Camus. That last sentence has the just-so feel of a well-made top fitting on a well-made box, the precision of an oiled guillotine. You feel there's nothing more to be said, no more worth saying. It's just the opposite with philosophical texts. They generally remind me of a crack Kafka made about Martin Buber: no matter how much he says, something's always missing.

I don't know if art is villainy but I'm certain that "Villainy" is art.

As for my friend the author, I can't wish him to be as happy as he wants, because I don't believe happiness is what he wishes for. So, instead, I wish he could be as happy as he deserves.

ON TWO SONNETS OF
ALEXANDER FERNLICHT

Sidney Fein arranged his papers by year and stored them in large accordion envelopes. These envelopes bulge with all sorts of items, from professional correspondence, birthday cards, and tax receipts to lecture notes, incomplete or abandoned manuscripts, and drafts of his books. Each envelope is a mine. When his daughter offered me the privilege of going through Fein's papers she handed me a license to dig with the injunction to prepare for the press any gems I could unearth, so long as they were not too rough and at least semi-precious. The discoveries have been worth the effort, such as finding out that Fein had invented a pseudonym, Klaren Verheim, and that he had written verse. Now I have discovered what I believe to be a second pseudonym and more verses, but a pseudonym quite distinct in character and purpose from Verheim and verses altogether different from the long, philosophical "Königsberg."

In Fein's file for the year 1980 I came across several pieces concerning one Alexander Fernlicht, described in one item as "a defrocked professor of history." Klaren Verheim became, according to Fein, a personality unto himself, a person quite apart from Fein. In "The Birth of the Author," Fein says of Verheim that he is not Fein but the means by which Fein might extend his authorship in otherwise inaccessible directions.

I believe Alexander Fernlicht to be a more conventional alter ego, precisely what Fein says Verheim is not: "a mere *nom de plume* behind whom Fein hides." In other words, while Verheim's role was to allow Fein to write things that Fein would otherwise never have written, I think Fernlicht was the means by which Fein could delve into episodes from his personal life.

In this pseudonymous Fernlicht work, Fein is Fein, but he exploits the tiny gap between himself and Fernlicht to deploy his corrosive, analytic intelligence by composing commentaries on Fernlicht and his works—that is, his own—even assuming the imperially critical first-person plural to augment the distance. What follows is a sort of diptych whose genre is hard to fix. From one point of view, Fein has written an ingeniously objective-sounding yet dreamlike exegesis of two sonnets as if he were a committee; from another, these are bits of speculative, semi-fictional autobiography; while, from yet a third viewpoint, what we have may be only superficially distanced revelations about Fein's marriage and a brief liaison.

Of course, the possibility remains that I am wrong and that Fein is not Fernlicht, not even a little. For instance, what is one to make of the fact that *Fernlicht* is German for *Distant Light* and that this is the title of a novel by his childhood friend Saul Mandelbaum? Could Fein have been writing a veiled account, not of his own life, but of Mandelbaum's? Or did he adopt the name as an homage to Mandelbaum after his friend's suicide in October, 1976? *Alexander* is Greek for *helper of man*. Fein saw Mandelbaum two months before he died and felt guilty for being unable to help his friend. The Editor is allowed an opinion and I have stated mine; but the truth is I cannot say with certainty what the true identity of Alexander Fernlicht is. Perhaps it is fitting that this introduction should end as indeterminately as Fein winds up the strange piece of writing that follows.

• • •

Two Inquiries Into Sonnets
by Alexander Fernlicht

1. The House Inside the House

By thorough examination of Fernlicht's letters and journals and thanks to the valuable aid of interviews with two people who prefer to remain anonymous, we believe we have been able to reconstruct the sources of his sonnet, "The House." This achievement may not be a signal one, but then, in the body of American poetry or even Fernlicht's oeuvre, neither is the sonnet. What perhaps will be of some interest is the process involved; that is, a kind of old-fashioned collusion among biography, literary criticism, and oneiromancy.

• • •

Fernlicht took one look at his wife's burning eyes and began to levitate. He rose from their queen-sized bed. With his loose robe billowing like a sail, he was wafted down the stairs and across the living room, coming to rest in the kitchen where a fresh pot of coffee simmered aromatically on the stove. Fernlicht filled the mug he found in his hand before slipping down the cellarway to the forbidding front door of his house, the secret, subterranean one. Carefully balancing the full mug, he took from the pocket of his robe a huge iron key and unlocked the narrow metal door, entered the narrow foyer, strode through the miniature parlor and climbed the stairs to his cozy wood-paneled study. Settling himself at his desk, he sipped the still-hot coffee and reached for a black-bound book. No sooner had he opened this tome than he heard his wife pounding on the steel door. "I can't live like this!" Trembling, Fernlicht pulled the window shade and crouched in the corner. His wife's voice arrived a little more faintly now. She was still screaming but less distinctly. She yelled a word that could have been *impossible*, *impoverished*, possibly *implausible* or even *implosion*. Fernlicht left his study and started down the hallway, going deeper into his house, further from his wife's voice. Doors opened on various rooms, each with its proper decor and function: an Edwardian nursery, a Turkish seraglio, a cell in the Château d'If, a Viennese drawing room, the red velvet upholstery of a Louisiana bordello, the strong room of a medieval keep. His wife's voice became ever more remote. He had never conceived the enormous size of his house, and he was both impressed and horrified by it. How could he have been so ignorant? The house was obviously much bigger than the regular one above and around it; but as he continued past a tiny lady chapel and the smoking room of a Dutch tavern, this absurdity struck him with less force than the conviction that, for good or ill, he was unlikely ever to leave the house.

• • •

We suppose that, as with most people, the dreams Fernlicht is able to recall are the most obvious and least deceptive. He himself once observed that Freud's interpretations are less astounding than his patients' power of recollection. Perhaps it is the transparency of their imagery that allows Fernlicht to remember dreams such as the above while he is certain to forget many more obscure and difficult ones that would do his unconscious more honor.

It is, of course, possible that Fernlicht overestimates the quality of his forgotten dreams, ascribing to them complexity, profundity, and power so that he might have something to hope or fear from them. After all, he cannot entirely escape what, with apparent contempt, he likes to call the most popular religion of any generation, which is superstition. We are, like Fernlicht, unable to take a decisively scientific view of where his verses originate. Nevertheless, in the present instance, we are satisfied that the dream and the sonnet are connected in the manner of a first draft and a finished text. Actually, we could also say there is a text lying *behind* even the first draft; that is, behind the dream. This would be Fernlicht's failed marriage, which began a year after his father's death and ended a year after he received his doctorate. The dream, in other words, is a first draft literarily speaking, but at the same time a mediator between an anterior actuality (his marriage) and the piece of artifice that eventuated from it (the sonnet). If we are correct, then it is revealing that all traces of the marriage, as well as the personality of the dreamer, have been ruthlessly excised from the sonnet. Fernlicht has also invented or rearranged details so that what began as the surreal imagery of a dream and the truth of a failed marriage winds up as metaphor in a deliberately flat and commonplace sonnet.

HOUSE

> The scholar leans into his lamp,
> lights up his pipe, digests the mood
> of cozy thought. The night grows damp;
> rain settles on his solitude.
> A conversation outside time
> as ears ignore the baffled noise:
> the scholar tacit as a mime
> attends the resurrected voice.
> The silence of soft rain, still night,
> concentrates upon the page
> the reader's eye, the shaded light,
> till mind is mindless of mind's rage
> and all the world could not arouse
> it from the house inside its house.

The ruling symbol of the dream is also its setting, a frighteningly vast, ostensibly infinite house with a door like a prison's and an unending jumble of historical rooms standing improbably in the basement of a normal suburban home uneasily shared by a husband and wife. The boundless yet cozy house of the dream becomes, in the final line of Fernlicht's sonnet, the modest metaphor of a scholar's mind. No grand claims are made for it. On the contrary. A house inside a house is a paltry thing compared with, say, Sir Edward Dyer's regal, if rather complacent, lines:

> My mind to me a kingdom is;
> Such present joys therein I find
> That it excels all other bliss
> That earth affords or grows by kind...

The impulse of withdrawal into bookish coziness and proprietorship, the library/study/mind as a uterus owned by a male—all this is like Sir Edward, but a few things have changed in the four centuries between Dyer writing about his "conscience clear" and Fernlicht dropping a phrase like "mind's rage." At least that is our opinion.

In the sonnet, the dreaming, levitating husband becomes a denatured scholar, complete with pipe and desk lamp. Meanwhile, the outer or *real* house has dematerialized completely, replaced by a conventional rainy night. Everything about the sonnet is emblematic, abstracted, banal. From one point of view, this makes the poem an evasion of the serious issues of the dream—not to mention the marriage—while, from another, the lack of concretion is really a sublimation of the dream's messiness and absurdity. The poem is, so to speak, as duplicitous in its simplicity as it is guilty in its innocence.

We are principally struck by one transformation of the dream into the poem. The reproving voice of the wife becomes "the silence of soft rain," but also, we think, the tension in the poem between "solitude" and "silence" on the one hand, "conversation" and "noise" on the other. This is no easy case of dualism, though: something versus nothing, the *crowded* versus the *vacant*. For example, the "conversation outside time" occurs because the "noise" is "baffled." It is solitude that allows the scholar to attend to that "resurrected voice." Whose is that voice, back from the dead? Prima facie it is the voice of the dead author of the book before him. This book, bound in black as a sign of its gravity, appears likewise in the dream. However, the dreamer never gets to bring the voice of his book to life. He is prevented from doing so by the raising of a different voice crying, "I can't live like this!" This wife's "noisy" voice contrasts with the calm, silent one of the dead author. It is accusing, discontent, frustrated, peevish—but "baffled," an acoustical metaphor which suggests her message is being blocked out but which also implies the dreamer's bafflement over what the voice is saying and its tone. The daily abrasions of the marriage have unexpectedly erupted.

We should not overlook the ambiguous threat to be inferred from the four "im" words of the dream which require close attention. They may constitute both a judgment on the marriage and a condemnation of Fernlicht, the dreamer/poet, and his way of life: *impossible, impoverished, implausible*—and that last suggestive possibility, *implosion*. With these possibilities in mind the sonnet loses its serene tone, for it could be the record of just such an "implosion," a turning away from the social world in favor of the double solitude of "the house inside the house."

The steel prison door of the dream provides yet another ambiguity as it keeps in as much out. Four of the half-dozen rooms that appear in the dream, perhaps all six, are traps of one sort or another, places of confinement: a nursery, a seraglio, a cell in a dungeon, an armory in a castle keep. Neither of the other two, which may at first appear to be sites of sociability (Viennese drawing room and velvet bordello), is innocent. On the contrary, it is easy to conceive how either might also be a penitentiary, the loneliness of decadent, purchased intercourse.

The one line in the poem we find truly arresting is not the last, the one that points so clearly to the sonnet's origin in Fernlicht's dream, but rather the twelfth: "till mind is mindless of mind's rage." The reiteration of *mind* here enforces the governing metaphor of the poem; it may even be a deliberate reference to Dyer's poem and the entirety of the vanished pastoral/humanistic tradition Dyer epitomizes. However, we find it remarkable that the line presents mind in three distinct aspects: first, as *mind* itself, the instrument of thought and of communion with the thoughts of others; second, *mind* in the negative sense of *mindless*, mind forgetting itself to find itself; and third, *mind* as a thing that *rages*, mind at odds with the tranquility the poem seems to celebrate. Save for this one line, and the conclusive word *rage*, the poem would be both trivial and dishonest.

Is "House," then, really about scholarly serenity or an ironic record of a desperate effort to evade the responsibility that begins in dreams? This question is not beyond speculation but we find it impossible to resolve and so we think it best to stop here.

2. ARRANGE YOUR OWN SONNET

As we see it, she was as unhappily married as he was irrevocably divorced. How long Fernlicht's *affaire de cœur* with Julia M. lasted we have been unable to calculate precisely, though surely it could not have been more than a matter of some months, approximately from January to May.

We are fairly certain that Fernlicht met Julia on a rainy night when, owing to condensation on the ignition wires, her car failed to start. We deduce it was probably in the parking lot of a suburban movie theater or shopping mall. It was unlikely to have been in the city as Julia was alone. Fernlicht would not have been able to start her car, given what we know of his limitations as a mechanic; however, neither would he have been able to take his eyes off her.

As always in such matters, more curiosity attaches to the ending than the beginning. Beginnings are generic, universal, self-evident, while endings are unpredictable and poignant. Our difficulty here is simple lack of documentation. We have only a single letter to go on, as well as the terror with which Julia M. rejected even our very discreet inquiry. What we would most wish to know, of course, is what this brief liaison reveals about Fernlicht's character. We have had no difficulty determining which of his sonnets can be traced to it. But who, for example, was responsible for breaking things off? What scruples, what *anti*-scruples, did each feel? Did the pressure of secrecy itself doom things, as often happens with conscientious people passionately caught up in the violation of a commandment? Was it mere infatuation that burnt itself out like a struck light bulb? Did one or the other endure recurrent nightmares of discovery, conscious moments of remorse? Did this or that party press for an open announcement, wishing to make the relationship into something consequential? And how did they cope with the final dissolution and disappointment? Was it a relief for one, a catastrophe for the other? Who got over it first?

As it happens, the one letter we possess, though undated, appears to have been written by Fernlicht just after the end of the affair, at a time when he obviously no longer cared much for either secrecy or tact. It is a perplexing letter consisting almost entirely of an introduction and two sonnets, or sets of verses. In so far as these sonnets are superficially clever they might be thought to display a certain bitterness, even rancor. But the cleverness lies only in the *ordering* of the verses, not in the lines themselves. Each line is for itself yet resonates with its partner in rhyme in a manner that bespeaks not cold indifference but authentic feeling.

The introductory part of the letter seems about equally divided between distance and intimacy; that is, distance gained, intimacy lost. "Dear Mrs. M.," it begins, "I am writing to you just this once and I hope you'll overlook my transgression. I will mail this to your work address, of course, and mark the envelope *personal* so you will be doubly safe, though how much safety one may expect in life I am not sure. When last we were together you said it pained you to have nothing to remember me by, no *souvenir*. That was your word, *souvenir*. I need nothing to remember you by. I simply remember. Right now I recall a great deal, practically everything, though later on I expect I'll remember less and less. This is not to say I'll forget you. Memory is like a filter. Much runs through and is lost, but what remains precipitates, hardens, can be held between the fingers and examined from every angle, like a diamond. I know you have no love of poetry, but since I can choose what you will remember me by, poetry is what I choose.

"The sonnet has always been a form for the expression of love, sometimes requited, more often not. Sonnets have fourteen lines (that is also a rule) and I have written you fourteen lines. But these lines can be rearranged and I am sending you two versions. The first is what is called a Petrarchan and the second a Shakespearean sonnet. Though you have no interest in such technical distinctions, I know that your mind is incisive so that you will understand what each means—means to *me*, at least. The privilege of employing the pronoun *us* is no longer mine."

There follow these two variations, both untitled.

> this long adagio, our history
> each day my first, each night our very last
> the present is all future and no past
> whose melody's a minor mystery
> a virgin bridge no car has ever crossed
> eagerness unanxious, ambition fresh
> whole-hearted as a lion tearing flesh
> was it you I found or was it I was lost
> on such a night it was our fate to meet
> to look, to see, before the silence falls
> the melting snow lays puddles on the street
> black looking-glass reflecting darkling walls
> all the steps I took, every breath I drew
> before I knew I knew you I knew you

•

the melting snow lays puddles on the street
black looking-glass reflecting darkling walls
on such a night it was our fate to meet
to look, to see, before the silence falls
whole-hearted as a lion tearing flesh
each day my first, each night our very last
eagerness unanxious, ambition fresh
the present is all future and no past
before I knew I knew you I knew you
a virgin bridge no car has ever crossed
all the steps I took, every breath I drew
was it you I found or was it I was lost
whose melody's a minor mystery
this long adagio, our history

Though we cannot have the same interest in these verses as Julia M., we nevertheless think we have grasped the nature of the intended contrast. The first, the "Petrarchan" sonnet, is an account of the start of the relationship. It is full of hope for the future and joy at what Einstein called in another context "finding without looking." At the same time, it conveys something of Freud's rather pessimistic and limiting definition of happiness as a sudden and unexpected gratification of long pent-up desires. The second, the "Shakespearean" version, is an elegy marking the death of the relationship. Thus, the first poem opens with the same line that concludes the second: "this long adagio, our history." *History*, of course, is a momentous word for Fernlicht, a professional historian. In the first poem, it refers to the lives of the couple *before* they met, before, that is, they had a history in common, and by extension to *all* of history, from its beginning down to the fatal moment in the parking lot. In the second version, "our history" is that of the couple's relationship.

The phrase "long adagio" also has a different meaning in each setting. In the first sonnet, it suggests the tedium of Fernlicht's solitary life and the existence of the unhappily married Julia M., a heavy, slow history that oppresses and seems without end. In the second, though, we are reminded that adagios, however lengthy, are movements in suites or symphonies, that they do end and the music goes quickly on. What, in the first version, is history about to be decisively transformed in the second is a history of mere months, a temporary implosion of the extraordinary, "unexpected gratification."

In the first version, the line that refers to their meeting ("the melting snow lays puddles on the street") comes in the sestet and thus leads up to the piercingly romantic and rather Platonic last line ("before I knew I knew you I knew you"). In the second, this line is made the first, for the chronological frame of reference has shifted and the sense of the whole affair being briefer than it ought to have been is powerfully conveyed—so brief was it that the whole of it can be encompassed in fourteen lines. Indeed, we suspect it was in part for its brevity that Fernlicht chose the sonnet as the most apt of *souvenirs*.

As to the effect of this intense episode on Fernlicht himself, apart from the existence of these verses, we are unable to conclude anything definite. Its melody remains a minor mystery.

FEIN RE-READS
DOSTOYEVSKY

YEARS ago I came across a four-box cartoon. First Box: one man declares with stunning candor, "I hate you." The second, clearly taken aback, asks, "Why?" Box Two: the first explains, "Because you're a Jew," and the other, visibly puzzled by such frank anti-Semitism or, less likely, because he's never encountered the phenomenon before, says "So?" (Impossible to tell from a cartoon but I like to imagine a *soupçon* of a Yiddish shrug in the intonation.) Box Three: the Jew-hater gets specific, "Because Jews eat Christian babies, that's why." The other's floored. "That's absurd," he retorts, eyebrows up, eyes wide. Final Box: The first, "Well, don't *you* eat Christian babies?" The other, "Certainly not! ...Well, just once."

Why is this funny? *Should* it be funny? I confess I laughed and, of course, the cartoon has proved memorable; but exactly what I was laughing at I'm not sure. It would be safe to say I laughed at the anti-Semite and surely that was part of it. After all, it's delicious for a Jew to laugh at an anti-Semite; what Fein would pass up the chance? What made him funny, though? Was it his credulity or his openness, his honesty? I laughed at the virtue of a foolish man who hates on bad authority. This rube, this moron, this gull not only believes Jews eat Christian babies, he actually says so to a Jew. He's got to be an idiot and so he's not to be feared but ridiculed. A dangerous anti-Semite would organize a pogrom or simply kill the Jew in front of him. The notion of a forthright, harmless anti-Semite who *discusses* eating Christian babies with Jews is funny. Two thousand years of atrocious nonsense are dispatched in four clever boxes. Hilarious. But what of the other, the Jew? What of his unexpected clincher, "Well, just once"? Why is *that* so comical? Why is it funny to mock the blood libel by pretending to confess to it—and to an imbecile accuser? The Jew is making fun of the accuser's gullibility and the charge's absurdity; but that is for *us*, not for the earnest bigot in front of him. *He's* not going to laugh. He's going to believe the Jew.

You can imagine the cartoon as a vaudeville routine. There's Groucho with a big Gentile stooge. Groucho mugs puzzlement, then indignation. "Who me? Eat babies? Not even kosher ones?" Then, in a whorl of cigar smoke and departing coattails, "Well, just once."

The aim of black humor is to make fun of what scares you. Ridicule the murderers; heap derision on them. If they're honest about their hatred, mock that honesty by pretending to share it. Or look at it another way: what if the Jew really did sample a bite or two of baby flesh, didn't care for it, never tried it again, got over it, gave up observing Passover, changed his nose, name, and day of rest. Is that also funny?

What provoked me to recollect that cartoon is re-reading *The Brothers Karamazov*. Like many Jewish boys I fell hard for Dostoyevsky in my teens. If I read a lot in those years, it's in large measure because of Raskolnikov. I devoured the long and febrile *Crime and Punishment* in tenth grade. The literature bug bit me as I was getting my learner's permit. While I read I too lived in a little room in Stolyarny Lane and evaded my landlady by slinking toward the Kamenny Bridge; I was living in New York City and simultaneously in St. Petersburg. Then it was *The Possessed, The Idiot, The Insulted and Injured, A Raw Youth, Notes from Underground, The House of the Dead*, the short novels and stories. I read them all. I couldn't get enough and delighted in their length; but I was too young to read properly. That is, as an adolescent I read good books in a bad way—thoughtlessly and for escape, just as an unhappy housewife will gulp down romances. As a rule, happy teenagers don't read Dostoyevsky. It was the prestige of *The Brothers Karamazov* that made me save it for last. He wrote it last, so I figured I'd read it last. But that was decades ago. I chose to re-read the novel just now to mark the centennial of its completion.

The gratifications of re-reading have often been extolled and, in my experience, they can scarcely be overestimated. I've even found it possible to recover much of the excitement I felt all those years ago, which means recapturing some of the innocence of first reading, when a tale is a journey and not a map. I know more now; but, in surrendering again to the alchemy of narrative, which means the annihilation of one time in favor of another, I'm happy to forget what I know. In re-reading Dostoyevsky I was not aiming at *studying* the text, only at giving myself up to it as I once had done. My reward was to be transported not only to mid-nineteenth-century Russia but also, to some degree, to a November afternoon on a wooden high-school chair beside a study hall radiator and the aroma of boiled iron.

You can't read Dostoyevsky in small snatches, the way I mostly read now, a chapter or two in bed before sleep. Dostoyevsky must be read in broad daylight and after midnight; you have to ride his elephantine roller coasters morning, noon, and night. I went through *Karamazov* in a week of intense reading and was mortified to find how distractible I've become. How had I read so much in my teens—Dostoyevsky, Wolfe, Joyce, Faulkner, Kafka, Flaubert, Gide, Cervantes—while keeping up with five courses and the demands of daily dread, social anxiety, hormonal frustration, one or two friendships, daydreaming, disgust, Oedipal skirmishing, discovering serious music, attending mandatory pep rallies, playing basketball, pool, and all the rest of what I remember as a dismal time? The answer is both negative and positive; that is, there was all I *didn't* do (television, movies, idle conversation, socializing, earning money and paying bills) and what I *did* do, which was to read for hour upon hour, honing my myopia.

Re-reading doesn't only furnish the pleasure of being reminded but also the humbling lesson of how much you've forgotten. I had a fair recollection of Fyodor Karamazov's lechery and sly buffoonery, Grushenka's numerous curves, Mitya's intemperate, incessant passion, Ivan's grave intelligence, even his devil's checked pants; I could summon up the *douceur* of Alyosha, Zosima's stench, and the Uriah Heepishness of Smerdyakov. But I had pretty much forgotten Katerina Ivanovna, the schoolboys, and the trial. Of Lise Khokhlakov and her mother I had retained nothing whatever. And so it came as a surprise as well as a shock to read the following exchange between Lise and Alyosha in Chapter III of Book XI.

"… Alyosha, is it true that at Easter the Jews steal a child and kill it?"

"I don't know."

"There's a book here in which I read about the trial of a Jew, who took a child of four years old and cut off the fingers from both hands, and then crucified him on the wall, hammered nails into him and crucified him, and afterwards, when he was tried, he said that the child died soon, within four hours. That was 'soon'! He said the child moaned, kept on moaning and he stood admiring it. That is nice!"

"Nice?"

"Nice, I sometimes imagine that it was I who crucified him. He would hang there moaning and I would sit opposite him eating pineapple compote. I am awfully fond of pineapple compote. Do you like it?"

Alyosha looked at her in silence. Her pale, sallow face was suddenly contorted, her eyes burned.

"You know, when I read about that Jew I shook with sobs all night. I kept fancying how the little thing cried and moaned (a child of four understands, you know) and all the while the thought of pineapple compote haunted me. In the morning, I wrote a letter to a certain person begging him *particularly* to come and see me. He came and I suddenly told him all about the child and the pineapple compote. *All* about it, *all*, and said that it was nice. He laughed and said it really was nice. Then he got up and went away. He was only here five minutes. Did he despise me? Did he despise me?

Tell me, Alyosha, did he despise me or not?" She sat up on the couch, with flashing eyes.[12]

Lise Khokhlakov is a precocious teenager and a nasty piece of work. Dostoyevsky portrays her as sick, hysterical, and knowing. The sort of thing she knows is what respectable people prefer to deny or conceal, such as that everyone in town participates vicariously in the parricide, even takes pleasure in it. (One can imagine Lise and a young Dr. Freud enjoying a profitable conversation.) Lise expresses her crush on Alyosha in a childish yet aggressive way, by teasing him without mercy; she considers marrying him, a proposal to which Alyosha, sent into the world by Zosima, agrees, though the notion is absurd. Anyway, the Elder tells Alyosha he has to live in the world but will do so "as a monk." Anyway, Lise changes her mind.

It's a capital error to see any of Dostoyevsky's characters, even the most obsessed, as absolutely single-minded, Lise included. She claims to have lost a whole night's sleep crying over the crucified child and, if true, that may be something in her favor. However, we aren't impressed by this, nor does Dostoyevsky seem to want us to be, not when he titles this chapter "A Little Devil." Lise may sympathize with the putative child; nevertheless, it's the pineapple compote that dominates her account and the reader's attention. She

---

12. *The Brothers Karamazov*, ed. Ralph E. Matlaw New York: W. W. Norton, 1976, pp. 552-553

is as interesting as any of Dostoyevsky's psychological grotesques and, in this respect at least, he could be said to make good use of the story of the four-year-old. However, for such a purpose did Dostoyevsky really require a Jew, severed fingers, and a crucifixion with four hours of moaning? In fact, wouldn't something genuine, something *documented*, a tale out of his and Ivan's dossier perhaps, have done as well or better? The passage arrested me. I could hear the iron doors of history crashing shut. It really looks as though Dostoyevsky went out of his way to introduce this story, rather as, on a far more exalted scale, he worked in "The Legend of the Grand Inquisitor" on the ground that he feared he wouldn't live to put it anywhere else. The two episodes have something else in common; both are attacks on non-Orthodox religions. The Catholics are on Satan's side and, as for the Jews, well don't we Russians know all about the Jews?

In their own ways to be sure, Ivan attacks the Catholics as Lise does the Jews. Both see devils. Lise's dream is of drawing demons to her again and again then driving them away with the sign of the cross. This resembles Ivan's own approach/avoidance minuet with belief in his conversation with his shabby devil. Lise and Ivan both reject faith, and so, for Dostoyevsky, it is axiomatic that they will be self-destructive. Each recognizes the Oedipal imperative and the unconscious sweetness of transgression. To Lise it tastes like pineapple compote, which Ivan admits to liking too. Though superficially paired off with Alyosha in the boy-girl arrangement of the novel, Lise is better seen as a sort of burlesque of Ivan. R. P. Blackmur covers this well:

> ... she loves disorder and wants to set fire to the house, to do evil of all sorts so that everything may be destroyed. And so on. The moments when everyone loves crime are every moment; everybody secretly loves Dmitri's killing his father. To all this Alyosha assents; it is part of his lesson. But it was Ivan whom she had sent for; and no

wonder—she was the pure expressive form of that which Ivan was only the critical form... She rejoices in what Ivan found intolerable. She believes where Ivan cannot believe. She has learned the harshness of love and the beauty of Sodom in exactly the sense represented when after she crushes her finger in the door she cries "Wretch wretch wretch," and watches the finger end blacken. [13]

What Ivan finds intolerable is the suffering of children. Lise finds delectable the drawn-out pain of a Christian child crucified by a Jew. Ivan's critique places morality above God and so he loses both. Lise expresses the condition of separation from God without Ivan's fancy scruples, and it's to Ivan she expresses it. Very well. Blackmur's analysis is clever, not excessively schematic, and I suppose it's true to Dostoyevsky's intentions. On the other hand, he says nothing about Dostoyevsky having introduced the story of a Jew crucifying a kidnapped Christian child, except as a general example of the torture of innocents, as if such a tale had even less significance than Ivan's accounts of the Turkish soldiers, the retired general, or the sadistic parents. But it has more. In fact, it matters more than the documented abuses that did happen because it never happened.

How did I react to Lise's tale of ritual murder when I read it as a raw youth? Apparently I had taken little notice, hastened irresistibly on by the fascinating fraternal troika, entirely enthralled. Nasty comments about Jews were hardly rare in my reading, given my tastes. The young readily forgive their heroes. Not that I was a careless reader back then. I may even have glimpsed something of the deep pattern Blackmur elucidates. I too was capable of putting one episode in the context of the novel, to me a complete world far away from that of Algebra II, study halls, and radiators. This was an inward world. I instinctively read the way I was told T. S. Eliot recommended: history and politics had nothing to do with litera-

---

[13.] R. P. Blackmur, *Eleven Essays on the European Novel*, New York: Harcourt, Brace, Jovanovich, 1964, 222-243

ture. Besides, writers were childish on such subjects, and whatever they said was inconsequential. Dostoyevsky constructed his own cosmos, a self-sustaining, roiling universe to which one responded inwardly and which told you about inward things. Besides, I knew only the *Classics Illustrated* version of Russian history: Ivan was terrible, Peter and Catherine great; Napoleon was defeated by the Cossacks and General Winter; the Decembrists were Romantic and failed; cavalry officers fought in the Caucasus, tossed rubles around, and drank gallons of champagne; the serfs were freed; some Russians wanted to be like the West and more didn't; the last Romanov Tsars were ruinous and provoked a couple of revolutions. It was something, but not much, and, anyway, most of it came from reading fiction. Now, however, re-reading *The Brothers Karamazov*, it is history—those clanging iron doors—that has made me linger mournfully over Lise's story.

Dostoyevsky completed his last novel in November, 1880. He died two months later, at the end of January, 1881. That same year Alexander II was assassinated and the first pogroms broke out. The following year came the May Laws forbidding Jews, already restricted to the Pale of Settlement, from living outside of towns. This was to prevent their owning land. At the same time the system known as *numerus clausus* was established throughout the Empire setting low quotas on Jewish enrollment in universities. According to some historians, Alexander's III's ultra-reactionary regime made cynical use of popular anti-Jewish sentiment to deflect criticism from itself and actively promoted this hatred through vicious propaganda culminating in the notorious *Protocols of the Elders of Zion*. This perennially best-selling fraud, beloved by Hitler, Henry Ford, and Arab sheikhs, first appeared in Russia in 1905.

Why did I think of all this history when I stumbled on Lise's anecdote? Rather ask, how could I help it. Once you know history it's a pitcher into which all sorts of formless things may be poured.

Konstantin Pobedonostsev (1827-1907) was over-procurator of

the Holy Synod, tutor to, then closest advisor of, Alexander III. He was Russia's arch-reactionary and authoritarian, not only attacking the nihilists and anarchists but reviling democracy, a free press, public education, and pretty much everybody who did not think as he did. With an irony I'd love to believe was intentional, some wit nicknamed him "the Grand Inquisitor." Dostoyevsky and Pobedonostsev were of the same generation, knew one another, and, by the 1870s, shared religious and political opinions. They corresponded. The author was eager to learn Pobedonostsev's views of the content of *The Brothers Karamazov*. In a letter to the publisher Lyubimov written while he worked on the novel, Dostoyevsky almost brags of his connection to Pobedonostsev:

> I was reproached for many figures in *The Possessed* as being fantastic but later, would you believe it, they were justified by reality, so they must have been apprehended correctly. K. P. Pobedonostsev, for example, told me of two or three incidents about imprisoned anarchists which strikingly resembled what I had depicted in *The Possessed*. (Letter of May 10, 1879)

You've got to wonder about this joyous affirmation, this validation "by reality." It has too much the ring of mutually confirmed prejudice. Did those "two or three incidents" really verify Dostoyevsky's story or did the novel, politically in harmony with Pobedonostsev's relentlessly anti-reformist, anti-Western, anti-anarchist, anti-liberal views, make the *éminence grise* see his opponents as a bunch of Kirillovs, Shatovs and Verkhovenskys? How delighted the former Siberian convict sounds ("would you believe it") to be "justified" by official Tsarist/Churchly authority. It's rather unseemly.

Three months later Dostoyevsky wrote to Pobedonostsev thanking him for approving of the portion of the novel that had so far appeared in print, up through Book V; that is, including "Rebellion" and "The Legend of the Grand Inquisitor." Whatever Pobedonostsev's praise may have been for this *pro*, it's clear that the

Censor was anxious about the persuasiveness of the coming *contra*. So was the author, and it is this concern his letter chiefly addresses. Dostoyevsky almost sounds as if he is defending himself *avant le fait* for not giving a direct, polemical refutation of Ivan. The artist even feels the need to apologize for being an artist:

> Your opinion of what you have read in the Karam-azovs (so far as the force and vividness of the published material is concerned) gratified me greatly. But at the same time you raise the *most crucial* question: my reply to all these atheistic propositions has not yet appeared, and it must be made. That's precisely it and my worry now and all my disquiet lies in that. For I proposed to make the sixth book, the Russian Monk, which will appear August 31, the answer to that whole *negative side*. And for that reason I tremble for it in this sense: will it be answer *enough*? The more so as it is not a direct point for point answer to the propositions previously expressed… but an oblique one. Something completely opposite to the world view expressed earlier appears in this part, but again it appears not point by point but so to speak in artistic form. And that is what worries me, that is, will I be understood and will I achieve anything of my aim? In addition there were the demands of art… I am very uneasy and would greatly appreciate your opinion, for I value your opinion highly. (Letter of August 24, 1879)

Did this deference to Pobedonostsev propel the comprehen-sively reformed socialist into the zealotry of reaction, even to the point of rabid anti-Judaism? Or was hatred of Jews a basis for their affinity rather than a consequence of it? I doubt that Dostoyevsky needed any help from the authorities to hate Jews. But I don't know. The historians are helpful, though they are far from speaking with one voice. According to several of them, Dostoyevsky approved of Pobedonostsev's plans for Russia's Jews; some claim he contributed to them, and one goes so far as to say he *advised* Pobedonostsev concerning Jews, which seems to me less than plausible. Konstantin Petrovich's idea was that Russia's Jewish problem could be solved by dividing the population, like Gaul, into three parts. One third, the least devout, would be assimilated; the second would emigrate, while the remaining third could be permitted to die out. Very tidy: assimilation, emigration, liquidation.

Despite all this, I think it's too easy to condemn Dostoyevsky over including Lise's story in his last novel. Maybe the pogroms and the Holocaust, about which Dostoyevsky didn't know, might have caused him to reconsider his position. Of course, that he couldn't know about the atrocities occurring after he finished his novel doesn't excuse him from contributing to them—if that is what he did. Men are not gods; authors are not paragons, and Dostoyevsky was nothing if not immoderate. No one can read his last book and fail to think that he is all the Karamazovs, with plenty to spare.

Dostoyevsky was an artist and not a politician or a theologian, though he obviously thought about politics and God in practicing his art; one led to the other. *The Possessed* was what emerged when he sat down to write a political polemic. His joy at finding what he had imagined there confirmed by Pobedonostsev suggests some surprise, as if he was pleased to be right about actuality but this wasn't his motive. Writers require material that suits them, subjects that will bring out their best. Ideally, such subjects will appeal consciously and resonate unconsciously. Jane Austen needed unmarried couples in English villages, not tales of combat from the Peninsular War. She knew her talent was for social satire, but the issue of marriage must have engaged more than her sterling neocortex. In the same way, Dostoyevsky required Dostoyevskyan subjects: extremist politics, debates between Westernizers and Slavophiles, fervid religious mysticism, and, according to Freud at least, parricide. He has a compulsion to turn mood into passion, feeling into idea, opinion into narrative, and to take things over the edge.

Kafka was an astute critic. In his diary there's a wonderful observation on Dostoyevsky's method. He is correcting his friend Max Brod's objection, that Dostoyevsky "allows too many mentally ill persons to enter."

> Completely wrong. They aren't ill. Their illness is merely a way to characterize them, and moreover a very delicate and fruitful one. One need only stubbornly keep repeating of a person that he is simple-minded and idiotic, and he will, if he has the Dostoyevskyan core inside him, be spurred on, as it were, to do his very best. (*Diaries*, II, 104)

What am I saying? That to get the best out of Lise Khokhlakov Dostoyevsky makes her identify with a crucifier of toddlers, that her blasphemy must take precisely such a form? Am I as eager to pardon Dostoyevsky now, *and with reasons*, as I was to overlook his flaws when I was sixteen? Apparently so.

Dostoyevsky is not Pobedonostsev, overripe with horrible certainty. He said the theme of his final novel was whether or not God exists, not the redemption to be had only from the Russian Orthodox communion and submission to the Tsar. The distinction between a dogma and a question, it seems to me, is not a small one. Dostoyevsky was, so to speak, a bigot with an open mind.

So far as Lise's story of blood libel is concerned, Dostoyevsky actually holds back in several ways. First, he doesn't include the story in Ivan's dossier. This would have given it an authority and emphasis it lacks. He keeps Ivan free of the stain of prejudice. Even the Turkish soldiers are offered as mere instances of humankind's abuse of children, not Muslim brutality. In fact, it's the respectable, churchgoing Russian parents that really get to Ivan. Furthermore, anti-Semitism is hardly promoted by implying that it appeals to the small and unreliable mind of Lise Khokhlakov; Dostoyevsky doesn't even say if the book in which Lise claims to have found the story really exists.

Second, though he needlessly includes the story, at least he doesn't dwell on it. Dostoyevsky just isn't at ease writing about Jews. His proper *materia poetica* is Russian: intellectuals, epileptics, officers, peasants, prostitutes, schoolboys, gentry, lawyers, monks, nihilists, gamblers, spongers, etc. Dostoyevsky gives the story of the Jew little attention. In my opinion, when he was writing the scene between Lise and Alyosha he probably wasn't focused on the anti-Jewish libel. Composing at speed and against a deadline, his concentration would have been on Lise, his little "she-devil," and how to fit her into the book's architecture. I can imagine him casting about for a crime in which she could find the sweetness of evil, an outrage which, considering that he would want an echo of Ivan in "Rebellion," had to involve the torture of a child. He needed a criminal for her to identify with—so why not a Jew, a ritual murder, an actual *crucifixion*? Lise kills Christ in her heart—get it? The author is in such a rush that he gets his ethnic slur wrong by choosing the incorrect holiday; Lise ought to be asking about Passover, not Easter. So, headlong he scribbles on, psychologizing about Lise revealing herself to Alyosha, linking her to Ivan. There's no reason to suppose he premeditated this stroke, much less that he interpolated the blood libel to gratify his distinguished friend Konstantin Petrovich. This is speculation, of course; but if my guess is right, then it is not an excuse but a mitigation of Dostoyevsky's responsibility to history.

Third and final point. The story of the Jew is in not of vital importance to the novel, not cemented to its plot and theme as "Rebellion" and "The Legend of the Grand Inquisitor" are, which is why I had forgotten it. The episode reflects on the author rather than his book. Putting it in may even, in the long run, have undercut Dostoyevsky's answer to Ivan about which he was so worried. If the positive riposte to Ivan's atheistic "negativity" is Orthodoxy and Tsarism, and if Orthodoxy and Tsarism entail not only bloody-minded anti-liberalism but brutal and credulous anti-Semitism, then Ivan Karamazov and Lise Khokhlakov aren't the only ones who are bedeviled.

Sidney Fein re-read *The Brothers Karamazov* in 1980 to mark its centennial, as he says. I found this essay in his folder for that year, the same in which he made his first notes for what was to become his own final book, *Aristocratic Democracy* (1983). There are two versions of the text, one handwritten and a typescript with corrections and documentation for his sources, which is unusual for Fein's rough drafts. There is no final, clear copy as he seems to have put the project aside. He may have intended to write more; for, at the end of the typescript, he added two questions in pencil: "How much does it matter that the reader is Jewish? What if he weren't?"

Fein's affection for Dostoyevsky's work is obvious from what he has written here and confirmed by the frequent appearance of *Notes from Underground* and *The Legend of the Grand Inquisitor* on his undergraduate syllabi. In an ethics course he taught in 1978 he included Camus' dramatization of *The Possessed*. It is also relevant that, in that same course, he assigned selections from Pobedonostsev's "Reflections of a Russian Statesman" (1896) in conjunction with Plato's *Republic*.

Fein's only significant mention of Dostoyevsky in his published work occurs in the chapter called "The Higher Parody" in *Diptych on Terrestrial Representation* (1973). This is a detailed comparison and contrast of the opening of *The Legend of the Grand Inquisitor* and the Prologue of Brecht's *Good Woman of Setzuan*.

Incomplete and ambivalent though this piece undoubtedly is, I thought it worthy of publication on the ground of intrinsic interest, also for the light it throws on Fein as a reader, and as what he called himself, "a typical deracinated Diaspora Jew." His daughter recalls that when, during his year as a visiting professor at Brandeis University, he was asked if were observant, her father replied, "Observant? Well, from a safe distance." Fein's Jewishness is as problematic as anybody else's. Something of his attitude may be gleaned from his view of Israel. He supported the Jewish state with contributions and even considered volunteering to fight for Israel in the days leading up to the Six-Day War of 1967, yet he never expressed any desire to visit the country. His daughter says she once asked him about this. "I don't know," he told her. "Maybe it's because I couldn't bear being in a place where nearly everybody's Jewish."

Fein certainly did not make much of his Jewishness. He married a Gentile, never joined a synagogue, nor did he provide a formal religious education for his daughter. On the other hand, he was fond of such books as Martin Buber's two collections of Hasidic tales, which he compared favorably to the best texts of Zen Buddhism. He never denied being a Jew, only being a good one. Of Franz Kafka, whom he loved, he wrote, "Kafka is the definitive Jew of the twentieth century."

I mention these remarks of Fein here because in these notes he is clearly writing as a Jewish reader who admires the anti-Semitic Dostoyevsky. Fein enjoyed re-reading, especially the books he loved in his youth. Each summer, for instance, he would pick up something of Conrad's. Re-reading Dostoyevsky also gave him great pleasure. But the shock of the gratuitous, almost nonchalant interpolation of the blood libel in *The Brothers Karamazov* pulled him up short and provoked an examination of the novel's context, the prejudice of a favorite author, how a great work of art can transcend its creator, and his own response to this collision between aesthetics and ethics, art and history, taste and conscience.

For Fein, this essay is unusually straightforward, without his customary theoretical playfulness and with less irony. Judging by the abrupt ending and those final, penciled questions, it was writing about his own feelings that proved most difficult for him. Fein must have felt the inadequacy of both the a-historical, a-political mode of reading which he says he had been taught in the 50s and the hyper-political exegesis of the 60s. Yes and no, he might have felt. Perhaps he even thought of his favorite sentence from

Saint Augustine, "These things are true in a way because they are false in a way."

Fein's wish, at least, is clear. He would like to let Dostoyevsky off. His struggle to do so puts me in mind of one of the Hasidic sayings from the collection he so admired:

> The rabbi of Koznitz said to God: "Lord of the world, I beg of you to redeem Israel. And if you do not want to do that, then redeem the goyim."[14]

14. *Tales of the Hasidim*, I, 289

ON IDOL WORSHIP

TWO weeks ago, the California Supreme Court issued its verdict in Tarasoff v. Regents of the University of California. The justices were divided; four found for the plaintiff, one concurred with reservations, two for the defendants. The majority opinion has received much attention largely focused on how it will alter the obligations of mental health professionals, replacing their obligation to confidentiality with a duty to protect potential victims of their unbalanced patients.

The facts of the Tarasoff case are not well known but ought to be because courts, like novelists, never contemplate questions in the abstract. On the contrary, judges are confronted with human beings and their particular narratives. Black robes and high seats notwithstanding, even the justices are not an abstraction called "the Court"; they too are flesh and blood and have stories. This is why the phrase "courtroom drama" is virtually redundant and why the Athenians' delight in the to and fro of public trials must have done much to inspire the invention comedy and tragedy.

Prosenjit Poddar, born a Dalit or "Untouchable" in Bengal, began graduate study at Berkeley in September 1967. That semester he participated in folk dancing classes at International House where he met Tatiana Tarasoff. They saw one another weekly thereafter and, on New Year's Eve, Tatiana kissed Prosenjit who misread it as proof of an emotional attachment. When Tatiana realized Poddar's mistake, she told him she was involved with other men and made clear she had no interest in an intimate relationship with him. Poddar cracked. He became depressed, neglected his appearance, studies, and health; he began speaking disjointedly, and frequently broke down weeping. During his occasional meetings with Tatiana he tape-recorded their conversations with the purpose of studying them to figure out why she didn't love him.

Tatiana went off to South America for the summer and, for a while, Poddar's condition improved a little, though not so much as to prevent a friend from persuading him to seek help. Poddar became a patient of Dr. Lawrence Moore, a psychologist at the University's Cowell Memorial Hospital. During one of their sessions, Poddar confided that he intended to kill Tatiana on her return. Moore had the campus police detain Poddar, recorded his opinion that his patient was suffering from acute paranoid schizophrenia, and recommended he be civilly committed as a dangerous person. Poddar was detained only briefly. It seems he gave such a good impression of being sane that Moore's supervisor, Dr. Harvey Powelson, ordered him released and not subject to further detention. Crucially, neither Miss Tarasoff nor her family were told anything about the threat against her.

By October, Tatiana was back. Poddar had given up therapy but not his plan to commit a thoroughly premeditated murder. To get at Tatiana he befriended her brother, then moved in with him. Before the month was out, Poddar murdered Tatiana. Her parents then sued Moore, Powelson, and the U.C. Regents in civil court. As for the criminal proceedings, Poddar was found guilty of second-degree murder but his conviction was overturned on the ground that the jury had not been given sufficient information. Poddar was then released on the condition that he return to India.

The Tarasoff case decided this month was the civil one about the failure of anybody to warn Miss Tarasoff or her family of the threat to her life.

The most difficult and influential cases, the ones we tend to retry, involve a conflict between two respected and cherished values. For instance, the recent affirmative action cases appear to pit merit against equality. I expect Thomas Jefferson was certain that in the new republic equality would ensure rewards would be based on merit alone, leading to a country governed by what he called "a natural aristocracy." Slavery either slipped the slaveholder's mind or he expected the nation to defer dealing with it for more generations than he cared to calculate. In most of their controversial cases, judges have to navigate between Scylla and Charybdis, aware, for instance, that we no more wish to dispense with equal opportunity than we'd willingly give up promotion based on merit. In the Tarasoff case the colliding values are, on the one hand, individual privacy and medical confidentiality and, on the other, public safety. Again, the issue has its origin in the rights and lives of individuals—Poddar's right to confidentiality and Tatiana's to be warned of a lethal threat. The cast of this tragedy is not limited to two; it also includes poor Dr. Moore, desperate to commit a deranged patient, the arrogant Dr. Powelson, who pulled rank and ordered the spurned lover set at liberty. Then there is Miss Tarasoff's family—bereaved, bitter, but ably represented in court.

KANT CONTRA IDOL WORSHIP

One of the cases ethical philosophers are perennially litigating is Relativism v. Absolutism. Should ethical issues be decided on principle or outcomes? Ought we to pursue purity of purpose or be pragmatic, apply a *thou shalt* or an *if/then*? Deontologize or consequentialize? Socrates argued it with the Sophists, Aristotle with Plato, Jeremy Bentham with Immanuel Kant, Idealists with Realists, Catholics with Protestants, some Jews with other Jews, and so on to this month. Discussions of the Tarasoff case have so far looked at it as one about applied ethics, which customarily follow theory. But I would like to reverse this order and deduce from the majority and minority opinions the philosophical theories behind each. This could be instructive, even illuminating.

Minority first for a change. Justice William Clark, Jr. rejected the idea that people like Miss Tarasoff have a right to protection by professionals that trumps their obligation to confidentiality. His approach to the clash of values is to deny that a conflict exists at all. In his view, the public will be protected *only* if confidentiality is strictly maintained. In making his argument, Justice Clark deploys a string of conditional verbs, revealing that he has applied what Kant calls hypothetical imperatives, future-oriented guesses at probable consequences. He supports confidentiality on grounds of social utility, contemplating the undesirable results of undermining it:

> ... a patient's rights are violated when rules of confidentiality are not observed... psychiatric treatment *would* be frustrated by non-observance... patients *would* subsequently lose confidence in psychiatrists and *would* fail to provide full disclosures, and... violent assaults *would* actually increase because mentally ill persons *would* be discouraged from seeking psychiatric aid.

I make that five future conditionals in one sentence.

A casual reader might suppose that it is Justice Clark who is the moral absolutist because he brooks no exceptions to the confidentiality rule. *Thou shalt not disclose.* And, in a sense, this is so, the sense being that he has elevated the American Psychiatric Association's book of ethics to a kind of idol, the sort that requires human sacrifice. But Clark's position is not one of moral absolutism because his argument is an instrumental one and because a moral absolute requires something of absolute value to ground it. According to Kant, without this invaluable something

> ... nothing whatever would possess *absolute worth*; but if all worth were conditioned and therefore contingent, then there would be no supreme practical principle of reason whatever.

Of course, Kant believed in just such a principle and called it the categorical imperative. This imperative Kant situated in the intellectual software issued with our mental hardware. It is one of the programs by which Kant figured we make sense of life, knowing that a disease has a cause, that everything doesn't happen at once, or that 2 + 2 = 4 and not 3 or 5, that they did so in ancient Egypt and do so now on Saturn. These organizing *a priori* principles include causality, time, necessity, universality, etc. With his idea that the mind comes with such categories, Kant synthesized the Rationalists' notion that all reliable knowledge comes from innate ideas with the Empiricists' insistence that everything we know derives from sensory experience. Kant resolved the epistemological impasse of his time by observing that for real knowledge neither innate ideas nor sense experience would be sufficient and that both are necessary. His categories are innate, but they are mere organizing principles rather than specific ideas about bridges and doorknobs. We pour what would otherwise be chaotic impressions and insoluble problems into these pre-existing molds. This explains why young children learn so quickly, a crucial adaptation for *homo sapiens*. A child who burns herself on a hot stove needn't repeat the experiment three times to figure out what caused the pain. According to Kant, we are also furnished with a mold into which we can pour our moral problems, a test for right action, a scale for measuring equity. As a father, I give Kant's view some credit. It certainly accounts for why it didn't take long for my daughter to register her first ethical judgment which, as it does with almost all children, took the form of a protest: *It's not fair.*

Kant knows that the bulk of our decisions aren't made by using his categorical imperative but hypothetical ones. He acknowledges that if/then decisions are just fine when choosing what route to take from Berlin to Königsberg for instance, where to invest our savings, whether to add just a bit more oregano or whether to ask out a supermodel. But calculating consequences will not do for moral matters where, according to him, our lodestar must be an imperative founded on something of "absolute worth."

Suppose we do have a pair of inborn scales. Suppose we place in one the APA's book of professional ethics and in the other the life of Tatiana Tarasoff. Which will weigh more? Perhaps idol worship is just choosing the less certain and more mutable, the lighter and lesser. Tatiana Tarasoff's life is singular, rulebooks of professional ethics legion. Among the dozens of biblical condemnations of idol worship there is this one which Ezekiel claims to have taken down from divine dictation:

> ... I the Lord will answer him that cometh according to the multitude of his idols; that I may take the house of Israel in their own heart, because they are estranged from me through their idols.

Justice Matthew O. Tobriner, who wrote for the Court's majority, is a man after Kant's heart. Not only does he use the categorical imperative; he applies Kant's first and second formulations of it.

> When a therapist determines, or pursuant to the standards of his profession should determine, that his patient presents a serious danger of violence to another, he incurs an obligation to use reasonable care to protect the intended victim against such danger.

The first form of the categorical imperative, Kant's sure-fire moral test, is to pretend the principle behind your choice becomes the rule for everybody and then see how you'd like to live with it. This, it seems to me, is precisely what Judge Tobriner has done. He states what the law should be and, because he's a Supreme Court Justice writing a majority decision, he has indeed universalized it, at least in the State of California. It's certainly a principle Tatiana Tarasoff might have lived with.

In his second formulation of the categorical imperative Kant fulfills the promise he made to himself after Rousseau shook him out of his Ivory Towery belief that intellectual attainment constituted the whole "honor of mankind." Kant couldn't give up on being an intellectual, of course, but he could have a bad conscience about it. And so, living at the time of the Revolution that was also inspired by Rousseau's ideas, he determined that the one way to redeem his privileges as a university professor would be to "advance the rights of man." This he does by stating his imperative in a way that has clear social and political implications:

> So act as to treat humanity, whether in thine own person or in that of any other, in every case as an end withal, never as means only.

Justice Tobriner implies that the U.C. mental health professionals did not treat Miss Tarasoff as an end but a means. A means to what? To upholding the stricture against violating Poddar's confidence. The Justice grants that confidentiality must generally be respected by physicians, but firmly declares that it ought to have been overridden in the Tarasoff case by a duty to Tatiana and, more generally, to the "protection of persons from violent assault." The word *person* is likewise an echo of Kant who used the word to distinguish between a means and an end. A hammer is a tool, a *thing*. We manufacture hammers as a means of pounding in nails. But an airline stewardess, for instance, should not be simply a means for beguiling middle-aged businessmen into buying tickets. I am thinking of those ads National Airlines recently ran in print, on TV, billboards, and radio: "*I'm Cheryl. Fly Me.*" Well, Cheryl is not a hammer, not a thing or an object, not created by our will as a means to our ends. Like Tatiana, she is a rational being and, as Kant says,

> [r]ational beings... are called *persons*, because their very nature points them out as ends in themselves, that is as something which must not be used merely as a means, and so far therefore restricts freedom of action...

Kant was writing in a world without airline stewardesses, but with plenty of servants and lots of slaves.

Kant's Idol Worship

A few weeks back, I got a call after dinner. I left my nine-year-old daughter watching TV in the living room to answer the phone in the kitchen. The caller wanted me to have dinner with him on Saturday and then go to a baseball game. I wasn't keen to do either; however, I also didn't want to offend my friend or, worse yet, hurt his already bruised feelings. His departed wife's infidelity was still a bleeding sore; in fact, in his fragile, self-doubting state he was unable to talk about anything else. I'd spent hours on the subject with him which is why the prospect of more of the same, even seasoned with home runs and hot dogs, wasn't appealing. So I said I couldn't come Saturday night because I'd be taking my daughter to New York for the weekend, to visit relatives. We said goodbye after agreeing on a vague raincheck. He was disappointed, but not hurt.

When I hung up the receiver I saw that Maya had not been watching TV but me. She stood in the doorway very still, looking at me with big, troubled eyes, arms crossed.

"We're going to New *York?*"

"No, sweetheart."

"We aren't?"

"Not this weekend."

"Then… you *lied?*" This was about ten percent question and ninety percent accusation.

There was nothing for it but to take one of those leaps parents sometimes have to risk. I began to draw for Maya the distinction between what I called "*social* lying" and "*real* lying."

"Let's say Julie just got a new party dress. Julie just loves this dress."

"Is it pink?"

"*Blindingly.* That's the trouble. You see, this electric pink of Julie's dress makes her look awful."

"Like a big pink pig?"

I nodded. "But remember, Julie *really* loves the dress. She thinks she looks just *terrific* in it."

Maya looked down sadly. "Poor Julie."

"Yes. But here's what I want to ask: Would you *tell* Julie her dress is horrible and that she looks awful in it?"

Maya considered the matter.

"Just suppose," I encouraged her.

"Well… I *might*. I mean you said I should always tell the truth."

"I know, Sweetheart. But maybe not *always* always. How would it make Julie feel if you told her that pink dress she loves so much makes her look like a pig?"

"Pretty bad, I guess. But maybe somebody *should* tell her so she won't go around looking so piggy with people laughing at her."

I got down on the floor. "Remember when Aunt Rachel gave you a set of blocks for your last birthday?"

"I'm *way* too old for silly blocks."

"I know. But you thanked her anyway."

"You told me I *had* to."

"And that was right."

"Even though it was a lie?"

"Remember when you said it was Freddy who broke that platter— that wasn't a good lie, a *social* one, was it? It was a *real* lie."

Maya giggled. "It was a whopper. You got *so* mad."

"Well, sometimes we tell fibs if it's going to hurt people not to. But the *rest* of the time we always tell the truth."

"Isn't a fib just the same as a lie?"

"Yes, it is."

Maya crossed her arms the way her mother used to and contemplated me with an alarmingly knowing look.

"You use me as an excuse to get out of things, don't you? Tell the truth, Daddy. I promise it's not going to hurt my feelings."

How could I deny what she'd just witnessed me doing? "Yes."

Maya uncrossed her arms, the frown disappeared, and she brightened right up. "*Fine*! Then I can use you *too*, can't I? That's just, like, I mean, fair."

And so, we made a pact, my daughter and I: if there's some invitation we want to reject, something social that we don't want to do, each of us has carte blanche to use the other as an out. We actually shook on it.

In the penultimate chapter of Kafka's *Trial*, a priest relates to Joseph K. the parable "Before the Law." The two then engage in a dialogue of exasperating Talmudic exegesis. After turning the story every which way, the priest at last tells K., "it is not necessary to accept everything as true, one must only accept it as necessary." To this K. objects sadly and perhaps a little indignantly, "A melancholy conclusion. It turns lying into a universal principle." This is just what Kant said any liar does when lying is subjected to his moral test. Just as a universal law that made fulfilling promises optional would contradict the very idea of a promise; so, for Kant, a lie contradicts the aim of communicating. Lies not only fail the universalizing test of the first form of the categorical imperative but also the second. To deceive a person is to turn him or her from subject to object, from end to means.

In 1797, when Kant was seventy-three, his attention was directed to an article by Benjamin Constant in the periodical *France 2*. Kant saw at once that Constant was challenging his absolutist position against lying. Constant's own stance is the same one I was compelled to take with my daughter.

> To tell the truth… is a duty, but is a duty only with
> regard to one who has a right to the truth. But no one
> has a right to a truth that would harm others. The moral

principle stating that it is a duty to tell the truth would make any society impossible if that principle were taken singly and unconditionally. We have proof of this in the very direct consequence which a German philosopher has drawn from this principle. This philosopher goes as far as to assert that it would be a crime to tell a lie to a murderer who asked whether our friend who is being pursued by the murderer had taken refuge in our house.

The example of the inquiring murderer presents an emergency like the one Dr. Moore encountered when his patient divulged his determination to kill Tatiana Tarasoff. Stories with actual people in them tend to blow away wispy philosophical abstractions; they can leave sticky matters of life and death.

The Prussian professor couldn't let this French challenge pass. Kant responded with a whole pamphlet. His lengthy answer is epitomized by its title, *On A Supposed Right to Tell Lies from Benevolent Motives.*

I certainly don't wish to be unfair to Kant. He will, I think, allow that a "social" lie may be, to use his word for acts aimed at positive results, "praiseworthy." But he will not permit even the best-intended fib to be deemed "moral." If we agree with Constant that "social lies" are essential to get along with one another, then Kant's insistence that scanting the truth is immoral would mean that social life itself is not moral. I'm entirely willing to grant this, especially when I consider how many vices are social and how few virtues—and how close the latter can be to the former. But perhaps a little face-saving hypocrisy is the blush on the cheek of a healthy civilization. Would you readily invite a remorseless truth-teller to be your houseguest for a long weekend, even if it were Socrates himself? Kant understands that sympathy, cunning, prudence, and calculation are praiseworthy qualities in doctors, hunters, financial advisors, and accountants. Efficient professionals with such qualities deserve appreciation, he says, just not respect. Well, respect is not a notably warm emotion. It seems to me a sort of amalgamation of love and fear—like one of Kant's own syntheses, made of both yet the same as neither.

And so Herr Doktor Professor Kant stamps his foot and insists that not to tell the murderer that Heinrich's hiding down in the cellar would be to heap the vice of lying atop the sin of homicide. Really, one wants to blush for Kant, to excuse him by claiming he must have been affected by the dementia that was soon to overtake him. But, in fact, in defending himself against Constant the professor wrote forthrightly and with his usual precision:

> The "German philosopher" will not take as one of his principles the proposition: "To tell the truth is a duty, but only to him who has a right to the truth." He will not do so, first, because of the ambiguous formulation of this proposition, for truth is not a possession the right to which can be granted to one and denied to another. But he will not do so chiefly because the duty of truthfulness… makes no distinction between persons to whom one has this duty and to whom one can exempt himself from this duty; rather, it is an unconditional duty which holds in all circumstances.

No doubt Kant would feel awful if a murderer he'd informed should find and kill his friend. I'm sure he'd be miserable, but then Kant associates morality with misery. He is not the first thinker to divorce being good from being happy; but he is the first to recommend being good *especially* when it makes you unhappy. Is there a more melancholy sentence about ethics than this: "Morality is not properly the doctrine of how we should *make* ourselves happy, but how we should become *worthy* of happiness"? This is nearly to say that only the unhappy deserve to be happy, like an abused orphan who suffers for hundreds of pages in a Dickens novel but comes into a fortune at the end.

The only way to win respect and moral authority is to pay for them. If you are so fortunate that your duty corresponds to your inclination, then, for Kant, there's little credit in carrying out that duty. We all think this way from time to time; for instance, I don't like to feel the University is paying me to talk to young people about books, something I enjoy doing; so I suppose the monthly check is for grading papers and remaining conscious through faculty meetings. Still, what Kant says is a formula for tragedy. It goes far beyond Shaw's quip about the Englishman who "thinks he is moral when he is only uncomfortable" or using Listerine and iodine because one tastes bad and the other stings.

I think the idol Kant ended up worshipping was his own theory; but what bothers me more is that, in elevating consistency above humanity, Kant betrayed that theory, that he commits, in effect, the very error he claims to abhor: inconsistency. His stubbornness is a reminder that virtue persisted in to excess turns into its opposite. The same Kantian argument that values the life of Miss Tarasoff more than the APA's rule book ought to make the life of Heinrich, cringing down in the cellar, outweigh the imperative to tell the truth, the whole truth, and nothing but the truth to everybody all the time. A dozen years before his reply to Benjamin Constant Immanuel Kant wrote this:

> If there is a categorical imperative, it must be one which, being drawn from the conception of that which is necessarily an end for everyone because it is an *end in itself*, constitutes an *objective principle* of will, and can therefore serve as a universal practical law. The foundation of this principle is; rational nature exists *as an end in itself.*

EDITOR'S NOTE

The California Supreme Court released its decision in the Tarasoff case on July 1, 1976, three days before the country's two hundredth birthday. As Fein says he was writing it a couple of weeks later, this piece can be dated to the middle of the month.

It is rare for Fein to respond to current events. The issue at stake in the Tarasoff case clearly stimulated him, perhaps because he connected it with being caught in a lie by the nine-year-old Maya. Above all, though, I think it was the connection he made to Kant that led Fein to organize his thoughts.

The title, "On Idol Worship," is mine. Fein merely scribbled "Tarasoff" at the head of his manuscript.

Sidney Fein thought highly of Kant. The syllabus of an introductory ethics survey he taught in the Fall of 1975 indicates that he devoted two and a half weeks to Kant, as much as he gave Socrates. Everybody else, from Plato to Nietzsche, got only one. According to the syllabus, the first week was reserved for "Kant's Epistemology and Kant and Rousseau." There are echoes of the classroom in this piece. According to some notes he made for a lecture, Fein felt a need to explain Kant's epistemology before his ethics: "Two hours just so they'll know what the *categorical* in categorical imperative means." Fein believed that reading Rousseau was a turning-point in Kant's life. He thought Rousseau's challenge to intellectuals provoked "the greatest mid-life crisis in the history of philosophy." It is typical of Fein that he was at least as interested in why the philosopher thought what he thought as in what he thought. The second week was given over to *The Foundations of the Metaphysics of Morals*. The extra half-week was spent discussing a movie, Peter Ustinov's film of the Coxe and Chapman play based on Melville's *Billy Budd* (1961). Fein, who called Kant "our first tragic philosopher," evidently saw in Captain Vere the ideal Kantian hero.

Idol worship seems also to have been on Fein's mind that summer. Accompanying his manuscript, in addition to a copy of the Tarasoff decision, quotations from Kant and Constant, are biblical passages from Exodus, Leviticus, Isaiah, Daniel, Jeremiah, 1 Kings, and 2 Chronicles. Perhaps Fein chose to cite only Ezekiel, Chapter 14, because it best suggests the broader, secular meaning of worshipping idols.

Though distinctive in some ways, in others "Idol Worship" has much in common with other of Fein's posthumous papers. Kafka is a familiar touchstone; an anecdote about Maya is not so rare, and the flexible but coherent structure is exceptional only for its two-part form.

As an instance of ethics applied as law, the Tarasoff case has turned out to be as consequential as Fein anticipated. By establishing a "duty to protect" that trumps medical confidentiality, it altered the obligations of mental health professionals and has made familiar the trigger phrase: "a danger to oneself or others."

As for Kant, Fein presents another of his cautionary tales for theorists. Fein mistrusted theory, even the theories of thinkers he admired, even one that proclaims human beings to be the paramount consideration. This same skeptical spirit is conveyed by one of Fein's characteristic aphorisms: "Virtue often consists only in a willingness to give in to the smaller vice."

ON BEING ALONE

EDITOR'S NOTE

Among Sidney Fein's papers for the year 1976 I found the following text in the form of mixed manuscript and typescript pages, all held together by a paper clip. The material has no title.

The four years between the publication of *Diptych on Terrestrial Representation* (1973) and *Want, Desire, and Need* (1977) were exceptionally productive for Fein. His annual files for the mid-70s contain the largest number of incomplete or discarded efforts, though in these years he was working hard on his second book, the most rapidly written of the three. The present material may originally have been intended for inclusion in *Want, Desire, and Need.*

In some ways, the pieces I have gathered here typify Fein's manner of working. It was characteristic of him to compose a series of fragments whose relation to each other is less than obvious, subsequently to organize them and provide transitions. Only at the last minute, so to speak, would he unify the whole.

Missing from "On Being Alone" are the transitions, the climactic concatenation, and the thesis. I am at a loss to say whether there is a thesis, an unstated tune behind these variations, as in Elgar's famous piece, or if they are random ruminations on distinct, though related, topics—Monsieur Teste, loneliness, Wittgenstein, solipsism, the ethical status of happiness. In selecting texts to prepare for publication, I have looked for those that are coherent enough to allow an attentive reader to figure out the connections and, if necessary, guess at the thesis. That is all I have done here.

Though typical in many respects, "On Being Alone" is unusual for its interpolation of a dialogue and a poem. On the manuscript of the former Fein has crossed out two possibilities for the speakers. One reads "Teacher and Student," the other "Self and Soul." In fact, Fein's manuscripts often include bits of dialogue, though few as sustained or perplexing as this one. The poem, as the text suggests, was almost certainly written contemporaneously with the other items; and, since it appears only in typescript, was certainly revised.

Finally, I would like to suggest a reason why Fein might have been preoccupied by solitude in the mid-70s. His marriage broke up in 1974, within months of the publication of the *Diptych*. There was, however, no divorce. Maya Nunfi Fein, who has requested me to undertake this editorial work, has given permission for me to include here what she knows of her parents' separation. When Fein's wife left him she agreed that the seven-year-old Maya could remain with him on condition that he not seek a divorce. Apparently, she did not want to go on being a parent but could not accept any legal declaration to this effect. Were Fein to sue for divorce, his wife promised to sue for custody and, given the prejudices of the courts at that time, she could be assured of winning. In his daughter's opinion, in accepting her mother's condition, Fein felt not only overwhelmed by the sudden responsibility of single parenthood but also that he was now barred from remarriage, that his life would thenceforth be built around his daughter and his work. Though nothing of these personal feelings is to be found expressed directly in "On Being Alone," Fein's daughter believes that during this period her father was a lonely man who expected to become more alone.

On Being Alone

Monsieur Teste, that thrice-distilled mentality, is far from resembling a convincing life-form. One supposes Valéry called him Mr. Head (*Tête*) because Teste's existence is almost exclusively cerebral. But the author named his alter-ego with wit. In Latin, *testis* is an ambiguous noun; it can signify either *witness* or *testicle*.

Looking on at life with the detachment of a perspicacious habitué of one of the fashionable cafés, this genuine witness with putative testicles has many fascinating thoughts about what he observes, himself included. One such is this:

> What really matters to someone (I mean the kind of someone who in his essence is unique and alone) is precisely that which makes him feel that he is alone.

The parenthesis seems superfluous; for how can those who really feel themselves alone help believing that to be alone is their "essence"? On the other hand, Teste might be right to specify the kind of person who cares about being alone. What he seems to have in mind is somebody who is alone whether in or out of company. Teste is not concerned with a person whose family happens to be away at the in-laws', who has no date for Saturday night, who is driving between the seething office and the crowded split-level. It is not *finding* oneself alone that he means, not the temporary condition of not being among others, because then there would not be enough to "matter." There would be no mystery, and being alone, even to the point of being lonely, would be trivial, a curable contingency. There is no question here of one's "essence," which is as much as to say one's fate. The distinction between being alone and being *essentially* alone is a valid one: if one really had such an essence it would be static and unalterable, and then one's fate would be how that essence compels the this-and-that of one's existence always in the direction of being alone.

So, Teste's observation raises two problems: a) the nature of the "someone" and b) the "that which makes him feel that he is alone." It's curious how the two seem to be distinct but are at the same time knit together by Teste's saying. A person and his or her mystery. Anyway, if it were truly somebody's essence to be alone, then for that person to be preoccupied by the nature of that essence would hardly be surprising. For this solitary, being alone is like being a woman for a feminist, Irish for a Fenian, a Trotskyite for a Trotskyite. Teste's "unique" someone might not talk about it so much, of course, though I don't doubt he could go on and on—if there were anyone to listen.

• • •

Two of the more intriguing causes or effects of being alone are solipsism and egoism, which can be mistaken for one another but are, in fact, almost opposites. The solipsist is humble, despairing, lonesome, disconsolate, and rare; the egoist is rancorous, arrogant, gregarious, and common. The solipsist has no other egos against which to push, while the egoist pushes for all he's worth against every other ego. The solipsist is a single atom of hydrogen in a vacuum tube. The egoist imagines himself the biggest ball on a pool table full of smaller balls. The solipsist sees himself as the end-point of inwardness; the egoist conceives himself as the outward limit of the material world. I cannot imagine a joyous solipsist, but the many egoists I have known are jovial people, so long as they are able to go on believing in their own superiority. Without obstacles, tribulation, dejection—above all without the pain of loneliness—the hero and heroine would not merit their happy ending, the union that rescues society by perpetuating it.

It is a melancholy inference, but one might almost conclude that people become worthy of companionship only by being alone and of happiness only by being unhappy.

• • •

-What does it mean to ask a question?

-You've already answered.

-Are you teasing me again?

-Again? Why, do I tease you that often?

-I'm afraid you do it even more than I notice you doing it.

-Don't sell yourself short.

-Then tell me about questions, about asking. I'm asking about asking.

-All right, I can give you my opinion if you like. The act of asking is different from, say, feeding a child or planting a beech tree. These acts are helpful. To ask is often only the wish to think instead of to help.

-Why? Is it wrong to want to understand feeding or planting? How can somebody feed or plant if he doesn't understand how to do them?

-Excuse me. As usual I've expressed myself badly. You're right, of course; it's always good to ask, where there's a genuine will to understand. Nevertheless, some things aren't understood by getting answers, let alone by the questions that evoke them. What did you really want when you asked me about asking?

-An answer.

-An answer is hardly ever enough of an answer.

-In that case, I'm not sure.

-Then perhaps it was only to feel less alone. That's another reason for asking questions.

-How could that be? After all, I'm here with you.

-True. And yet *I* feel alone.

-That's not very flattering; but, if so, then maybe that's why you answered, so as to talk to me instead of yourself.

-Well that too can be one of the meanings of asking, so why not of answering as well? I sometimes think questions and answers are things people use to propel their conversations forward like ships. The passengers and crew need to feel connected to the port they've left behind and the one towards which they're steaming. The moment the engines stop everybody on board feels how alone they are. Adrift.

-You know, you're awfully fond of metaphors.

-Perhaps. It's really very hard to make purely factual statements. All language is metaphor; it's almost as if it were not in our nature to stick to the facts. Facts haven't any meaning; they lack value and quality. So, as meaning-loving creatures, we feel compelled to do something with them, to *arrange* them. "The facts lay between us like flowers on a table." I once read that sentence in a novel. It's a good sentence. Like orchestras, facts need conducting; like dreams, they yearn to be interpreted. Haven't you felt how much there is to disappoint in an array of facts? This is why people speak of "fleshing out" a story limited to a few facts. Facts are dry as bones, brittle and juiceless. All the same, flesh without a skeleton is even worse.

-What brought *that* on?

-You did.

• • •

To the one who feels himself alone what makes him feel alone probably does count for more than anything else. This would explain why solitary people are less alert than one might expect. That they overlook things must be either because they are concentrating on something else (their personal version of Teste's *that which*) or because nothing outside of their condition matters enough to arouse their attention. Fed by self-absorption, the ego can begin to swell immensely despite being unloved, even by itself.

In ancient times, megalomania was limited to rulers and warlords; now it is a disease of modernity. The pressures on the ego seem to be increased both by conditions of freedom (Pascal: "The silence of these infinite spaces frightens me") and of oppression (Sade: "It was necessary to call hell to the rescue, and to find, in the world of nightmare, images adequate to the history of man in this Iron Age"). Where the rational, socialized citizen insists on his rights, the irrational, isolated individual proclaims himself beyond good and evil. No wonder Nietzsche in his final madness took to signing his letters "The Crucified One," or that Camus should have written his first play about the emperor Caligula.

Say a woman is lonely and longs to be married, to be half of a couple. What a preoccupation she can make of it, and how many forms her sense of deprivation can take, anything from fantasizing about her heart's desire to becoming a man-hater. Yet even if she struggles toward resignation, her sense of being alone will matter more to her than anything else.

Suppose a man cuts himself off from everyone, lives by himself, joins in no one's joys or sorrows and will not share his own. Is such a hermit rebelling against the human condition, the condition of a social species, or is he only being more honest about it, that humans are not ants or bees and, at bottom, we are alone? I imagine that sooner or later, if he remains on his own, he will arrive at the latter position. "My condition may not be a happy one," he will say to himself, "but at least it is more truthful than that of those who believe themselves happy at some dinner party. The nothing I have is more honest than the pitiful consolations of... *next* to nothing."

Such a person is suspect, already on his way to misanthropy, megalomania—or to solipsism, which is the philosophical form of being entirely alone. Aren't the worst of our criminals always called "loners"?

Apparently, solipsism has been on my mind. I've written a long poem about it. The speaker of this poem, it now occurs to me, is a solipsist who wants very much to escape solipsism, or at least is disgusted by it. The poem is full of springtime but lacks any expression of the season's joy, conveying a resignation that would like to be stoical but isn't. The speaker is only resigned to what he calls that "smudge of consciousness" which, his claim to the contrary notwithstanding, he fails to keep from fouling whatever happens.

ACCIDERE

Of all the things that might have happened
nothing did. No one rang his bell; in spite
of provocations riots didn't break
out, not so much as a cocktail party,
nor was war declared, so he was not called
up. Inert, he made no sacrifices,
gathered no affection, organized no coups.
When something happens it so often
seems forced upon the world that behind all
acts one hears the echo, not always faint,
of some turn of violence—Huns swarming
over the Apennines; Montezuma
fatally subdued—yet all prepared in
advance by snarled skeins savants pick
apart as soon as the happening stops
and cannot go on happening, when
it qualifies as one more vanished corpse
to memorialize with static dignity
in the encyclopedic cenotaphs.
But it isn't wholly true even
on this emptiest of spring Sundays that
nothing happened. *It* happened; in fact,
it loved to happen. Marcus Aurelius
noted thus his moment of satori,
Imperial and Stoic. Yet loving
to happen must mean that it loved its own

actualization as an infant
its evacuation, vainly, with an
awful but forgivable complacency,
as the wind heedlessly delights to blow.
And since it loved best to happen clean of
every smudge of consciousness, vacantly
he watched irises unfold, red robins
pause to feel the worms under blue milky
clouds beneath which to happen wants no
meaning since it simply loves to happen,
so he kept still as ivy stretched out tendrils
then commenced its green and pointless climb.

The bravado of that "kept still" isn't going to take anyone in. A lonesome poet has written a lonesome poem.

• • •

Ludwig Wittgenstein must have proved his sincerity even to the unimaginative when he gave away a fortune. Did this show that what he said about the material world "lacking value" was an anti-metaphysical declaration or only that it lacked all value to *him*? Was Wittgenstein making the point that everybody's happiness lay elsewhere or trying to make good on the expectation that his might? His high morality is lonely, even disconsolate, far from that of the sociable Socrates in his agora. As he says, "It is clear that ethics cannot be put into words."

In all his photographs Wittgenstein looks haunted, as if he is aware of being a member of a doomed generation. The Wittgensteins were Jewish, rich, gifted, musical, and unfortunate. The suicides. The brother's lost right arm. It was the family wealth, Paul's war wound, plus his courageous determination to which we owe the left-handed concerti of Ravel and Prokofiev.

Wittgenstein understood much to begin with and then he learned more; he was flexible enough to produce an intellectual biography with a second, even a third act. He was always going off by himself—to obscure villages, to fjords—a mystic ascetic celebrated by the crassest of materialists. He deserves to be listened to.

In accordance with his two opinions, Wittgenstein developed two styles. In the *Tractatus* he is precise, atomistic, Talmudic, Euclidean; in the *Investigations* desultory, discursive, anecdotal, nearly nonchalant. And how well each style suits each aim, each theory of language and the world "as he found it." It would be a strange genius who can obsess about language while failing to be thoughtful about the use he makes of it. What really *convinces* in each book is, in fact, Wittgenstein's style, as though the form of his utterance determined his arguments rather than vice versa. In Aubrey's *Brief Lives* there is a good story about Thomas Hobbes. In his fortieth year, Hobbes happened to be in a private library when he chanced to look at an open copy of Euclid's *Elements*. He read the forty-seventh theorem of Book One. "By God," he is supposed to have exclaimed, "this is impossible." Hobbes then read the demonstration which referred him to a previous proposition, that to another, and so on until he arrived back at the self-evident axioms. Hobbes at once fell in love with Euclid's method and did his best to imitate it.

Reading at random in the *Tractatus* makes one feel like Hobbes in that nobleman's library, and not only because of Wittgenstein's irritating, though unimpeachably rational, device of numbering his propositions.

> 5.64 Here it can be seen that solipsism, when its implications are followed out strictly, coincides with pure realism. The self of solipsism shrinks to a point without extension, and there remains the reality coordinated with it.

This really does sound like Euclid, with its unextended point and coordinated reality. As to the plausibility of Wittgenstein's proposition, I also want to cry out, "By God, this is impossible."

The solipsist holds that the only certainty is that he exists and so the existence of everything and everybody else lies in his own consciousness. Like all dead-end theories, solipsism is feared and despised, mentioned in the history of philosophy chiefly as a position to be assiduously avoided. It is generally agreed that solipsism is one of the illnesses of idealism, of which realism is, of course, the opposite. A realist believes that the condition of his knowing anything is an object independent of his knowing. The solipsist says, "That chair exists only in my mind as does the impression that it is supporting my weight." The realist says, "I see the chair because it was there before I put my rear end on it; moreover, the chair will still be here after I've gotten up and left the room." The solipsist lives in a vacant universe with a multitudinous mind; the realist in a bustling cosmos with a comparatively empty, albeit highly receptive, mind. For the latter, there are other people galore; for the former, less society than Crusoe found on his island.

So how can Wittgenstein assert that solipsism "coincides with pure realism"? How can inescapable solitude accord with hectic sociability?

For Wittgenstein, the abrogation of metaphysics banishes value from the world. To him, the end of metaphysics is simply what science must insist on—exploding Aristotle's qualitative hierarchies in favor of quantitative descriptions. Science demands, he feels, the abolition of ends in favor of processes. The planets have orbits an astronomer can calculate, but to what purpose they go round and round is simply not *knowable*. What I like about Wittgenstein is that he never doubts what is unknowable is of the greatest importance, and yet he insists it is unknowable. Science is all *how* and no *why*; all matter, but nothing of *what* matters in Monsieur Teste's sense. The things our senses tell us about the world, how tart things taste, what is terrifying or beautiful, what our hearts desire from the world—all this practically ceases to be real when Wittgenstein accedes to the strictures of science. But what is unreal is not unimportant. Wittgenstein is far from giving up on what matters but he sees it as displaced, as superlunary, so to speak. Can there be a sadder proposition than this: "The sense of the world must lie outside the world"?

Wittgenstein can say, "The subject does not belong to the world; rather it is a limit of the world." (This is not altogether unlike my poem in which consciousness is a mere "smudge.") Wittgenstein does not mean the world excludes subjectivity. On the contrary. In fact, he must mean that the "world" is *not* the only reality, just the only one Wittgenstein thinks we can talk about sensibly. Fences are no less real than fields. They define the fields. The self, the "limit of the world," is no less real than the elements of the Periodic Table. The self is distinct from the world only in the sense that the eye can see everything but itself, that the hypersensitive brain is itself insensate. Holding that the world is the facts but not the perception of them doesn't mean that the world isn't full of perceivers—subjects who can suffer, hope, wallow. They too are facts.

The solitary perceiver, then, even should he be a solipsist, sees exactly the same facts as the realist. Solipsism isn't megalomania, but its obverse. Overwhelmed by the world it sees and smells, the isolated self "shrinks to a point without extension, and there remains the reality coordinated with it." This reminds me of Kafka's glum advice: "In the battle between yourself and the world, back the world." Megalomania is what the solipsist shrinks *from* as soon as he tries to express himself. He can only express "the world." The world matters to the solipsist because, for this most solitary being, as for Monsieur Teste, the world is precisely "that which makes him feel alone."

Conclusion? More certain of the existence of the metropolis than that of our shriveled selves, we're all alone in the big city.

ON EMMA AND ANNA

S IDNEY Fein was interested in literary problems for extra-literary reasons. He loved many poems, plays, and novels for their own sakes; nevertheless, he hoped to realize un-literary gains from his examination of them. Fein might have approved of Eliot's dictum that the greatness of literature can only be apprehended by reference to values other than literary. I say maybe because Fein shared neither Eliot's religious beliefs nor his critic's anxiety about assessing greatness. What Fein seemed to like were the problems posed by stories and poems and the way they led him to find things out. This search for problems and their enjoyment animated Fein's reading no less than his writing.

In his first book, Fein agrees with Aristotle's opinion that litera-ture is more philosophical than history, but not the philosopher's reason for saying so. While Aristotle argued that literature gave us general cases rather than specific ones, and so the universal rather than the actual, to Fein it was the concreteness of literature that told the most:

> History doesn't care if it is understood. History is a hard knot made of tangled and unreckonable contingencies. Who can unravel them? The concreteness of literature, on the other hand, is the product of thought and, unlike history, it yearns to be understood.

Fein relished this "reckonable" concreteness of literature. He uses it heuristically; he speculates, digresses, and generally romps around in it.

Had Fein completed the notes below we might have learned something weighty and philosophical. Even as they stand, he seems to have been aiming beyond his ostensible targets, the two great adulteress-heroines. Any reader accustomed to the apparent non-sequiturs of his style is bound to wonder whether Fein's meditation over the corpses of Emma Bovary and Anna Karenina was part of a trajectory of thought that would overshoot comparison and contrast. Any reader of Fein will wonder what he was getting at.

It is a privilege to edit Fein's posthumous papers and to bring some of them before the public. Still, I cannot rid myself of the misgiving that publication may be a betrayal. Fein would certainly have supplied a greater sense of order and, as he so often did in his completed work, some final declaration that would wipe away any sense of fragmentariness. Like Dickens, Fein was fond of good housekeeping on virtually moral grounds. Perhaps it was preserving an orderly intellectual headquarters that freed him to attempt so many daring maneuvers. My greatest scruple about this editorial work is the unavoidable worry that the pieces I have put together are unfinished. It is not that they lack resolution, for most of them are resolved. The distinction between the almost-completed and the finished is more subtle. The difference is like that between a fine and well-made but not-yet-assembled chest-of-drawers and one that is sturdily doweled, well glued, and polished to a high finish.

That said, my study of Fein's papers convinces me that his work is, in a sense, *all* fragments. I believe he seldom knew where he was going when he began to write. I think that Fein wrote to see where his pen would lead him. That his finished work strikes people as premeditated is a successful illusion. The good craftsman wants to show off the lustrous bureau, not a workshop full of sawdust and discarded stock. Many other thinkers also work fragments up into wholes, of course. Fein's distinction was not to plane down the surfaces of his writing, not to sand the joints into seamless transitions. His trick lay in convincing readers that these fragments are not random but disposed in accord with a plan that only becomes clear at the end.

The following manuscript, held together by a large paper clip, was deposited in Fein's folder for 1977. The two extended quotations describing the heroines' corpses are typed, but the rest is handwritten with interpolations and corrections. By 1977, Fein's marriage had broken up and he was raising his daughter Maya on his own. He had recently invented his pseudonym Klaren Verheim whose first excursions into fiction also date from this time. It seems likely that Fein's personal situation prompted his interest in adultery, while Verheim's fiction suggested the issue of a novelist's attitude toward his characters. I see no need, however, to look for autobiographical motives behind these notes. My own opinion is that Fein began with a daydream of a tea party in the afterlife where Anna Karenina entertains her impossible-to-please guest, Emma Bovary. It is typical of Fein that a serious and solid essay should begin with a whimsy, grow from gossamer. As he himself once wrote: "All heaviness begins as lightness and how quickly it can evaporate into lightness again."

On Emma and Anna

To know if an author loves or despises his main character is already to know a good deal. But what if the character should also know?

Flaubert and Tolstoy feel differently about their heroines. Tolstoy loves Anna. Lionel Trilling goes so far as to say that he has an "almost sexual love for his heroine." As for Flaubert, satire and scorn are heaped so thickly above whatever compassion he feels for Emma that he appears simply cruel. I can easily imagine Anna forgiving

Count Tolstoy for everything he puts her through. (Her lovers are both Counts with seven-letter surnames.) On the other hand, I picture Emma nursing an undying resentment of Flaubert.

I imagine them in a garden. It is Anna's garden and it looks perfect enough for the last act of *The Importance of Being Earnest*. Tall shrubs, bleeding hearts, gladiolas, clematis, great blue hollyhocks, a stand of dark cypresses at the verge. There are ornate white lawn chairs and, atop a round table, a huge silver samovar which Emma eyes covetously.

Emma begins insistently, puffing herself up while simultaneously attempting to appear refined.

> Emma: We were ahead of our time. It's only our deaths that seem dated now.
>
> Anna: More tea, dear?
>
> Emma: No, thank you.
>
> Anna: Well, I won't say you're wrong, Emma. And yet our deaths do imprison us. Suicide invariably does.
>
> Emma: But that's so unjust. It's unfair to judge people by their deaths, as if that colors everything that came before.
>
> Anna: I'm afraid that's exactly what suicide does.
>
> Emma: Lovers, husbands, children, priests, the outbreak of war—nothing could have saved us. We were doomed from the first. *They* doomed us.
>
> Anna: Doomed? Well, I suppose we are victims of literary composition, my dear. But isn't it nice here? All these flowers and no men at all.
>
> Emma: We weren't victims of literature but of wanting, of wanting *more*. Victims of Flaubert and Tolstoy, you think? No. Our sin was just that—*wanting*. The punishment was for that,

laid out for us from the first.

Anna: As you say, laid out in advance, like the sin of Oedipus. Well, in the end we both wanted to die, didn't we?

Emma: I wanted to die but also *not* to die. I wanted to die and then watch them cry and then come back and have everything transfigured. At the last moment, I repented.

Anna: I'm sure you did, dear.

Emma: And you? Did you too repent at the last instant?

Anna: Oh, no. I just threw myself away. It felt like the period at the end of a long, dreary paragraph.

Emma: Still, we scared them, didn't we?

Anna: Scared who?

Emma: Oh, everybody who longed to condemn us. All those men in black.

Anna: That's very near a tautology, Emma.

Emma: No more than Flaubert's monstrous boast.

Anna: What was that?

Emma: You know. It's become famous. He claimed to be me! Can you imagine? *Madame Bovary, c'est moi. C'est monstreux!*

Anna: Oh yes, I did hear about that. Just the right words, as usual.

Emma: I'll never forgive him. What gall! What a boast! It's as if he were saying I'm so small while he is so large. It's like being eaten up.

Anna: But don't you think it might have been something other than a boast?

Emma: Flaubert, that vain and cynical man? That philanderer. What else could he have meant?

Anna: Well, perhaps it was a defense. A defense especially of you, Emma. Perhaps he meant to take responsibility for you.

Emma: But that's still *more* insulting. Besides, he was only defending his reputation. He had no thought of me. The Madame Bovary he had in mind was a book, not a human being.

Anna: Are we human beings then?

Emma: Certainly we are. We exist and we are human. Who is more human?

Anna: Oh, Emma. You're so unhappy. You must try not to be bitter, darling.

Emma: I have a right to be unhappy. I was never loved—not as you were. My whole life was consumed by deprivation and bad luck. Oh, how I envy you!

Anna: Me?

Emma: Oh, yes.

Anna: I assure you I'm unworthy of your envy, of anyone's. I'm nothing at all. Did you know that some wag has reduced me to the last line of a limerick?

Emma: A limerick?

Anna: He sums up the whole book, its hundreds of pages. I come at the end, of course.

Vronsky's suicide was all in vain.

Karenin's too cold to complain.

Levin and Kitty

Flee from the city,

Then Anna jumps under a train.

• • •

Emma's envy, bafflement, and frustration are etched deeper by Anna's compassion, grace, and natural superiority. Emma was born twenty years before Anna but she is hardly twenty years older. Anna is a mature woman, while Emma has never left adolescence. Anna is a *grande dame*. She cannot help but condescend—at least that is what Emma feels. Anna is the kind of woman she would like to have been, has had the sort of life she craved. And, ah, what a magnificent *bouilloire* she has!

Emma resents that Flaubert should judge her without seeming to do so. According to her lights, he simply despised her. Tolstoy, on the other hand, does not hold back from judging Anna and yet, because he adores her, this judgment is softened without being blunted.

Emma would like to say something like this in order to overcome her sense of inferiority: "They both of them licked their lips over our moral disintegration and then they killed us off." But she cannot stop thinking of how Tolstoy's passion led to greater violence but also yielded a real Russian love. "Flaubert is a species of chemist," she says acidly. "To him I was always half dead, whereas your Tolstoy worships you even after he's torn you to shreds. He leaves your beautiful head untouched just so he can go on mooning over your hair."

• • •

While it is not attractive, there is justice in Emma's resentment. Taking her hint, we are tempted to begin our lecture morbidly, by comparing the two passages that describe the women's corpses. Both bodies are presented from the point of view of men who had been intimate with them, for whom these bodies cannot be matters of indifference. Flaubert chooses Bovary, the most unimaginative possible narrator, while Tolstoy shows us the body of Anna through Vronsky's eyes. If only to focus the class's attention, the lecturer might claim that what is said of the dead bodies reveals much about the two fictional women and the two fictional men but also the two non-fictional novelists.

Flaubert first.

Emma's head was turned toward her right shoulder. The corner of her open mouth was like a black hole in the lower part of her face; her two thumbs were bent inward toward the palms of her hands; a kind of white dust powdered her lashes; and the outline of her eyes was beginning to disappear in a viscous pallor, as though spiders had been spinning cobwebs over her face. From her breasts to her knees the sheet sagged, rising again at her toes; and it seemed to Charles that some infinite mass, some enormous weight, was pressing on her.

Thus Flaubert displays for us the dead Emma. Never mind that she is in her own bed; she might as well be on a cold metal table in front of an anatomy class. All those semi-colons mark off physical details recorded with the chilly blankness of an autopsy report. Even Charles' dim sense of a weight pressing on her does not relieve his practically clinical detachment, which is precisely that of an incompetent doctor. Charles is not given to poetic diction and so what there is here must be put down to Flaubert's eagerness to make a point. The lecturer would point out, for example, how uncharitable, how full of disgust Flaubert's description of Emma's mouth is, a "black hole" opening to an essential hollowness. Nor is he satisfied to disgust us with the image of cobwebs overspreading her face; we must also imagine the spiders spinning them. The sheet that covers Emma Bovary's corpse does not flow, conforms to no feminine curves; rather it *sags* from breast to knee, falling to a nadir at her sex. Such writing is so oppressive that one cannot escape the thought that the weight that presses on Emma is not the ennui of the provinces but of Monsieur Gustave Flaubert's thumb.

Then the lecturer might pause and brighten as he turns to the way Tolstoy shows off the dead Anna. It is no matter that she lies on an actual table rather than a bed or that she has been killed by a locomotive rather than poison, that her death has been much more violent than Emma's—and for that reason more heroic—and her "shameless" position much less decorous than Emma's beneath that sagging sheet. Anna seems scarcely to be dead at all.

> ... on the barrack table, shamelessly exposed to strangers, bloody, yet still full of the life that had scarcely left her; the untouched head, thrown back, with its heavy plaits and hairs curling at the temples, and on the charming face, with its half-open rosy mouth, a frozen strange pitiful expression on the lips, and a terrible look in the fixed, open eyes, as if expressing in words that terrible thought—"that he would repent of it"—which she had said to him during their quarrel.

The lecturer would invite the class to consider those mouths more closely. While Emma's is "like a black hole," Anna's is "half-open" and "rosy" and still merits the adjective "charming." Flaubert is parsimonious with adjectives but Tolstoy heaps them up almost recklessly. Anna's expression is "frozen strange pitiful." Vronsky's guilt in the face of this face reminds me of the other great looking-a-corpse-in-the-eye scene in Tolstoy, when Peter Ivanovich is momentarily frightened by the "reproach and warning to the living" on the aspect of the defunct Ivan Ilych. No doubt it was of these two scenes that critic was thinking when he observed that Tolstoy's corpses seem more alive than the healthy characters of lesser writers. Nothing more typical of the Antaeus of world literature than to say of a beautiful woman mangled by tons of rumbling steel than that "the life... had scarcely left her." Neither Tolstoy nor Vronsky can bear to part with that life. Emma, on the other hand, is as dead as Eeyore's burst red balloon.

• • •

Consider, says the lecturer, Emma and Anna as representative women in a period of transition. Adultery still matters economically as well as emotionally, though the former is diminishing. Flaubert, of course, strictly binds Emma's affairs to her debts; they are the strands of rope making up the noose. They have the same source in her longing for elegance, adventure, and distinction. The dreams of Emma may be cheap but they are aspirations all the same. In male characters like Don Quixote and Jay Gatsby the purity of aspiration exceeds its object. The same, apparently, does not hold for women.

Adultery was originally an economic sin, a function of the agricultural or pastoral community's obsession with the ownership of land and livestock. Economically, there is no comparable patrimony Emma's adultery could misdirect. She is not portrayed as Bovary's property either, not even in the limited sense that Anna's virtue nearly makes her Karenin's chattel. It is easy to see that adultery is on its way to becoming merely an emotional shock, a betrayal that is sexual but no longer one of property, or of vows that even the wedding party does not take seriously. Today too, the lecturer might observe in a lowered voice, adultery remains serious business, very serious, but people are hard pressed to say why. Adulteresses no longer drink poison or launch themselves under express trains. The victim is less the husband than the "family," though people say it without a whole heart in an age when you can get even odds on any given marriage ending in divorce. As work requires less upper-body strength and the middle class needs two incomes to stay in the middle, "the family" is likely to become an increasingly abstract designation. Already its definition is up for grabs.

All the same, we still read the stories of Emma and Anna with understanding and empathy. Longing, the need for love, the desire for more life, the risks of moral disintegration and ostracism—all these we still grasp, even if we are not social historians—or shepherds.

Freud believed that as civilization matures men neglect their women for other cultural activities such as war and business. He supposed that their wives and mistresses would resent this and turn into enemies of civilization—anarchistic golf widows, so to speak, on the sexual warpath. This opinion seems quaint nowadays when a woman is as apt to abandon hearth and home as a man. But Anna and even Emma may well be the sort of women Freud had in mind. It is curious that, after more than a century, Emma Bovary can start to look like a giantess of authenticity.

• • •

Adultery: personal and linguistic.

My wife was an adulteress. I have been an adulterer. About adultery, then, I ought to have something to say. And yet, though adultery is among the most culturally drenched of sins, I can think of surprisingly little to say except that it isn't what it used to be.

Adultery, like the loss of virginity, can become a legal fact only in the crudest way. But extra-legally, and also like virginity, there are what we might call shadows of the fact. In my youth, there were so-called technical virgins. Just so, there can be technical adulteresses. A glance is enough.

In its purest or "classical" sense, adultery denotes pollution of the genetic stream, the substitution of 23 unauthorized chromosomes in a zygote and potential heir. But it would be obtuse to say there can be no adultery without procreation, even that there can be no adultery without intercourse. I would also argue that there can be adultery without marriage. If adultery is a betrayal of commitment, of fidelity, of the exclusivity of sexual and emotional access in accord with implicit as well as explicit contracts, then why not? If so, then adultery exists on a continuum of human sexual behavior and can only be defined socially, not biologically. (Monsieur Foucault might award me a gold fleur-de-lis for this thought.)

As a sin, adultery is as archaic as the wooden plow. People in the industrialized West no longer commit adultery; they merely have "affairs"—a term that suggestively mixes the sexual with the commercial. Old-fashioned adultery remains a lethal offense in places like South Asia and the Arabian Peninsula. This is one of the ways we know we are different from the Hindus and Muslims, or rather that they know they are different from us. Their "revenge killings" publicly horrify and privately impress us. "Can't we discuss this like civilized people?" is the giveaway cliché of the West where being "civilized" often means being relativistic and cold-blooded. Certainly, men slaughter hecatombs of women in the West, but we no longer see the crime of passion quite as we used to do. We call such acts by a revealing phrase, domestic violence. (Can violence be domesticated?) The ultra-sophisticated read about the latest *crime passionel*, click their tongues, and say with Huxley's Lenina: "All that fuss about having a girl."

Like tragic drama, adultery can still be consequential. Mere affairs, though, are inconsequential, comedies of good and bad manners. Tolstoy reminds us of this in his novel's second and third sentences, which sound like the exposition of a farce (please take note, class, of the former governess' nationality):

> Everything was upset in the Oblonskys' house. The wife had discovered an intrigue between her husband and their former French governess…

No liberated woman commits adultery. The unliberated may still do so—in order to become liberated.

Is adultery a paltry subject for literature or a powerful one? This depends on the attitude and the skill of the author and the social condition of the reader. It requires no great act of imagination to grasp that what may be a black sin in one age is a solecism in another. Behind Emma and Anna one glimpses the figure of Hester Prynne standing still, silent, and admirable indeed. The nineteenth century loves both its comic and tragic adulteresses and surely some portion of that love is sadistic.

Lysistrata is the earliest comedy that really counts for us. Is it still true that a female rebellion not linked to sexuality loses half its force?

●　●　●

An adulteress's valentine.

Emma and Anna are married women; their lovers are single. How different their stories would be if it were the other way around. Emma and Anna are wives and mothers, not homewreckers, not *femmes fatales*. Because Anna is a good mother readers will forgive her anything. Emma is less likeable in part because she is such an indifferent mother. Her capacity to love we think of as stunted by fantasy and selfishness. In other words, motherhood trumps both adultery and virtue. So, the suicides mean different things, at least to men. Without even mentioning motherhood, J. P. Stern puts it this way:

> The *form* of Anna's death, suicide, is determined by her psychological and social situation. So is Emma's suicide ... But only of Anna's death can we say that it is the vindication of a law, since it is only she who has drained the cup of human passion.

Stern seems to be saying that Emma thirsts merely for refinement, Anna for love. But for readers the acid test of their capacity for love remains maternity.

Imagine an adulteress of the more customary sort. I mean a "kept woman." Her life is like her boudoir, sealed-off. Love isolates her but, if she loves, she accepts the bargain. She will be an anti-Emma because it is the ordinary for which she longs. That's where the grass is greener. One February night, triumphing over her sorrow and loneliness, she writes some verses to her lover, who, it almost goes without saying, is unworthy of them.

> All that we cannot have, breakfast,
> a public appearance, union that is not
> reunion, a quiet evening, a flamboyant trip,
> the whole ineffable quotidian, wet weekends,
> boredom, a joint return, a life steeped
> from the bag of mere banality,
> the commonplace of hampers and toothpaste,

beyond appreciation by those who have it—
une vie qui est dans le vrai, said Flaubert—
must be weighed (and it is) against
the thing we have. (I weigh it, I do.)
I listen for the music in our silences. The
loveliest of grace notes that I catch
just because they're never played
please because you hear what's in the mind.
The missing pearl glitters brighter than the ruby
you own. To understand food, try starving.
So let's be one another's Valentine, further
even than what proclamation can proclaim
or a social contract with two witnesses.
We are a secret, a secret like a room in
which no secret can exist and where nothing's
withheld but the room itself, its curtains
drawn to rule out the precious light of
ordinary days, to close in this subdued,
cloistered, unacknowledged gloom
where I can hear each unplayed note we play.
Dear, I'll be your Valentine as best I can.

As a term of opprobrium *adulterer* never carried anything like
the weight of *adulteress*. It is the Hesters who wear the scarlet letter,
never the Dimmesdales whose guilt is, so to say, optional. Can this
tendency to blame the female over the male be due entirely to the
double standard? Is it owing to the facts of biology? (From Nature's
point of view, what is sexual intercourse but a technical innovation
making evolution more efficient?) Is it all in Strindberg's anxious
line, that "the father can never be sure"? Shouldn't we also count in
the fear of sexual autonomy in females which runs deep in possessive men, right beside their jealousy of other males? After all, the
possessive are always insecure. No doubt a case could be made by

the reductionists for a genetic imperative on the part of the male to ensure that it is his genes alone that make it into the next generation. No matter what it says, reductionism always leaves something out.

If the cuckold is a fool and a victim, then the adulterer is neither. The cuckold is his wife's victim though his honor may depend on pretending that it is the adulterer who is to blame. According to Nietzsche, "Slave Morality" altered the conception of virtue (Gk. *arête*, where Ares' name is still detectable) from strength in a man to chastity in a woman. The adulterous male can still call on the earlier idea of virtue ("he's good *with* the girls") while the adulterous woman cannot. On the contrary, she has "lost her virtue." It is easy to see the injustice here, the repression of women, at least those who have something to repress. Yet the ages of the Greek queens, of the Canaanite goddesses, of the matriarchal Old Religion lie below even Nietzsche's atavistic "Master Morality." Wise women know this very well. Were they to read Nietzsche they would guess that his secret is a fear of their powerful, annihilating giggles.

Thanks to their authors, adulterous women like Emma and Anna in the end cannot giggle and have nowhere to turn. That is how Flaubert and Tolstoy arrange matters. The highly conditional compassion of the one and the judgmental adoration of the other wind up at exactly the same point, self-murder. What liberated man-hater would not point and nod and gloat? Emma and Anna have fallen into the hands of patriarchs. A female writer, Kate Chopin for example, has no difficulty arranging quite a different outcome. In her genially subversive story "The Storm," adultery is, so to speak, a win-win proposition.

• • •

Anna captivates Vronsky but she also flirts with Levin. Tolstoy knows already how to be Vronsky but he is trying to be Levin. Levin is the Tolstoy who resists, the incipiently puritanical Tolstoy who some years later will compose "Why Do Men Stupefy Themselves?"

and "What is Art?". Tolstoy had a nature rich enough to spread over a dozen time zones. No wonder Matthew Arnold thought *Anna Karenina* not a work of art at all but "life itself." *Madame Bovary* seems to suffer by comparison, yet this is only because Flaubert is ferociously faithful to the actual. Arnold wanted art and life to be rich and beautiful and edifying all at once. He mistrusts an art like Flaubert's; besides, as an Englishman he is bound to look askance at anything French. However, a Russian, far to the East and so on the outskirts of European civilization, is virtually beyond critique. Tolstoy can be celebrated as a force of nature who makes Arnold succumb to Anna's "charm":

> ... *Madame Bovary*, with this taint, is a work of petri-fied feeling; over it hangs an atmosphere of bitterness, irony, impotence; not a personage in the book to rejoice or console us; the springs of freshness and feeling are not there to create such personages. Emma Bovary follows a course in some respects like that of Anna, but where, in Emma Bovary, is Anna's charm? The treasures of compas-sion, tenderness, insight, which alone, amid such guilt and misery, can enable charm to subsist and to emerge, are wanting to Flaubert. He is cruel, with the cruelty of petrified feeling, to his poor heroine; he pursues her without pity or pause, as with malignity; he is harder upon her himself than any reader even, I think, will be inclined to be.

Arnold is so deliberately and even naively chivalrous that he claims more compassion for Emma than her creator. It seems an odd claim, though. Can a reader feel more deeply, let alone better comprehend, a character than her author? Can even Matthew Arnold outstrip Flaubert's "*Madame Bovary, c'est moi*"? In any case, I don't think Emma would be pleased by Arnold's remarks. I believe she would prefer Flaubert's cruelty to Arnold's backhanded sympathy.

• • •

Civilized people routinely betray in private what they espouse in public. Less obvious is that they themselves accede to the very restrictions they violate. It cannot be argued that people do not support a rule simply because they violate it. Even in a permissive society there is always plenty of room for hypocrisy.

Freud saw human society under threat because it requires what he called the "inhibition of aim." It likewise demands a lot of lying and this too causes hostility to civilization, and not on the part of the unruly beasts, but on the part of the upright. Among the peculiarities of human society is that impudence in the violation of rules is more readily condemned than the transgression itself. Sins and crimes, after all, can be forgiven if they are acknowledged with remorse; they may even be overlooked if they are committed with proper discretion. But the sinner who neither repents nor bothers to conceal her sin will not be ignored or forgiven. Ostracism is the usual result, particularly on the part of those who lack not the inclination but the courage to sin themselves. That sort of honesty infuriates. It is too wild, while shame serves as a token of tameness. Don Giovanni is just such a monster of impudence—heroic and lost. Mozart closes his opera with everybody singing a jolly ditty over the pit into which the Don, defiant to the end, has been dragged. These singers constitute a civilization that is righteous, relieved, restored, looking down on the repressed as if waking from their own libidinous dreams.

Very well. The social is not the moral in so far as the former demands concealment and the latter revelation: the truth, the whole truth, and nothing but. Naturally, then, Anna fares worse in a social sense than Emma but better in a moral one. I like the way J. P. Stern puts it:

> It is significant that, quite unlike Emma... Anna does not have to go through a degrading phase of lies and subterfuges. She tells her husband of her adultery, she forces him... and therefore all of society to recognize and

even to accept what she has done… And such a situation is difficult to imagine with Emma, if only because the secrecy of her love-affair is an integral part of that turgid sensuality on which she lives.

Unlike Emma, Anna is moral in her immorality. Or, you could say she attempts to rescue her soul from her immorality by publicizing it while her concealment further sullies Emma's. Twist this idea a little further and you get an inversion of Kant's dictum that the best test of the morality of an act is a willingness to make it public. Kant probably couldn't imagine a time like ours, dense with unwanted confessions, when publicity would, in effect, displace morality.

Since everyone sins, Anna's ostracism must be the consequence of her nobility more than her sin. In a sense, Karenin is able to retain his icy dignity because of her sacrifice, her *virtue*, whereas it is impossible for Charles Bovary to look anything but a fool.

• • •

Emma's hands play with her dress, the fringe on her shawl; she fingers the damask tablecloth and stares at the silver samovar shining in the sun. Anna sits calmly, superior without in the least trying to be. Her voice is deeper, her posture straighter; even her French is more correct than Emma's. How exasperated poor Madame Bovary is by all this, and how eager not to show it. She had accepted the invitation with the pleasant thought of their having so much in common. Nevertheless, all afternoon long it has been only of their differences that she can think or speak.

She looks at her hostess with narrowed eyes and says spitefully: "Oh, if only I'd been you. If I'd only been *you* I'd never, never have told!"

EDITOR'S NOTE:

The following sources are cited by Fein:

Arnold, Matthew, *Essays in Criticism: Second Series*, London, 1898

Freud, Sigmund, *Civilization and Its Discontents*, trans. James Strachey, New York, 1961

Stern, J. P., *Re-intepretations*, New York, 1964

Trilling, Lionel, *The Opposing Self*, New York, 1955

ON DICKENS AND MILL

The answer to anyone who talks of the surplus
population is to ask him whether he is the surplus
population...

-G. K. Chesterton

EDITOR'S INTRODUCTION

Sidney Fein affixed a couple of notes to the manuscript from
which I have assembled the following essay. While such notes are
uncharacteristic, in fact Fein was doing something fairly typical:
thinking on several planes at the same time. His central preoccupation was the contrarian one of showing the kinship of Dickens and
Mill, interesting in its own right, but perhaps more so in conjunction with the two notes.

It would be fitting had Fein written the first note in advance of his
essay and the second after abandoning it. In his file for 1976 both
notes follow the essay but this proves nothing. Fein would have
placed the essay first if, as I believe, his intention were to return to
it and prepare it for publication.

In 1976, Fein taught his first course on ethical philosophy, a night
course that met once a week from six to nine. The students were
mostly adults who had already put in a full day's work, evidently
making them a little slower and sleepier than they might otherwise
have been. In the first note, Fein describes how this course became
the occasion of his essay.

Note One:

Two commonplace pedagogical propositions: a) teachers learn from their students; b) the best way to master a subject is to teach it. Seldom mentioned is how the first may derive from the second; I mean that the learning of teachers can owe as much to the sluggishness of their students as to their unspoiled insights. Simply by sitting silent and perplexed dull students can spur their teacher to toil like Sisyphus as he tries to push them up Mount Anagnorisis.

Judging from their essays, my night students are bright; however, in class they are so weighed down by weariness that some evenings this intelligence of theirs might as well not exist. From six to seven they would profit more from a nap than a lecture. The slower they think the more desperately I do.

This week brought such an emergency. I wanted them to grasp Mill's egoistic altruism, how, on a view of human nature as selfish and pleasure-seeking, he prescribes that the highest and most durable pleasure lies in promoting that of others. Mill's elegantly precise and reasonable English either baffled or failed to persuade them and my rendering in plain American was no more successful. It was owing to professorial frenzy that *A Christmas Carol* popped into my head. I asked if they all knew the story, which they did, though some knew only the Mr. Magoo version. What followed was pure improvisation; I'd never before thought of Mill in connection with Dickens' tale yet the moment I did—right there in front of those twenty-three ambitious but drowsy students—the correspondences were obvious.

I went to the board and drew two cartoons. The first showed Scrooge scowling in nightcap and gown, hunched in on himself, clutching a money bag; in the second, Scrooge sported an expansive smile and was leaping merrily in the air, flinging about pound notes and half-crowns. Under the first I wrote "12/24," under the second "12/25". As I scribbled the dates I quoted Thornton Wilder: "Money's like manure. It should be spread around to help young things grow." Then the class began to work and then… etcetera.

The second note paints with a broad brush. Fein drops names like ponderous rose petals, anticipating some of what he was later to develop in his last book, *Aristocratic Democracy*. He also makes a prophecy. Evidently the train of thought suggested by his class on Mill chugged into the future as he anticipates a kind of replay of the mid-nineteenth century crisis on a planetary scale.

Note Two:

As the seventeenth and eighteenth centuries are to epistemology and politics, so the nineteenth is to economic thought, not merely as specialized theory (specialization being the specialty of our own century) but in the broadest sense, which means with no separation from ethics. I would even argue that no matter the theory—whether that of Smith, Malthus, Ricardo, Mill, or Marx—the *ethical* aim was always the same. It is the one formulated by Bentham: the greatest happiness for the greatest number. This offended the great anti-utopian individualists of the spirit, like Kierkegaard and Dostoyevsky; but the real opposition to such general benevolence lay with Spencer's Social Darwinism and the heroic immoralism of Nietzsche insisting that the individual always comes before the group. Still, it is the optimistic Adam Smith who provides the baseline to which all the others react. Smith failed to foresee the misery the policy of *laissez-faire* would produce once industrialization took hold and was conjoined with the repressive politics deployed to sustain it. It's not his fault, but Smith implied three decades of Metternich's world order. The accumulated excrement hit the fan in 1848, the year of both Mill's *Principles of Political Economy* and Marx and Engel's *Communist Manifesto*. Smith, Mill, and Marx—these remain the three essential alternatives that have dominated economic debate ever since: unregulated free markets in everything from coffee to wages, the so-called "mixed economy" of regulated or even Keynesian capitalism, and central planning—the first and last being the most repressive. The West has largely opted for the wishy-washy middle ground, with North America inclining toward Smith and Europe toward Marx.

As businesses spread over the earth, I expect the old debate will be renewed, perhaps under different names. Multinational corporations will favor ruthless *laissez-faire*, provoking a Marxist, anarchist, or socialist opposition. As for the liberals in the wealthy countries, they will call for regulation on a global scale and redistribution, restrained by the cost to their standard of living. The debate might also be overtaken by events, such as a world-wide economic collapse induced by protectionism redux, some environmental cataclysm, or big wars between rich nations competing over resources or between haves and have-nots armed with weapons of mass destruction.

The most reasonable alternative, now as then, the happiest, most moderate, least repressive and theoretical—that is to say, the most *English*—is, of course, Mill's, or Dickens'. "We must love one another or die" is too vague. Scrooge has to love Tiny Tim or else.

DICKENS AND MILL
Over Port and Cigars

TO commemorate the eightieth anniversary of the publication of *A Christmas Carol*, the public was presented with a facsimile edition, preceded by a rip-roaring introduction by G. K. Chesterton. Chesterton so combines liveliness with conviction that it is easy to be carried away by him. His chief claim even has a kind of glamour. This is that Dickens, the anti-Grinch, single-handedly rescued Christmas. From whom? Chesterton mentions two would-be Yulicides, "the seventeenth-century Puritans," who simply failed to kill off the holiday, and "the nineteenth-century Utilitarians" who were presumably frustrated in their aim by the immensely popular story of Scrooge. But for Dickens, he writes, "The very word Christmas would now sound like the word

Candlemas. Perhaps the very word carol would sound like the word villanelle" (vii).

Sometimes we simply agree with a text, but often we insist a text we happen to love agrees with us, even if it doesn't. This must be especially true for people whose sympathies are broader than their opinions, like the reactionary Chesterton. So, he sees Dickens as a Chestertonian, fighting "the final pitched battle against the new theories (ix)," an indignant looker-backward, a stout hold-out, like himself, against a soulless, joyless, vicious modernity who favors a merrier, more Catholic Olde England. Frankly, this doesn't sound quite right. The denomination of Dickens' Christmas has always seemed to me Victorian rather than Catholic or even Anglican. Still, Chesterton is certainly right about Dickens' promotion of the holiday; in fact, merchandisers really ought to put up a bronze plaque in his honor in every department store.

What is provoking about Chesterton's comments is his insistence that the unregenerate Scrooge is the embodiment of Utilitarianism. Everybody is sure that Dickens hates Utilitarianism. Even Dickens is certain of it, and he set out to prove it in *Hard Times*. But, to me, it is precisely the redeemed Scrooge who ideally exemplifies the internal sanction and universal ethical hedonism prescribed by the still Utilitarian and pre-socialist John Stuart Mill in his essay of 1863. Chesterton makes his point this way:

> ... [T]he old miser has the new arguments. Scrooge is a utilitarian and an individualist; that is, he is a miser in theory as well as practice. He utters all the sophistries by which the age of machinery has tried to turn the virtue of charity into a vice. (ix)

Of course it is possible Chesterton is thinking of Bentham's cold calculation rather than Mill's "love of loving," the former's relentlessly quantitative ethics rather than the latter's sympathetically qualitative kind. However, when he wants to show Scrooge's superiority over the "enlightened" employers of the twentieth century, who would deny the poor even "their Christmas ale," Chesterton backhandedly compliments what he calls Scrooge's individualism. Here it seems clear that it is not Bentham but the Mill of *On Liberty* he has in mind:

> [Scrooge] believed at least in the negative liberty of the Utilitarians. He was ready to live and let live, even if the standard of living was very near to that of dying and letting die. He partook of gruel while his nephew partook of punch; but it never occurred to him that he could forcibly forbid a grown man like his nephew to consume punch, or coerce him into consuming gruel. (x-xi)

Chesterton must have been a brilliant dinner companion. I can imagine his dazzling discourse over the roast beef and Yorkshire pudding continuing during the retreat to the billiard room. But still, I would want to resist him. "Oh, come now, Chesterton," I see myself retorting over port and cigars while affecting an Oxbridge accent. "That's a bit thick. Gruel or punch, live and let die, miserliness as Utilitarian dogma? You're a great man, Gilbert, and I'm sorry to have to say it, but you're committing a vulgar error. I can only conclude that you're so offended by Mill's atheism that you willfully overlook his humanity, and so enchanted by Dickens' humanity that you imagine he's as ultramontane as yourself. If you want my opinion, Dickens, whom you revere, has *exactly dramatized* in advance what Mill, whom you detest, was to write twenty years later." After that, I would be wittily put down, of course, but not, I think, refuted.

SCROOGE AND MARLEY AND
MALTHUS AND MILL

I can be schematic. *A Christmas Carol* is the perennially appealing tale of one man gone right but also an allegory aimed at inspiring a class, an entire society, to go right. The symbolism is as transparent as Dickens' biographer Edgar Johnson says:

> Dickens—as always when he is deeply moved and most profound— is speaking in terms of unavowed allegory... *A Christmas Carol* is in reality... a serio-comic parable of social redemption... Scrooge is the embodiment of all that concentration upon material power and callous indifference to the welfare of human beings that the economists had erected into a system... The conversion of Scrooge is an image of the conversion for which Dickens hopes among mankind. (489)

As Johnson airily observes, "What could be simpler?" The contemporary economists who appeared to make a system of selfishness—not just the red-meat free marketeer Herbert Spencer but also the well-meaning rivals Malthus and Ricardo—were challenged also by John Stuart Mill who, with no hope in supernatural intercession but just as much humanity and bluntness, also calls for a conversion of the capitalists. Mill is all about the transmutation of individual psychological hedonism into the universal ethical variety, making a selfish altruism the base on which both public policy and private charity ought to rest. In Chapter Two of *Utilitarianism*, he sums up both his program and Dickens' theme:

> The multiplication of happiness is, according to the utilitarian ethics, the object of virtue: the occasions on which any person... has it in his power to do this on an extended scale, in other words to be a public benefactor, are but exceptional; and on these occasions alone he is called on to consider public utility; in every other case,

private utility, the interest or happiness of some few persons, is all he has to attend to. (26-27)

Scrooge seems too indelible a character to be a mere allegory; and yet that is what he is, an incarnation of that depressing theory of Malthus that prompted Carlyle to nickname economics "the dismal science." But Dickens is a marvel, and he can enliven even the most dismal theory. In introducing his protagonist, he deploys five active participles to reinforce Scrooge as Hand, the rough side of Adam Smith's famously invisible and providential one:

> [He] was a tight-fisted hand at the grindstone, Scrooge! A squeezing, wrenching, grasping, scraping, clutching, covetous old sinner! (3)

Malthus and Ricardo sound cold, but no more than Scrooge, who "iced his office in the dog-days; and didn't thaw it one degree at Christmas" (4). So insensitive is the man of business that he feels the winter weather as little as the way he is ignored on the street. Scrooge's foil is, of course, his nephew Fred, who on his first appearance is described as if he were a cheery fire:

> He had so heated himself with rapid walking in the fog and frost ... that he was all in a glow; his face was ruddy and handsome; his eyes sparkled, and his breath smoked again. (Ibid.)

Scrooge's incarnation of cold and insensitive economic theory becomes explicit when he replies with rhetorical questions to the two gentlemen collecting for the poor:

> "Are there no prisons? ... And Union workhouses? ... The Treadmill and the Poor Law are in full vigour, then?" (13)

These words will be thrown in his face by the Spirits; but still more telling is what Scrooge says to the gentleman who objects that many would prefer death to the workhouse:

"If they would rather die... they had better do it, and decrease the excess population." (Ibid.)

The excess population. Here is Scrooge summoning up Malthus's gloomy calculation that population increases geometrically while cultivated land expands, at best, arithmetically. Before Malthus, nobody conceived of a surplus population; indeed, population was thought to be the real "wealth of nations." The Reverend Malthus put paid to that blithe notion and began to intone like John on Patmos. "The view," he wrote, "has a melancholy hue." Robert Heilbroner sums up Malthus' grim prospect:

> [T]he larger portion of mankind would forever be subjected to some kind of misery or other. For somehow the huge and ever potentially widening gap must be sealed: population, after all, cannot exist without food. Hence among the primitives such customs as infanticide; hence war, disease, and, above all, poverty. (90)

Thomas Malthus was not an inhumane man and he did not relish what he had discovered; but he's nonetheless relentless:

> Famine seems to be the last, the most dreadful resource of nature. The power of population is so superior to the power of the earth to provide subsistence... that premature death must in some shape or other visit the human race. The vices of mankind are active and able ministers of depopulation... But should they fail in this war of extermination, sickly seasons, epidemics, pestilence, and plague advance in terrific array and sweep off their thousands and tens of thousands. (Quoted by Heilbroner, Ibid.)

My point is simply that in Dickens' allegory the "excess population" is epitomized by the weakest, apparently most useless, and least fit to survive. Dickens certainly knew what Malthus wrote.

Malthus was generally reviled and universally quoted at the time. Dickens also knew that the sufferings of "thousands and tens of thousands" move us—and will move Scrooge—less than one brave, cheerful, crippled little boy whose very crutch is more full of life than most subway cars.

Scrooge is famously transformed overnight, but he isn't changed at once. His redemption requires a whole curriculum and the process is exactly the one outlined by Mill.

The program Scrooge gets with on Christmas Eve is a course in what Mill calls the two sorts of sanctions, external and internal. Of the former Mill says, with an uncharacteristic nod to religion à la Dickens':

> They are the hope of favor and the fear of displeasure from our fellow creatures or from the Ruler of the Universe ... (39)

The external sanction is the fear of pain or the loss of love and the hope of pleasure or of winning affection: the electric shock or the biscuit. Freud says the same thing and so do trainers of cocker spaniels. Of course, Mill understands that the weakness of the external sanction lies in its being external; it can't obligate us to caring about others' happiness. A student who doesn't cheat only because the proctor is hovering over her is prudent, not ethical. Cowardice is not morality. Mill is almost dismissive, then, of the external sanction. To him it isn't enough that we be frightened of acting like Scrooge; however, again like Freud and the dog trainer, he admits that the internal sanction of feeling for humanity is only the internalization of the external, though he is quick to correct the idea that it is therefore purely artificial:

> If, as is my own belief, the moral feelings are not innate, but acquired, they are not for that reason the less natural...
> [The] moral faculty, if not part of our nature, is a natural outgrowth from it... (44)

Writing of the same process, Freud fixes the business of socialization with a memorable military metaphor:

> The tension between the harsh super-ego and the ego that is subject to it, is called by us the sense of guilt… Civilization, therefore, obtains mastery over the individual's dangerous desire for aggression by weakening and disarming it and by setting up an agency within him to watch over it, like a garrison in a conquered city. (84)

Once you've got one, the superego is like Joe Louis and your ego like Max Schmelling; you can run but you can't hide. Scrooge has misplaced his superego, or rather has turned it into the principle of profit and cheapness. The internal sanction is what Freud calls aggression channeled against oneself; its strength comes not from the strictness of one's upbringing but the strength of one's own aggression. Scrooge's miserliness is a form of aggression directed against the world in general and the Cratchits in particular. The difference between external and internal control of aggression is chiefly a matter of range of motion. The mother needs to control the child. When he is still an infant she can do so physically; a toddler can be commanded by her loved and feared voice ("People won't like you if you don't share… Stop hitting your sister!"). But as the child's activities extend beyond the reach of hands and voice, the mother needs an implant. In effect, her voice becomes the child's own. Freud calls this voice the superego, Mill the internal sanction, and Disney Jiminy Cricket. In Dickens, it is Scrooge's rectified heart. The internal sanction may be only a continuation of the external one, but it is still vastly different in quality. The child who is spanked by his mother is not the same as the one who punishes himself. Depending on how you look at it, the latter is civilized, moral, or neurotic.

Since *A Christmas Carol* recapitulates this process rather strictly, Dickens starts Scrooge off with the external sanction. Marley may be Scrooge's savior, or his intercessor (Marley-as-Mary), but his *initial* function is to threaten: if you don't mend your ways you'll wind up like me. Throughout the story Dickens animates objects— Scrooge's house, the door knocker, Tiny Tim's crutch. I particularly like his description of Marley's chain:

> It was made... of cash-boxes, keys, padlocks, ledgers, deeds, and heavy purses wrought in steel. (25)

This commercial chain is a sort of charm bracelet, a synecdoche for the sins of Scrooge's class as well as the punishment that awaits him, implying not only the cosmic spanking that is at hand but the reasons for it:

> "I wear the chain I forged in life... I made it link by link, and yard by yard; I girded it on my own free will... [W]ould you know the weight and length of the strong coil you bear yourself?" (25)

Marley's Utilitarian lesson couldn't be clearer; for he says he is "doomed to wander through the world... and witness what [I] cannot share, but might have shared on earth, and turned to happiness" (30). Dickens' anticipation of Mill's ethics is complete when Marley adds:

> "Not to know that any Christian spirit working kindly in its little sphere... will find its mortal life too short for its vast means of usefulness... Mankind was my business. The common welfare was my business..." (33)

Marley, like Mill, knows that he can't scare Scrooge straight. Fear is merely a prologue, the introductory lecture that sets up the course but converts no one to the discipline. Therefore, the task of the three spirits is to implant the internal sanction. "Without their visits... you cannot hope to shun the path I tread..." (35) Scrooge must learn in his old bones that the worst of hell for the countless specters he sees outside his window is the unhappiness of being unable to make others happy. For Mill, too, the conversion must be to a new form of happiness:

> [E]ducation and opinion, which have so vast a power
> over human character, should so use that power as to
> establish in the mind of every individual an indissoluble
> association between his own happiness and the good of
> the whole... (24)

The happy Utilitarian is not dour but hearty, not ascetic but generous to others and himself.

ONTOGENY RECAPITULATES ONTOGENY

Scrooge has to re-live his childhood because it is in childhood that the moral feelings are implanted. Scrooge's journey is propelled by sentiment. To prepare for it, the Spirit of Christmas Past literally touches his heart, reviving that shriveled organ: "Its gentle touch... appeared still present in the old man's sense of feeling" (49). But feeling unfocused is not in itself going to promote general utility. For active compassion imagination is indispensable. The degenerate Scrooge is not only a miser but a philistine. So, Dickens shows Scrooge his boyish self, alone in the musty schoolroom on Christmas Eve, but happily picturing scenes from *The Arabian Nights* and *Robinson Crusoe*.

This episode puts me in mind of Mill and his own education. In his estimation, the breakdown that he suffered at twenty-one was a function of his father's extraordinary home schooling. James Mill too was a "tight-fisted hand at the grindstone." The curriculum is well known: Greek at three, Latin and math by eight, logic mastered at twelve, economics at thirteen, no holidays and no pals. Music was actually forbidden and when any poetry was assigned it was sure to be accompanied by Bentham's dictum: "Quantities of pleasure being equal, push-pin is as good as poetry." Of his father, Mill wrote that he "regarded as an aberration of the moral standard of modern Romantic times the great stress laid upon feeling." Emotion was too unreliable to promote general utility; only reason would do. Dickens understood that frigidity in the pursuit of virtue is as unprepossessing as cold selfishness, especially to children. It took Mill until he was twenty-one to arrive at the same insight.

It was over a sentimental incident in a novel (not one of Dickens', of course, but it might as well have been) that the Benthamite house James Mill had made of his son's mind crashed. Mill wept, realized that even achieving a society decent in every way wouldn't make him personally happy, and determined that he was not "a stick or a stone." What saved him is what saves Scrooge, a conversion, an immersion in feeling—first the poetry of Wordsworth and then the affections of Harriet Taylor, an attachment Mill's father also abhorred. Poetry, which Mill called "the very culture of the feelings," he now rated not merely on a par with ethical philosophy but its *sine qua non*, a prerequisite. There is a personal, not to say Oedipal, element in Mill's vehement revisionism, as there is rebellion in his passion for Mrs. Taylor. To Rousseauian compassion Jeremy Bentham and James Mill had preferred stolid British self-interest, albeit socially enlightened. Mill, the converted Romantic, made feeling the pin in the pinwheel of his emended Utilitarianism, and these are the same feelings that people look for in their annual reading of *A Christmas Carol.*

Dickens' faith is more in childhood than Christianity and so, once he thinks about the one he missed, is Mill's. The degeneration of Scrooge from sensitive boy and Fezziwig's cheerful apprentice to the young man who chooses money over love, the useless citizen and miserly exploiter, is nicely outlined in Chapter Two of *Utilitarianism*:

> Capacity for the nobler feelings is in most natures a very tender plant, easily killed, not only by hostile influences, but by mere want of sustenance; and in the majority of young persons it speedily dies away if the occupations

to which their position in life has devoted them... are not favorable to keeping that higher capacity in exercise. (14-15)

The moral risk of business is that business will be all. Poor Scrooge failed to take to heart the example of his first employer. Watching Fezziwig's Christmas party, Scrooge is not only recapturing his earlier self but getting a second chance at an object lesson in humane business practices and the Utilitarian union of ethics and economics. "During the whole of this time, Scrooge had acted like a man out of his wits. His heart and soul were in the scene, and with his former self" (62). It is all arranged so he will learn the Utilitarian lesson, that his own happiness depends on the happiness of others. The Spirit is so confident of the lesson that he can afford to tease:

"A small matter," said the Ghost, "to make these silly folks so full of gratitude."

"Small!" echoed Scrooge. (63)

Feeling, generosity, imagination, his sister's tenderness, boyhood associations, Fezziwig's gladness—all are essential to Scrooge's re-education, just as Mill's rebellious conviction that quality of pleasure is more important than quantity was to his: "It is better to be a human being dissatisfied than a pig satisfied..." (14). For Mill, dissatisfaction is an engine of progress. Dissatisfied human beings are the ones who write Child Labor laws and worry about Tiny Tim's health.

The lesson is ruthlessly reinforced. Fezziwig shows Scrooge how to be the ideal boss of a patriarchal capitalism; the dowerless fiancée bitterly hopes money will comfort Scrooge when she does not; he sees her among her children and, having none himself, is enchanted by her eldest daughter. Overwhelmed by his loneliness, Scrooge cries out like Gertrude riven in twain: "I cannot bear it!"

It's interesting, though, that Dickens should give us a hint of what, apart from simple avarice, so altered the young Scrooge. After all, why *did* Scrooge change? On the personal level, there's the hint that his father, like Mill's, could be an ogre; for when Fan comes to fetch him home from school she says, "Father is so much kinder than he used to be, that Home's like Heaven!" (54). But we hear nothing further of Scrooge père. More serious is Scrooge's harsh judgment of the world he lives in, the world of *laissez-faire*, the Corn Laws, and David Ricardo:

> "There is nothing on which [the world] is so hard as poverty; and there is nothing it professes to condemn with such severity as the pursuit of wealth." (67)

To Dickens this worldly wisdom is sophistry, for it does not take into account the effects of pursuing wealth to the exclusion of all else and does not oppose to the relentless external sanction of poverty the mitigating internal one of duty and love. It's the latter—though not without years of protest and struggle—that has given us minimum-wage laws, workman's compensation, Social Security, and the five-day week.

SCROOGE RISES WHEN HE FALLS FOR TINY TIM

Scrooge's bourgeois unhappiness, the misery of a Hobbesian pool ball sealed off from and merely colliding with other pool balls, is precisely the one described by Mill:

> When people who are tolerably fortunate in their outward lot do not find in life sufficient enjoyment to make it valuable to them, the cause generally is, caring for nobody but themselves. To those who have neither public nor private affections, the excitements of life are much curtailed, and in any case dwindle in value as the

time approaches when all selfish interests must be terminated by death; while those who leave after them objects of personal affection, and especially those who have also cultivated a fellow feeling with the collective interests of mankind, retain as lively an interest in life on the eve of death as in the vigor of youth and health. (20)

The ground of feeling having been prepared, Scrooge next needs an outlet for his new-found empathy. The Ghost of Christmas Present takes Scrooge to observe the Cratchits keep the holiday. Here all is activity, joy, and mutual affection in the face of poverty. It is significant that Scrooge's first reaction to watching the Cratchits' Christmas dinner is: "Spirit, ... tell me if Tiny Tim will live." The Ghost throws Scrooge's words back at him: "What then? If he be like to die, he had better do it, and decrease the surplus population" (96). Malthus's theory the Spirit calls "wicked cant" and he reminds Scrooge that, "It may be, that in the sight of Heaven, you are more worthless and less fit to live than millions like this poor man's child..." (96-97). If a crippled child is a surplus, what is an unfeeling miser?

The Spirit whisks Scrooge on a tour of miners on a moor, a barren lighthouse, a ship at sea, and finally to his nephew's party, where the company is laughing at Scrooge. What's to be done? Fred gives the answer, reminding us that *miser* and *miserable* share an etymology: "... his offences carry their own punishment... His wealth is of no use to him. He don't do any good with it" (107). Such was Mill's carrot for the captains of industry. But there was a stick too, another kind of external sanction—bloody insurrection. And this too Dickens anticipates when, at the end of the tour, the Ghost pulls two wretched, starved allegorical toddlers from the folds of his robe, Want and Ignorance. Do nothing to repair them "And bide the end," he admonishes Scrooge and all the plutocrats of Britain (118). Utilitarianism implies that only reform can save capitalism from merited destruction. In 1852, Mill said that if he had to choose between the current state of affairs and communism, he'd go with the latter, a point whose force depends on knowing how little the speaker cares for communism.

Dickens and Mill are hardly revolutionaries. Scrooge should pay Cratchit better and allow him more days off; the capitalists should pony up for sewer systems, public education, and imported grain; but neither Dickens or Mill questions the *right* of Scrooge to decide, neither gives up on private property; they want it used for the public good. Both understand the power of self-interest and so the effectiveness of a profit incentive to generate new wealth. In fact, the sharing out of private wealth is what both understand by a happy ending. There will be no expropriating of the expropriators. Mill remains English, not Continental, an empiricist and no rationalist in love with theory. He understood the dangers of ideas like Marx's and that communism could turn into a tyranny of surveillance and conformity: "No society in which eccentricity is a matter of reproach," he wrote, "can be in a wholesome state" (see Heilbroner, 132). Here is a pair of authentic Englishmen: Dickens is the world's champion manufacturer of eccentrics, and Mill preferred them to the risk of turning the Greatest Happiness Principle into an inefficient and totalitarian program distributing dwindling wealth. Better that Cratchit should be grateful to Scrooge and see him as his benefactor. Better patriarchal capitalism than everybody anxiously calling everybody else comrade. So let Scrooge's hand remain on the tiller so long as it is an open hand, not a grasping fist. In Utilitarian economic theory as well as in a Dickens' dénouement, *amor vincit omnia*. Scrooge has to love Tiny Tim. They are, in a sense, one. As the Ghost of Christmas Future reveals, they can save one another from dying on the same day.

As an economist, Mill's great insight was the one implied by Dickens, that economic laws should govern production but not distribution (see Heilbroner, 128). Economics provides the money to buy the prize turkey but Scrooge is free to decide to give it to the Cratchits, to make sport at his nephew's party, and to use his cash to save Tiny Tim. Though less moving, Mill's version is every bit as clear:

> The distribution of wealth... depends on the laws and customs of society. The rules by which it is determined are what the opinions and feelings of the ruling portion of the community make them, and are very different in different ages and countries, and might be still more different, if mankind so chose... (Quoted by Heilbroner, 129)

The finale of "A Christmas Carol" is as flamboyantly congenial as it should be, concise, unforgettable, and almost more dream-like than the dreams that precede it. The language of the Scrooge who awakes on Christmas morning is that of rebirth; he even speaks in the short sentences of a child: "I don't know anything. I'm quite a baby. Never mind. I don't care. I'd rather be a baby." He is filled with the happy anticipation of doing good to others, especially to one particular other. It's a nice touch to have him crow over the prize turkey he intends for the Cratchits by exclaiming, "It's twice the size of Tiny Tim" (156). So, Tim doesn't die and the human face Mill sought for capitalism turns out to be that of Ebenezer Scrooge.

A BIBLIOGRAPHICAL NOTE:

A Christmas Carol belongs to all humankind who neither can nor want to resist it. The tale has come to function as a modern myth, like those of Faust and Don Juan, a common shorthand available to be alluded to on appropriate occasions. In fact, Scrooge is the antithesis of those heroes because he is saved and they are damned. Faust and Don Juan wind up as high-brow operatic heroes, while Scrooge gets a musical, a popular carol written in a major key. Like the Ghost of Christmas Present, *A Christmas Carol* sheds general joy, fulfilling Mill's injunction by promoting the greatest happiness of countless numbers of audiences. But the fate of the original manuscript offers a fitting irony all its own.

According to B. W. Matz, editor of the facsimile edition, Dickens presented the manuscript of *A Christmas Carol* to an old school fellow named Thomas Mitton, who sold it to a London bookseller from whose hands it passed into those of a Mr. Churchill (not the famous one), after which it landed with a bookseller in Birmingham, who sold it to one Stuart Samuel and this Stuart Samuel sold it to J. P. Morgan (xiv).

WORKS CITED

Charles Dickens, *A Christmas Carol*, facsimile edition, London: Chapman and Hall, 1923

Sigmund Freud, *Civilization and Its Discontents*, New York: W. W. Norton, 1961

Robert Heilbroner, *The Worldly Philosophers*, New York: Simon and Schuster, 1953

Edgar Johnson, *Charles Dickens: His Tragedy and Triumph*, New York: Simon and Schuster, 1952

John Stuart Mill, *Utilitarianism*, London: Longmans, Green, 1897

ON PHILIPPE
LECONTE DUPARC

One of Teste's pet notions, and not his least fanciful,
was his wish to keep art itself—Ars—and yet do
away with the illusions of artists and writers. He
could not stomach the stupid pretensions of poets—
nor the vulgar pretensions of novelists. He insisted
that clear ideas about what one is doing lead to far
more surprising and widely valid results than all the
humbug about inspiration...

- Paul Valéry

O N Friday, December 9, 1938, Philippe Leconte Duparc was joined in matrimony to Leah Oppenheim in the Registry Office at the Hotel de Ville in Rouen. It was the only occasion on which they met. At the time Leah was stateless, a refugee in double trouble: Jewish like Walter Benjamin and, like Bertolt Brecht, a Marxist. The marriage provided her with French citizenship and so saved her from being deported, which was its purpose. The bride was twenty-four, the groom thirty-nine. The couple who had chanced to mention Leah's plight to Duparc, and had thus brought them together, lived in Rouen, made the arrangements, and served as witnesses. Immediately following the ceremony, the groom returned to Paris, while the bride and her comrades enjoyed a good lunch.

Apparently Duparc never spoke about this generous act, at least not in public; however, he wrote many letters to Leah over the next four years, the shortest and last begging her to leave France, but most comprised entertaining narratives of his life in Paris and miscellaneous *jeux d'esprit*. It seems Duparc liked to make up plots of imaginary American films and devise hilariously candid political speeches which he put into the mouths of Chamberlain, Churchill, Hitler, Goebbels, Stalin, Roosevelt, and a shoal of French ministers—prime, secondary, and tertiary. Duparc could be deliciously acerbic, and found fault with everybody save only the abandoned Czechs and the ill-placed Poles. Overdogs did not appeal to him; underdogs sometimes did.

The longest of these letters describes an alternate universe in which the Germans do not invade, or even exist, where Duparc and Leah become a thoroughly bourgeois couple with three healthy children, two girls and a boy, whose charms and deficiencies are laid out in detail. In this version of history, the couple own both an apartment in the Troisième Arrondissement and a summer house in Aix-en-Provence. They form the hub of a circle of well-placed, eccentric, talented friends in the arts, business, and politics, all of whom have amusing problems. Not only are the couple's circumstances entirely different, so are their tastes and personalities. Leah becomes a moderate conservative while Duparc is disgusted by everything published after *Notre Dame de Paris*. In none of these letters can one find a single poem of Duparc's. In fact, it is conceivable Leah Oppenheim, his wife, was unaware of his literary work.

Leah saved all of Duparc's letters and had them returned to him by a couple from Carcassonne with whom she deposited them days before her arrest. Her final letter to Duparc was enclosed with them. It consisted of a single sentence: "It would appear you were right."

By the time Duparc died in 1956 he was pretty much forgotten. In those fractious years leading to the end of both the Fourth Republic and the French Empire, when political significance was ascribed to every gesture and France had almost as many political parties as cheeses, neither the Left nor the Right wished to remember, let alone claim, Duparc. Anyway, he had never been more than an outlying bulb in the cultural chandelier of the inter-war years.

I had never heard of Duparc at all until I chanced on a paragraph of his in a collection of essays on modern French poetry. The essay is not by Duparc, but the author reprints what he had to say in 1926 on the topic of writing poems about summertime. The comments piqued my interest. They struck me as weirdly apodictic yet curiously persuasive; moreover, I liked that I couldn't say how serious Duparc was when laying down the law.

APROPOS LES POÈMES D'ÉTÉ:

The ratio of adjectives to verbs should never fall below 3:1. The ideal summer day is spent at ease looking appreciatively at vegetation, all that blooms, soughs, bends in the breeze, all that flutters, dresses skimpily, lies still. A line of at least five stresses should always be chosen to accord with the *chaise longue*, a slim sunbather stretched full-length on her towel, a dozing retriever breathing slowly on its side. This line should convey the hula-like undulations of foliage, clouds languidly gathering for a refreshing late-afternoon storm, the aroma of privet hedges and wet tiles. The poetry of summer must describe all things patiently, lingeringly, as if it were too sultry for the least haste. Never anything staccato or too clever. Each season possesses its own melancholy and summer's may be insinuated; however, this must be accomplished with nearly weightless touches. In the end a sunny, airy mood should prevail, as in Mozart a major dominant will triumph over a minor tonic. As for oppressive heat, glare, and the listlessness induced by sodden air, one should resist the temptation to yield to prefabricated, infernal metaphors. In fact, it is preferable to dwell on the coolness of the indoors, shaded patios and broad-leafed trees. Always bear in mind that summer is the season of positive hedonism, as winter is of the negative. Summer poetry should have a sound-track made of bird song, the chirring of insects, the noise of happy children. There will be flowers in profusion, plants in general, but they will only be vivid if one uses their precise common names. Queen Anne's Lace, Black-Eyed Susan, Bee's Balm. Everything should be done to immerse the reader in nature at her most dense and intrusive, to convey a vitality and fullness consistent with stillness. Nothing need be excluded except bloodthirsty mosquitoes, poison ivy, and sunburnt adolescents.

Early in 1939, the anti-Semitic Comtesse de Mornay conceived a passion for Duparc. He was content to satisfy her desire but always remained icily silent when she started in on the Jews. According to a confidant who wrote about this episode after the war, Duparc dealt with the woman via sexual games. He would *pretend* to be Jewish: "After all, I'm circumcised; it shouldn't be so difficult for you." In this way, the lady could enjoy being dominated by a lower order of being or, conversely, dominating and "torturing" the Christ-killer. According to my source, the affair ended when Duparc went too far with the game of Jew-ravishing-Christian and when he told her the story of Heinrich Heine's wife, who complained to a visitor from Germany that she couldn't comprehend why "Henri" always hung about with so many Jews in Paris.

In 1926 Duparc was a member of one of those manifesto-issuing movements that cluttered and enlivened French cultural life at the time. It was a disorganized sort of movement and never succeeded in becoming an *ism*. It did issue a Latin motto, however: *Ars Sine Leges Vanum*, something like that. Many of Duparc's rules for the writing of poetry were produced for the two numbers of the group's journal, *Vituperatio*, which I suppose was from the Latin for *stricture* rather than the root of *vituperation*—not that these semi-serious enthusiasts couldn't whip up a dollop of vituperation when they wanted. Their short reviews of work by non-members are vitriolic. With the help of the Alliance Française, I have been able to obtain a microfilm of the two numbers. The cover of the first has a perfectly realistic picture of a nude woman divided into small squares, as if neatly diced. It begins with the manifesto which runs to three pages of breathless claptrap. The general idea seems to have been to call for *restriction* in art (as if art could manage without restrictions or keep itself from violating them); however, this call for limits seems more subversive than, as one might expect, conservative. The great point is that only restrictions that are self-imposed are valid. That which is not chosen is anathematized as *inauthentic*. Restrictions, however, need not be invented by the artist. One may choose to write a sonnet or a sestina, heroic couplets or a Homeric epic in hexameters. Tradition is the enemy of creative freedom only if it is an imposition. Restriction is understood broadly: "*Vers libre* is neither more nor less valid than *terza rima*. An artist must be free to make new choices, even unprecedented ones. Needless to say, a poet may write *against* poetry, so long as the result is a good poem in which case it is not against poetry but for it. The poet may elect any style except no style at all." Rules seem to matter immensely to these people, but more as a conception than in any practical sense; they are pretty vague about what the rules are.

Duparc's contributions, on the other hand, are comparatively clear. The following is from the second and last issue of the journal. My apology for the translation, a poor one but mine own.

EN ÉCRIVANT LES POÈMES D'AMOUR

Sincerity is as fatal to love poetry as original love poems are lethal to passion. Yet, love *without* poetry is dumb, inelegant, senseless. This appears to be a problem. The love poem that fails to persuade us that someone loves somebody else is simply ridiculous; but a poet, even a poet in love, is not a diarist or a journalist. The truth of sentiment is no better justification for bad verse than for any other crime of passion. It is notable that the greatest proportion of good love poems concerns the unrequited variety. This is scarcely surprising, since unrequited love— with its longing, pining, aching, yearning, reproaching— sharpens the senses, focuses the mind, and hones diction; moreover, denial of the physical leads one to the spiritual, as Plato said. The truth is that gratified love has too little to say for itself, and a good thing too. Requited love is smug, complacent, and overweight; moreover, to speak much of satisfied love is in poor taste, a form of protesting too much. Clean linen does not require airing and ought to be worn next to the skin, under the clothes. Frustration is bad for lovers, good for poets. Is there a single decent poem about married love? Such misbegotten poems offer merely the reiteration of stale feelings poured into the mold of banal conventions. It is imperative for good love poetry to convey at once involvement and detachment. That is to say, good love poetry is essentially dialectical, drawing power from the tension of disharmony while marriages are unlikely to survive such tension. If you mean to write a poem expressing love be sure that the emphasis only appears to be on the object of your desire; take care that, in reality, the klieg light falls on the nature of your desire. Half of all bad love poetry is subjectivity masquerading as objectivity (as in the tediously familiar metaphors for the beloved's lips, voice, hair, etc.); the other half is objectivity passing itself off as subjectivity (as in the no-less-tedious formulae concerning the peregrinations of the lover's "heart"). A hundredweight of love sonnets is not unlike a hundredweight of chocolates. They are all more or less the same and, taken collectively, disgustingly cloying. It is the pain of love, its cheating allure, its undoing, above all its loss that works on the page. The beloved, like the lady on Keats' urn, must always elude the lover, at least if the lover intends to set up as a serious poet. Women of sensibility thoroughly understand this and so are never seduced by good love poems. Bad poems can, however, sometimes work, because the badness is in direct proportion to the lover's sincerity. Love requires some poetry but the reverse is equally true. Nature's arrangement for perpetuating the species is the most potent of all the poetry-inciting emotions. Love must bear the responsibility for more wretched poetry than anything else. If the poem is merely a means to an end, like two glasses of champagne, then the quality of the poem need not be of the *premier cru* to achieve its effect. In fact, the worse the wine and the poorer the poem, the better their chances. I will grant that a good love poem may begin with genuine feeling— where else could it receive its impetus? —but then the serious poet must at once begin to stray from this coarseness of feeling. He will be like the ship that makes a half-degree error in setting its course and winds up at a more exotic destination, perhaps on another continent. This is only to say that words will concern such a poet more than the sentiment that sought them out. There are exceptions—Shakespeare's sonnets, for example. Nevertheless, even here, it is the pain and abasement of the Dark Lady poems that linger with one the longest. *Th' expense of spirit in a waste of shame is lust in action* is surely among the best and most sincere of love poems. Next to it, even the sublime but conventional praise for the young man pales—as, one suspects, the young man's perfections did beside the Lady's vastly superior defects. She, in short, is real, whereas the boy evanesces into "pure poetry." When

hunted and *hated* coalesce into the unstated *haunted* one
thinks, here at last is a love poem that tells the truth.

To many of his contemporaries, Duparc looked like an oppor-
tunist, an unreliable man who would change opinions and sides
depending on need or advantage. He married a Jewish woman and
never slept with her; he slept with an anti-Semitic aristocrat and
never married her. He preached the virtue of regulation, of limits,
yet subverts orthodoxy and jumbles tradition into the cigar box
with Surrealism and Dada. Is he a man of the Left or the Right?
In Duparc's time, even more than ours, it mattered. It mattered to
Duparc too. One of his better aphorisms is this: "Certainly politics
is a form of ethics—unfortunately, it is the very worst form."

What appeared to be opportunism was, in my opinion, Duparc's
perpetual striving after balance. In his way, he was a radical moderate,
one who took into account the ethical imperfection of his species,
including himself, much as Monsieur Teste does here:

> I do good and evil. The same mind, the same hands, the
> same goads, do both. And the man I am when I do good
> is not absent in the man I am when I do evil. For I have
> but two hands and one mind; and it is not I who defined
> the two attributes of human conduct, good and evil. It is
> some stranger to me, and to us...

This is why I find Duparc's most characteristic poem—morally
and aesthetically—to be *L'Art du Funambule*, here rendered by a
translator far nimbler than myself:

THE ART OF TIGHTROPE WALKING

The unbalanced extol balance
rigor and flux
lean this way and that, arms out
head and heart

equipoise escapes us anyway
female and male
we feel it as a just rebuke
wrong and right
or worse, think That's it as we drop
motion and stillness
down and up, now and then, left and right
true and false
to grant each opposite its due
suave and gauche
season blandness with lemongrass
sweet and savory
and fill all time zones with our breadth
here and where
assent to every counterpoint
lucid and dim
leaven solemnity with wit
lofty and low
poke around the poles but unite
raw and cooked
our riven selves' extremities
foot and mouth
perceive the form yet kick the thing
ideal and real
never to totter or tumble
naive and knowing
in untidy drawers or passions
apathy and love
balance is a mode not a mean
deficiency and glut
calm perhaps, never quite serene
open and shut.

The trick of tightrope-walking is simply leaning to the left, then to the right. Duparc attempted to maintain a satisfactory equipoise by embracing self-division, laid out in the even-numbered lines of his poem. As for good and evil, these he regarded as attributes of conduct and he acknowledged that his conduct could go either way. As Teste says acutely, the same *goads* may push one in either direction.

One day, Duparc read in the newspaper of a street peddler who had been arrested and charged with the theft of a valuable necklace from a jewelry store outside of which he happened to have set up his table on the day of the crime. This peddler, Borescu, was a Rumanian refugee and while the necklace, described in glittering detail in the article, was not recovered, the man was a convenient target for the police. Now, Duparc had seen just such a necklace adorning the throat of a wealthy young lady known to him and a few others to be something of a kleptomaniac. At a dinner party he attended, the woman behaved like a child with a new toy, inviting people to admire her necklace. Duparc took it on himself to have a word with a certain *juge d'instruction* with whom he had been at school.

"It must be done discreetly, you understand, but I expect she'll pay up or return the goods. Either way, Borescu should be released."

"And if the lady denies it?"

"I'll hire a lawyer for the fellow. A good one who'll know how to show your lot up."

The *juge*, who related the story to a journalist after the war, wished to know how sure Duparc was. The woman was, after all, the daughter of an influential industrialist.

"Let's say I'm a great deal more certain that the lady lifted the necklace than you can be that the peddler did. Will *that* do, Monsieur le Juge?"

Around the same time Duparc was doing this good deed, he got wind that a journal planned to publish an essay by a young leftist poet and critic. Word got out that the piece was to be an assault on Duparc's entire generation of poets, arraigning them for the crimes of formalism, political disengagement, aestheticism, and self-absorption. Duparc approached the editor and promised him a new story by Charles Avensœur, then very much *à la mode*, if he would withdraw the piece. What Duparc promised to Avensœur is unknown. The essay was not printed while an Avensœur story was, albeit a second-rate effort. Duparc's action did not remain secret and hurt his reputation, especially when the young poet/critic blew himself up during the war and became a hero of the Resistance.

Baudelaire: "Commerce is in its essence *Satanic*… [T]he least infamous of all businessmen is the one who says: Let us be virtuous in order to earn more money than the fools who are corrupt. For the businessman, honesty itself is a lucrative speculation."

Duparc wrote occasional essays, like Montaigne, though his real topic is not always clear. One of them appears to be about business, in particular business and morality. He begins by citing the above passage from Baudelaire, who also wrote of business that it "is *natural* and therefore *infamous*." Duparc wryly observes, "The consummate dandy is at pains to maintain a pose his existence undermines. He despises nature but cannot manage without her oxygen and vegetables; he disdains business yet finds agricultural surpluses and haberdashers indispensable. Moreover, for the dandy whatever is *infamous* will sooner or later become attractive." Notwithstanding this demurral, Duparc goes on to support Baudelaire's point about commercial honesty with a story.

A wealthy friend of his, "a great name on the Bourse, but far too well-read and agreeable a fellow ever to talk shop," was begged at a dinner party by less affluent men to confide the secret of his success. "Reluctantly, my friend the mogul agreed but warned the company that they were unlikely to find what he told them pleasing. 'Go on, go on,' they said." Duparc says that he alone remained silent.

He admits that he is fond of the magnate and esteems his success, but insists that he shares Baudelaire's temperamental distaste for money-making. As for his saying nothing, Duparc characterizes his silence in the spirit of his tightrope-walker: "My silence in that company was not so much real silence as the vector of two contrary, unmade speeches."

The businessman relates how, at the start of his career, he had persuaded a dozen investors to put substantial sums into a canal-building project.

"I acted in good faith, you understand. It was supposed to speed up shipping on the Danube and it might have done so too, if only it had actually been dug. As it turned out, I had been naïve. The bulk of the money was siphoned off by crooked contractors. However, things had been arranged in such a way that my fee was paid before the work began—so I could easily and with impunity have realized a small fortune from the deal. But I chose not to do so. In fact, I took my fee, mortgaged my family house, and liquidated my family's holdings to pay back those investors."

The men at the table gasped and put down their cognacs. "You ruined yourself?" one exclaimed.

"Oh, on the contrary," replied the millionaire complacently as he cut the end off a Havana cigar, "though I admit I couldn't positively *know* it at the time, and my family called me all sorts of vile names, including the worst of all—*romantic*." Here he paused to light his smoke then proceeded. "I sensed that my decision was prudent. And so it proved. Such a story always makes the rounds. People believed, like you, that I had ruined myself to pay off a debt of honor. It made my reputation. Never since have I had the least difficulty in raising capital or securing partners for any enterprise."

The moral Duparc draws at the end of this piece returns not only to Baudelaire but poetry. "As in commerce, so in poetry: form is an honorable and tactical scruple, faithfulness to the rule the most prudent speculation. The writer who proves himself both competent and true to his chosen principles gains our trust—Baudelaire himself is an excellent example—and then there is nowhere we will not follow him."

Duparc evidently admired Baudelaire who is given a star turn in another of his amusing directions for writing poems, this one regarding poems about cats.

Sur Les Poèmes Félins:

It is to be deplored but, sooner or later, most poets are reduced to writing at least one set of verses about a cat. A few such indiscretions can be overlooked but it is sad when a poet writes compulsively about cats; one senses the cat is his sole companion, both subject and muse. It goes without saying that, in general, the urge to write about cats ought to be repressed. As a subject, the cat is too "poetic" to generate good poetry. It is possible to write a quite decent poem about, say, a steam engine or a retaining wall by setting down the essence of the object. Through poetry alone we are able to do what Kant said we can't and grasp the *Ding-an-sich*—but, as a subject ,the cat is too suggestive, too prefabricated: a cat is, so to say, born an animated metaphor. Still, since there seems to be no avoiding the cat poem, a few strictures may be laid down. Item: never anthropomorphize cats. To do so is a capital error that lands the poet in a bog of mawkishness, a thicket of obscurantism, a miasma of sensuality. Second, be definite about your cat. Only objectivity can save you. Make the reader see just this cat and nothing else. Third, the movements of your cat should be at the core of the poem; never begin with the cat-as-icon or, worse yet, cat-as-correlative. A dog may remain motionless and still proclaim its caninity, but a cat that is absolutely stationary ceases to be fully feline, loses her flexibility and hardens to a mineral—or, still worse, an Egyptian statuette. While the cat may be used to suggest mystery—I allow that is permissible—it should never mystify. Your cat may be described as a companion, but bear in mind that it will take great skill and some measure of sincerity to persuade the reader that a cat can really make a satisfactory companion. In *Les Fleurs du Mal*, Baudelaire includes no less than three sonnets about cats. The best by far is the first (no. 34). It is also the only one devoted to a *singular* cat.

> Come to my amorous heart, my lovely cat.
> Into your soft paws retract your sharp claws
> And let me plunge into your fine eyes,
> Admixtures of metal and of agate.

I find this alloy of metal and agate particularly admirable. The other two (nos. 51 and 66) are about plural cats, thus cats abstracted into a sort of hyper-poetical felinity. Though I say it with compunction, for me, these fall flat, peopled and catted as they are with theoretical cutouts:

> Fervent lovers and austere scholars
> Both love, in their mature season,
> The powerful gentle cats, pride of the house,
> Which like them are sensitive to the cold and
>   sedentary.

Too sedentary by half. As for kittens, obviously they are off-limits. If one must write about a cat at least make sure she has arrived at her majority, as Baudelaire did in the magisterial mode of No. 34. "Le Chat" is not merely a good poem about a cat but a sublime sonnet in which the poet contrives something alchemical, transmuting cat into mistress, mistress into cat:

... from your paws to your head,

An astute air, a perilous perfume,

Wafts about your brown body.

Duparc was neither wealthy nor poor. He inherited a decent sum from his mother, invested it wisely, and eked out his living by writing. During the Occupation, he published a series of genre novels under pseudonyms—mediocre detective stories and historical romances, satisfying the time's understandably escapist urge—while writing poetry for himself and those clever letters to Leah Oppenheim Duparc. The poems of the war period are mostly lyrical, in minor keys. Here and there a note of protest or indignation can be heard, now and then a breeze of anger blows through the refined and stuffy room, but then futility takes over again and these impulses are smothered under a static and indifferent beauty.

There are few published interviews with Duparc perhaps, in part, because he gave journalists a hard time. Asked by one if he were a neoclassicist, he answered with a Gallic shrug. Asked if he were of Israelite descent, he replied with a Yiddish one. Asked how he would describe the kind of poetry he wrote, he retorted dryly, "Contemporary French poetry."

Despite his pose, Duparc's intellectual attachments ran fairly deep. In one interview he briskly summed them up: "In poetry an errant Parnassian, in temperament a would-be Stoic, in diet a lapsed vegetarian, in politics a convinced Epicurean, and in religion a faithless Kierkegaardian." Of all these aspirational witticisms the one that really counted, given the times in which he lived, is the obscure one about Epicurean politics. Duparc was not being cynical. Epicurus believed in the rule of law, a social contract, and justice as mutual advantage. These are reasonable, moderate positions, not idealistic or ideological ones. But underlying them is Epicurus' belief in the futility of public life in general and political hope in particular. All of Epicurus' views are defensive, whether he is speaking of the gods (they don't care, nothing to hope or fear from them), ethics (being good is not violating the law, since breaking it brings more pain than abiding by it), physics (nothing out there but matter in motion in a void), diet (fruit, bread, water), or death (being dead's just what it was like before you were born—remember?). Epicurus is the philosopher of middle-aged hedonism whose game is avoiding anxiety and pain, not pursuing joy or pleasure. He recommends intellectual pleasures only because they produce no hangovers, spread no venereal diseases, and clog no arteries. Epicureanism is a colossal defense mechanism, a huge trench work, the template for all rationalizations of life.

Epicurus' father was an Athenian colonist in Samos. From him Epicurus inherited Athenian citizenship and so owed the city two years' military service. When he was eighteen he traveled to Athens for training. This happened to be in 323 B.C., the year Alexander the Great died—by poison, as I believe. When the news arrived from Babylon, the patriotic Athenians rose up against their occupiers to reclaim their liberty but were crushed by the Macedonian phalanx in a matter of months. Perhaps, then, Duparc's mention of Epicurean politics is an indirect comment on the Resistance, a justification for his own detachment. It suggests that he, like Epicurus, was not so much a defeatist as a man without faith in the public world or those who professed faith in it. In his way, he too sought *ataraxia*, a negative freedom from pain and anxiety; however, Duparc was not a philosopher but a poet. Conscience, vanity, and enthusiasm easily got the better of him.

One of Duparc's last poems—it would be fitting were it the *very* last—is a commentary whose two titles are made from Epicurus' aphorism on the mortality of body and soul, both of which he conceived as organized atoms that, in death, disintegrate.

So Long as We Exist, Death is Not With Us

You on a motorcycle, I in a balloon.
The road moved, and the clouds.
We moved. You fast and low,
I palely high and wanly slow.
My Uncle George ate a spoilt oyster.
Your grandfather went mad.
Two and a half wars broke out
like Cousin Corinne's acne, very bad.
You showed me me in a photograph;
it's a sort of proof, a negative,
you said, ocular proof, you said.
Somebody had a child or two
and one of them dropped dead.

But When We Are Dead, Then We Do Not Exist

Silence isn't silent, sleep isn't sleeping,
darkness isn't dark, meaning isn't meaning.
The sandals on my feet I will not feel,
the blushes on the beach I will not feel.
History comes to many ends
by several means, you said:
that was your invariable lesson.
Shall we lie down now, shall we?
See? the bed is well made now.
Don't worry, you said, because the
coffee is already cold. But I'll miss
the breezes I'll miss, I said. I will.
Bonne nuit, you sighed, then gave me a kiss.

I discovered this essay in Fein's folder for the year 1982. It is a holograph; Fein never typed it up, though he may have intended to do so. He seems to have been interrupted, first by an urgent request for a review, then by returning to work on *Aristocratic Democracy* (1984), to which the political elements in the essay are perhaps related.

I have been unable to find any record of a Philippe Leconte Duparc. I believe Fein made him up. It might be objected that Fein was writing about a real person and simply changed his name, choosing the middle name "Leconte" as an allusion to the nineteenth-century Parnassian Leconte de Lisle, whom Duparc somewhat resembles and claims to emulate. However, I have also been unable to trace any of the writings of Duparc cited in the piece or the putative, ephemeral journal *Vituperatio*. My conclusion is that Fein has written an appreciation of a poet-critic whom he invented in order to appreciate.

The question, then, is why Fein should do such a thing. I can think of three possibilities: a) as an exercise, b) as a *jeu d'esprit* à la Duparc, or c) to get at something more serious, to work out some problem. The three motives hardly exclude one another. In fact, it is characteristic of Fein to approach a problem in a spirit of playful experiment. I believe the real incentive behind the essay is the last, while the other two are not motives but methods. I admit that the problem behind the essay is never stated, but this is as typical of Fein as he says it is of Duparc. Unlike a classical composer, Fein liked to wait until the end to state his theme.

The epigraph from Valéry's *Monsieur Teste* provides a clue. Teste is in favor of *Ars* but unenthusiastic about the pretensions of the artists who produce it. Fein probably meant that Duparc felt the same way. Monsieur Teste comes close to being pure mind and this may also reflect Duparc's detached approach to living. The second quotation from Teste concerns moral ambiguity and the dangerous idea that standards of conduct are alien not just to him but "to us." I feel certain that Fein would not have agreed with this. So, it seems reasonable to suppose that what was on Fein's mind was the vexed relationship between art and ethics—and, given Duparc's historical situation, politics as well.

Teste wants art to be preserved but not "the illusions" of artists. Possibly Fein himself felt the same way at times and yet his account of Duparc suggests the impossibility, the inhumanity, of insisting on the distinction. Duparc is more implicated in the emotional untidiness of life, including "the illusions of artists and writers," than he preferred to be. No doubt the pretensions of artists can be tiresome and make one yearn for "clear ideas," but then one is on the way to becoming a mathematician. Duparc, unlike Teste, is a poet, and this in itself diminishes his detachment from the messiness of making art. He is also entangled in his time, however reluctantly, and this is a hindrance to his moral disengagement. Duparc marries out of spontaneous indignation; he repairs an injustice done a refugee because he can and therefore must. Yet, out of vanity, he interferes with the publication of an essay critical of him and his friends. He carries on an affair with a despicable woman to humiliate her. Duparc tries not to take sides when not to do so is almost criminal. Perhaps Duparc is Fein's portrait of Baudelaire's dandy in the twentieth century. Like Teste, the splenetic author *Les Fleurs du Mal* also comes in for two mentions.

Fein says Duparc's most essential metaphor about himself, his most "existential" statement so to speak, is not the leap of faith (he is "a faithless Kierkegaardian") but the opposite: balancing on a tightrope, leaning two ways at once, or being silent as the vector of two contrary speeches. Very likely Fein meant to create an alter-ego for his own high-wire act. Sartre said of Baudelaire that his attitude was that of "a man leaning on himself, like Narcissus." Like Baudelaire and Monsieur Teste, Fein and Duparc understand themselves to an exceptional degree; they lean on themselves and nothing else. All three scrutinize themselves acting and thinking and then write about it. Duparc wants contrary things because his nature is contrary, contrary to itself. The tightrope-walker who commits himself fully is bound to fall. Fein, however, was too humane not to be skeptical about such athletic skepticism.

Taken as a whole, though, the heft of this peculiar essay is more light than heavy. If it is at all serious, then it is a serious *jeu d'esprit*. Fein is having fun here, especially with Duparc's rules for writing poems. Like the essay itself, these regulations are not to be taken in earnest but then neither can they be laughed off either.

ON IRREVERENCE

Not Elijah

"So, how old are you? Five? Six?"

"I'm eleven, actually."

"As old as that? And you don't even have your own apartment? Why, at your age I'd been evicted from three of them. Okay. So, what's your line of work?"

"You're very silly. I go to school."

"No, *Still* in school? And you call *me* silly? By the time I was your age, unless you're exaggerating about being eleven, I'd already been fired as a stoker on the Queen Mary and was well into the last half of a career as a stockbroker. You don't mean to say you haven't failed at *anything* yet?"

"My grades are pretty good. So, no, not so far."

"As the Arkansas groom said to his twelve-year-old bride, time's a-wastin'. Do you at least have some *prospects* of failing?"

"No, but I suppose it's not unlikely."

"Not unlikely, eh? Well, I'm *not unsurprised* you speak *not unpompously*, what with all those *not bad* grades. Still, what you said is profoundly true if not truly profound. Like they say in the Bronx, you can't win 'em all, but out in Chicago they know you *can* lose 'em all. Myself, I'm a perfectionist."

"You mean you're a Cubs fan?"

"My dear old bean, the Cubs are like the Church. They haven't got fans, just devoted flagellants, half-hearted masochists, the kind of people who can't kick a habit."

Nowadays Jerry Teitelbaum is a big-shot microbiologist, which means he knows a lot about life from the ground up. I've heard that within his field Jerry can't be surprised. But he can surprise me. For example, it was a shock to learn he didn't agree with a famous colleague, a doughty ecological campaigner who's always reminding us polluters we're just part of nature. "If that were entirely so," mused Jerry, "then we couldn't be responsible for nature, could we?" Jerry's good at gossip. He told me that at a conference on global warming this celebrated sage opined that the most efficient way to save the planet would be to shoot Americans. "When he called for questions, I asked—very politely, of course—if he would care to begin with himself." It's always a treat to grab lunch with Jerry. He's like a heart surgeon who can tap dance.

We touched base last week at a deli over corned beef on rye and pickled tomatoes. I confessed how, when I was a kid, I thought "kosher" was an ancient Hebrew method for extracting the flavor from food. This turned the conversation to childhood cuisine and that led Jerry to his Proustianly detailed recollection of a fifty-year-old seder in Albany. The guest-in-chief at his family's house that Pesach was Groucho Marx. It was a memorable lunch of memories and we both laughed more boisterously than is becoming in middle-aged fathers of daughters.

Now, back to Jerry's Seder story.

There was this formidable woman at the dinner, Viola Malkin, my grandmother's best friend. She drove a red Cadillac convertible, kept all the dietary laws, and wouldn't touch meat. This she announced proudly to Groucho while passing him the platter of lamb.

"Well, Viola," Groucho said as if meaning to be gallant, "if I ever become a cannibal, I promise to eat only female vegetarians. Orthodox ones."

Mrs. Malkin giggled nervously. I don't think I'd ever seen her giggle before. Her face looked like it might shatter.

"You mean your mother didn't keep kosher, Mr. Marx?"

"Well, we were all bottom-feeders ourselves but, as these things go, I guess Minnie kept *fairly* kosher. We never had a pork roast. My brothers, of course, are a different kettle of gefilte fish. When he wasn't chasing shiksas, which wasn't often, Chico couldn't get enough Italian sausage. Sweet or hot, made no difference to Chico. And Harpo would gobble up Canadian bacon like a lumberjack, even when we weren't playing Saskatchewan. As for Zeppo, he'd hop the *Hindenberg* to Westphalia for just one bite of their ham. And we *all* love jumbo shrimp, the jumboer the better. Even Gummo, who's something of a shrimp himself. So, you see?"

Mrs. Malkin looked scandalized. This suited her better than mirth. "And your mother *accepted* this?"

"Minnie? 'You boys break my heart,' she'd cry out. She cried it out like Big Ben, every hour on the hour, and we'd cry back, 'Yeah, we boys, you Jane.' So, tell me, Viola, do you come here often or just when your husband's messing around with his secretary?"

Jerry swore he wasn't making it up, said all these vignettes from that evening flooded back as he talked, that his memory was apparently studded with shallow graves.

I asked how people reacted to Groucho's performance, how he did.

Jerry grinned. "Well, everybody knew who Groucho was, of course, that all those Marx boys were sex maniacs, allergic to inhibition, anarchists in perpetual rut, hostile to authority. My mother was completely serene. She sat the foot of the table like a treasure chest watching Long John Silver. Treasure chests don't get hanged. Pirates sometimes do, but they make entertaining guests. I'd say pretty much everybody went along. I mean the men behaved as if being insulted by Groucho were a real distinction. As for the ladies, they acted as though getting felt up by him was an honor—and *not* was a disgrace."

"What about you? You were eleven. Did you think it was just some kind of floor show?"

"Now, that's an idea—a floor show for Seder. But, look, I'd seen *A Day at the Races* so I was in awe. No, that's not right. What I felt was that Groucho was more of a child than I was. Forget the cigars, he had that knack. I wasn't in awe of *him* but of his effect on the *adults*, especially since our Seders usually oscillated between boring and stiflingly sanctimonious. In the movie, Groucho played a veterinarian passing himself off as a doctor. He was a false authority, a deceiver, an incompetent. There was nothing sweet about him the way there was with his brothers. Harpo and Chico always had scenes with adoring kids, enchanting them by playing harp and piano. Not Groucho. *His* thing was perforating grown-ups. In the movie, all these adults had it coming. But this was our *Seder*, you know? I expected *some*body to object, to stand up and point a finger like Jeremiah; but the truth is they *loved* getting punctured."

"So Groucho was invited to be irreverent? Did he at least dial it back during the service?"

Jerry cut a slice of green tomato, forked it into his mouth, chewed it ruminatively.

"On the contrary. He couldn't have been more relentless if he were getting paid for it. Since I was sitting next to him he directed a lot of his wisecracks my way, but always loud enough so that everybody could hear, even deaf Uncle Nathan. I'll give you an example. After I'd done the Four Questions he said that even if I *was* the youngest *he* had four questions too. I remember one was about Elijah. He asked me if, when I opened the door for Elijah at the end of the service, the prophet actually showed up—if for some mysterious reason he picked Albany for his comeback—he'd get three glasses of wine to catch up. Oh, I just remembered another. He wanted to know what the Angel of Death did about Egyptian twins and whether manna came both seeded and seedless. Then there was *Dayenu*. That was another routine. He sang his own version. It went something like this: If He'd sent the Babylonians, *Dayenu*; if He'd sent the Assyrians, *Dayenu*; if He'd sent Haman, *Dayenu*; if He'd sent the Romans, *Dayenu*; if He'd sent the Inquisition, *Dayenu*; the pogroms and the Nazis and the Arabs, *Dayenu*—but why Molly Goldberg and Herman Wouk? Wasn't *dayenu dayenu*?"

I told Jerry the story about the priest who accosted Groucho in a hotel lobby and asked for his autograph. "It's for my mother, Groucho," said the priest. "She's your biggest fan." "Really?" Groucho shot back. "I thought you fellas weren't allowed to *have* mothers."

Jerry chortled. "A little masterpiece."

It was this lunch with Jerry, who once enjoyed a Seder with Groucho Marx, that's gotten me thinking about irreverence.

SPECTRUM OF IRREVERENCE

Like light, political opinion, and complaining, there is a spectrum of irreverence. At one end is profanity, at the other vituperation. Blasphemy is an assault on perfection; irreverence is an assault on the *claim* to perfection.

Irreverence in a vacuum is feeble and insignificant; that is, it only flourishes in a context of reverence, just as lying requires the expectation of truthfulness. It is no accident that the great age of European irreverence (and pornography) was the end of the Victorian period which gave us Shaw, Wilde, Sacher-Masoch, de Kock, but also Freud and Picasso. *Les Demoiselles d'Avignon* is an irreverent picture; *The Interpretation of Dreams* demolishes the veneration of family life and childhood innocence. Decades of religious and social pieties were required to produce the irreverence of modernism. At its finest irreverence is a corrective; it restores balance. What good is it to run about with a fistful of sharp pins if there aren't any balloons? Groucho needs Margaret Dumont, a bearded faculty, a thousand stuffed shirts, but they need him, too. I expect Jerry Teitelbaum, precocious though he doubtless was at eleven, did not find it so easy to distinguish scurrilous ill-nature from a well-placed puncture wound, to tell the difference between a Groucho-as-Thersites and a Groucho-as-Undershaft. He must have been perplexed by the adults' licensing of all those insults. No doubt some of them were cowed by the comedian's celebrity, but at least a few—maybe the serene Mrs. Teitelbaum—sensed his indignation was with human-kind and knew there was nothing personal in his insults. Groucho explodes self-importance, puffed-up Platonic types, unwarranted self-esteem. But at that Seder he was not insulting people he actually knew and maybe that is why they could glory in his acidu-lous attention. The Fool is permitted to mock Lear, but he never denies his master's royalty. Impersonal irreverence is often enter-taining and salutary; the personal kind, less so. This will account for why Groucho Marx's wives and children do not seem to remember him as kindly as the rest of us.

All reverence is either religious or modeled on religious subordi-nation. But irreverence is not always antagonistic to religion. In fact, irreverence in its very highest form is a religious attitude. Religious people can be magnificently irreverent, especially when provoked by the nominal devotion of sleep-walkers calling themselves believers.

Religious irreverence is not only remedial; it is edifying, as it is aimed at razing the false so as to build up the true. Pious irrev-erence is the last recourse of the believer, the furthest point of a once-moderate argument. That great paradoxophile Kierkegaard complained that it is all but impossible to be a Christian in a Chris-tian country; that is, one where everybody is sure they achieved this status when a few drops of water were dripped on their heads at the age of fourteen days. He is infuriated at seeing what he deems the most difficult of tasks dismissed as the easiest—and, worse, one to be gotten beyond. It is Kierkegaard's wrath as much as his ideas that made him beget Existentialism. It was his fury that drew the attention of his countrymen; I mean his act of public irreverence in attacking the just-deceased, highly esteemed Bishop Mynster, head of the Danish Lutheran Church. Kierkegaard said the old man might have been eminently clubbable but he was certainly not, as his eulogist put it, "a witness for the truth." To Kierkegaard only a felt idea counts, only concepts so passionately lived that they cease to be concepts. Kierkegaard was endlessly sarcastic about Hegel, but he was far more irreverent about the counterfeiters of what concerned him most. One of the last things he wrote, just after he had completed the tenth and final installment of *The Instant*, is this elegant Parthian shot aimed at the state-supported professional Christians of the tidy Kingdom of Denmark:

> The actor is an honest man who plainly says, "I am an actor."
>
> One never gets a priest to say that, at any price.
>
> No, the "priest" thinks he is the very opposite of an actor. Entirely without prejudice (because he knows that it does not apply to him) he will raise and answer the question whether an actor may be buried in Christian ground. It never occurs to him (a masterpiece of scenic art, if it is not stupidity) that he is cointerested in the decision of this question, yes, that even if it is decided in favor of the actor, it nevertheless might be doubtful whether it is justifiable for the priest to be buried in Christian ground.

Another sort of religious irreverence is common in Zen Buddhist texts where the masters do not address those who are indifferent to enlightenment, or who simulate it, but sincere seekers going down the wrong path and whose reverence is therefore an error. An example, concise even by Zen standards, is the answer of Wen-yen to a novice's question, "What is the Buddha-nature?" "A dried stick of dung," he replied. No doubt the novice was anticipating something rather different—say, "The Buddha is like that white cloud floating high above the Blue Mountains." Such an answer would have divided the world when the point is its unity, that the Buddha-nature is in everything. Conceive it as a cloud—pure, weightless, clean, above the earth—and the chain is broken. But if the Buddha-nature can be in a stick of dried dung then it is also in the cloud, the Blue Mountains, even in the novice.

The irreverence of the reverent is not mockery but therapy. It is not set up against reverence but misapprehension. The Hasidic zaddiks are like the Zen masters in provoking sudden enlightenment through conversations with misguided seekers. Consider this reproof from Rabbi Menachem Mendel: "When a man makes a reverent face before a face that is no face—that is idol worship." Martin Buber's *Tales of the Hasidim* is studded with pious irreverence. Rabbi Moshe Leib made a typically Jewish moral point, but did so by praising atheism, which must have startled his davening, kosher-keeping, phylactery-and-yarmulke-sporting disciples out of their self-satisfaction:

> [T]o what end can the denial of God have been created?
>
> This too can be uplifted through deeds of charity. For if someone comes to you and asks your help, you shall not turn him off with pious words, saying: "Have faith and take your troubles to God!" You shall act as if there were no God, as if there were only one person in all the world who could help this man—only yourself.

INVERTED AND AMERICAN IRREVERENCE

A kind lady once charged me with false modesty. She meant, of course, to pay me a compliment, or at least to insist that I accept the one she was offering. I demurred. "False modesty," I tried to explain, "is something to which I can only aspire."

Consider somebody who, despite being acclaimed and extolled, cleaves to a relatively accurate self-knowledge and a just self-appraisal. Irreverence for such a person could be a saving grace, a cure for the seduction of seigniorial comportment.

In America, irreverence is almost a founding principle. After all, the nation began with an irreverent letter to His Majesty, George Rex. Democracy is not a political arrangement which encourages reverence. Plato, a descendant of kings, knew how to affect the grand manner and was an aristocrat of the intelligence. Living in the world's original democracy he wrote of its lack of reverence irreverently: "... a charming form of government, full of variety and disorder, and dispensing a sort of equality to equals and unequals alike." Democracy is entirely compatible with boasting and tall tales (Mike Fink, Pecos Bill, Paul Bunyan) and with serious eloquence (Lincoln, FDR, M. L. King, Jr.) but it cannot do without irreverence. President Kennedy, asked how he liked his new job, replied, "The pay's good and I can walk to work." Any President who can say that is unlikely to subvert the Constitution. Richard Nixon would not have been capable of it. This is because Nixon was too reverent; but what Nixon revered was Nixon.

America is the land of Billy Sunday and Billy Graham, and what could be more American than Christian Science? But America is also *Elmer Gantry* and H. L. Mencken. It is our good fortune to have spawned both Theodore Roosevelt and Mark Twain and in almost the same generation. The former was a great man who set out to become a Great Man. In the name of Christian virtue, he banned Tolstoy's *Kreutzer Sonata* and thought well of the Philippine War. Twain is the tonic to TR's dominant. It was Twain who nailed a certain Southern blowhard by calling him "a good Christian in the worst sense." Midwesterners like Twain, Will Rogers, and Kurt Vonnegut sweep from the plains with sharp pins for the grandiosity of the coasts, the zeppelins of high culture. Toward the end of his life Twain received a state visit from Rudyard Kipling, author of "The White Man's Burden" and not one to hide his light under a bushel. As the two were international celebrities, the press gathered outside the door of Twain's Connecticut house, awaiting a joint communiqué. At length, the authors stepped out on to the porch. I don't know what Kipling said—probably a lot—but Twain summed up the summit in a couple of sentences that simultaneously heaped irreverence on the press, Kipling, and himself: "Between us we divided all the world's knowledge. He knew everything, and I knew the rest."

Marx Brothers' movies take place in specially constructed worlds where no authority is worthy of respect but all insist they are. About these films the assiduously impudent Antonin Artaud was hilariously reverent: "... if there is a definite characteristic, a distinct poetic state of mind that can be called *surrealism, Animal Crackers* participated in that state altogether." That's a French anarchist for you—loads of theory and no sense of fun. "If Americans... wish to take these films in a merely humorous sense... so much the worse for them..." Even T.S. Eliot, no Gallic dramaturge, corresponded with Groucho. Apparently, brilliant irreverence can inspire a pretty high-toned reverence.

Irreverence is bracing only if it is not perpetual. Even in comprehensive Marxist send-ups like *A Night at the Opera* and *A Day at the Races* there is always a conventional romance, which the clowns abet. They are on the side of Young Love and so, their own polymorphous libidos notwithstanding, they respect it. Indiscriminate irreverence cannot be a norm without losing its force. Pins are not blunt instruments. It's obvious that Lear needs his Fool, a little less so that the Fool needs his Lear.

Inverted irreverence is a sign of health, of proportion and lucid self-assessment. The mad scientist—the mad *anything*—is only one who suffers from an excess of reverence for himself and all he does. Bertrand Russell understood this pathology very well: "One of the symptoms of an approaching nervous breakdown is the belief that one's work is terribly important."

IRREVERENT RHETORIC

Once upon a time there were magnificent blasphemies, oaths which released great jets of language, the pipe organ of transgression with all its stops pulled out. Certainly, there is a music of irreverence, from diapason to sixteenth-note. Here is an example of the latter. Asked to name the greatest poet in the French language, the courteous André Gide replied, "Victor Hugo, hélas." In just *trois mots justes* Gide burst the blimp of bloated Romanticism and his nation's *amour-propre*.

Irreverence tends to be expansive. As an attitude, it has no fixed boundaries so that even an epigram can seem to be a camel's nose threatening the tent. Theocratic regimes criminalize even minor expressions of irreverence and will not scruple to execute those who use them, at least in public. These governments are as earnest about their dogmas as Artaud is about the Marx Brothers' putative surrealism. George Orwell, always a salutary guide, sets the tone for his "Reflections on Gandhi" with a general marker of level-headed, cautiously paradoxical irreverence: "Saints should always be judged guilty until they are proved innocent..." Saints may be guilt-ridden by their colossal superegos, by all the aggression Freud insists they've internalized; but they may also be inflated by their admirers into swollen icons before whom Orwell, an impeccably sane thinker well provided with pins, is disinclined to bow without solid arguments. He knows that, in the end, idols always demand human sacrifice. Reverence, in short, is more lethal than its opposite.

The explosion of outmoded pieties at the end of the nineteenth century proceeded with pin-thrusts, the irreverent epigrams catalogued by Bartlett. Between Wilde and Shaw and their forebears yawned the gap between the buckboard and the Buick. Both gave lectures that resembled stand-up routines and wrote irreverent plays because humor is an oral art. When you hear a good joke, you can't help wanting to tell it to somebody. While Wilde's irreverence is aesthetic, Shaw's is ethical and political. It is because Shaw thinks big that he deploys a form of irreverence that is agglomerative, swallowing more and more, building like a tsunami or a fugue, accumulating energy before it crashes on the shore and inundates everything he deplores. These speeches would be sermons if it were not for the wicked joy Shaw got from writing them, actors from declaiming them, and audiences from hearing them. Where Wilde's wit moves from paradox to paradox, *bon mots* set up like pictures in a gallery with the portrait of Dorian Gray at the far end, Shaw's wit has a theory behind it. Wilde's humor is pointed, but Shaw's irreverence has a point.

My two favorite examples of the Shavian tidal wave are from the Preface to *Major Barbara* and Act Three of *Man and Superman*. While the first is technically not part of the play, it might as well be a speech by Undershaft. After all, Shaw's gigantic prefaces are barely distinguishable from the rhetorical set-pieces delivered by his alter-egos in the plays. Here Shaw characterizes both himself and his society *in propria persona*:

> Here I am... by class a respectable man, by common sense a hater of waste and disorder, by intellectual constitution legally minded to the verge of pedantry, and by temperament apprehensive and economically disposed to the limit of old-maidishness; yet I am, and have always been, and shall now always be, a revolutionary writer because our laws make law impossible; our liberties destroy all freedom; our property is organized robbery; our morality is an impudent hypocrisy; our wisdom is administered by inexperienced or malexperienced dupes, our power wielded by cowards and weaklings, and our honor false in all its points.

Irreverence is here conveyed not by asserting that the most respected institutions of the British Empire are weak and in need of adjustment, but that they produce exactly the *opposite* of what they promise. With comprehensive irreverence, Shaw declares that the Fabian has become the revolutionary, but his way of saying so shows that the public lecturer has merely relocated from the auditorium to the theater.

More rhetorically potent still is Don Juan's indictment of the ladies and gentlemen of Satan's Epicurean-Edwardian high society which, with ascending adjectival gaiety, gathers together everything Socrates might ever have said to exasperate the Athenians, all anyone *can* say about the contrast between worthy substance and revered appearance:

> Pooh! Why should I be civil to them or to you? In this Palace of Lies a truth or two will not hurt you. Your friends are all the dullest dogs I know. They are not beautiful: they are only decorated. They are not clean: they are only shaved and starched. They are not dignified: they are only fashionably dressed. They are not educated: they are only college passmen. They are not religious: they are only pew-renters. They are not moral: they are only conventional. They are not virtuous: they are only cowardly. They are not even vicious: they are only "frail." They are not artistic: they are only lascivious. They are not prosperous: they are only rich. They are not loyal, they are only servile; not dutiful, only sheepish; not public spirited, only patriotic; not courageous, only quarrelsome; not determined, only obstinate; not masterful, only domineering; not self-controlled, only obtuse; not self-respecting, only vain; not kind, only sentimental; not social, only gregarious; not considerate, only polite; not intelligent, only opinionated; not progressive, only factious; not imaginative, only superstitious; not just, only vindictive; not generous, only propitiatory; not disciplined, only cowed; and not truthful at all: liars every one of them, to the very backbone of their souls.

Selah.

A Short Note on Bad Irreverence

The refusal to respect what is respectable, honor what is honorable, the urge to defile what is innocent—this is irreverence decayed into easy cynicism, the language of the radio talk show. Irreverence misdirected loses its therapeutic value as a corrective and is merely corrosive, an assertion of egoism, the indulgence of a pose, invective rather than satire, with none of Kennedy's witty humility, Gide's polite regret, Shaw's delicious cataloguing. Even unbelievers should be able to distinguish between irreverence and nihilism.

John Wilmot, Second Earl of Rochester, was a master of irreverence, at least of disappointment. He was a proud courtier who put his trust in a capricious prince and ended by writing "Upon Nothing," a sort of topsy-turvy, grudging ode to Nihilism's black hole:

> The Great Man's gratitudes to his best friend,
> Kings' Promises, Whores' Vows,
> tow'rds thee they bend,
> Flow swiftly into thee, and
> in thee ever end.

A cynic is a reformed idealist who misses seeing the world as it is, first by revering it too much and then too little. Vituperation has a mean mouth and blasphemy generally revenges itself. Proper irreverence is a sovereign restorative, a wellspring of wholesome jollity, a petard to explode pretension, a tool for separating the respected from the respectable, a weapon for humiliating those lacking in humility. Bad irreverence is no use at all.

Envoi

I like to imagine Groucho at the open door, irreverent to the last, a sort of Elijah in reverse, bidding adieu to the Teitelbaums with this deathless line: "I've had a perfectly wonderful evening; unfortunately, this wasn't it."

Works Cited

Artaud, Antonin, *The Theater of Its Double*, trans. Mary Caroline Richards, New York: Grove Press, 1958

Buber, Martin, *Tales of the Hasidim: Later Masters*, trans. Olga Marx, New York: Schocken, 1948

Kierkegaard, Søren, *Attack Upon "Christendom,"* trans. Walter Lowrie, Princeton: Princeton University Press, 1968

Orwell, George, *The Orwell Reader*, New York: Harcourt, Brace, Jovanovich, 1956

Plato, *The Republic*, trans. Benjamin Jowett, New York: Modern Library, 1960

Shaw, George Bernard, *Major Barbara*, New York: Penguin, 1977
_____, *Man and Superman*, New York: Penguin, 1972

Suzuki, D. T., *Studies in Zen*, New York: Dell, 1955

Wilmot, John, Earl of Rochester, *Poems*, London: Routledge and Kegan Paul, 1964

Editor's Note

I found "On Irreverence" in Fein's folder for 1979. The manuscript is typed, without corrections or marginal notes, complete with title and the list of cited works. It is exceptional to find a piece Fein evidently considered finished among his papers but not unique. Why wasn't "On Irreverence" published? Well, Fein might have decided that, even though finished, it was not worth publishing. It is also possible that he did send it out and it was rejected. In some cases—and "On Irreverence" may be one—I believe what he had brought to completion was not intended for publication but was written as a kind of occasional essay to be presented to one reader. In this case, there is reason to think Fein intended the essay for the friend who initiated it, the late Gerald Teitelbaum, yeast geneticist and pioneer of recombination technology.

It could be said that "On Irreverence" is less an essay than an anthology, a building made of bricks with Feinian essayism as the mortar holding them together. Fein was obviously fond of subversive Jewish humor, an early fan of Woody Allen and a lifelong one of Groucho Marx. Clearly, he relished their irreverence. But here he expands that category to comprehend everything from Hasidic tales and Zen *mondo*, from a Gide *bon mot* to Shavian stemwinders. Fein finds irreverence in low jokes about sex but also in the sublimities of religious faith. By the end of the essay, the word feels so stretched that a reader might wonder if Fein has rendered it useless. I think, however, that what Fein aims at portraying is not a genre but an attitude, one that he sees as—to use his term—a *corrective*. He casts a wide net for his examples but what he admires in each is irreverence used as a tool to restore balance, never as an end-in-itself. What Fein calls irreverence is distinguished from mere buffoonery, facetiousness, or mockery. Feinian irreverence falls on a spectrum within a still broader spectrum. This is why the tone of his essay is hard to fix—at times serious, at others frivolous, concerned with the aesthetics of the zinger but also the ethics of a humane intelligence. As he says, irreverence is a useful pin in a world with no dearth of balloons.

ON KAFKA'S SENTENCES

SOME time ago I had to deliver a lecture on Oscar Wilde. Unable to come up with anything that wasn't humiliatingly dull, I conceived the fancy of writing a lecture on *The Importance of Being Earnest* as if I were Oscar Wilde. He, I reckoned, was never boring and would hardly speak tediously about his own play. Wilde believed the first priority of a literary critic was to be interesting. The exercise required me to think about how Wilde wrote, and I soon realized he composed at the level of the sentence. This is rarer than might appear. Of course, all writers have to put sentences together, but most seem to think in paragraphs or whole slabs of prose. It is their argument or their plot they have in mind; the fashioning of one-liners would only slow them down. Comedy writers, however, must take care with each sentence. Wilde's famous *bon mots* are also *des phrases bonnes*.

> The only difference between a caprice and a lifelong passion is that caprice lasts a little longer.
> As long as war is regarded as wicked, it will always have its fascination.
> If this is the way Her Majesty treats her prisoners, she doesn't deserve to have any.

George Bernard Shaw was born within a year and a half of Oscar Wilde, the 1850s being an exceptional decade for Irish wit. Though he works on a broader canvas, Shaw likewise does so one brushstroke at a time—admittedly, often rather lengthy strokes. In *Answers to Nine Questions,* he described the formula of a serious humorist: "My method is to take the utmost trouble to find the right thing to say, and then to say it with the utmost levity" (Bartlett, 719). It would have been superfluous for Shaw to add that his success lies in being not just cleverly paradoxical but elegantly succinct—for the sentence itself demonstrates this. So, the brilliant humorist's lathe turns out well-made, cunning sentences.

I was recently reminded of this art of crafting sentences while re-reading Kafka's *Castle*. This book is at times humorous—Thomas Mann called Kafka "a religious humorist" but it is scarcely the comedy of Wilde or Shaw. If Kafka is a humorist—and we are told he often broke up while reading aloud to his friends—then he is a transcendent and a terrifying one, certainly not the sort to have written for Henny Youngman.

So there I was, moving right along at the side of Land Surveyor K. through his baffling adventures in the snowy village, when I was stopped dead by a single sentence. I couldn't go on; I felt compelled to re-read this sentence (to re-read my re-reading) and then to write it down. I felt moved the way a perfect poem moves; the sentence cast about itself a spell of silence in which all I could do was admire the truth of its beauty.

Kafka is among my favorite writers. I loved him from my first adolescent reading; that is, long before I had any idea of how to interpret his work. My teenage self couldn't begin to fathom *The Trial* or "In the Penal Colony" but he knew they were good, better than good, original, but not merely eccentric, anything but, in fact. I can remember the sensation. I felt I had stumbled across a masterpiece from another planet, a world startlingly like the one I was living on and yet... not. Re-reading *The Castle*, despite all I had learned in the meanwhile about the author and his work, I experienced again some of that naïve excitement, as I can with any of the books that meant most to me between the ages of fifteen and twenty-five. Perhaps this recaptured innocence is why I was in awe of the aforementioned sentence and it led me to think about Kafka as a writer of sentences. I put aside what I had learned, thoughts of

Oedipal psychology, the engagements, the tuberculosis, the ambivalent Jewishness, the vegetarianism and Mitteleuropean angst—not only the sows' ears but even the silk purses. I turned from thinking at the macrocosmic level of interpretation to the microcosmic one of particular sentences and was surprised by how many I could recall, how deeply they had sunk into not only me but our culture. I began to imagine a Kafka story as a beach whose entire meaning could be found in one grain of sand if one could only somehow grasp its exquisite perfection and discern all its facets.

Of Kafka's sentences the most famous are certainly his openers, astounding information delivered matter-of-factly: "As Gregor Samsa awoke one morning…" "Someone must have traduced Joseph K…" "Dearest Father, you asked me recently why I maintain that I am afraid of you…" Even his less peremptory beginnings can burrow their way into the imagination. Heinrich Böll admitted to being so enthralled by the first lines of *The Castle* that he modeled the start of one of his own novels on them: the arrival at night, snow, an invisible presence.

Many of Kafka's first sentences have two faces. One is that of a creature pulled from bloody depths, a writhing newborn, authenticated by the pain and the naturalness of its delivery. What Kafka writes in his diary about his breakthrough story, "The Judgment," reveals what his standard for writing would henceforth be: "… the story came out of me like a real birth, covered with filth and slime, and only I have the hand that can reach to the body itself…" A genuine writer is mother, father, and midwife to his work; to start a story is to go into labor. And so you feel nothing could be more personal, more subjective, than what will follow one of these first sentences. For Kafka, an opening sentence is an eruption from what, in a later diary entry, he called his "dreamlike inner life," the wellspring of all his gushers. This is a Romantic, expressive, virtually unconscious view of what happens to Kafka when he begins a story. But Kafka is not an Expressionist or a Surrealist and his openers have another face, a contradictory one. Passionate, slimy, bloody they may be but at the same time they are abstract, clean, as detached as the first line of a legal document or—better still—an algebra problem.

Let X = 5. Let a traveling salesman turn into an insect. Kafka's first sentences often feel like the premises of logical discourses, instances of a generative *What if?* He elevates the petty and overscrupulous language of his insurance office into a perverse sort of poetry: think of the explanations of court procedure in *The Trial*, Bürgel's soporific monologue in *The Castle*, the Officer's account of justice in the Penal Colony. This kind of writing includes its own pedantic commentary—most famously of "Before the Law" in *The Trial*—and is usually thought of as Kafka's mordant commentary on bureaucracy, a parody of official prose, which is fair enough. Yet one too easily forgets that Kafka was trained as a lawyer and that he is always writing about laws or, more majestically, "the Law."

What kind of lawyer was Kafka? The answer depends on your point of view. If you think a good lawyer is one who does his utmost in the interests of his client—in Kafka's case, the Workers' Accident Insurance Institution for the Kingdom of Bohemia—then he was not a good lawyer. However, there is no question that Kafka was a lawyer who was good. If I needed another reason to admire him, then there is what Gustav Janouch's father told his son about his colleague, the Institution's token Jew. What is humanly impressive is that Janouch should praise Kafka to a son who has just become enthralled by him; a lesser man might have considered Kafka a rival and done his best to diminish his son's respect. Kafka's job is usually thought of simply as a distraction from his writing, albeit one that taught him about bureaucracy. But, to me, Kafka's day job weighs heavily on his fiction, helping to account for why he wrote as he did, how he could conceive first sentences like "Before the Law stands a doorkeeper"; "Our laws are not generally known... "; or "'It's a remarkable apparatus ...'" Kafka's work seems to have convinced him of the inhumane logic of the Law itself, which can stand for a father's judgment, one's own guilty conscience, and the will of an unintelligible god. It is the saints, Freud pointed out, who suffer from the deepest sense of sin because they have the most powerful superegos. In *Conversations with Kafka* Gustav Janouch's father says this to his son:

> Kafka personifies patience and kindness. I cannot remember an occasion when there was trouble in the Institution on his account. Yet his approachability is not a sign of weakness or a desire to please. On the contrary; he is easy to get on with because, by being completely fair, just and at the same time understanding towards others, he commands a similar response from everyone around him. People speak freely to him, and if they find it hard to agree with him they prefer to say nothing rather than disagree. This happens in fact quite often, because Kafka expresses unpopular views which are completely his own and contradict accepted opinion. The people at the Accident Insurance Institution don't always understand him. But all the same they are fond of him. For them, he is some strange kind of saint.

So this is how Kafka conducted himself at work and how he was seen by his co-workers: respected both for and in spite of his differences from them, hard to understand yet easy to approach, operating on an ethical level far loftier than the Company's. To confirm Kafka's saintliness, Janouch tells his son how Kafka went about litigating on his company's behalf. Apparently the tale was not unique.

> Not so long ago an old labourer whose leg had been smashed by a crane on a building site said to me: "He's no lawyer. He's a saint." The labourer was to receive only a paltry pension from us.

> He brought an action against us which was not in the

proper legal form. The old man would certainly have lost his case, if at the last moment a well-known Prague lawyer had not visited him and—without being paid a penny by the old man—had not expertly redrafted the labourer's case, so that he helped the poor devil to win it. The lawyer, as I learned later, had been instructed, briefed and paid by Kafka, so that, as the legal representative of the Accident Insurance Institution, he might honourably lose the case against the old labourer.

Kafka's scrupulous self-consciousness was without bounds. He knew what it was like to be the man from the country but also to be a doorkeeper. If he could be a punctilious lawyer he was also a man with antinomian proclivities; and it seems to me that his opening sentences emerge from both impulses of his character.

"The Problem of Our Laws" begins with the first-person-plural narration that Kafka often employs to establish the universality of his theme. "Our laws are not generally known; they are kept secret by the small group of nobles who rule us." Well, aren't there plenty of days when this seems to capture matters? Here also is a good example of what I meant by comparing Kafka's openers to algebraic propositions. He lays down the conditions of a problem which cannot be appealed—there may be laws but we don't know what they are; we only know the nobles who may or may not abuse these laws—and then proceeds to look into the implications, the various theories of the Law, and political proposals about what to do. He works out the permutations, all of which derive from this opening sentence. But Kafka's final sentences are no less remarkable than the first ones. This little story concludes with an interesting one: "A writer [and there is little doubt about who he is] once summed the matter up in this way: the sole visible and indubitable law that is imposed upon us is the nobility, and must we ourselves deprive ourselves of that one law?" Should this conclusion be taken as a rejection of nihilism, of revolution, of relativism? At least one can say that the connection between the opening sentence and the last is relentlessly logical: the story states a problem, examines it in excruciating detail, finds the situation to be impossible but nonetheless true and irremediable, then settles into a statement by "a writer" about the human condition announced at the outset. Though the story is brief, one could even dispense with everything between the first and the last sentences without altering either its meaning or its power.

A story with a similar relation between its first and last sentences is "An Old Manuscript," one of Kafka's Chinese tales and a little masterpiece of polysemous symbolism. It begins with this sentence: "It looks as if much had been neglected in our country's system of defense." Against what must these people erect their great walls? Are the bestial barbarians outside of them or inside? Are they repressed impulses? Are they beasts or gods? No matter, we civilized souls need our defenses; that is precisely our situation. Again, the story concludes without any change in conditions, but with Kafka etching his picture of it more deeply. "This is a misunderstanding of some kind; and it will be the ruin of us." The position is unsettling for these "artisans and tradesmen," for the ego, for the *homme moyen*; it is one of perpetual tension, like that of Heisenberg's electron twitching between valences. Kafka is a master of uncertainty. Just consider how he will drop "nearly" and "almost" into his declarative sentences. "I almost pledged my solemn word of honor," says the Chief Clerk in *Metamorphosis*, sweeping away with one hand what the other has appears to give, conveying at once the yearning for faith, the fear of it, and the suspicion that faith can never discover its object.

There are some notable last sentences among the short pieces of Kafka's first publication, *Meditation*. Three of them form a characteristic cluster: all serve as final paragraphs, are impersonally addressed, universalized but also directed specifically at the reader ("you" or "one"). All are like descending elevators, bringing us down from flights of the spirit to an earthly fate—both ours and the author's—down to a world of bodies, wry little morals, tiny grimaces.

> All this is still heightened if at such a late hour in the evening you look up a friend to see how he is getting on. ("The Sudden Walk") A characteristic movement in such a condition is to run your little finger along your eyebrows. ("Resolution")

The most poignant is the conclusion of "Bachelor's Ill Luck":

> That is how it will be, except that in reality, both today and later, one will stand there with a palpable body and a real head, a real forehead, that is, for smiting on with one's hand.

The first two examples resemble the brief observations in Kafka's diaries, but the last foreshadows the long breaths and tactical subordination of the complex writing to come. The virtuoso example of what Kafka could accomplish with a run-on sentence is "Up in the Gallery," a later story in which Kafka playfully puts Georges Seurat's painting into motion, following each semi-colon with a verb, raising the action to something like frenzy. As with the examples from *Meditation*, there is an elevator at work here too. The piece's two paragraphs are only two sentences, the first puffing up the exalted fantasy of "the young visitor" who would like to intervene on behalf of the "frail, consumptive equestrienne" who is virtually a hunger-artist condemned to circle the big top "in the infinite perspective of a drab future"; the second, for all its frantic movement, "sinking into the closing march." It is a playful exercise but, as always, expresses Kafka himself. He is both the artist in the ring and the young man who dreams of saving her from "the bursts of applause that are really steam hammers." Everything happens suddenly, in only two sentences, which is just the sort of thing that transpires when one is drawn into a picture, when its stillness moves.

"At this moment passed over the bridge a truly unending stream of traffic." In his diary Kafka noted that this final sentence of "The Judgment" was written just before six in the morning on September 23, 1912, "as the maid walked through the anteroom for the first time." This diary entry alone would make the sentence noteworthy because it shows the story was, in a sense, written virtually in "real time." At dawn Kafka writes that Georg carries out his father's verdict while thinking lovingly of his parents as the early-morning traffic streams across the bridge. Kafka concluded the glorious all-nighter with his own parents sleeping just a few feet away. The writing of "The Judgment" was a matter of precipitation, as in chemistry, with Felice Bauer as the catalyst that in a flash fused all the elements in Kafka's inner life in a work of what Coleridge called the esemplastic imagination. But what earns the story's concluding sentence a special place for me in the Kafka canon is not that it gives us an early glimpse of twentieth-century rush-hours or that the English translators chose to retain the German sentence structure, but a comment the author made to his friend Max Brod about it:

> Kafka told me, in fact, and to the best of my recollection, more or less in so many words, "Do you know what the last sentence means? When I wrote it, I had in mind a violent ejaculation."

The sentence records an expulsion: Kafka has finally found a way to write about his relation to his father, to get it *outside* of himself at last. But the comment is also a reference to generation: Kafka has created his first real work of art and feels in himself that power. And yet everything in the story is about him, his longings, guilts, self-divisions, sexual anxieties—all about him, and so the ejaculation is also masturbatory, a burst of relief and yet one that is unsatisfying. Then again, the entire blurred night of writing was leading up to Georg's condemnation which is felt literally as a climax. The comment to Brod about ejaculation isn't so surprising. Kafka was unable to speak about the story without mentioning sex; it is all birth, blood, ejaculations. Creativity for him, after "The Judgment," is an elemental experience; it is to be taken by the spirit, less cerebral than biological. The last sentence of "The Judgment" is an onanistic *Liebestod*. All this was not so disgraceful that Kafka was ashamed to tell his best friend about it. On the contrary, the evidence is that he felt exhilarated, grateful, and fulfilled. There may even be some hope in the stream of traffic being "truly unending," hope that this last sentence would lead to new first ones.

Some of Kafka's last sentences resemble one another; that is, they make characteristic gestures. For example, the last sentences of *The Metamorphosis* and "A Hunger Artist" have always seemed to me essentially the same. As images of Kafka—suffering, degraded, ill, yet seeking spiritual advancement—Gregor Samsa and the Hunger Artist create around themselves a claustrophobic arrest of space and time, as if the world were holding its breath and cannot move forward so long as they remain in it. They are themselves the disease that sickens existence. The moment they are removed, robust life rushes in and is a relief—attractive, not least of all, because of its shallowness. The transformation of Grete from sympathetic little sister and budding musician to triumphant sibling rival and nubile marriage material is how Kafka ends *The Metamorphosis*. What begins with Gregor's transformation ends with hers:

> And it was like a confirmation of their new dreams and excellent intentions that at the end of their journey their daughter sprang to her feet first and stretched her young body.

Gregor never could find the food he needed—perhaps it was music rather than milk—and that turns out to be the Hunger Artist's secret too. Not to find anything in this world to take into oneself so as to nourish one's being is to become a husk, an empty carapace, dry as the straw with which the Hunger Artist is swept away, just as Gregor's desiccated corpse is "dealt with" by the charwoman. As Grete's body replaces Gregor's in the family cage without any loss of freedom because she now dominates it, so a young panther takes over the Hunger Artist's. The panther is the anti-Hunger Artist: "… the joy of life streamed with such ardent passion from his throat…" The onlookers are shocked: "But they braced themselves, crowded round the cage, and did not want ever to move away." After prolonged suffering, Kafka instinctively winds up with these sentences about young bodies, animal spirits. We too feel relieved, grateful for the sight of a good-looking girl or a sleek panther. Yet these vigorous finales are ambivalent. Neither succeeds in making us comfortable about preferring health to disease.

The composer Aaron Copland once said, "We all know how to get a big hand at the end of a piece by making a loud noise with a big drum." The well-fed panther is not such a noise, nor is the stretching Grete. Kafka's last sentences are never so vulgar; yet his endings can be expansive, tremendously so, albeit in his own style. For example, he achieves mighty effects by shifting his perspective from intimate close-up to the long-focus of infinity. His memorial to the coal shortage in Prague, "The Bucket Rider," ends with just such a sudden shift. It is also beautiful and ineffably sad:

> And with that I ascend into the regions of the ice mountains and am lost forever.

The first-person narrator has just been telling off the coal dealer's mean wife. He is freezing. His bucket is so light and coal-less he can no longer control it. And so he floats away, but not just skyward, not just to the mountains, but "into the regions of the ice mountains." The frigidity of that Prague winter—of business-men's wives, of life—is bitter and vast enough to swallow any of us. The narrator's voice, we realize at the end, has been coming to us from this infinite nothingness. Because the story is so concise, Kafka concentrates his imagery in this wonderful sentence until it attains the non-biodegradability of poetry.

To be lost on the heights is also what happens to Josephine in the final sentence of Kafka's last story of all. Again, the protagonist is exalted and vanishes. In this last of his last sentences the consumptive Kafka manages to draw a full breath to describe the only sort of immortality to which he or any artist can aspire:

> So perhaps we shall not miss so very much after all, while Josephine, redeemed from the earthly sorrows which to her thinking lay in wait for all chosen spirits, will happily lose herself in the numberless throng of the heroes of our people, and soon, since we are no historians, will rise to the heights of redemption and be forgotten like all her brothers.

Now, the sentence from *The Castle* that has given rise to these reflections is neither the book's first nor its last. It is the fourth sentence of the eighth chapter. In fact, this may be why the sentence pulled me up; I mean, precisely because I was not anticipating anything special. We are conditioned to have high expectations of first and last things—including sentences in novels. So a reader might easily overlook this one. I had certainly done so when I first read the book in my teens, thoroughly confused, uneasily delighted. I don't imagine Kafka had any wish to draw particular attention to this sentence. It is entirely possible that it held no more significance for its author than any other. He would not confide to his friend what he was thinking as he wrote it, and it is not at all like those characteristic gestures of contraction or expansion mentioned above. I think it was just because I was re-reading the book that the sentence attracted me so much. First readings are linear, drives through new territory; but subsequent ones are like looking over a map of an entire country. One can assess the relation between one locale and another.

The sentence put me in mind of the tiny bit I know of fractals, such as that the shape of a small piece of coastline or a flower's petal can reproduce that of the entire coast or the whole bloom. Because I had already read *The Castle*, had motored through it, albeit without really grasping where I was, the sentence yielded a sort of illumination, an anagnorisis. It seems to concentrate as much of the meaning of the whole book as can conceivably be packed into forty-three words. Again, I don't propose that Kafka meant to do any such thing; yet, because his stories are more about conditions than actions, any given sentence can represent the whole if it embodies the essence of the given plight. For me, this is exactly what the following sentence from *The Castle* does, incarnating the truth of K.'s whole position and, what's more, implicating the reader in it —that is, all of us:

> The Castle, whose contours were already beginning to dissolve, lay silent as ever; never yet had K. seen the slightest sign of life—perhaps it was quite impossible at that distance, and yet the eye demanded it and could not endure that stillness.

Kafka prolongs this sentence, first with a respectable semi-colon, then a more casual but at the same time nervous dash, finally with a comma. This extension, it seems to me, is what gives the sentence its satisfyingly complete trajectory. The semi-colon and the dash link three independent clauses. The final comma might have been replaced by a period, yielding four sentences. Any of these could stand alone and I can imagine a foolish editor suggesting just that; but, if so, none would be really complete, let alone achieve the poetic dimension their fusion does; for it is the relationship of the clauses that is essential. The first one is objective, laying down the facts of the shrouded Castle and its eternal silence. Anyone with eyes and ears could register these. The semi-colon connects these suggestive but, still merely factual, details (silence, near-invisibility) to K. and so conveys his subjective response to the fact of the Castle's impenetrability. Not stopping there, Kafka imparts the more profound effect of this prospect of the Castle on K.—and not only on the Land Surveyor. It is not *his* eye that is aggrieved by the Castle's stillness, that makes the demand for movement and some acknowledgment from on high, but *the* eye; that is, a generalized human eye, anybody's eye.

It is significant that Kafka introduces the phrase "never yet" into this remarkable sentence, an epitome of all those around it. K. has ostensibly been in the village only a matter of days, yet the phrase suggests almost a whole lifetime spent contemplating the Castle, scrutinizing it through binoculars like a sniper, confronting it as a supplicant with his demands and hopes—and ours as well.

WORKS CITED

Bartlett, John. *Familiar Quotations*, Boston: Little, Brown, and Company, 1938
Brod, Max. *Franz Kafka: A Biography*, New York: Schocken, 1963
Janouch, Gustav. *Conversations With Kafka*, London: Andre Deutsch, 1968
Kafka, Franz. *The Castle*, New York: Alfred A. Knopf, 1962
_____. *The Trial*, New York: Modern Library, 1956
_____. *Letter to His Father*, New York: Schocken, 1966
_____. *Diaries 1910-1913*, New York: Schocken, 1965
_____. *Diaries 1914-1923*, New York: Schocken, 1949
_____. *The Great Wall of China*, New York: Schocken, 1960
_____, *The Penal Colony*, New York: Schocken, 1960
Mann, Thomas. "Homage" in *The Castle*, New York: Alfred A. Knopf, 1962

EDITOR'S NOTE

I found this piece in Fein's folder for 1980. The typescript was left with corrections but untitled.

Sidney Fein's enthusiasm for Franz Kafka began, as he says, early and endured all his life. According to his daughter, Fein first read Kafka in high school, not for a class but on the cunning recommendation of an English teacher. Apparently, this talent-spotting teacher detained Fein after class and asked if he had any plans for his future. Wishing to appear to have given his future some thought, Fein replied with what he thought was a safe answer; he said that he was thinking of going to law school. The teacher blandly observed that quite a few writers were also lawyers and dropped, among others, Kafka's name. He left it to Fein to follow up. It was the book he bought in tenth grade—the old Schocken collection published as *The Penal Colony*—that led him to tell this story to his daughter. She had come across the book and wondered why he kept a dried-out, jaundiced, disintegrating copy of a book of which he had two newer editions.

Fein relished his re-readings of those classics he had loved most in his youth, and these re-readings sometimes led him to write about them (see for example "Fein Re-Reads Dostoyevsky"). The syllabi of those courses he occasionally taught often include something of Kafka's but never *The Castle*. He told Maya he had not liked the book when he read it in his teens, far less than *The Trial*, *The Metamorphosis*, and the shorter works. He even said he had picked it up once, re-read a couple of chapters, then gave up. But in 1980 he re-read the whole of Kafka's last novel and this essay was the consequence.

For Fein, Kafka was not only a favorite writer but, as he once wrote, his "favorite Jew." His interpolation of the story from Janouch, which seems like a needless digression from the subject of the essay, is really essential to it in that it presents Kafka as an exemplary human being whose scrupulousness was at odds with the career path Fein had once thoughtlessly told his teacher he intended to take.

Perhaps Fein had come to read *The Castle* with more under-standing, or—since our relations to books can be reciprocal—it could be that the book read an older Fein better than the younger one. Fein's attraction to one sentence became the catalyst for an appreciation that is both aesthetic and ethical; that is, to adopt Fein's word, "microcosmic," as it is limited to single sentences, but also "macrocosmic"—for Fein has here written what is virtually an assessment of Kafka's entire oeuvre.

ON CONTRACTS

M Y good neighbor, Mrs. Ardekian, is a cheerful widow. She lives alone, but her children and grandchildren visit regularly and, when they are coming, she cooks for days in order to stuff them with delicacies. I'm usually offered some too. My favorites are *lahmajoons*, a sort of meat pie that I cannot get enough of and which I had to be forgiven for the grave solecism of once calling "Armenian pizza." Then there is Mrs. Ardekian's wonderful *doma*, and her sublime desserts—*souberog* and *mamoouls*. *Mamooul* is a perfect name for these nutty cookies sprinkled all over with confectioner's sugar like grandmotherly love.

Mrs. Ardekian lives in a ranch house, everything on one floor, and she keeps it as tidy as if it were a yacht owned by Joseph Conrad. She herself is a tidy person, though never formal or stuffy. She is fit, trim, with neat white hair. She favors jeans, sweatshirts, and tennis shoes. Mrs. A. keeps up with the news, reads biographies and popular fiction, and socializes with two other widows. One of these has recently moved to what, with lowered eyes and voice, Mrs. A. referred to as "a facility," as if it were the knacker's. Mrs. A's real passion, though, is birds. She can identify pretty much anything feathered.

This May, an unfamiliar bird appeared on my lawn and I rather fell for it, and wanted badly to know what it was. This compulsion to name goes back a long way, right to the beginning. It seems to have amused the Creator to have Adam label everything in Eden. I've always liked this passage in Genesis, which is also about the invention of language and the power that naming confers:

> ... out of the ground the Lord God formed every beast of
> the field and every bird of the air, and brought them to
> the man to see what he would call them; and whatever
> the man called every living creature, that was its name.

It makes you picture the Deity as a playful father, setting novelties before his son just to see what he'll call them, then adopting his childish names, the way doting parents do. This was just before God made Eve. Coming out of anesthesia, perhaps feeling for his missing rib, Adam called the marvel that had been fashioned from it "woman."

So, I spotted a lovely bird on my lawn. It caught my eye, a real beauty. It wasn't flashy, on the contrary. It was gray and black. The gray was the color of a pair of kid gloves Anna Karenina might have worn in her salad days. The black sat like a yarmulke on its head and matched the color of its perky tail. When I looked harder I saw the black wasn't black at all but a much deeper gray. The two colors harmonized so well that they seemed like the same tune, done first in a major, then in a minor key. The bird's grace fascinated me. I had never thought hopping could be such a fluid, balletic movement. At rest, the bird was sleek as a parked Maserati. I spotted it three days running, watched it hunting worms and bugs, and thought it a privilege to do so. As I say, I needed to put a name to the charmer. And so, when I saw Mrs. Ardekian taking a walk, I decided to ask her, knowing it would give her pleasure to tell me. The difficulty lay in describing my bird to her.

"What's it look like?" she asked sensibly.

"Well," I stalled. "It's gray with a black cap and tail, except the black is really dark gray. It looks something like a robin—same diet too, I think—except that next to it any robin would look like an oaf."

She laughed. "What you've got is called a gray catbird. As in *the catbird seat.*" Then she made bird noises, as if she were reporting the last parliamentary address by my catbird.

She invited me to walk with her and we began by discussing the origin of the phrase "sitting in the catbird seat." I recalled that James Thurber had written a short story with that title but she knew that Thurber had swiped the phrase from Red Barber, who deployed it colorfully in calling baseball games. We both figured it must be a Southernism (I later learned that Barber said he'd picked it up in a poker game in Cincinnati). Mrs. Ardekian explained: "Catbirds like to settle on the highest point available in a yard or a field, you see. Tallest shrub or tree. See? The catbird seat—on top, able to look everything over."

"That, Mrs. Ardekian, is an explanation as elegant as the bird itself."

"*Her*self," she corrected. "What you've seen is the female. The male would be a bit stockier and you'd probably notice he's got a red bum. Watch out for him—he's certainly around somewhere. Some of them have *harems*, you know."

It pleased me that the affection I felt was for a female.

"You know, if you enjoy birds, you should feed them."

Mrs. Ardekian herself had half-a-dozen feeders stocked with a variety of seeds; she also put out suet and furnished her avian spa with a pair of concrete birdbaths. "But, you have to keep the feeders stocked year round," she cautioned. If she was torn between the desire for me to share her enthusiasm and the wish to preserve her monopoly, she didn't show it.

"Why do you like having the birds around?"

She paused, probably because of the stupidity of the question. "They delight me," she said with a girlish giggle. "You see, we have a contract, my birds and I."

It was this comment of Mrs. Ardekian's that has got me thinking about contracts.

When Mrs. A. claimed that she had a contract with her birds, she may have been speaking metaphorically but I could tell she meant it. She wanted to express the reciprocity of her relations with the birds: she provides them with food and, in return, they give her the pleasure of watching them consume it. The question that occurred to me was: can there can be a contract if one party—or even both—are unaware that there *is* a contract? Mrs. Ardekian might like to fancy that her woodpeckers, goldfinches, and nuthatches know about the deal, are pleased with it, and believe they're getting the better of the bargain; however, the birds don't know there is a contract, only that there is easy food to be had in her yard. It is to the food they are faithful, not a contract. On the other hand, Mrs. Ardekian's metaphor doesn't seem to me far-fetched. Her warning that one must always keep the feeders stocked is saying that I must uphold my end of a covenant. Without seeds and suet, the birds will not visit; from the birds' point of view, I would have broken a contract, so to speak. The idea that human beings can have contractual relations with animals seems entirely plausible. We don't know whether birds are aware of the reciprocity of a contract, but what of cows and horses, dogs and cats? People develop complicated relations with their pets and livestock. Do human-animal contracts really exist or is it just that humans are inclined to impose a legalistic framework on *all* their relationships? Did dogs originate in a contract we made with wolves? Certainly, the idea of a contract between willing parties is useful in many situations because it rationalizes what would otherwise be untidy or sentimental. A contract is practical—a guide to practice—laying out what must be done, or not done, by the parties to fulfill mutual obligations, with prescribed benefits and penalties. Perhaps this is why philosophers and lawyers, those of our species most devoted to reason, are so dedicated to the concept.

Adam and Eve had a deal with God, though there were no more negotiations than Mrs. Ardekian had with her sparrows. In fact, this ur-contract—as one would expect from the Almighty—is imposed and, to speak frankly, has the feel of a set-up. There is a good deal of theological as well as psychological force in Kafka's saying that the original sin is man's insistence that the original sin was committed against him.

The next biblical contract is the one God makes with Noah after the Flood, suggesting the Deity might have felt some remorse. But this contract is not merely with Noah and family, not even just with humankind:

> Then God said to Noah and to his sons with him, "Behold, I establish my covenant with you and your descendants after you, and *with every living creature that is with you*… I establish my covenant with you, that never again shall all flesh be cut off by the waters of a flood to destroy the earth."

Like Mrs. Ardekian, God includes animals in the deal. No more mass extinctions, God promises, at least not by water. In return, all men have to do is refrain from killing each other and "not eat flesh with its life, that is, its blood." The pattern is set; the Deity will look after us if we follow the rules, including the dietary ones. God seals His pledge in celestial style, with a rainbow. We sign on by eating dry meat and trying not to be murderers.

The Hebrews like this way of putting matters. Abraham is the prototypical monotheist, also the first human to negotiate with God, which shows just how close Abraham and God become. It is a great moment when this human being stands up and intercedes, however fruitlessly, for Sodom: "Wilt thou indeed destroy the righteous with the wicked? … Shall not the Judge of all the earth do right?" And the contract negotiations are off and running, Abraham bargaining God down to sparing the city if he can find just ten good people in it. Perhaps God gives in so quickly because He knows Abraham isn't going to find even one.

Abraham's relation to God is explicitly described as a contract between them:

"I am God Almighty; walk before me and be blameless. And I will make my covenant between me and you, and will multiply you exceedingly."

Abraham knows about this contract, even if, like Adam and Noah, he didn't negotiate it. He sticks to it too, through the awful twenty-five year wait for Isaac (imagine the nightly conversations with Sarah about having intercourse in their seventies and eighties!). He adheres to the contract even when the awful command to cancel it comes. He obediently climbs on his donkey and rides off on the three-day journey to sacrifice the miracle child. The contract between Abraham and God is personal, yet one of the key tenets of Judaism is that it is also general, transferable to the unnumbered generations that will descend from those forty-six chromosomes, including millions who know nothing about it. However, another way of looking at the matter is to say that it is these later generations who thought up the contract and projected it back onto a legendary progenitor. They really want a deal with God, a collective contract.

The desire for a collective contract is powerful for a people intent on seeing themselves as "a people." This collective contract is renewed and sealed at Sinai, where its true nature becomes clear. In Exodus, the covenant between created and Creator turns into what will later be called a *social contract*. The covenant ramifies, its strictures ever more numerous and legalistic. First, there are the Ten Commandments. Even these are chiefly social, more concerned with humans' relations with one another than with God, whose role is that of sovereign enforcer. After the Commandments, most people stop reading and so neglect the ensuing avalanche of rules governing all sorts of situations and social relations:

> When a man sells his daughter as a slave, she shall not go out as male slaves do... Whoever curses his father or mother shall be put to death... When a man leaves a pit open, or when a man digs a pit and does not cover it, and an ox or an ass falls into it, the owner of the pit shall

make it good; he shall give money to its owner, and the dead beast shall be his...

And so, on and on and on to the number of six hundred and thirteen.

It was philosophers who secularized the contract, making of it a formidable and durable political idea. In a theoretical sense, all this was accomplished at a stroke by Socrates—or Plato—in the *Crito*. To persuade his old friend that evading unjust but legal punishment would be wrong, Socrates conjures up a conversation with "the Laws," a dialogue within the dialogue. Incidentally, the passage always reminds me of Job because in both texts Power insists on obedience and reverence, never accounting for its injustice. In this fantasy conversation—a largely one-sided affair—Socrates adumbrates the idea of a contract between the individual and the Laws, or the State. What is often overlooked is that he simultaneously invents civil disobedience.

Socrates has the personified Laws ask lots of rhetorical questions, just as he habitually did. For example, the Laws inquire whether, because they have injured him, Socrates can injure them in return:

"... And was that our agreement with you?" the law would say; "or were you to abide by the sentence of the state?"

The Laws enumerate the blessings of civilized life from which Socrates has benefited for seven decades and observe that these were conferred on him because of them:

"Do you imagine that a state can subsist and not be overthrown, in which the decisions of law have no power, but are set aside and overthrown by individuals?"

It is a notoriously odd argument, seeming to suggest that one superannuated gadfly skipping town could overturn the Athenian constitution, albeit only "as far as in [him] lies." The argument appears to undermine Socrates' life of non-conformity, his role as dissenter and social critic, which he had just eloquently defended at his trial. Well yes, Socrates does say there exists a binding social contract between him and the state and even awards the greater status to the state for, as in the Bible's covenants, it is clear which party has the standing to set terms. The Laws are indeed godlike. They ask, "In the first place did we not bring you into existence?" and, in the same vein: "… you are not on equal terms with us; nor can you think that you have any right to do to us what we are doing to you." Socrates even has the Laws call him "our child and *slave*." The contract is clear: Socrates gets the benefits of life in Athens, the Laws demand in recompense that he abide by them. I have heard these passages invoked to the un-Socratic end of stifling dissent, which is why the following passage seems to me so significant. Socrates has the Laws say to him that a citizen "… must do what his city and country order him; *or he must change their view of what is just…*" This is where Socrates confirms the meaning of his life and also invents the idea that inspired Thoreau, Gandhi, and King. Socrates can establish his moral authority to question the govern- ment only by submitting to the Laws. By submitting to an unjust punishment he can make clear that the injustice is not in the Laws but the human beings who misapplied them. Another implication of the dialogue is that Socrates did not believe the social contract guarantees justice to the individual in return for obedience. The Laws promise only a just *system*, the rule of law, but not justice itself.

I think the idea of a social contract is dear to philosophers simply because it is a philosophical idea, because it is *their* idea. Perhaps philosophers are aware of the extent to which it is a sort of legal fiction, handy for purposes of analysis and political progress but not good history. Thomas Hobbes, the greatest of social contract theorists, walks right up to this telling admission when, immedi- ately after his indelible depiction of the horrid State of Nature, he writes:

> It may peradventure be thought, there was never such a
> time, nor condition of war as this; and I believe it was
> never generally so, over all the world…

Yet he quickly recoils from this revealing disclosure by means of an ignorant error, ascribing to Native-Americans (Hobbes' favorite representatives of the "savages" just as they were a century later for Rousseau) a lack of political organization, "except the government of small families, the concord whereof dependeth on natural lust…"

Still, Hobbes' idea of the social contract is both powerful and seminal. It begot Locke and Rousseau and, arguably, a couple of revolutions. The irony, of course, is that Hobbes was a Royalist who intended *Leviathan* as a gift to the Stuarts, a stainless steel, up-to-date, state-of-the-art, secular, scientific justification of absolute sovereignty. That there is no such justification is just one problem; a worse one, from Hobbes' point of view, is that his logic justifies people pulling out of the contract, opening the way for revolution. It wasn't just Hobbes' deductive logic that led to this, of course. He was an Englishman and the limitation of governmental power was part of his heritage. Magna Carta, however fitfully applied, had been around for over four hundred years when he wrote. All the same, whether deliberately or inadvertently, Hobbes included in his contract something neither the Bible nor Socrates did, an escape clause.

Since, by Hobbes' theory of voluntary motions, we are by nature isolated balls of pure selfishness, we only join society the better to enjoy our lives, liberty, and property and are willing to renounce those rights (to Hobbes every law is an ex-right) that make this enjoyment insecure. The first obligation of the state, then, is to maintain these individual rights. Should the government fail to do so, let alone violate them itself, it can be justly overthrown. Hobbes never says this; he was a Royalist, after all, but he couldn't avoid implying it. Because Locke had no such reluctance he gets all the credit for inspiring the Declaration of Independence.

My point, though, is not to give credit where it's due, but that social contract theory is not a credible description of history. Hobbes' story of isolated individuals gathering in a field, clubs at the ready, agreeing to laws, giving up freedom and equality, and choosing the tallest fellow with the biggest club to enforce the rules, get called "Your Majesty," live in a palace, be bowed to, and accept everybody's collective sovereignty as his alone, so long as he can enforce the rules ,is absurd. The theory is compelling, not because Hobbes accurately described human behavior in the past, but because he deduces his historical myth from a plausible psychological theory; that is, the theory of a reciprocal contract is useful in analyzing the present. Hobbes was a man of his time. He knew many of the great early scientists and admired their work. In Paris, he sat on a committee to examine Descartes' doctrines. He traveled to Italy and Germany to visit Galileo and Kepler; Mersenne and Gassendi were personal friends. He pretty much adopted the latter's neo-Epicurean materialism along with Galileo's "bodies-in-motion" view of the universe. His contract theory answers the needs of both individuals and states in his time, when Protestantism, capitalism, nationalism, and imperialism left both nations and individuals on their own, insecure and in need of social structures to replace discarded ones like feudalism and Christendom. The idea of rights maintained through a compact between the individual and the state, also of contracts between states that grew out of Grotius' ideas and bore fruit in the Treaty of Westphalia, is a modern idea, one that not only suits modernity but contributes to it by putting politics on a rational footing. Hobbes' notion of universal war in a state of nature replaced by civil peace is not historically *correct* but it is politically *true*.

Time to get back to the original question suggested by Mrs. Ardekian: can there be a contract if all parties are not aware that one exists? Well, we never actually sign a social contract, and the idea that merely passing through the process of "socialization" constitutes our subscription is hardly satisfactory. Children and people who have lost their minds are also covered by the social contract, in some way or other, but have even less of a conception of such a thing than Mrs. Ardekian's sparrows, who will cavort on her feeders only if she fills them with food. Are most citizens aware of a contract between themselves and the government? It seems to me not a matter of whether, but of when and why they are aware. It is in the nature of a successful social contract that it should be taken for granted, just like a sound electrical grid and functional sewer system. We become aware of these arrangements only when they cease working. I know some people to whom being deprived of electricity and water for an hour would seem like a return to the state of nature; but, to everyone, life without law and order really is. Cities are complicated places and many work amazingly well; but, as Hobbes more or less said to those who accused him of cynicism, just take the cops away for a few days and watch what happens.

The *Leviathan* was not inspired by anthropological research, but by an experience that was *post*-social rather than *pre*-social, the collapse of the British government and the civil war of the 1640s. In the circumstances of Hobbes' time, his analysis makes excellent sense. It is the breakdown of the law—the uninvestigated crime, the unfilled pothole—that makes us mindful of a contract. We stop at red lights and pay our taxes, so why are the bridges falling down? It is a Thirty Years War that makes us dream up a Treaty of Westphalia and two ruinous world wars that make us want to give Leagues of United Nations a shot. Social contract theory is not really about the building of societies from an original chaotic state populated by armed, self-sufficient egoists. It is prompted by existing societies that have plunged into dysfunction. The Declaration of Independence is essentially a bill of particulars telling George III how he had not held up his end of the deal. The Founding Fathers did not build a new nation from scratch. If the seeds aren't there, if the baths are dry, the finches will opt out of Mrs. Ardekian's back yard. It is tempting to say that wherever there is reciprocity there too is a contract.

I've been meandering but haven't forgotten the original question about contracts of which the parties may be unaware. Perhaps underlying all the contracts of which we are aware is an archaic, fundamental contract that, as we say with charming anthropomorphism, evolution stumbled upon, the benefit to a single organism of joining with another for something other than sexual reproduction: the primeval form of giving-to-get. On average, cooperative species did better than those that produced loners. Wolves have complicated social contracts. The lone wolf may look cool, but he is not in an enviable position.

I cannot say Mrs. Ardekian is wrong to think of her relations with her birds as contractual. It is, after all, a good way of understanding matters. After the Flood and the rainbow pledge, God could look down on the ceaseless blood-shedding and, like Mrs. Ardekian at her kitchen window, think of His contract, though those creatures down below are oblivious to the averted danger. A good governor should also look down from his or her corner office and think of what is owed to all those commuters, policemen, and homeless derelicts on the park benches. The contract is no less authentic because nobody remembers it until the hurricane or the tornado, the riot or the crime wave. Was it really so different in the days of the Mandate of Heaven and the Divine Right of Kings? Even before popular sovereignty, reciprocity was crucial. On the gates of Persepolis, the subject peoples were promised peace and security in return for submission to the King of Kings. Bad, corrupt, and incompetent autocrats could be removed with or without the pretext of divine displeasure. In choosing their successors, genes were generally less important than ability to Roman emperors while Chinese ones often passed over their feckless children in favor of efficient ministers when choosing their replacements. I imagine they thought it their contractual obligation to do so.

Suppose I sign a book contract but neglect to read all its provisions, having been assured by the publisher that the language is "standard boilerplate." The major points are clear, though: I supply

On Contracts

the finished manuscript, the publisher undertakes to publish it by a certain date, and we divide up whatever proceeds might eventuate according to some formula. Now suppose the publisher changes his mind; he no longer wants to publish my book and, even though I have fulfilled all my obligations, he cancels our contract without fulfilling his, pointing to a clause on page twenty-three that states he can pull out at any time and for any reason. There is no clause allowing me to do the same. The contract is, perhaps, not a good one, neither reciprocal nor symmetrical; yet it is still a contract. And I signed it.

This is a bit like marriage which is often conceived as a contract. Written marriage contracts are still common in many cultures. In many cases, the contractees are the couple's parents, so those most concerned may be entirely ignorant of the contract's provisions— dowries, property rights, business mergers—including escape clauses. Save for the rich and famous who go in for prenuptial agreements, in our society the escape clause is usually unstated because it would be tasteless to include it among vows that still include the phrase "till death us do part." The public declarations at a wedding are themselves a sort of contract. One sometimes worries that the more sincere they are the more unreliable they will prove.

Mrs. Ardekian is happy watching over her birds. I take pleasure in the feeling she has for them. A few days ago she and I and another neighbor, Mr. Lundberg, met by the mailbox and the talk turned to birds. Mr. Lundberg, it turns out, is a bit of a birder himself, though, next to Mrs. Ardekian, merely a dilettante. He makes no contracts; a freeloader, he looks without feeding. Lundberg listed, as if it were a personal merit, the most colorful and unusual birds he had spotted so far this spring. He claimed to have seen a titmouse, a flicker, some purple martins, any number of goldfinches, a red-tailed hawk, and four indigo buntings.

"Which birds are *your* favorites?" he asked Mrs. Ardekian rather condescendingly.

"Oh," she said, "I love my brave little sparrows best."

One day in Hebrew school Rabbi Weiser asked us boys what the most important holiday was. Most said it was Yom Kippur, the Day of Atonement, highest of the High Holy Days; a few argued for Rosh Hashanah, the New Year, kickoff of the Days of Awe. One candid boy said that the most important holiday was obviously Chanukah because you get money and presents and it lasts for eight nights, too.

The old rabbi just shook his head at us and, without troubling to explain why, said, "No. It's the Sabbath."

EDITOR'S NOTE

I found this piece in Fein's file for 1983, the year before his death. The manuscript is rough, mostly corrected typescript but partially handwritten. It is untitled; I am responsible for the admittedly inadequate "On Contracts." I have prepared it for publication with some compunction because it is obviously fragmentary and, even more than other posthumous pieces I have seen through publication, in an unfinished state. Perhaps if he had lived Fein would have returned to the essay, but it seems to me even more likely that he simply abandoned it. He may have despaired of its rambling nature, as he himself admits to "meandering." I have to admit that its point is elusive, even with the reiterated question about a contract between parties unaware of its existence. That might be a theme, or at least a motif, but here Fein seems to resemble a pianist improvising on a nebulous tune. Digression characterizes a good deal of Fein's writing but he usually pulls things together in the finale, often delightfully. Many of his essays resemble boots that have been loosely laced, with a final cinching at the end. Here he concludes with the touching memory of a rabbi teaching that what is most holy is what is most commonplace, not what is most grand or exceptional—Mrs. Ardekian's sparrows, not Mr. Lundberg's indigo buntings. The faithful attend to the weekly Sabbath rites, the pretenders only the High Holy Days. But what this has to do with the Flood and Abraham, with Socrates and Hobbes, I'm not entirely sure.

Fein's interest in social contract theory is easily accounted for, though. It is owing to his recent stint teaching ethical philosophy as a visiting professor at Brandeis University. To judge from his syllabus and the assigned readings, he gave a lot of time to political theory.

The somewhat bitter paragraph about marriage may be read as a reflection on his own experience or on the spike in the divorce-rate during the 1970s. Fein had commented on this phenomenon before, in *Want, Desire, and Need*, published in 1977, four years after his own marriage fell apart. Here he noted the high number of divorces among the educated class during the years following 1973, from which he dates the start of the Women's Liberation Movement. He stresses the significance of that year, calling it "the real end of the sixties." He observes the coincidence of Women's Lib with the withdrawal from Vietnam, the first oil embargo, a stubborn recession accompanied by equally intractable inflation, the resultant pressures on families to generate two incomes in order to remain in the middle class, and the transition from a manufac-turing economy to one based on managing information with keyboards. Fein considers that the majority of these divorces were initiated by women, and he expresses sympathy for their position, their "peculiar identity crisis," the pressure not to resemble their mothers. He notes that most of the divorced men he knew remar-ried within a couple years while most of their ex-wives struggled on alone. When the book came out he was asked by an interviewer whether he had also remarried. Fein replied dryly: "The contract of marriage is both holy and wholly unreliable. As for me, I have too high a regard for the institution of matrimony to mar it by my further participation."

ON FERNLICHT ON
FERNLICHT

I MET Alexander Fernlicht at a Grand Central ticket window in the late winter of 1974. It was rush hour and all six-foot-three of him exuded desperation; even in his crisp blue IBM suit he looked frantic. I was third in line when he broke in and began to plead with the clerk. He knew this was useless, but there are times when one can't help oneself from trying even the futile and humiliating, if only so nothing will be left out. Fernlicht was as willing to abase himself before that clerk as a Dostoyevsky character before his worst enemy.

"Look," he implored, "I've lost my wallet. Or it was stolen. My ticket was in it, my money, credit card, everything. I've got to get the train to Norwalk. You understand? My little girl's waiting for me."

The two people in front of me, also anxious to get tickets, suggested he get lost and worse.

So, I bought Fernlicht a ticket.

It's normal to feel affection for those to whom we've done a good turn; it's usually the recipient who resents the obligation. But Fernlicht's relief and gratitude were whole-hearted. We sat together on the train and got on very well very quickly. The swiftness had to do with his daughter, Hannah. Hannah was the one thing, apart from his gratitude to me, about which Fernlicht was never half-hearted. He explained that he was a single father.

"Me, too," I said. We were in the same situation and of an age.

"Hannah went to a friend's house after school and she's expecting me to pick her up. I can't be late. You know?"

I nodded. I was familiar with the way blood pressure rises at rush hour when there's a little girl waiting. In those days Maya and I were living just outside New Haven and I had to go into New York fairly often. Alexander and I would meet for lunch now and then in midtown. I invited him and Hannah up to our place for a Memorial Day weekend. The visit was not a success. Maya, two years younger than Hannah, had behaved badly, which I ought to have anticipated. Maya was irritated by Hannah's ladylike perfection, and my appreciation of it only made things worse.

I remember Alexander making a joke of it. "Of course Hannah's good. She can't afford to alienate me"

"Oh? Well, Maya seems to get a kick out of provoking *me.*"

He smiled sagely, both superior and sympathetic. "It happens."

"What?"

"Oh, blaming the parent who isn't gone for driving away the one that is."

Fernlicht majored in English literature at Penn. But he had a knack for computers. He understood them, grasped their potential, took some courses at the Moore School, was unexpectedly recruited by IBM, and accepted—all in a half-hearted way. Fernlicht was often less than dedicated perhaps because had so many interests; he was an accomplished hobbyist. A near-scratch golfer and cyclist, he had earned some color belt in martial arts, and did a little wood-turning. Once in a while, he'd write a poem. The poetry he divulged reluctantly after he'd read one of my books. He didn't bring it up to be competitive; in fact, he seemed more embarrassed than proud, as if writing a poem were some sort of social failing, like flatulence. He would never accept that he was a poet, a title he conceived of existentially, not practically. To him a poet wasn't just somebody who composed verses; a poet had to be some kind of exalted creature. "Jesus, I'm not Wallace Stevens," he said over Katz's corned beef, fingering his rep tie.

Like most people you feel deserve happiness, Fernlicht wasn't happy and he grew less so as Hannah edged toward college age. It was as if he had slipped his mooring and lost his rudder. Our affinity was a circumstantial one: coincidences of age, background, education, a fondness for words—above all, our recovered bachelorhoods and only daughters. According to Fernlicht his marriage began to end the moment his wife discovered she was pregnant. Apparently, she didn't want a child. "Maybe a sister," he said, "but certainly not a daughter."

What to me was solitude was loneliness to him. I don't think Fernlicht missed his wife any more than I regretted mine; however, the man badly needed a woman in his life. The trouble was he only managed… women. I met a couple of them. His romances were akin to his hobbies, a sort of rambling from country to country in the hope of finding oneself a citizen in one of them. His activities— so various, always well done but never fulfilling—were efforts at gap-filling. He confessed as much to me when he asked if I got satisfaction from my work. When I said I did, he replied that he wished he could. "I don't get any from work. Not a lot from play, either."

Fernlicht loved literature but couldn't live for it. Like me, he was a Kafka fan. I remember Kafka coming up during a lunch we had at Kepler's in SoHo. "You know," he said while nibbling one of Kepler's elliptical doughnuts, "Kafka said anything that wasn't literature bored him. Shocking candor, don't you think?"[15]

An association of ideas grabbed me. "That reminds me of something. You remember the old British actor George Sanders? Master of supercilious languor? Well, Sanders took sleeping pills in

---

[15] Kepler's, Home of the Elliptical Donut, was a gathering spot of "typers" in what became known as the Typewriter Underground, a contemporary group devoted to resisting the rise of the word processor.

his mid-sixties and left a note that read something like *"Dear World, I'm leaving because I'm bored."*

"Kafka didn't kill himself."

"No. On the contrary, he tried his best to stay alive. By the way, he also said that it's possible to extract a lot of books from life, but hardly any life from books."

"Then maybe he valued life so much because he wanted to extract books from it. Imagine living with a mind like that," said my friend with glum admiration.

I examined Fernlicht's long face, saw ciphers in it I imagined I could decrypt. "You too have weapons," I quoted.

"What?"

"The last words in Kafka diary. *More than consolation is: You too have weapons.*"

Why I said this I'm not sure. I guess I wanted to Fernlicht up, keep him safe in harbor.

Fernlicht was good at his job. I picture him as exceedingly patient with people frightened of computers, but short with those who pretended to know what they didn't. He was a melancholic man who yearned to make a meaning for his life, one of those who need a cause to die for—or somebody to live for. He was too wise, decent, and humane to place much-loved Hannah in the impossible position of being responsible for him. Exactly the opposite. Fernlicht would get down on his knees before a ticket seller not to keep her waiting or—worse yet—worrying about him. While Hannah was still in his charge, so long as he still felt himself *Hannah's father*, he was all right. I knew things had changed when he said "Being Hannah's father was my best gig ever." Fernlicht went through parenthood with a clenched fist, a straight back, anchor and tiller squarely in place. But that was just it: to be Hannah's father was to him not *being* but *doing*; it was bathing, carrying, playing, feeding, instructing, driving, listening, consoling, advising, comforting, entertaining, dressing. When he had inevitably to give up that "gig," fissures broke out all over the retaining wall.

Like the majority of poets—that is, minor ones—Fernlicht had more sensitivity than talent. However, it was a distinction that he never confused the one with the other. Perhaps that is the deeper reason why he refused to think of himself as a poet; I mean because his verses were never crafty but the residue of an inundation of feeling. It was Hannah, engaged now, who, with surpassing kindness, sent me the following document. The two parts, a poem sandwiched between its exegesis, were both written by her father. She found them on his desk, Hannah said in her note, neatly typed, addressed to no one.

FERNLICHT ON FERNLICHT

"Nada" is a less than satisfactory poem that appears to be both the record of a black mood and of a struggle—hard to say how vain— against it. A black mood? Moods are passing events, at least once they have passed. It is clear that the author of "Nada" would like what he is describing to be a mood; he tries to shake himself out of it. This measure of resistance may well be to his credit; but there is no evidence that the emptiness is filled at the end, at most that he is trying to find reasons not to give in to it. If the poem's subject is not a mood, then it must be a situation, one that is personal, persistent, potentially universal, familiar enough not to require naming. The gap between "clinical depression" and "*la condition humaine*" may be no more than a hair's breadth, one deep breath.

Context counts. For example, if we knew the poet had been diagnosed, his despondency transfixed by some pointed psychiatric label, we would find it difficult to put that fact aside while reading read "Nada." Or, if we knew the author of the poem to be a witty, jolly fellow leading a rich and balanced life, a good chum and pillar of the community, then "Nada" would mean something quite different to us. And if the first word of the poem were "She" and we knew the author to be a woman who had just given birth, we might well find in it something postpartum.

Nothing. *Nichts. Rien.* An empty set. An erased memory. Zilch. An utter absence. "A Clean, Well-Lighted Place." The final chapter of a textbook on Atheistic Existentialism. *Nada*—two minimal syllables that rhyme, noises a baby might make. Watch out the rhymes.

NADA

1.
He sits himself down at his desk like an
atheist awaiting the descent of grace,
prepared to propitiate, bargain, sacrifice,
whatever it takes for a vacuum to
suck up this vacuum he abhors.
On the beach the bathers
turn on their towels and sigh;
the teacher at the blackboard
explained how but never why.
In the lounge ladies clink their ice cubes
and nod; in the park kids are getting high
on pot, glue, worse; before their cathode-ray tubes
the old breathe the stale, ostracized air.
As for him, he feels full of nothing,
nothing on a chair.

2.
There's nothing inside the nothing inside
but nothing, and this nothing swells like a
diapason, adds weight like a careless
jockey, declares it's both process and thing,

neither fair flower nor foul wind but mere
blankness, white whale's flank, space left by last year's
celosia, the heavy hush after the
final waltz. It grins sullenly then yawns,
a maw fit to swallow selfish prayers, baffled
lust, elegant or crude philosophies—
in fact, it gobbles up far more than these,
eats everything that Polyphemus sees.

3.
Children and lovers, scholars in full spate,
an oboist squinting hard at her score,
a sturdy slugger pounding on the plate—
I swear, there are plenty more
to reknit the world, ravel up those rents
through which vacancy peeks—perhaps even you,
feeling senseless and yet making sense,
struggling from your oubliette and seeing blue.

The rhymes are interesting because they are irregular yet deliberate, as if the poet intended something by them. Part One sets up
the expectation of a loose, parasitic blank verse in its first five lines.
Then, unexpectedly, the thing breaks into a kind of jig. The lines
get shorter; six and eight have end-rhymes, making a quatrain, as
do lines nine through twelve. *High* rhymes with *sigh* but then also
with *why*, so the two quatrains are merged into an octet, almost a
ditty, except the expectation is violated when nothing rhymes with
air when we anticipate something should. And yet, with nothing
(*nothing*) intervening, *air* is picked up in the devastating final verse,
which is half the length of the initial ten-syllable line: *nothing on a
chair. Air, nothing, chair*—these words round out the picture of the
poet sitting down to work, or trying to work, hoping against hope for
something, *anything* to vacuum up a vacuum, as if, under the aegis of
a willing muse, two nothings could cancel one another out.

Despite being an "atheist," the poet is prepared to undertake any ritual by which "grace" might descend. At first, "Nada" seems the consequence of a poet employing the deplorable device of overcoming writer's block by making it his subject, and the "grace" for which he waits seems to be inspiration. However, the language is too suggestive, and radiates too far, for such a self-absorbed, negligible purpose. And, in fact, what ensues in the jigging section is a kind of ode to meaninglessness, to emptiness and how people rush to fill it with anything from sunbathing to natural science—the latter being superb with *hows*, but useless on *whys*. Then there are social drinking, drugs, TV, the palliatives of the adolescent, middle-aged, and senile. Though the feeling of nothingness originates with the poet, belongs to him, he presumes that others suffer from it too; that everybody does. Emptiness surrounds our planet and permeates us—or at least him, who is the "nothing on a chair" inditing all this. Why? Just to make himself feel better? But, if that is what he was aiming at, *nothing on a chair* sounds as if he missed. But if the poet was attempting to externalize his discontent, his impatience with life, then, out of generosity, we may allow him some modicum of success. We can even imagine him enjoying a gratifying moment when the phrase *nothing on a chair* popped into his head, grace showering the atheist with *les mots justes*.

The poet himself is absent from Part Two, which is a definition rather than a lyrical complaint. The noun that comes up three times in a line and a half, making up half the syllables, is here personified and set it in motion. *Nothing* is busy and attracts a plethora of verbs. *Nothing* swells, adds, declares, and grins; it yawns and gobbles. Rhyme is nearly absent, as if the poet feared it might distract from the breathless enjambment, the sheer bustle. So, it is a surprise when the last three lines are an emphatic, rhyming tercet: *philosophies, these, sees*. Ravenous nihilism consumes everything, like a black hole; but what nothing eats is nothingness and all it sees is itself, for the black hole is also Polyphemus's ex-eye.

In Part Three ,the poet tries to transmute negative lead into positive gold. By this cultural alchemy tragedy confers dignity, suffering breeds consciousness, pain teaches joy, and death is the mother of beauty. Here are things that are *not* nothing, which are so *gut-an-sich* that Nothing cannot chew them up. In the black year 1941, Paul Valéry wrote *Mauvaises Pensées et Autres* in which may be found the famous aphorism: "God made everything out of nothing. But the nothingness shows through." The poet alludes to Valéry's witticism when he claims—without, it must be said, notable conviction—that the goodness of life can "ravel up those rents/through which vacancy peeks…"

It is presumably to fortify this effort to *reknit*, to *ravel up* life's torn sleeves, that the poet composes his finale so conventionally: eight ten-syllable lines in an *ababcdcd* rhyme scheme, deploying regular uses prosody as a way of "feeling senseless and yet making sense." Yet the sunshine does not quite break through. It is blocked by one crucial word, an archaic term for an archaic punishment. An oubliette, from the French verb "to forget," is a concealed dungeon at the bottom of a castle with a trap door in the ceiling as the only opening. The "you" who is down in the secret dungeon, quite forgotten, is the poet himself. He dreams of liberation of clambering up and standing erect under a light-filled, cloudless sky. But the whole point of oubliettes is that nobody climbs out of them.

Is "Nada" a suicide note written by a man who would prefer to go on living? "Of Suicide" is one of David Hume's posthumous— that is, suppressed—essays. It is not an argument in favor of killing oneself, but a defense of the right to do so. Hume opposes the general opinion that choosing to end one's existence is at once a crime and a sin. He not only respects the Stoic solution but approves of it under certain circumstances.

> A hair, a fly, an insect is able to destroy this mighty being whose life is of such importance. Is it an absurdity to suppose that human prudence may lawfully dispose of

what depends on such insignificant causes? . . Do you
imagine that I repine at providence or curse my creation,
because I go out of life, and put a period to a being,
which, were it to continue, would render me miserable?
Far be such sentiments from me… If suicide be supposed
a crime, 'tis only cowardice can impel us to it. If it be
no crime, both prudence and courage should engage us
to rid ourselves at once of existence, when it becomes a
burthen…

True, the author of "Nada" makes no mention of suicide, yet his
poem is steeped in the thought of it. He believes the world has
somehow emptied out and feels himself hollow too, a minor Kurtz,
a petty Ahab, reduced to the solipsistic corner lit by a desk lamp
and the perverse urge to write down these verses which, in the end,
are addressed only to the nothing he has become.

So ends my friend's commentary on his last poem, his effort at
a detached, objective evaluation of his condition. That he calls
the poem "unsuccessful" might be just another expression of his
modesty; or, it could mean he found the poem aesthetically unsatisfactory; or, and this thought has troubled my sleep, what he meant
was that poetry couldn't save him. And, of course, it didn't.

It's too simple to say that Alexander wanted to elevate his depression to something cosmic by a sort of negative sublimation. There
is no reason why the personal and universal should *not* coincide;
in fact, they must. We don't live among abstractions but crawl our
way toward them through real dirt. Nevertheless, when Fernlicht
invoked that famous *bon mot* of Valéry's about the *Nihilo* showing
through Creation, I heard a wrong note. It isn't just that my friend
really was an atheist who didn't believe God created anything, even
with holes in it. "God created" is merely a way of speaking for
men like Valéry and Fernlicht, not a confession of faith. No, the
false note comes from the sentiment itself, which is too chilly and
remote, like outer space. Closer to Fernlicht's particular brand of

unhappiness is this sentence written by the same Paul Valéry two years later, in *Tel Quel*. It too begins with God making something:

> God created man, and finding him not sufficiently alone, gave him a female companion so that he might feel his solitude more acutely.

EDITOR'S NOTE

I found the above manuscript in Fein's folder for the year 1979.

The structure of the piece makes one think of Chinese boxes, Russian dolls, the frame of *Frankenstein*. Fein introduces Alexander Fernlicht, Fernlicht his poem, then, at dead center, sits "Nada," the poem itself, followed by Fernlicht's critique (in which he does not identify himself), and, finally, Fein reflects on it all, though so briefly one wonders if he gave up writing, unwilling to find out where it might lead.

Fein wrote down two titles at the head of the first page of the manuscript: "Nada" and "Distant Light." Both are crossed out. The present title has been provided by me.

Did Alexander Fernlicht exist? Was he a real person or a creature of Fein's like Klaren Verheim and Mr. Ponderoff, like Philippe Leconte Duparc? When I first came across the manuscript I felt pretty sure that Fernlicht is, like these others, an imaginary character. Fein's imaginary people are not characters in works of fiction. They serve a different function. They are more like specific stimuli for thought-experiments Fein invents to work through something. With Duparc it was aesthetics, with Verheim critical theory, with Ponderoff pseudonymity. Nevertheless, I diligently checked the public records for Alexander and Hannah Fernlicht. I even contacted IBM. I found what I expected to, nothing.

Alexander Fernlicht and his poetry appear in another of Fein's papers, the one I titled "On Two Sonnets of Alexander Fernlicht. The Fernlicht that emerges from the two essays, is the same, an amateur poet with romantic problems.

What did Fernlicht mean to Fein? An editor can only speculate. One answer is that he is a version of Fein's friend Saul Mandelbaum, who committed suicide. Another is that Fernlicht is an alternative ego, a Fein who composed verses, a Fein who chose a career in business, one who couldn't bear solitude and whose daughter was always perfectly behaved—above all, a Fein who succumbed to despair, like Mandelbaum, whose death shook Fein. Fernlicht may have been a way of exorcising despair. Perhaps he served the same function for Fein as Nietzsche said the thought of suicide did for him: "... a powerful solace: by means of it one gets through many a bad night."

ON ZEICHER'S
ESSAY IN ETHICS

EDITOR'S INTRODUCTION

On Wednesday, April 23, 1980, T. H. Humphrey, a twenty-four-year-old graduate student whose dissertation on the 1833 Frankfurter Wachensturm had been rejected ten days earlier, walked into a classroom in the Rabb Graduate Center at Brandeis University and began firing a Beretta pistol he had purchased four days earlier in Mason, New Hampshire. His fiancée had broken off their engagement on April 12. Humphrey's intention was to kill his dissertation advisor; however, in his disordered condition, he burst into the philosophy class of Assistant Professor Paul Zeicher whom he had never met.

Two students were struck, one in the stomach, the other, fatally, in the head. Zeicher leapt toward Humphrey. He took a bullet in the chest but still managed to fall forward, tackling the gunman and slamming his arm to the floor, so that he dropped the pistol. Two male students then subdued Humphrey; a young woman, screaming all the way, rushed to the first-floor office to call the police and summon medical help. Paul Zeicher died of his wound in an ambulance less than an hour later. He was twenty-nine years old.

During the academic year 1979-80, Sidney Fein, then thirty-seven years old, served as Visiting Professor at Brandeis.

I found the following text in Fein's file for 1980, leading me to suppose it was written either immediately after the tragic event of April 23 or over the summer. Fein typed out what he wrote, with corrections, paper-clipped it together, but left it untitled The title below is mine.

Fein's relationship with the younger man seems ambiguous, close and distant at the undated same time. That may account for why Fein sometimes refers to him as Paul, at others as Zeicher. It is as if Fein himself is unsure about how close they were.

This little memoir may be the sole record of Zeicher's work. I can find no record of a book by Paul Zeicher titled *Essay in Ethics*. Evidently, the manuscript was never published, and it may well have been lost.

On Paul Zeicher's *Essay in Ethics*

My first encounter with Paul Zeicher was a matter of inadvertent eavesdropping. This was in early September, on the first day of classes. My ten o'clock Philosophy 420 class was scheduled to meet in the same room as his nine o'clock 100-level introductory class. As always on these occasions, I felt a slight nausea and wondered if this was to be the year when I would be found out. I was also feeling a little ridiculous too, because the role of professor has something comic about it, at least when I'm cast in it. So I was anxious and eager and wanted to avoid that chilling grand entrance when the waiting students turn en-masse, like a shoal of piranha, to fix their stares on the grade-giver rushing through the door. Some tender unearned respect, some look cowed and others preemptively resentful, but most are just skeptical. The consequence of my impatience was that I was standing in the corridor as Zeicher, who never closed his door, wound up his first class with his two dozen freshmen.

As everyone knows, first classes are rituals: "I am Professor… My office is in Room… My office hours are…" Then there is the calling of the roll with awkward mispronunciations, followed by the handing out of syllabi, holding up of books, inane generalities about the goals of the course, a first reading assignment, and a welcome dismissal. I suppose Zeicher had been through this; all I heard was the way he ended the class. From that alone, though, I could tell that this was an engaging and engaged man, one for whom teaching was a calling rather than distraction from career-building research. For this one, I thought, teaching is a personal undertaking. This enthusiasm is admirable but it is also risky—too much dedication being as bad as too little. Zeicher concluded whatever had preceded with a version of a Hasidic parable, fitting for Brandeis:

> Once upon a time a man lost his way in a dense forest. An hour later a second person wandered into the forest and likewise became lost. By sheer chance they bumped into each other. The second person, assuming that he was not also lost and must know the true path, asked the first the way out of the woods. "I don't know the way out," replied the man. "I can only point out the ways that lead further into the thicket. So, it looks as if we'll have to try to find the way out together.

These days I'm often asked about Zeicher. People suppose that he and I were closer than we were. Well, perhaps they aren't entirely wrong. While we had only a few conversations, they were not wasted on academic small talk; in fact, all of them are memorable. The first was when he came to my office with a copy of *Want, Desire, and Need* held in both hands, like a tea-tray. He said some gratifying things about the book without stooping to flattery. He also told me candidly with which of my ideas he disagreed and why. He asked me to sign the book, which I did quickly, without any personalized message, and with the usual feeling of embarrassment. I have a distaste for dedications, those vestiges of the old fulsome expressions of feudal dependence.

Zeicher had another agenda item.

"I'm in my fourth year," he said. "Tenure review's just a couple of years off and I need a book even to have a chance."

"Have you got one?"

He blushed. "It's pretty much finished."

"Your dissertation?"

"No," he said, paused, and gave a dry little laugh. "The truth is I can't stand my thesis. I dredged two articles from it but I'd be content never to lay eyes on the thing again."

I asked what the thesis was about.

He rolled his eyes. "Hegel."

"Ah, I see. And the book you'd like to publish?"

"It's about ethics. Much better than the dissertation. Alive, if you know what I mean. I wasn't written as just a means to an end. But I really need to find a publisher."

"You've sent out inquiries, I suppose?"

He nodded his head then hung it.

I hesitated. "And you're wondering if maybe I can help?"

Though Paul was outgoing in his classroom, outside it he was downright bashful. And, when he was embarrassed, as I think he often was, he avoided speaking. He nodded at me.

"Would you maybe read… some of it? I mean, just an excerpt. I wouldn't want to take up your time. Of course… I understand if you're busy." He looked around my empty Visiting Professor's office. "You must be terribly busy."

This speech was almost too much for him; he barely got the words in a whisper.

He's supposing I know the way out of the forest, I thought.

"Sure. I'll be glad to take a look."

After several abject expressions of thanks, the conversation reverted to my own book—and, to my surprise, the one before that as well. For a moment, I wondered if Zeicher might have boned up for our conversation but dismissed the idea. Paul was a thoughtful man but not really a calculating one. Where tenure was concerned, though, he was desperate. This wasn't because he craved a raise and a title; he was terrified of being banished from the classroom, from his students. Academic jobs were scarce and those who failed at the only hurdle that mattered rarely got a second chance.

In our second conversation, he offered me a confession: "Teaching," he said, "is the only form of social life I really enjoy." This was quite an admission and not altogether in his favor. But it was made by a thinker who wrote in his book of Marx, Nietzsche, and Freud that:

> They have bequeathed us powerful flashlights with which to search the basement of our motives—class interest, power, sex. Still, a flashlight is not a skeleton key to reality; it is properly a thing we look *with*, not *at*. Unconscious urges may seem to invalidate ethical reflection and undermine our freedom of choice; but buried motives can be dragged out into the light. In fact, that is precisely the accomplishment of all these modern excavators.

Imagine a young teacher who believes in all simplicity that he is involved solely in the educational transaction described on his course syllabus. Then he reads Nietzsche and is stunned to realize that it isn't teaching he loves, nor his students, but the power to preach at and overawe the young. What a crisis! But how much worse if he is persuaded by Freud's analysis of the erotic transference that can taint pedagogical no less than psychoanalytic relations. "You say you love your students, Professor; but have you examined carefully in what sense?" Paul Zeicher had conducted that examination, of course, with the conscientiousness of a Talmudist working out a tangled midrash or a Jesuit performing his spiritual exercises. For Paul, young as he was, such self-examination would indeed have been a kind of spiritual exercise, except that, to judge by his book, he didn't believe he could purify his motives, just that he could make himself cognizant of their complexity and that they might not be entirely knowable.

I suspect Zeicher was more frank with me than his departmental colleagues because I was just passing through and had no vote on his tenure. After all, the junior faculty are all competitors and senior ones all judges. I was neither the one nor the other; I had one foot inside and the other outside the door. I was there, yet I was also an outsider. Also, he had enough respect for my work to dispute it.

When Paul gave me a typescript of the entire book, per my request, I asked why he chose to call it *An Essay in Ethics*. "Were you being modest or thinking of Locke and Hume?"

"As I like to tell my students," he said, sitting up straighter, "*essay* only means *attempt* and the best of these attempts always seem like a journey where you're not sure exactly where you're going to wind up."

I liked this and agreed. "Students confuse essays, which ought to be alive, with reports, which are dead. I think the infection might be contracted somewhere around the eighth grade."

Zeicher's smile was suddenly displaced by a serious look: "Do your students have trouble getting down into things—I mean, developing a paragraph? Mine sure do."

I nodded. "And how do you fix that?"

"Well, I don't, of course, not always. What I tell them is to try behaving like an annoying three-year-old."

"How's that?"

"Write a sentence, then ask *why*. Answer with the next sentence, then ask *why* again. And keep it up until asking why's either meaningless or exasperating. Then start the *next* paragraph. It works, too. Sometimes."

This made me think of Maya ten years ago. *Why? Why? Why?* It really could get exasperating. On one occasion, I told my curious daughter a joke she loved and often asked me to repeat—and now I told it to Zeicher.

"A father's walking his little girl down to the beach. 'Daddy,' she asks, 'why's the grass green?' 'I don't know,' he says with a shrug and they walk on. 'Daddy, why's the sky blue?' 'No idea, Sweetheart,' he says and leads her on to the sand. 'Daddy?' 'Yes, dear?' 'Why's the ocean blue?' 'Haven't the foggiest,' he admits, spreading out the beach towel. They sit down and after a moment the little girl looks up at her father. 'Daddy,' she says, 'I hope you don't mind my asking you all these questions.' 'Oh, not at all, darling,' he says. 'How are you going to learn if you don't ask questions?'"

Zeicher didn't actually laugh, but he said it was a good joke. Then he asked why I thought Maya had liked it so much.

"Because the father's an ignoramus."

"And because hers *isn't*?"

"Oh, but he *is*. I can't explain why the sky's blue to a three-year-old. Can you?"

"Yes," he said, ironic and earnest at once. "And even why sometimes it's gray.,"

"And why it's black at night?"

"Yep, that as well."

Zeicher never spoke to me about his private life, his childhood, his family, his marital status. So far as I knew, he could have been a polygamist and the product of parthenogenesis. Our relationship was circumscribed, professional; it was the sort self-contained two pool balls might have, meeting once in a while and bouncing off one another. I never invited Paul for dinner and, of course, was never invited to his home. After his death, though, I drove by the place. He had lived on a short street in Waltham called Woerd Avenue, the name an odd alloy of *weird* and *word*. He rented the second floor of a little house set among alders, and willows, and heavy brush.

There was a small frog pond next to it, a stagnant little finger of the Charles River. I presumed Paul would have chosen the room with the river prospect as his study. If so, as he worked he had a good view of Mount Feake Cemetery spread out along the opposite bank. If you happened to be near-sighted and couldn't make out the tombs, it would look bucolic and restful.

An Essay in Ethics is short, only 178 pages, and that is just one of its virtues. When he handed it over, in a black spring binder, Paul warned me not to expect anything grand or original.

"I sometimes find that originality's a kind of perversion, or rather the cause of it. Know what I mean?"

"When it becomes a motive, yes."

He nodded. "Exactly. It's the same with popularity and teaching, as I tell my students."

As I tell my students. Zeicher was always quoting things he had said to his students. He couldn't help it, I think, because he was never so mentally alert and eloquent as he was in front of a bunch of undergraduates. I've experienced it myself, the way one's brain speeds up in front of a class, its conductivity souped-up by the terror of silence.

I saw at once why Paul had trouble finding a publisher. He had shared with me his failure and frustration by showing me the dismissive readers' comments from the four university presses who had turned him down. Why? To gain sympathy, to see if I'd agree, or out of an impulse to humiliate himself? The reports were certainly of the ego-crushing variety: "Derivative... uninteresting... wishywashy... takes no account whatever of recent contributions of French post-structuralism... unlikely to find an audience... not a real contribution... eclectic to a fault..." The book lays out a moral position that is indeed eclectic and, if read superficially, could be mistaken for a nebulous mélange of more famous work. I found his position to be both eccentric and admirably honest.

Zeicher accepts that there is no abstract good, only what he calls *good for*. He criticizes absolutism for a peculiar reason:

> Moral absolutes are dangerous because of the ease with which they turn inhumane; nevertheless, one should be prepared to act as if there were indeed an abstract and universal good. Human rights, for example, though rooted historically in the Reformation and the West's five centuries of slow political progress thereafter, are good for the vast majority.

Reasoning in this fashion, Paul attempts to reconcile the absolutism he partially rejects and the relativism he finds suspect. He's not the first to attempt this and one could (like the reviewers) dismiss it as a mug's game. There are in his position elements of pragmatism, utilitarianism, echoes of Epicurus and his modern avatars, all of which he makes scrupulously explicit in copious footnotes. But there are distinctive applications. A good example—poignant now—is the way he addresses the use of force which he sums up in a single sentence: "The resort to violence is always an ethical failure, a short-circuit—unless it isn't." "There's no system here at all," one reviewer had scoffed, though another entered a verdict more generous and measured, if grudging: "The author describes what we mean by an ethical being, the sort of decent person we admire and would even—on our best days—strive to become." What I think Zeicher really does, as much by accumulating illustrations as by discursive argument, is to compel a deep consideration of ethics while renouncing the temptation to offer any moral prescriptions. His cardinal virtue is alertness. This accords well with the two sentences he chose for the book's epigraph, drawn from Gustav Janouch's *Conversations with Kafka*, a book whose authenticity has never been finally established—unless you love Kafka and read it carefully. Young Janouch asked Kafka about a recent book by Leonhard Frank with the optimistic title, *Man is Good*. For his epigraph Paul chose Kafka's reply:

Most men are not wicked. Men become bad and guilty because they speak and act without foreseeing the results of their words and their deeds. They are sleepwalkers, not evildoers.

While I was reading Zeicher's manuscript I was, perhaps because of this epigraph, reminded of a couple of Kafka's late aphorisms:

We are sinful not merely because we have eaten of the Tree of Knowledge, but also because we have not yet eaten of the Tree of Life.

There is a goal, but no way; what we call the way is only wavering.

Zeicher's book is that of a young man, though hardly as naïve as Leonhard Frank's. ("Nothing makes me more pessimistic than optimism," wrote Ionesco.) Many of the book's shortcoming are owing to Paul's not yet having eaten of the Tree of Life. But, as for what Kafka calls "wavering," Zeicher, unwilling to prescribe a way, seems to embrace it.

Paul proposes that one is an ethical being in much the way one is blond or French or Jewish—that it is a part of what he calls one's "distinctive identity." It's what one is rather than what one thinks that counts for him. In his distinctions, he reminds me of Kierkegaard.

To be an Aristotelian, a Kantian, a Utilitarian means to adhere to an idea more than to live it. One can extol and defend the Golden Mean, the categorical imperative, the Greatest Happiness Principle without actually living by any of them. And this will not even be hypocrisy in so far as one's intellectual commitment is genuine.

Karl Marx must have had something of the same notion. Having lived long enough to hear his name become an adjective, he once said, "I am not a Marxist." As Zeicher might see it, Marx wasn't just making a joke or taking exception to his disciples; he was declaring that he was alive and so not yet that finished, dead thing we are accustomed to calling "Marx."

A passage I particularly liked must have come straight out of the classroom. I can see him making inspired use of the props at hand, like Jesus holding up a mustard seed or Eliot posing as a Hebrew prophet showing his generation fear in a handful of dust. I can see him pointing to his upholstered teacher's chair, the molded plastic of the students' unyielding ones.

> Plato the aristocrat is a moral absolutist with rigid precepts; for him, one size fits all in ethics as in politics. For him, our job is to wedge ourselves into a seat designed for the one ideal rear end. His middle-class student Aristotle sees the world differently. His chair is still firm but has a good deal of give in it so as to compromise with our imperfections.

I like also this one-liner on the two philosophers: "Any sensible person would choose to read Plato but live like Aristotle."

T. H. Humphrey brutally ended two lives, ruined his own, and even that was a botch—the blind vengeance of a rejected Ph.D. candidate, a spurned lover, vain as the *coup de main* at Frankfurt on which he had wasted three years. How much of the responsibility belongs to his parents who decided to name him Troy Hector? It is no more than a passing irony that Humphrey's thesis and Zeicher's book should both have been turned down. Zeicher died defending what, in the end, meant most to him, his students. Now he's being called a hero, of course—as Hector was—but the *mot* doesn't feel quite *juste* in Paul's case; it seems to me a false attribution, the usual journalistic simplification. Certainly, he acted bravely, and effectively too. I can't say I would have done the same and I'm aware that a small change in the University's class schedule might have had me facing the gunman on April 23. But no, Zeicher was better than the kind of hero he is being hailed as. This was a momentary thing, nearly an accident, even if it was also the fulfillment of a devoted

teacher's fantasy that also revealed the man's character and, lamen-
tably, fixed it forever. In accord with his own ideas, Paul Zeicher
was not a hero but a decent and humane man, keenly aware of the
imperfections of our messy selves and an indifferent world.

ON MYSTERY

ONE of the things I did on my summer vacation was wonder what the publisher would come up with by way of a cover for *Aristocratic Democracy*. According to the managing editor there has to be some sort of illustration and, by contract, I have no say in the matter. Long ago, when I had not published so much as an epigram, I told myself that, should I ever get so far, my books would all have a standard format and nothing on their covers but words, in the style of my beloved, inexpensive, but hardbound Everyman and Modern Library editions. That was then, as they say; that was adolescent dreaming.

I tried to think of a suitable picture for the new book, something that would suggest its insides in a clever, commercially irresistible way. I accomplished this thinking in various locations—the shower, the car, in the kitchen while making a stir-fry, in bed in lieu of falling asleep. Wherever I was, I drew a blank. Perhaps if what was being published were a work of fiction it would have been easier to dream up a cover; but then I suppose it would also matter more because a cover illustration is bound to guide a reader's imagination, often promising more than there is. In the end, I felt relieved that the responsibility isn't mine, not for the cover, the font, width of margins, or rag content of paper. As a physical object, *Aristocratic Democracy* will have nothing to do with me.

Memory is layered, like the Grand Canyon, a wedding cake, or a parfait. Whatever's down at the bottom grows invisible, crushed under pressure. We presume such things are "forgotten," only to find out they aren't when they suddenly erupt to the surface, sometimes with astounding accuracy. It was while I was fruitlessly contemplating the book cover question that I had such an experience: I recalled a letter of Kafka's I must have read at least two decades ago. Of course, it was about a cover illustration.

Those who can console us always assume great authority and that's what Kafka does for me.

On October 25, 1915, Franz Kafka addressed the following letter to Kurt Wolff Verlag:

> Dear Sir,
>
> You recently mentioned that Ottomar Starke is going to do a drawing for the title page of *Metamorphosis*... It struck me that Starke, as an illustrator, might want to draw the insect itself. Not that, please not that! I do not want to restrict him, but only to make this plea out of my deeper knowledge of the story. The insect itself cannot be depicted. It cannot even be shown from a distance... I would be very grateful if you would pass along my request and make it more emphatic. If I were to offer suggestions for an illustration, I would choose such scenes as the following: the parents and the head clerk in front of the locked door, or even better, the parents and the sister in the lighted room, with the door open upon the adjoining room that lies in darkness.

Ottomar Starke was only three years younger than Kafka, but he lived until 1962, the year of the Cuban Missile Crisis. He was a maker of woodcuts and a set designer but is best remembered as the creator of covers for Wolff's *Jüngste Tag* series—above all, of course, *The Metamorphosis*. Kafka's first book, *Meditation*, had no cover illustration, nor did *The Stoker*, the first published in the *Jüngste Tag* series. They are just like my dear Modern Library and Everyman editions. I expect Kafka was pleased by this, as I would have been.

But the next book, *The Metamorphosis*, was to have a cover illustration whether he liked it or not. Judging by the tone of alarm in his letter, Kafka didn't care for the idea one bit, but, like me, he had signed a contract. The suggestions he offers are *faute de mieux*, not as bad as what he feared, though not better than nothing. Starke was probably shown the letter because what he devised, though not exactly what Kafka proposed, does reflect the author's suggestions. His cover depicts a male figure in a bathrobe who is taking a step away from a door. The door is ajar so that we see only a sliver of the interior, and it is jet black. He holds his head in his hands, covering his eyes. Who is this man? He seems too young and slim to be Herr Samsa and the Chief Clerk would not behave so, nor would he be wearing a dressing gown. It's not a great illustration. Kafka's ideas were better but there is, at least, no depiction of the bug.

Der Jüngste Tag series was a remarkable enterprise born in a world of empires about to tear themselves to bits, on a continent that had been stable for so long that only the most sensitive seismographs sensed how precarious its balance was. Several of these were writers published in Kurt Wolff's series. The books were to be short as well as cheap: "… epitomes of their creators' ideas." The project was begun in 1913 and announced in a prospectus written by Franz Werfel.

> *The Newest Day* will be more than just another group of books, but less than a [formal] library. It is to be a series of creative works by our latest authors, produced out of the common experience of our time… we shall publish at intervals and at a low price (80 pfennigs for the paper-cover edition, 1 1/2 marks for bound copies)…

Surprisingly, the War didn't kill series. It lasted all the way to 1921 and put out eighty-six small books, of which Kafka's, of course, are the only ones to have become world-famous. Wolff had two talented assistants, Franz Werfel, who knew Kafka, and Kafka's best friend in the world, Max Brod. *The Newest Day* was not only a great moment in modernism but also in networking.

Kafka's proposal to depict either the parents and clerk before the locked door or Gregor's family gathered quietly under the light that will set off the darkness of his room, good as it is, strikes me as desperate. Whatever Starke might end up drawing, the really essential thing for Kafka was clearly this: *The insect itself cannot be depicted.* Notice that "cannot" (*kann nicht*) may mean either *must not* or *is unable to.* I believe Kafka intended both. The metamorphosis itself must be preserved as a void, a mystery. This is not to deny it meaning; just the opposite. As a mystery, what happens to Gregor is free to be a symbol with unconstrained significance: tuberculosis, religious conversion, artistic talent, amputation, Jewishness, self-hatred, materialism, Oedipal war, masochistic guilt, sexual frustration, disgust with family and commercial life, and so on. The ripples can multiply; they can swell to breakers. Depict the insect, sketch us a cockroach or dung beetle, and audacious metaphor pales to pitiful simile. Dostoyevsky's Underground Man feels himself "*like* an insect" whereas, now that it is the twentieth century, Gregor really *is* one. *The Metamorphosis* is the "epitome of an art" indeed, one that knows what not to reveal. This is why Camus said Kafka's art "consists in forcing the reader to reread." Just imagine if the Officer in *The Penal Colony* were tried for insubordination or, even worse, that Joseph K. were hauled before a district court and charged with embezzling from his bank.

Kafka writes of mysteries without ever transgressing into mystification, which is just what his imitators invariably do. Mystery enhances and runs deep; mystification, like any fraud, diminishes both those who perpetrate it and those taken in by it. Mystery leaves you pondering; mystification swearing. Mystery begins by accepting, even insisting that there is something that *cannot be depicted.* Mystification holds back what can and ought to be revealed. Mystification is pretentious, hollow; it is found in bad screenplays, bad detective novels, bad ghost and science fiction stories, and in tales that are "dream-like" without ever persuading you they could be actual dreams. Of mystification ("… and so we never did discover who the real murderer was…") there is nothing good to say. About mystery, though, one can speak endlessly, because what *cannot be depicted* is hardly, for that reason, beyond interpreting. Kafka has a knack for finding in what has never happened to anyone what happens to just about everybody. His works constitute a kind of Modern Everyman Library.

The etymology of *mystery* is religious. The Greek word *mysterion* refers to secret rites (e.g., the Eleusinian). *Mystes* means an initiated one and *myein* to perform the initiation. To the Romans, *mysterium* meant, in general, "supernatural thing." The early Christians, sponges who could turn anything to their ends, used the word to signify something like "divine secret."

The so-called mystery plays dramatized biblical events, especially from the life of Jesus, to instruct and awe an illiterate medieval laity. In Roman Catholicism, *mystery* came to have two specific meanings: a) a sacrament, especially the Eucharist, and b) one of the fifteen episodes in the lives of Jesus and Mary that serve rosary-sayers as topics for meditation. False mysteries are, of course, mystifications. In my opinion *mystification* is what ought to have been written on the forehead of the Whore of Babylon hefting her golden goblet overflowing with abominations.

There is no religious mystery or mystification in the Homeric epics. Both are, so to speak, nullified. The gods' motives are all too comprehensible. These are nature-gods, anthropomorphized, and so the supernatural is really the natural. That is why Socrates could say that he believed in the gods in a higher sense than his accusers; it is why he mocks the credit Euthyphro childishly gives the old myths. Socrates, the supreme rationalist, despises mystification, yet he believes in mystery.

In Greek tragedy, the mystery is Fate, but it is a mystery shared by all, albeit some stories are stranger, more ironic or thrilling than others. It isn't true that in Greek tragedy Fate overrides responsibility; in fact, it might be better to say that a hero's fate conspires with his character. Still, I've always felt sympathy for the dying Oedipus at Colonus shaking his fist skywards and whining that it wasn't his fault.

Kierkegaard has something interesting to say about these matters.

> In Greek tragedy concealment (and therefore recognition) is an epic survival based on a fate in which the dramatic action disappears from view... This is why the effect produced by a Greek tragedy bears a resemblance to the impression given by a marble statue that lacks the power of the eye. Greek tragedy is blind. Hence it takes a certain abstraction to appreciate it.

It seems to me the same thing could be said of Kafka's work. The real mystery isn't the appearance of the insect. Picturing the latter can only undermine the former. Kafka does his best to tell the story as if it were literally true yet he doesn't want the reader to see it that way. Gregor himself is on the verge of turning into an abstraction. The metamorphosis is the *donnée* of his story, as Oedipus' parentage is of his. Both fates are established before the stories begin, just as the mystery of the Big Bang—or, better still, what preceded it— ended long before the invention of bagels and bicycles, yet is their *sine qua non*.

Kafka is anxious for his reader, and this is why he was jumpy about *The Metamorphosis* being published with an illustration on its cover. Every writer considers his or her readers, even as absent abstractions, even authors who claim to write for no one but themselves, but especially bad authors who think like con-men and consider their readers as targets for mystification. Kafka worried about how *depicting the insect* would prejudice the reader's mind. Thus, the insect *cannot be depicted*.

ON MYSTERY

In modern drama, what passes for mystery is psychological. As Kierkegaard sees it, all drama is built on a structure of concealment and revelation, pretty aesthetic illusion displaced by gratifying ethical disclosure, "warts and all." In Greek tragedies, neither concealment nor revelation is in the hands of the hero; in modern drama, both are. It's up to Nora to sit Torvald down and have it out with him. Hamlet feigns madness but reveals his sanity in the end. Ricky spots Lucy in the chorus line and calls her out. They are all revealed, uncovered; they have to show themselves. After all, *theater* means "place for showing." It derives from *theasthai*, to behold. All drama is show biz, including the courtroom variety. Non-Kafkan courts of law are supposed to be places for showing the whole truth and nothing but the truth. In either kind of theater, all mystery is dispelled, save for those deep enough to outlive the dénouement or verdict—"the rest" that "is silence."

As a psychological state, guilt too can be a mystery; it is the one on which Kafka is the supreme expert, in fact. It can exist independent of responsibility. Guilt can shrug off even an exculpatory verdict. Kafka gives us our modern epic of polysemous guilt in *The Trial*. Like *The Metamorphosis*, it too begins immediately following a mystery, the accusation against Joseph K. One man goes to bed human and wakes up a bug; another goes to sleep innocent and wakes up guilty. Life really is like that.

The nature of Kafka's religious beliefs is mysterious; however, all his best stories have a spiritual aura about them. His mysteries are more archaic and run deeper than the positivistic mysteries conceived by Poe and Conan Doyle or the psychological extravaganzas of Gothic novels from *The Castle of Otranto* to *Dracula*.

The divine mystery and the murder mystery are linked by nothing more than semantics. Murder mysteries are locks with keys, both manufactured at the same time. They had better have a key or what we are left with is a thirteen-line sonnet. You might suppose that the best of such stories would be those with the cleverest plots;

but, in fact, the unlocking is secondary to the locksmith. What we want is to sit alongside our favorite detective, to have a drink and a smoke with him. He reassures us. He sets the world to rights, fingering the innocent as well as the guilty, making sense of it all. What he dispels isn't mystery, though, but mystification. That is an ethical act, not a spiritual one. The facts of the case must not only be worthy of the detective but fitted to his or her style. Miss Marple would be, not out of her depth perhaps, but certainly out of place on the mean streets of Los Angeles. Sherlock Holmes needs his London and its fog. As dissolvers of mystifications, detectives are hard-headed, thick skulls around Cartesian brains. The problems they solve have no spiritual dimension; however, the best detectives always do. This is because they see and suffer from a human condition they know more about than those around them. Only the most diabolical villains can approach them in this regard, like Moriarty, that mathematical immoralist.

Drop Hercule Poirot into the world of *The Metamorphosis* and both would be shattered. The murder mystification is devised to be explained. Kafka's mysteries are not, in accord with Klaren Verheim's proverb: "Whatever can be explained can be explained away." An unsolved murder in a detective novel is simply a cheat. There's no use claiming that the daring author has transcended convention by violating our expectations when what he's really done is fail to fulfill convention's just demand for justice. Such an author would be attempting to get credit for a course he hasn't taken—and extra credit, at that. It is much the same with religious mystification, the charlatanism of the spirit, meretricious shows of ritual, incantations, smells and bells. The state of California churns out spanking new religions at almost the same pace as flashy movies, the kind that, even in its Golden Age, a bitter Scott Fitzgerald dismissed as "wet goods for children." Bad movies and bad religions depict their insects because it's all gotten up, a "special effect." There's really no bug there at all.

Historical mysteries result from our inability to establish objectively the causes of events. History means "inquiry," but into what? Into past events, one says, though this is no real answer. After all, history is not chronicle, not this event then that one, any more than a series of unconnected events constitute the plot of a story. History is a tale of causes-and-effects and so must be shaped by the minds of historians and these seldom limit themselves to what can be objectively established. Where's the fun in that, after all? In one direction historiography dissolves into psychological speculation, what is called psycho-history; in another, it devolves into docudrama.

Heinrich von Kleist, among Kafka's favorite authors, gives an example of how a historical mystery may be clarified by psychological speculation. He does this in his essay called "On the Gradual Fabrication of Thoughts While Speaking." Here Kleist examines the source of the Comte de Mirabeau's consequential speech of June 23, 1789. It's notable that, up till then, all the Count's speeches before the estates had urged moderation. In effect, Kleist ascribes one of the principal sparks detonating the French Revolution to Mirabeau's almost inadvertent inspiration, provoked by the appearance of the Marquis de Dreux-Brézé, the King's Master of Ceremonies.

> The King having enjoined the estates to adjourn, his Master of Ceremonies later returned to the hall to find the members still present, and asked them if they had not heard the royal command.
>
> "Yes," answered Mirabeau, "we have heard the King's command…" I am certain that he made this affable start without the faintest prescience of the bayonet thrust with which he was to conclude.
>
> "Yes, Monsieur," he repeats, "we have heard it…" Clearly he has no idea of what he is about.
>
> "But by what right," he continues, whereupon a fresh

source of stupendous ideas opens up to him, "do you proclaim commands to us? We are the representatives of the Nation!" This is exactly what he needs, and leaping to the pinnacle of audacity, he cries, "The Nation *issues* commands. It does not *receive* them. And to make myself absolutely clear to you"—only now does he hit on the words that express the total opposition for which his soul stands armed—"you may tell your King that we will not leave our places except at the point of the bayonet."

The mystery: why did Mirabeau invoke the bayonet? The answer: simply because it tore out of the momentum of his own words. Well, why not? As an inquiry into a turning-point in history, what Kleist tells us is more penetrating than what the textbooks have to say.

Mysteries are ubiquitous. People are called mysterious when their origins are unknown; because of this their motives are considered, at the least, suspicious.

Twain had good reason to call his last novel *The Mysterious Stranger*. Its hero is Satan.

Sex is a mystery to virgins, one that even experience may not dispel.

Genius too is a mystery. If it were explicable we would call it talent.

According to Kafka, the real mysteries of life aren't hidden at all, are not the clever, oddly reassuring crimes of the detective novels. They are the accusations lodged against us, the secure job we cannot quite manage to clutch, the metamorphoses we undergo. These we have to endure but it is hard to understand or depict them because they are always before us.

When I was a boy, the local shoe store had a fluoroscope, a contraption about the size of a washing machine. You'd try on your new Keds, stick your feet into a pair of slots, push a button, and you could see all the bones inside your feet inside the sneakers. Highly dangerous, but a good afternoon's entertainment—instructive, too.

EDITOR'S NOTE

I discovered these untitled and uncorrected notes in Fein's file for 1983. As *Aristocratic Democracy*, the last of his three books, came out in October of that year, the notes probably date from the end of August or early September.

In many respects, what I am calling "On Mystery" is typical of Fein's posthumous papers: free-floating, preceded by no definite thesis, yet conveying a sense of unity. As in many of Fein's writings, Kafka looms large.

The personal nature of Sidney Fein's affection for Franz Kafka is apparent. He says Kafka had been a consolation to him even before he understood anything about Kafka and his work. "I couldn't grasp anything; I only knew it was good," he wrote elsewhere. Fein shows what a large return a living reader can earn on the sympathy he invests in a dead writer. Kafka felt the same about Kierkegaard. Though in his letters to Max Brod, Kafka is sometimes harshly critical of the Dane, he was fascinated by him and read every one of Kierkegaard's books he could lay his hands on. In his *Diary*, Kafka says of Kierkegaard, "He bears me out like a friend."

These notes contrast the mysteries to be found in Kafka to what is called the mystery novel or the detective story. Fein's penultimate paragraph sums up this theme by reporting the way Kafka saw the matter. I believe he is alluding to a passage in *Conversations with Kafka* where the author teases young Janouch for reading a detective serial and also for being ashamed to be caught at it. When Janouch hastens to dismiss the story as "rubbish," Kafka ribs him: "Do you call rubbish the literature which earns the editor most money?" But then he turns serious:

Detective stories are always concerned with the solution of mysteries which are hidden behind extraordinary occurrences. But in real life it's absolutely the opposite. The mystery isn't hidden in the background. On the contrary! It stares one in the face. It's what is obvious. So we do not see it. Everyday life is the greatest detective story ever written. Every second, without noticing, we pass by thousands of corpses and crimes. That's the routine of our lives…

Fein felt much the same way, apparently. Kafka's heroes—the two K's, Gregor, the Officer—each is blinded by routine. All are caught in the mystery that stares them in the face but which they fail to see.

A final note: In the end, Fein's publisher decided that *Aristocratic Democracy* would have no cover illustration.

ON SIDEKICKS

YESTERDAY, I looked through an old photo album, the sort of thing you do once a decade or so. The album is covered in cracked brown leather; the black-and-white snapshots have those little triangles at each corner to hold them in place. On the second page is a photograph I recalled my father once made a point of showing me, with commentary. The picture is of my great-grand-father, Elias Fein, standing in front of his place of business. He has on a black suit with a high white collar; his arms are crossed. He isn't smiling proudly but stands there grim and pugnacious, the immigrant who has staked his claim and isn't just prepared but eager to defend it.

"That's exactly how I remember him," my father had said.

Elias emigrated from Colmar in Alsace; it isn't hard to figure out why. Colmar is usually in France but has sometimes been in Germany; it depends on who won the last war. In 1349, the Christians of Colmar massacred the Jews of Colmar. Napoleon Bonaparte was a liberator of Jews—he's a hero to many still —but he didn't love them. He turned on the Jews of Colmar by freeing the Gentiles who owed them money of their debts. In 1848, there were anti-Semitic riots in Colmar as in so many other civilized spots in Europe. Alfred Dreyfus came from Alsace too, from Mulhouse, right down the road from Colmar. He was accused of being born with double disloyalty: a German sympathizer by location, by heritage an alien Jew.

I visited Colmar once, just to see the place. The town looks *echt*

Deutsch, a sort of Grimms theme park, featuring half-timbered buildings with high-pitched roofs leaning over cobbled squares. St. Martin's Gothic church dominates the town's modest skyline; it looks German too, big and stolid, without French grace. It was begun in the 13th century on the remains of an older church. Perhaps the Carolingian chapel looked more French. Even the wines of the region are German—Riesling and Gewürztraminer. Alsace was hospitable to both French and German anti-Semitism—a tradition that, like haute cuisine, Oktoberfest, and Brooks Brothers, never goes out of style. Easy to understand why Elias would want to head for a new world. For his longing, we American Feins must be grateful.

Great-grandfather Elias wasn't a money-lender but a tailor. He settled in the Tioga section of Philadelphia and started up a business in cheap women's dresses. He did all right; but, when his elder son Reuben took over the business it took off. Reuben was a real go-getter. Reuben had vision. He opened new markets and hired a lot of competent and diligent women who, according to family lore, he encouraged to join the Ladies Garments Workers Union. His younger brother, my grandfather Emmanuel (the name of a messiah), could have joined the business but had no interest in it. Instead, he convinced his father to send him to Penn Law. He became famous and/or notorious as a crusader who took on liberal causes. He ran for mayor once. Instead of being proud of this, my father dismissed it as a ploy by the bosses to flatter Emmanuel's vanity and divide the Jewish vote. My father Henry, Emmanuel's only son, was as disgusted by the prospect of becoming a lawyer as his father had been by a future in the dress factory; he wanted no part of crusading, nor would he consent to be a doctor, or even a dentist. Perhaps owing to some atavistic impulse, or well-aimed Oedipal thrust, what my father chose was business, to make lots of money and to do it without pretensions.

My father valued personal virtues but didn't believe in collective ones. Politics he considered a stew of empty clichés, phony promises, and grubby motives. His father's reputation as a do-gooder might have intimidated but it didn't impress him. "The difference between God and a social worker is that God doesn't pretend to be a social worker," he once cracked. Yet he was offended if anyone called him cynical. On the contrary, he claimed it was the politicians who were the cynics, lying and bamboozling and trying to hold on to office long enough to be called statesmen. "*I'm* the idealist," he declared, "but the practical kind." So, Father joined his Uncle Reuben at Female Thrift Fashions, Inc. and, after a few years, was running the place. Like Reuben, he had vision, a vision so large it required a bigger city. "Philadelphia," my father said when explaining why I'd have to leave my friends, "is one big inferiority complex." I was twelve, he moved FTF and us to New York, where he made it big. "That's why you've got the means to be a decadent intellectual," as he reminded me recently.

Before I was whisked off to Brooklyn Heights, there were several occasions when I was left to spend an unkept Sabbath at my grandfather's office. I loved being there. The place had a legal smell of old wood, rows of musty law books, a motherly secretary/receptionist, and a man who wasn't any kind of father but a friend. Grandfather kept interesting objects on his desk, including a shockingly big copper shell-casing he said was from the Civil War. My visits always started off well enough, with him asking about my week, about what I was learning in school; but in no time he was delivering lectures on plutocracy, racism, the countless venal and mortal sins of bankers, realtors, corporations, the nation's hypocritical foreign policy, and the awful things going on in City Hall, right under William Penn's nose.

Even as a child, it was clear to me that Grandfather felt betrayed by my father, who had chosen his brother over him. I expect he had looked forward to his son becoming his partner, fighting injustice at his side rather than, as he once bitterly put it, "hawking shoddy *schmattes.*" I suppose in his eyes it was a step backward for the Feins, from the professions to trade. To fill the void left by his son, my grandfather took on an associate, Bernard J. Black. Bernie was somebody's nephew, so giving him a place was an act of kindness. Bernie was certainly grateful—more than grateful—but he was not a surrogate son. He became something else. Bernie Black was Grandfather's sidekick—and my friend.

My memories of Bernie are all fond ones. He was much warmer toward me than Grandfather, and he was fun. He didn't spout sermons and screeds; he asked me questions I couldn't answer but liked being asked: Was I happy? What were my *two* favorite books? Did I think my school was really trying to integrate the wave of new students who'd fled the South? He was always asking me silly riddles. "What gets wetter the more it dries?" (A towel.) "What's the difference between a piano, glue, and a tuna?" (You can tuna piano but you can't piano a tuna!) "That's good," I said, "but what about the glue?" "Sorry, Sid. I'm stuck on that!"

During my visits Grandfather soon handed me over to Bernie who took me to lunch at the Horn & Hardart automat. On one of these occasions, Bernie asked whether I had a girlfriend and, picturing pigtailed Caitlin O'Brien, I blushed. "So, it's a secret, eh? Good, secrets are okay. But look, maybe I'll tell *you* a secret." He glanced around the crowded restaurant and whispered, "But later, not here." When we got back, he ushered me into his little office, shut the door, sat me down, and with great solemnity, said what he was about to tell me was his "most secret secret." It turned out to be that his real family name was Blechschmidt.

"Ugh! It means tinker—you know, tin-smith. But blech can *also* mean nonsense. Just imagine having to go through life as Bernard J. Blechschmidt, forger of tinny rubbish."

Bernie was excellent company, one of those rare adults who have the knack of treating children as equals; but what I had a hard time figuring out was his attitude toward Grandfather. At times, it seemed simply unalloyed adoration but, at others, a sort of wry, though unshakably loyal, skepticism. He was proud of my grandfather and his crusading, but not so much that he couldn't make a joke now and then about both—or appreciate one made by somebody else. When I told him what my father said about God and the social worker, Bernie broke up.

Like many pale, ectomorphic urban boys of my generation, I loved the old B-Westerns. Heaven knows how many of these Hollywood cranked out during the Depression and the war—so many that they were bound to be formulaic, like concerti grossi.

All the usual things captivated me: the empty plains that signified a fetterless freedom not to be found in Brooklyn, not even in Prospect Park. Then there were the horses, the romantic adventures, the shoot-outs and showdowns where the bullets never exploded flesh or struck the hero. I also liked small, odd details, things you couldn't really talk about: for instance, that the cowboys never had to go to the bathroom, change their clothes, wash their hands before dinner, brush their teeth, or shave; that they were never short of cash, lived on a diet of beef and beans and seemed to have no parents, as if they'd been born in their prime. The heroes were not only relative-free but always on the move. While I was anchored to my home, they were homeless, which I also thought of as liberation. The exception was Roy Rogers who owned a beautiful spread and had a cowgirl wife. Dale Evans was the first married woman I encountered who didn't take her husband's name. What you wanted from Roy and Dale was for them to adopt you. I liked the heroes' intimacy with their horses, who had dignified names like Champion, Silver, Trigger, Black Jack.

Almost all of these cowboy heroes had sidekicks; but I hadn't thought much about them until the day it struck me that a sidekick is what Bernie Black was—Emmanuel's Andy Devine and Smiley Burnette, Grandfather's Gabby Hayes, his Slim Pickens. This cast that my grandfather into the mold of Whip Wilson, Hopalong

Cassidy, Rocky Lane, Tim Holt, Bob Steele, the Durango Kid, Sunset Carson, Rex Allen, and the Cisco Kid. It seemed improbable, and yet, like them, he fought injustice, albeit unmounted and in the Wild East. And, like them, he had a sidekick.

I've tracked down two etymologies for the word sidekick. One traces it to 1896 and the slang of pickpockets. The "kick" was the front side pocket of a pair of trousers, the hardest to pick, the safest. So, says the lexicographer, a "side-kick" was a person's closest companion. This seems fanciful. The alternative derivation is simpler, older, and feels more like it. This source says the term was first used in 1886 to mean "side-pal" or "side-partner"— a wingman, so to speak. The source is American, obviously. There was still plenty of Wild West around in 1886.

Sidekicks, being of a type, resemble each other. However, some famous sidekicks, especially from more civilized Europe, are different from those in the Westerns. Dr. Watson is a sidekick, but who can imagine Gabby Hayes writing up Hopalong's adventures or Pancho with a medical degree upbraiding Cisco for downing too much tequila out of ennui? Doc Holliday was more gambler and gunfighter than dentist, and only a temporary sidekick for Wyatt Earp. He was also an actual person, while real sidekicks—by which I mean fictional ones—stick around. If the hero loses his sidekick, he quickly gets another one. When Chester left *Gunsmoke*, Festus, an even more sidekicky sidekick, turned up the next week.

Cowboy movies seldom explain how or why the hero acquired his sidekick, why the sidekick sticks by the hero, or which needs the other more. This need, like the relationship, is simply a *donnée*, part of the formula. Yet the implication is that, in addition to providing an occasion for a bit of dialogue between action sequences, the needs of hero and sidekick are mutual. I suppose as a child I felt this vaguely; now I think that the sidekick grounds the hero who, for his part, needs not only an anchor, but a subordinate, someone whose anti-heroism will be a foil for his conspicuous valor. The sidekick initiates nothing; he is literally along for the ride. He may, like Bernie, be skeptical of his pal's knight-errantry and not so happy with the danger it puts him in; but sidekicking is better than homesteading, preferable running a dry goods store. So, he attaches himself, makes a profession of it—just as the old character-actors made their careers by hitching their chuckwagons to a star.

Are these relationships homoerotic? Only the most willful of psychoanalytic critics would push the point. Still, the bond of hero and sidekick does mirror many childhood and adolescent bonds, not only for boys but for girls as well, children in the stage of "best friends," when boys useless at sports fasten themselves to stronger, more athletic ones and unprepossessing girls shadow cute, popular ones. And yet nobody would wish to be Nugget Clark Waller; everybody wants to be Rocky Lane or Tim Holt. The hero always has a fancier outfit, a better mount, shinier six-guns. Westerns are puerile fantasies, wishes fulfilled in ninety-minute vacations from the ordinary. Wyoming was, for me, an alternate universe. But then there was also the suspicion, quickly repressed, that, if I could actually move into that world, I wouldn't be a hero at all, that the best I could hope for was to be a sidekick. Maybe this is what Bernie Black felt about his fate. Being Grandfather's dogsbody in pursuit of mostly lost causes, standing by his side (actually, a little behind) for the Right and Good—this was much better than writing wills or doing title searches. Sidekicks want adventures, but they know their limits. That's what makes them sidekicks rather than heroes.

Sidekicks are like the B-sides of hit 45 records. They are played by actors whose faces you recognize but whose names seldom make it off the tip of your tongue. But they possess an individuality that's deeper and more human than the heroes, who are defined by signature gimmicks—Hoot Gibson's ten-gallon hat, Lash LaRue's bullwhip. Sidekicks aren't so brave or fast on the draw as the heroes, not as eloquent, sharp, charismatic, or flashily clad—yet they are reliable, faithful, and they have two feet on the ground, unlike their *Luftmenschen* companions. If you think about sidekicks at all, you might wonder what they were like ten years earlier. You might wonder if they made jokes about the hero behind his back.

The relation between the Western hero and sidekick is not that of master to slave. Rather, the affiliation seems to me more like the one between knight and squire, or one particular knight and one special squire. I am thinking of Cervantes' sublime satire, *El ingenioso hidalgo don Quijote de la Mancha*. For me, the ur-sidekick is Sancho Panza.

Like Sancho, a good sidekick is completely sane, even if he'd prefer not to be; and, like Quixote, the hero is slightly mad, driven by his cause and addicted to conflict. Heroes never claim to be heroes for the same reason that people suffering from delusions don't claim to be deluded.

The relationship between Bernie Black and my grandfather must have been to some degree like that between the Don and his squire. Emmanuel was famous for his speeches in court, just as Quixote mouths the bombast of his beloved romances. Bernie was different; he was plain-spoken, unoriginal, but always made sense. Sancho has a bottomless bag of proverbs, the common wisdom of the common man. *Rain in May makes bread for the whole year. Dainty dogs may eat dirty puddings. He whose father is a judge goes safe to trial.* Some of Sancho's proverbs strike me as especially suited to sidekicks, such as *It is other people's burdens that kill the ass* or *The bay horse thinks one thing, the man who saddles him another.* A sidekick resembles that ass, is like that bay horse. He too is subject to the commands, whims, and burdens of another. Sancho must know that Quixote is crazy but he follows him all the same. Like all good sidekicks, he is in love with a madness he doesn't share, partially deplores, yet constantly abets. It's so much more fun to be Quixote's squire than to be Panza the family man or Sancho the stay-at-home, that he eagerly lays aside his own sanity until it is needed. So, it makes perfect sense that, when Quixote recovers his mind, it should be

Sancho who pleads with him to sally forth once more, to return to madness.

The most profound and also the most playful commentary on the sidekick's relationship to the hero is Franz Kafka's tale in *The Great Wall of China*, "The Truth about Sancho Panza". This two-sentence masterpiece was first published in 1931, well after Kafka's death, by his own sidekick, Max Brod, who gave the parable its title:

> Without making any boast of it Sancho Panza succeeded in the course of years, by devouring a great number of romances of chivalry and adventure in the evening and night hours, in so diverting from him his demon, whom he later called Don Quixote, that his demon thereupon set out in perfect freedom on the maddest exploits, which, however, for the lack of a preordained object, which should have been Sancho Panza himself, harmed nobody. A free man, Sancho Panza philosophically followed Don Quixote on his crusades, perhaps out of a sense of responsibility, and had of them a great and edifying entertainment to the end of his days.

Well, what else but romantic demons were Crash Corrigan and Whip Wilson? And what else but puerile editions of Sancho Panza were the sidekicks who accompanied them on their adventures? Was it like this for Bernie Black? Was my grandfather in some sense *his* diverted demon, the source of endless edifying entertainment, a master to be served because Emmanuel, messianic tilter at windmills, was, in some sense, Bernie's responsibility?

I can imagine a reversal of Kafka's story. Here it is the sidekick who is the demon, a dull, normal, limited, second-rate demon conjured up by a hero who is anxious that—without such a one to remind him of what it truly is—he would lose his purchase on the world even as he went about setting it to rights.

I found this text in Fein's folder for 1973. There is a holograph, with revisions, stapled to a typescript. As Max Brod gave Kafka's story its title, I have done the same for Fein's essay.

Emmanuel Fein died on September 29, 1963. According to his daughter, Fein believed the Sixties began on November 22 of that year, the day John F. Kennedy and Aldous Huxley died. He regretted his grandfather missed a decade he would have relished, one in which many of his lost causes were won, or at least reconsidered: red-lining, police brutality, manifestly unfair sentencing, bigoted zoning, industrial pollution, deceptive advertising, violations of labor law. Had he lived, Emmanuel Fein's career of defending the indigent and going after the affluent would have been celebrated. Even as it was, *The Philadelphia Inquirer* reported that his funeral attracted a couple thousand people. The eulogy was delivered by the head of the NAACP.

"On Sidekicks" is also a memoir, a "Feinian" one in its unexpected digressions, with an appearance by Kafka at the end. What is not typical are its revelations about family history, the author's child-hood, his love of the old B-Westerns, even the name of a girl on whom he had a prepubescent crush. Fein was rarely so open about himself in his writings, which tend more toward abstraction than confession.

It is never easy to say just what Fein's intentions were with his unpublished papers, or even why he chose to leave them unpub-lished. "On Sidekicks" may have been put aside with the intention of returning to revise and reorganize it—but, just as likely, it is merely a set of free associations and variations on a theme, observa-tions without any special focus or real unity. Nevertheless, that Fein revised and typed up what he wrote suggests a serious purpose.

As an adult, Fein liked movies, his taste maturing as he did. His daughter recalls his telling her that the first time he realized film could be an art-form was when he saw *The Seventh Seal*. Bergman's masterpiece was released in the U. S. in October, 1958, when Fein was sixteen. His comments here on the Westerns of his childhood indicate that he saw a lot of them but looked back on them as childish and formulaic, debased, melodramatic versions of *Don Quixote*; yet, as a boy, he loved them and, at thirty-one, thinking of his forebears, and especially of his grandfather's associate Bernard Black, wrote of them with affectionate nostalgia.

While Fein has a good deal to say about the men in his family, there is not a word here about the women, no mention of a grand-mother, mother, or aunt. I think the explanation is not that Fein was indifferent to women or unfamiliar with matriarchs—he had plenty to say of the former in *Want, Desire, and Need* and of the latter in *Aristocratic Democracy*. I believe he was concentrating here on the exclusively masculine worlds of the old Westerns and his grandfather's law office, the friction between fathers and sons, but, above all, on the bond of hero and sidekick, and his inability to be either one or the other.

IN TREVISO

CLAUDE was waiting for us outside the trattoria, just as he had promised when he suggested we drive up from Rome and spend a few days in Treviso. There he was with two newspapers, lounging at a table underneath the inevitable Cinzano umbrella.

"Oh, come," he'd said. "It'll be a kick to see you and Maya and you could show her Tuscany on the way. Come on Tuesday or Wednesday. Nora and I are a little cramped, I'm afraid, but I'll arrange for you to stay at this sweet *pensione*. It's right in the middle of town. We can rendezvous in the piazza. Trattoria Pontini. It's right next to the Palazzo—a bit to the left, like me. Can't miss it. I generally settle in from two to four." Maya, who had been bored in Rome and was no more eager to return home than I, leapt at the prospect of a road trip. "Oh, Daddy, rent one of those cute Italian cars." We took our time, leaving the *autostrada* for stops in Florence, Assisi, and Modena. By the time we got to Verona, Maya refused to go into any more churches or museums. "Mothers and babies, mothers and babies," she whined.

Treviso is small, feels hospitable, and all roads lead to the Piazza. We parked at one end of the square which was dominated by the ponderous Romanesque Palazzo dei Trecento. Maya spotted the Trattoria Pontini at once.

Claude wore a linen jacket draped over his shoulders, Italian style, and loose white trousers. His hair was much longer than I remembered, still smooth and black. He parted it high on the left so it fell over the right half of his face in a way that looked nearly natural and almost concealed his receding hairline. He was clean shaven and looked as if he'd modeled himself on Marcello Mastroianni in *La Dolce Vita*. In our student days, he'd always appeared as if he'd forgotten to shave for three or four days. "It's a *look*," he'd explained to me with that mock-earnestness of his. "You know, too caught up in work or play to bother—too inspired, or too dissipated." Did any other college freshmen use the word "dissipated," speak French laced with Italian—or vice versa—know all about the market in Leger lithographs, quote *The Magic Mountain* in German, reproduce entire Lenny Bruce monologues, or tap dance in the Quad? Could any others produce a cheese *soufflé* on a hot plate?

Claude rose to greet us, wrapped his arms around Maya, and lifted her high into the air, which, to my surprise, she not only tolerated but seemed to enjoy.

I noticed he was sporting a pair of tan slip-ons, *sans* socks. When we were freshmen, Claude had taken me into Macy's and bought a pair of wing-tips of the kind I associated with London bankers. Florsheim's price floored me.

"Never ever skimp on shoes," he'd said as if he knew very well I would but also that I'd never ever forget his advice not to.

Claude Kaplan had gone off to Europe around the time of the invasions of Cambodia and Laos in 1970, though for personal rather than political reasons. His first marriage to Phyllis—Philly—had ended with his losing custody of their two children and half his trust fund.

It was back in our junior year that Philly claimed to have become pregnant and Claude had determined to marry her, even when the pregnancy evaporated. He had discovered a yearning for domesticity. "Solves the whole sex issue and, besides, you know how I love to cook," he explained when he invited me to the City Hall wedding and the post-nuptial feast at the Capital Grille. "I'm buying Philly and me a condo. At last I'll have a proper kitchen!" Philly liked being married too, just not, eventually, to Claude. She came to see him as a grown-up child spoiled by too much money who would never do anything but indulge himself and others. She phoned me when the marriage was cracking up, maybe out of some self-justifying impulse, or because she felt I was owed an explanation. I tried to explain that it wasn't the money that paralyzed her husband but guilt over being adopted by a Chicago heiress and raised according to her mood swings. "Stop that stuttering or I'll nail your tongue to a board," he'd told me his right-wing grandmother once threatened during a family dinner. Ever witty, Claude always referred to the old lady as "the John Birch Society." "He *still* stutters," said Philly resentfully. His mother had sent Claude to a shrink when he was six, the kind who makes things worse. One morning during our sophomore year, his adopted father, a stockbroker, walked in front of an express train. His mother overdosed on sleeping pills three times before, perhaps owing to miscalculation, she took enough of them. "Well," Philly said in a hard-edged voice, "*I'm* not going to save him and I'm sure as hell not going to see my kids ruined."

Claude phoned me after the divorce decree came down and said he wanted out, that he was leaving the country, but would keep in touch. "Thought I'd do it the old-fashioned way, take a ship the way our forebears did, but in luxury and in reverse." On the voyage over he met Nora, who went after him. Claude was sophisticated in all respects except with women. He suffered from an unfortunate combination of acute shyness and libido. When I met Nora, I was struck by how much she resembled Philly—tall and blonde—only she was less courteous and more mercenary.

My own marriage blew up the same week the *Diptych* came out. My wife left a note for me, wished me well, said she didn't want any money, that she'd just made other plans. These didn't include Maya. She preferred liberation to custody. When I was invited to speak at a conference in Rome in June I decided to accept and took Maya along. Like my friend, I wanted out, at least for a little while. I had Claude's address in Venice and sent him a copy of the book.

It followed him to Treviso where he'd settled in for the summer and the last act of marriage number two. He phoned to congratulate me on the book and, when I mentioned Maya and I would be in Rome, he invited us to Treviso.

Claude put Maya down but held on to her hand and smooched it so theatrically that she giggled. "*Signorina Maya e molto bella! Parla Lei inglese?*"

Maya took back her hand and proudly retorted with one of the half-dozen sentences she'd memorized on the plane. "*Lo dica in inglese, per favore.*"

Claude and I laughed and Maya looked jollier than I'd seen her in a year. She and Claude were clearly determined to charm one another.

We sat down. "So, do you sit here swilling espressos every afternoon?" I asked.

"Oh, every now and then a cappuccino."

"Treviso was bombed in the war," said Maya who had gone at the guide book methodically. "I read about it."

Claude motioned widely. "Well, as you see, Signorina Maya, it's been cleaned up for you. I told them you'd be coming. It was all I could do to talk them out of the brass band."

The piazza was filled with dazzling sunlight but the heat was dry and bearable. "Summer in Venice," Claude had said, "is too hot even for Rimbaud."

An ancient waiter reluctantly sauntered out of the shade to ask what we would have. I ordered a Coca-Cola for Maya and an iced tea for myself.

"So, where's Nora?" I asked.

Claude shrugged indifferently. His indolence always pained me, made me think of the waste of his talents. He had been a good painter and a clever student when he bothered to pay attention. I had to wake him for his physics final by turning over his bed; he took the exam in his pajamas. After graduation, he did two years in architecture school—Le Corbusier was, for a time, a religion with Claude—then, with a year to go, he dropped out. This was the last straw for Phyllis. Then he went into what I thought of as his Mr. Toad phase. He designed inflatable furniture, worked on a scheme for farming lobsters, started then abandoned a book about currency collapses, collected early nineteenth-century reticules, then antique Caucasian rugs. He had introduced me to Debussy and Fragonard, to Handel and Mies van der Rohe, Heine and Gide, burgundy and Beaujolais. I also learned from him that the rich, like the poor, think about money almost all the time. Claude made me rejoice to be middle class, an ant to his grasshopper. If only he'd been poorer, I thought, he'd have achieved great things. Claude was my best friend from college days; so, even long after idolizing turned to deploring, he could always rely on my sympathy.

"Liked the book," he said. "You're a lot smarter than I thought. Passed it on."

"Oh?"

"To a young American woman I ran into here—*right* here, in fact. She's a bohemian, a semi-hippie, I guess, but very intelligent and so intense it's scary. Pretty too. But not to worry. I've ordered another half-dozen copies of *Diptych on Terrestrial Representation*—it's a mighty title, Dr. Fein. In German, it could flatten a barn."

"Nobody says 'Doctor,' Claude."

"Over here they do. Italians adore titles. *Dottore*. *Dottoressa*, which I like even better."

"Is the woman at our *pensione* a *dottoressa*?" asked Maya just because she was feeling neglected.

"Well, she ought to be. It's because of her that I put you there. Signor Muscato is so happy to leave the work to her that you never see the fellow at all. You've seen her so you know that Signora

Muscato looks like Gina Lollobrigida but she also cooks like Julia Child."

"*Bon appétit!*" cried Maya, who recognized the second name.

"*Buon appetito*," Claude teasingly corrected, with a raised finger. "Now, how about a tour? Stretch the old legs. Not too road-weary are we, *bella signorina?*"

"Oh no," said Maya *con gusto* and leapt up.

"You dropped off your bags at the *pensione*, yes?"

"At the desk. The room wasn't quite ready."

"Good, then off we go while the incomparable Signora Muscato lays on the finishing touches."

We took a turn around the Piazza dei Signorini. "They light it up every night," Claude confided to Maya, "like Christmas at Mulberry Street and Grand. It's magnificent, you'll see." We strolled the Passeggiata Lungo, then I Buranelli with its Venetian canal. "You can see we're in the Veneto," said Claude. Maya fell in love with the Isolotto della Pescheria, but was wilting all the same. "I guess I *could* do with a little nap at our *pensione*." She enjoyed saying the word *pensione*.

Claude sympathized. "*Povera piccola ragazza.*"

"I'm only seven," she explained.

"*Che? Sette? Gia! Impossibile!*" cried Claude and performed a little *salto* of disbelief.

Before we separated Claude insisted we come to dinner.

"It's a party and I'll be doing the cooking, of course—supplying the wine too, so dress casually and bring big American appetites. You'll be meeting that young woman I mentioned, the one who admires your book."

"You didn't actually say she'd read it."

"Didn't I? Well, apparently, she was bowled over by it. You'll like her, I think, and her name too; it's got three barrels. Leda Steinberg-Barrantes. A walking Greek-Ashkenazy-Mexican melting pot. Young, gifted, and named for a myth. What's *not* to like? Oh, and there'll be this Italian couple, the Parellas, pals of Nora's. We owe them a supper. Otto runs the toniest *schmatte* shop in town and Luciana's a clothes-horse. You can guess how they met. They seem to despise each other in a co-dependent kind of way."

Maya treated us to one of her baby hippo yawns.

"Signorina, are you by any chance partial to *osso buco*?"

We arrived for supper at sunset. Claude and Nora inhabited half of an ancient building on one of Treviso's canals. "Gutted and dolled up," Claude commented, "like a carp in a Chinese restaurant. It's comfortable. Everything new, except the walls—nice, thick ones they are too, cool as a cathedral." Then he made some zippy introductions and vanished.

The dinner was to be elaborate; Claude's cuisine always was. He fussed over it in the kitchen and we scarcely saw him before it was ready. Nora was left to preside but was uninterested in the job. She gave me one smile and about a minute of small talk before focusing on the Parellas. She entirely ignored Maya, who grew fidgety. I asked Nora if she could perhaps explore the apartment. Five minutes later Claude ducked his head out of the kitchen to inform us that Signorina Maya had graciously volunteered to act as *sous-chef*.

"He *always* does this to me," grumbled Nora to the Parellas and resumed gossiping with them. Luciana Parella wore something in yellow chiffon. Otto, who was built like a linebacker, stretched out a polo shirt and blue slacks. He directed asides to his wife under his breath and in rapid Italian to which she retorted just as quickly in a serpentine *sotto voce*. It took me a while to realize they were having an argument in *italiano piano*. But to Nora they spoke in *inglese forte* and their manner was nearly sycophantic.

Leda arrived late, for which Nora chided her. The Parellas looked her up and down and hardly acknowledged her. She wore a T-shirt and jeans and looked about sixteen. Shrugging off her hostess's reproaches, she appropriated me at once.

"Oh, your book, your book," she began in a high, breathless, Midwestern voice.

I waited for a predicate.

"I'm thrilled to meet you. Really. You're a kindred spirit, Mr. Fein." She spoke ingenuously, sure that she could pay me no higher compliment.

Leda Steinberg-Barrantes' large eyes were the color of dark chocolate, her eyebrows almost black. Her long blonde hair was pulled up into some sort of braid that unraveled by stages through the evening. She was pretty, just as Claude said, but then I've always found the combination of dark eyebrows and light hair attractive. Her face was that of a lost child who was too brave to care about being lost. She twisted in her seat, crossed and uncrossed her legs, rubbed her ankle, so restless that I wondered if she might be on something. She had no small talk and recognized no boundaries.

"Claude says you're a single parent. Doesn't that keep you from working? Do you ever resent your daughter? Where *is* she, anyway? Do you miss being married or do you feel liberated? Couldn't your wife understand your work? Do you think sex is a trap—you know, nature getting what it wants by tricking us into thinking we're getting what *we* want? Who's your favorite director? *Bergman*? I knew it! Do you think a genius can sometimes be astoundingly stupid? I tried to read Heidegger but gave up. I suppose I can see why he turned Nazi in 1933—conformist imbecility, good career move—but how could he *stay* one? I mean, did he confuse the Third Reich with the Ground of Being or what? You made a good point in your book when you said that people insist on being treated as subjects but love being complimented as objects. Do you think that's more true of women than men? I'd like to make a film about female-objects… maybe starring that Mrs. Parella over there."

I learned later from Claude that Leda was twenty-two, had run away from NYU's film school with the son of a big-shot anti-war Quaker, himself an erstwhile graduate student. "I think she said his field was classics or it might have been the ancient near-east—anyway, either Romans or Hittites. Apparently, he translated things brilliantly. Also he drank. She got away from him in Paris after he beat her up. Somehow she wound up here in Treviso. Her family sends her money but not very much. It's an act of charity to feed her body and her ego. She wants to make movies—oh, pardon me, not *movies* but *experimental films*. But I suppose you heard all about that."

I had, of course, because Leda had seated herself beside me at dinner and went on talking non-stop. Listening was not her forte. By the time we got to the *cassata torte* I was pretty much worn out. Maya sat by Claude and threw me jealous looks. Nora and the Parellas drank a lot of wine and more or less ignored the rest of us. "Yes, Claude really is an obsessive cook," she said when I complimented the meal. "I'm sure he's sublimating something awful but, heaven knows, it's not sex." At this, Signora Parella laughed more loudly than necessary..

Maybe being ignored by Nora reminded Maya of her absent mother. She threw one of her tantrums that night, albeit a relative short one. I calmed her by reading to her from a book of Italian folk tales that all end with *and from that time on they were always together and as happy as happy could be*. I promised her that we'd go hiking when we got home and go to the amusement park. I reminded her that in August she'd be spending a week with her grandparents who were staying up late inventing up new ways to spoil her. She listened to all of this in clenched silence; and, after I'd kissed her good night, she looked at me with narrowed eyes and, as she often does, said what was on her mind: "You *made* Mommy leave."

Thanks for sharing, I thought, but just tucked her in.

We were late getting up the next morning and, when we came

downstairs, the voluptuous Signora Muscato told me Claude had phoned and asked that I call him back.

"Look," said Claude, "I'm a defrocked father in exile. How about lending me Maya for the day? I'll take her into Venice and show her around. I'll watch over her like the crown jewels. Of course, only if she wants to and if you're willing. You could spend some time with Leda. I don't know if she's nuts about you or just nuts but last night she begged me to ask. *I absolutely have to talk to that man about my work.* That's what she said. Talk *more* about it, I guess. Did she use you all up during dinner?"

Maya leapt at the idea of a whole day in Venice with Claude, especially when I told her he'd promised a gondola ride up the Grand Canal. "Please, Daddy? *Please?*"

I gave in and spent the morning looking into shops. I bought a short leather jacket and a pair of sunglasses for Maya—wildly reckless without her there to try on two or three dozen. In an antique shop, I picked up a magnifying glass with a mother-of-peal handle and an edition of Dante bound in calfskin and so old that it felt almost spongy.

Claude had arranged for me to meet Leda me at the Pontini at one, when I could buy her lunch. She was right on time and gave me an unexpected hug. She sat down and beamed at me while I smiled back stupidly. We decided on a pizza but agreed it was disappointing, that real Italian pizza usually was.

"Imprinting," she said.

"Pardon?"

"You know, like ducklings. Your first pizza's the standard against which all others are measured. Even if you should find one that's better—objectively, I mean—your first one's always going to be the best. For me, it's Rizzo's on Homer Street."

Leda tended toward the apodictic in her pronouncements, but they were interesting. Her gush of speech was inexhaustible, nearly manic. She told me she liked Marx's cultural criticism but had no patience for his economics or politics, which reminded her of the phony revolutionaries she'd met at NYU.

"Narrative's absolute, of course, but it's true that the mode of delivery really is relative to the means of production and who controls them. A warrior aristocracy produces *The Iliad* for after-dinner entertainment, democracy the *Oedipus* cycle and hard seats costing one drachma; an urban bourgeoisie craves books like *Pamela* and *Tom Jones*, and the industrial age *Gone With the Wind* and *Les Enfants du Paradis*. Knowing modes of production and distribution is useful in understanding forms of expression, but I'm interested in what transcends them, in what Marx denies, the a-historical. For instance, I believe storytelling's always ambiguous—I mean it's always collective and private at the same time. You know, you sit in this theater with a hundred strangers and yet you're locked up in your own chamber of imagery. That how Ezekiel puts it. *Sure*, I read the Bible. A director can learn a lot from the Bible because its stories are so concentrated, like freeze-dried coffee. You kind of have to add water. Anyway, what I mean is that we're connected through stories yet isolated by them. That's fascinating. And it isn't limited to film or drama; early novels were read out loud. All those edifying family novels with young people making it to financial and marital security. The literate and the illiterate all need narra-tives as much as vitamins and minerals. We all like being read to, sung at. We all like to *watch*. Didn't some scientist prove that if you can't dream you'll go mad? That's so, isn't that so? I think you said something sort of like that in your book, didn't you?"

After this breathless lunch, Leda asked me to come to her apart-ment. I went reluctantly. It was a two-room affair in a squalid back street half a mile from the piazza. One room was taken up by a hot plate, a tiny refrigerator, two chairs and a card table, a 16mm camera, and piles of books. The *Diptych* lay on top of a tottering stack of film cans. I wondered if it had been left there deliberately.

The second room was wall-to-wall bed, plus a floor lamp with a purple cloth over it. The bed was strewn with satin pillows, round ones, squares, oblongs.

"I was going to show you one of the shorts I made in New York but now that you're here I'm ashamed of them. Five-finger exercises, juvenilia. If it's okay, I'd rather just tell you about a couple of projects that are still in my mind. Big ones—bigger, at least. And then, if you like, we can go to bed. You've really got to be a *little* sex-starved."

I was stunned, maybe a little offended, but also a little bit amused. To Leda, sex was apparently just a thing you did, a way of collecting experience, a trip to the gym, a sight-seeing tour, a pastime, collecting. To her, I supposed, men were simple creatures who never said no. It occurred to me that Claude must have said yes. His charity was not so pure. Recalling how Nora had treated Leda, I realized that she probably knew. As a seductress, however, Leda was inept. I'm no prude, but I saw that she was indeed lost.

"Tell me about your projects," I said gently and evasively. This was what she really wanted anyway, not a meaningless coupling.

"Okay. Pull up a chair. She sat down and we were knee to knee.

"The first is about Hansel and Gretel."

"The fairy tale?"

"It's fascinated me since I was a child. I mean, there are the great details, the witch and her house and that oven, the chicken bone, the feckless father and the nasty stepmother, the clever, resourceful kids, the bread crumbs, the treasure. But the happy ending never made sense to me. There was something wrong about it. I really brooded over it. The grown-ups were no help; I mean, they just *accepted* it and laughed off my questions. So what I want to do is my own version. I want to make it, you know, *realistic.*"

"A realistic fairy tale?"

"Don't be coy. You know very well how real fairy-tales are, how we never entirely outgrow them. They're lodged in our psyches and become part of us. That's what they're *supposed* to do. Tools of socialization, especially for little girls. Still, I always felt *Hansel and Gretel* had been cleaned-up, that it was, like, an *official* version of another story. A darker one."

"Darker than abandoned children, cannibalism, an old woman burned alive?"

"Yep, exactly. My film will begin with Gretel, Margarete on her deathbed. She's a famous old woman, a heroine, but now she's confessing the truth to an astonished priest. Most of the film will be a flashback."

"So, what really happened?"

"It's all about the stepmother, actually. In case you forgot, in the official version she's just conveniently dead when the kids get home. No explanation given. Their father's there but all we hear of the stepmother is that she's kaput. The witch is dead and so's the stepmother. Happy ending for the little ones."

"You think they're the same, then? Two versions of the bad and threatening ersatz mother?"

"That's too clever by half. Too clever. No."

"Then?"

"The way I see it, when Hansel and Gretel get home their father's out looking for them but the stepmother's right there in the house and, of course, anything but pleased to see them. Knowing her greed, they show her a little of the treasure and entice her to follow them to the witch's house to fetch back the rest. You see, they've planned it all out, made notches on the trees through the forest and everything. So, they take her back to the little house in the big, black forest. They tell her they think there's more treasure in the loft and, while she's up there, the children lay wood and kindling in the oven, right on top of the old woman's bones and ashes. Then they call up and say that the oven's full of gold coins. She rushes down, shoves them out of the way, and sticks her head in the oven. Hansel pushes her in and Gretel lights the kindling, then they slam the over door and run."

"But that's terrible."

"There's more," Leda said quickly, caught up her story. "The kids rush away, putting their hands over their ears to mute the stepmother's screams. They rush home, find their father, and tell him everything. He's horrified. The children make him agree to their story—what becomes the official version—and move into town where they buy the biggest house. The story circulates and the children become famous. The father, terrified of his children but subservient to them, with nothing to do, no wood to cut, wastes away. Johannes takes his share of the loot and moves to Thuringia, where he buys up land, rises to the rank of Junker, and oppresses the peasants. Margarete founds an orphanage and devotes herself to good works. The only true thing about the official story—the one every child in Germany knows—is the old woman's treasure. Margarete tells the priest the truth she's come to understand. The witch was simply a lonely old woman, miserly but the kind who says to cute children that she could 'just eat them up.' She did offer her and Hansel sweets and they told themselves, as children will, that she really did mean to eat them. She asked them to stay with her and help with the chores. And, of course, they really did kill her. But all that business about Hansel being locked in a cage and Grete giving him the chicken bone—all that was fabricated. Margarete has spent her life trying to make amends. She tells the priest she prays every day for her brother's soul and begs him to pray for hers... So, you see? The *real* story's about how poverty, hunger, unkind stepmothers and whipped fathers deform the souls of children. That's what Gretel came to understand. What I have, anyhow."

"What'll you call it?"

"*Johannes and Margarete*, of course." She frowned and added gloomily, "If I ever make it."

I suppose Leda would have liked me to declare that of course she would produce many films, that they'd be wonderful and make her famous. Don't all spirited young people like to bask in assurances to match their yet-to-be-thwarted ambitions? Leda certainly shared her generation's romantic attraction to movies and the glamour of celebrity; yet I'm sure she promised herself never to do anything for the sake of popularity. Maya liked Disney's concoctions and perhaps, when she was seven, Leda did too. But now she had taste and was determined to be original, worthy of her heroes—who were directors, not actors. She was one of those few who didn't merely long to *be* an artist but to *make* art.

"Anything everyone praises, even if it is good, is already played out," she said. "You quote somebody in your book who said the one thing that can't be imitated is the truth."

"Yes, because then it ceases to be true. An old rabbi said that."

She cocked her head like a sparrow and smiled. "Aren't *all* rabbis old? Especially the young ones?"

I laughed.

That first and last joke of hers broke the tension I had been feeling ever since she had called me sex-starved. Instead of going to bed, we went for a walk and ended up back at the Isolotto della Pescheria which Maya had liked so much.

Islands can provoke fantasies of snugness, of being an island oneself. I once dreamed of being home sick as a child. I was staring out my bedroom window at gigantic snowflakes falling over a silent world, safe on an island in a sea of snow. Of the stories I made up for Maya one of her favorites is "The Little Island." It seemed to me that Leda too craved an insular refuge. Her promiscuity was a mistaken tactic for dealing not just with men but the world outside her own skin. Perhaps she believed it was a way to distract her demons and so preserve her inner world inviolate, that later, when she was older and less fetching, there would be other ways to secure herself. Yet islands are eminently invadable, vulnerable to everyone and everything. The original Leda was queen of landlocked, inward-looking Sparta yet nonetheless a rape victim. This Leda looked outward from her harbor, like maritime Athens, yet she too had been abused. Where are women safe? Only on legendary islands like Lesbos or Wonder Woman's Paradise Island?

If I'd taken Leda up on the offer to share her bed she'd have revealed less to me. It was on that little island in Treviso that she told me the idea for the film she most wanted to make. We sat beneath a grassy bank and, shading our eyes, gazed out over the dazzling water. Even with my sunglasses I could barely stand so much Italian light.

"The working title's *Possibility*. I've got it all worked out, more or less. It'll run for sixty minutes, in five sections, not counting the opening credit, and each will be half as long as the preceding one, so it speeds up the way time does—you know, like when you're five and a year's twenty percent of your life but when you're twenty…"

"Or forty."

"Stop it. You're not *that* old. Well, anyway, the protagonist's name is Alexander. We see him first behind the credits when he's ten years old and staring dreamily out the window of his bedroom at a snowfall. French piano music, light and a little sardonic—Poulenc or Satie.

"The first full section lasts thirty minutes. It's based on a short story I wrote a couple years back. Here we see Alexander at twenty. He's sharing a seedy apartment with two young men and a young woman. *La Vie Bohème*. Alexander composes music. Two of the roommates are painters and lovers, but it's a difficult relationship because they're also rivals. The third young man's a writer and grad student. He's working on both a doctoral thesis and his first novel. He's our anchor, our stage manager, or Nick Carraway, the most together of the lot, pessimistic about his roommates' chances yet a little envious of their freer spirits. Alex is struggling with a violin concerto and his related infatuation with a talented young violinist.

He works part-time at the Conservatory and is giving her private lessons. Her father is in oil, in Houston, fabulously rich and has plans for his daughter; he's no fool either. When he learns of the relationship—which isn't even one yet—he flies to New York to disapprove in person. It's a big scene. Alex explains to the millionaire that his concerto is for his daughter; that it'll be her portrait in music, the expression of his adoration of her. Then there'll be short scenes from all the painters' lives accompanied by voice-overs from the author. He'll be reading from his novel, which is based on them. The novel's tragic. All the characters fail; one dies, and the rest live unhappily ever after. In real life, however, it's exactly the opposite. The two painters make a baby and score a joint show at an upscale Midtown gallery. The writer finishes his dissertation and publishes his novel, which makes the *Times'* bestseller list. The composer finally goes to bed with the rich girl, who refuses her father's demand that she return to Texas. He completes the concerto and, in the last scene of this part, she performs the premiere and it's a *succès d'estime*. I'll draw the soundtrack from Berg's *Violin Concerto* and parts of Prokofiev's *Second*. Do you know the Berg?"

"Yes."

"Good. Okay. The second section's fifteen minutes. Alexander's thirty and he's given up composing. He's working for a maritime insurance corporation, wears suits and detests his job, though he is good at it. He commutes from one of those beige suburbs where everything's *nice* and nothing's *good*. He's married but not to the violinist, and that's as much of a deadening routine as his commute. He works himself up to the decision to quit his job and divorce his wife; but, on the day he intends to submit his resignation, he gets this big promotion. They've picked him to head up the office in Antwerp. In the last shot he's holding the appointment letter in one hand, his letter of resignation in the other. For the sound track I'm thinking Bach's *First English Suite*.

"The third section will last seven and a half minutes. Alexander's thirty-five and opening a shop, a bookstore/café. He has a partner. They're best friends. Then they fall for the same woman, a customer who buys only French books. The partners fall out; the bookstore closes; the woman moves to Grenoble. For the music I'm thinking of either the waltz from Berlioz's *Symphonie Fantastique* or Martinů chamber music. Martinů's a happy hybrid, a Gallic Czech."

"I like Martinů too."

"That's reassuring. Okay. The fourth section runs three and a half minutes. We see Alexander at forty, looking tough. He's in a room across from police headquarters in a Middle Eastern country. Through the window he watches men in uniforms come and go. He carefully unpacks a sniper rifle. He has his orders. But he's been betrayed and the scene ends in a shoot-out. The music will be the *presto* from Beethoven's Opus 130 quartet."

"He escapes?

"Of course he does. And in the fifth section—running time, ninety seconds—he's fifty and eating an elaborate meal in a fancy Viennese restaurant. He takes notes for his column. The staff eyes him anxiously. He's a well-known food critic. Always dines alone. The music will be from the *Das Diner* section of Strauss' *Bourgeois Gentilhomme*."

"Very amusing—Viennese table music, but still a little French."

"The final section will be thirty seconds. Alex is sixty. We're in his study—a heavy desk, wood-paneling, lots of bookshelves. He's put on a recording of Mahler's *Das Lied von der Erde*. The last movement. For twenty seconds, we see only his face; the camera moves in for a close-up then a close-up of the close-up. All the little lines and pouches. He's staring at the camera. His expression's blank, unreadable. Then the camera pulls back and we notice he's holding a pistol in his lap. He raises it just a little and shuts his eyes. And that's it. *Fin. Fine. Finito. Das Ende*. That's all folks."

Leda was almost panting.

"Such serious music," I wanted to say. "What? No blues? No Stones or Beatles?" I very nearly asked, "Why not the *Liebestod*?"

But before I could say anything, Leda started rattling away again, asking me about this scene or that one; but, afraid of what I might say, hardly giving me a chance. "Of course I'll need to work out lots of details. I just wanted to give you an idea— you know, like what they call a treatment. So, well, what do you think? Is it a good concept, halving the length of each section? Not too precious?"

Auden remarked the only mistake one can make in assessing the efforts of young poets is to say something to stop them from writing. Sincerity comes a distant second, commandment-wise.

"It's powerful and it's interesting," I said. "I do like the idea of halving the length of the episodes. And then the music, of course. It sounds terrific, Leda."

She was turned away from me, so I was watching her profile. No smiling; just the tiniest twitch around the mouth. She looked more exposed than ever, almost like the coast of an uninhabited island. Maybe she wasn't buying my praise, or perhaps she was just anticipating more and better. To the young, praise is the only constructive criticism.

She began to tremble and still wouldn't look at me. She spoke almost in a whisper. "You know, I'm more like Claude than like you."

"Meaning?"

"Meaning that I'll never accomplish anything, not really."

"But Leda, you're just starting out. Your ideas are wonderful; you're bursting with them. You'll achieve—"

She got to her feet. "For God's sake, don't *encourage* me."

I stood too and now she turned toward me. I thought of Maya and how much more I had to do than just keep her alive. "Sure, I'll achieve what I *can*, yes. I certainly won't be spoiled by having too much money, and I won't be distracted by men either. Even failure isn't going to deter me." The bitterness of her tone took me aback. "I'm from pioneer stock, from the prairie. I come from a small town in Michigan, and I've been trying to escape it since I stopped being a healthy little animal, since I developed this illness. You might as well call it consciousness. I wanted an *interesting* life, but what I've gotten is a lonely one. I've built one of those lopsided castles children make out of popsicle sticks. Not exactly stable."

"Maybe you ought to go back. Not home, not to Michigan, but to school. Life isn't just a series of adventures."

She gave a little laugh. "Hah! You know, my parents liked to say I had an artistic temperament. 'Our Leda's got an artistic temperament,' they'd say. That was their way of not understanding me. They meant to encourage me, like you. But there's no such thing as the artistic temperament. The whole idea's just a dodge, an excuse for—for instability."

"You *are* an artist," I said lamely.

She crossed her arms. "Nora's going to take Claude for a lot of money. I'm not the reason, but I *am* the excuse, and I don't know squat about terrestrial representation."

After that, we left the island and headed back toward the piazza. Leda wouldn't let me walk her back to her apartment but she did smile at me, maybe a little wistfully, and took my hand in both of hers. "I think I'll go to Germany next. Tried love in Paris, and I've been to Venice. Maybe I'll give death a shot in Berlin."

And there was the *Liebestod*, after all.

"Please don't talk like that, Leda," I said. She gave me a chaste peck on the cheek then walked off, waving but not looking back.

> *When did the Lovedeath turn to the death of*
> *love, the death of love to the love of death?*
> *Was it in the middle of a sentence*
> *or in the silence between breath and breath?*

I made my way back to the *pensione*. Claude had phoned from the train station in Venice and left a message for me. He reported that he and Maya had had a swell day, and I should meet them at his place around five, then we'd all go out for a big banquet at Il Basilisco.

When I arrived, Maya was waiting on the terrace. She ran to me, threw herself into my arms. "Oh, Daddy. They've been just *yelling* at each other," she exclaimed into my chest and broke into tears.

Inside, Nora screamed something. A door slammed. Claude swore.

There was no banquet at Il Basilisco.

That night, I made the flight reservations and loaded up our rented Fiat in the morning. As Maya absolutely refused to come with me, I left her with Signora Muscato while I went to say my goodbyes to Claude. He looked drawn and he needed a shave. "Awful sorry, old man," he said as lightly as if we were still freshmen. "Not that I didn't see it coming. Look, give me a call when you get home. Okay? And please give my love to Maya. All my love."

Just past noon, Maya and I boarded a plane at Venice's airport which is named for another restless spirit, Marco Polo.

Six months later Claude phoned from the house he'd just bought in Pennington, New Jersey. The divorce was a done deal, and even more expensive than the first one. "I'm seeing somebody," he said, "terrific woman, a sculptor." He'd met her at Sotheby's, where she had a day job. I asked if he had any news about Leda.

"As a matter of fact, I do. She sent me a letter. It followed me from Treviso but took more than a month to find me. Did you know she went off to Germany right after you left? Well, apparently she had some sort of breakdown in Berlin. The hospital called the embassy and *they* called her parents who came over and took her back home. Said she was feeling so much better and planning to leave soon, because there was still so much she wanted to do. Her plan was to finish up at NYU and then she thought she might try Mexico. There was something about making a documentary about peyote-eaters or the people who smuggle stolen American cars. But, to be honest, I've got my doubts. Her handwriting looked pretty weird. You know, shaky. Look, gotta go. Love to Maya."

Fini. Das Ende. That's all folks.

EDITOR'S NOTE

I found this piece near the top of the second of Fein's thick files for the year 1973. It was among the last things he wrote during that exceptionally productive year; it almost certainly dates from late December. Fein did not take the trouble to type up a fair copy yet the text shows numerous corrections. The most noteworthy of these is the curious interpolation of four lines of verse. I only appreciated its significance, and that of Fein's allusion to Wagner's *Tristan*, because in the first file for 1973 I discovered a poem dated February 13; that is, around the time that his marriage ended. Here is the complete text of this uncharacteristically revealing and intimate poem:

LIEBESTOD

The still bedroom was dimmed by blue drapes.
Though they were outside time it mattered
it should be a November afternoon
when exertion brought its own reward.
He was an expiring salmon expending the
last erg of energy in the sweet water
of his birth; wave on wave buoyed him
then dropped until he plumbed the
matrix of all metaphor, perishing

with limbs of lead into the dusky void—
only to renew the compulsive cycle
of recurrence heralded by Nietzsche,
framed by Klimt, explicated by Freud.
Was it the love of death,
the death of love, or merely one
soul lost in the release of spirit,
the love that feels like death?
Memory shuffles delight up with regret.
When did the Lovedeath turn to the death of
love, the death of love to the love of death?
Was it in the middle of a sentence
or in the silence between breath and breath?

Fein seldom wrote lyrical poems or, for that matter, memoirs. He did not keep a journal, but it is clear that his brief sojourn in Treviso moved him to write about it months later, probably just after he received the phone call he mentions from Claude Kaplan. I think this was owing not only to the poignant visit with the freshman friend he so admired and his encounter with the unstable Leda Steinberg-Barrantes, but also because of where Fein found himself in his own life. Like Claude, he had inherited money and gone through the dissolution of a marriage. Like Leda, he had cultural ambitions he feared might exceed his ability and self-discipline.

Another reason why Fein might have memorialized the 1973 visit to Treviso is that the year marked the end of an era. The year was a significant one for America. Fein himself thought of it as a transitional moment, the real end of the Sixties. In his opinion, spiritually speaking that decade began with the assassination of President Kennedy in November 1963 and ended with the withdrawal of U.S. troops from Vietnam—along with the eruption of the Women's Liberation Movement, the Arab oil embargo, and the post-war inflation, all of which came in 1973. The year was also a turning-point in Fein's life. It began with the simultaneous publication of his first book and the end of his marriage, making him at once an author and a single parent. Maya Fein tells me she has retained a few memories of that trip in June of her eighth year. She remembers nothing of their time in Rome but does recall the long, interrupted drive to Treviso, also her day with Claude in Venice, which she describes as "hot but thrilling." Claude Kaplan was a very good companion for a child, apparently, at least for a few hours. "He bought me a leather purse—my first real handbag—and a straw hat I thought quite stylish." But what she recollects most vividly is the explosive scene on their return to Treviso. Her own parents, Maya told me, had done all they could to shield her from their arguments, to mitigate the tension in the household; Nora and Claude Kaplan had no such scruples. She describes their fight as "terrifying and operatic. I felt I was seeing a grotesque version of my own parents, of *all* parents. It was all about that hippie girl who'd been at dinner." Evidently, whatever scabs had formed over Maya's wounds were ripped off in seconds.

Claude Kaplan's third marriage proved more enduring than the first two. It seems to have had a settling effect on him. After buying the Pennington house, he invested what remained of his inheritance in a six-story building in Tribeca. With the rental income, he lived the life of a gentleman of leisure in New Jersey horse country. His wife had a studio and two cats, which seemed to content her. They had no children. He sold his building during the first of Manhattan's gentrification booms after which he and his wife traveled widely. They moved to Palm Beach in 1995, where he died in 2003.

The only facts I have been able to determine about Leda Steinberg-Barrantes are that she returned to New York University in 1975, suffered another breakdown, failed to complete her degree, and died in 1982, in Michigan. The obituary is brief and gives no cause of death.

FEIN ON FAULK

I NEVER knew Ben Faulk but I did meet his remarkable fourth and final wife, Estella Gismondi. "I was his Catherine Parr," she told me.

This was last year when the Museum of Modern Art mounted its Faulk retrospective. Most people thought the widow was credited as co-curator to secure her cooperation or just as a courtesy. In fact, it was Estella who arranged every detail, just as she had organized her husband.

On my own I would never have gone to see what was allitera-tively billed as "The Four Phases of Faulk." I'm ashamed to confess that I dislike museums, especially big ones. The pocket museums I saw in Europe—the Munch in Oslo and the Musée Matisse in Nice for instances—appealed to me. One can concentrate in such places; there's an end to them that you can see, and the senses aren't so overloaded. I once told an art major that my ideal gallery would have only a single picture in it. Misunderstanding me, she earnestly asked, "Which one?" The truth is that, like shopping malls, museums weary me almost as soon as I step over their thresh-olds. It isn't just the sensory assault, though. Art affects me with the same kind of bafflement my college physics text did. Of course, there are pictures and statues I love, monuments, emblems; and I'm not utterly ignorant about art history, though in the detached way I'm informed about the Roman Republic. Perhaps I suffer from an impaired visual imagination—whatever that is. I need pictures and installations and performance art explained to me and I'm grateful to the articulate experts who can actually do it—that is, not the connoisseurs who lean backwards and admiringly mumble "there's a sort of Bonnard quality," "obviously derivative of the work of Manicotti Delacorte," or "did you notice the heroic placement of that dab of red?"[16]

I only went to the MoMA because my friend Hallinan phoned and begged me to go with him. Since Harry's wife read Betty Friedan and left him—"on principle," he had said—he's been so forlorn that it's hard to refuse even the largest of his requests and this was a small one. He said he needed to see the show but couldn't face going on his own. I asked why he felt the need to go at all. He said it was because he had met Faulk and his wife back when he and Helen were living out in Southold, where Ben Faulk had set up his studio. The Faulk spread had been featured in *Life*. "There were pilgrims," said Hallinan.

"You knew the Faulks well?"

"A couple of dinner parties. I knew the wife better, liked her more too. Faulk I never got much of a fix on. The man liked to keep his mouth shut."

"Inscrutable genius, eh?"

Hallinan paused. "No. I'd say more like distracted or just plain uninterested. I had the strange notion that he might be, you know, stupid. Ridiculous. He was famous; but he just sat there and, you know, it wasn't like a *brilliant* silence. Estella was the really intelligent one, in my opinion. A formidable woman. She moved Faulk around the way you might a mannequin on wheels."

I chuckled. Hallinan had a gift for such metaphors. "Was he senile, ga-ga?"

"Don't think so. He wasn't that old and he was working all the time."

"Mannequins aren't inscrutable."

[16.] Delacorte's work is examined admirably in fragment XIX, Manicotti II, in Felt's *First Folio*, Felt Collection, New York City.

"No, not even absent-minded. But they sure aren't *sociable*, either."

"Maybe Faulk just didn't care for Long Island dinner parties. Did *you?*"

"Mannequins can't *bathe* themselves either," was Hallinan's answer. "Look. Is eleven okay?" He wanted to get off the phone even more than I did. Perhaps that's why he neglected to mention that we had a rendezvous with the formidable Estella Gismondi.

At the entrance to the four large galleries an aluminum table had been set up and covered with green baize. It held brochures arranged in fans, like canasta hands. These reproduced one of Faulk's most famous works from each period of his career, included a brief biography that listed the artist's accumulated honors, thanked lenders and donors by name. Behind this table a diagram of the exhibition had been painted right on the wall. It featured several quotations from critics about Faulk's work. These were rich in superlatives but not notably informative.

I had just picked up one of the brochures when Harry cried, "Ah, *there* she is!" He did this loudly and not looking at me, the way people do when they want the person indicated—the "she"—to hear, an indirect greeting. A striking woman in a well-tailored suit (jet black) and imaginatively coiffed hair (silky white) was seated on the banquette nearest the entrance. She had been observing the visitors but turned to look our way. *The Spirit of Manhattan*—as if she were an allegorical monument—that was my initial impression. She projected elegance, restraint, self-assurance, worldliness and wealth. Her face was an intelligent one, uniting astute, impregnable sophistication (Upper East Side) with bohemian acumen (Green-wich Village). Her age was hard to fix, but not because she'd had herself fixed. She was too at ease in her skin for that. Whatever her age, you could see the intimidating beauty she must have been twenty years ago. She didn't get up or lean forward but remained seated, legs casually crossed. The smile she gave Hallinan seemed to hold back a good deal in the warmth department. When Harry introduced us, she took my hand like a queen who's worked at mastering the common touch. I felt about sixteen years old.

"It's a pleasure to meet the author of *Diptych on Terrestrial Representation*. Your book's not just stimulating but full of surprises, Mr. Fein. I could never guess where you were going to fly to next. Quite the *title*, by the way."

She'd read my book? A mumbled "thank you" was the utmost I could manage in the face of such unexpected and ambiguous praise. I thought of Hallinan remarking on how much brighter this woman was than her celebrated, inarticulate husband, and I believed it.

"When Estella phoned me about the show, she mentioned she'd been reading this unusual book," said Harry. "I told her the author was an old chum of mine. That's why I asked you along. Didn't I say?"

Apart from my editor, I had never met anybody who had read my book, nor had I ever expected to do so.

Four galleries. Four Periods. Four Wives. The scheme was so well known even I'd heard of it. First came the "Series of Series" (sections of 1940s cars, teenage dancers, not-quite-possible houses); next, the extreme, nearly abstract landscapes (arctic, desert, surreal, maybe extraterrestrial); then the brief departure into so-called "environmental installations"; finally, the portraits of "Invented Worthies."

The tour began briskly, with our widowed guide commenting in just the fashion I like, presuming nothing, going straight at the point of each painting. "Those cars are from his childhood, already outmoded when he painted them. That was in the second half of the Fifties. He adored the hulking things like a child. Collected pictures of them and hung them like pinups. Those cars were aesthetic touchstones for him. They represented beauty and money—beauty bought for money. In Binghamton, only the rich could afford Plymouths, Oldsmobiles, and Hudsons—let alone Cadillacs. Look like they're made out of cast-iron, don't they? That was on purpose.

The grills really thrilled him. Plutocratic smiles, capitalist grimaces. He loved the curves, too, the—what do you call them?—the *skirts* and the big white-wall tires. Come closer. See the brush strokes? Caresses. The colors are feelings. Joy, envy, admiration, jealousy. Red, yellow, black, pink and orange. Ben's father did piecework in a shoe factory. There wasn't much money. He liked to say his brushes saved him from the shoes. Reminding himself to be industrious, to justify every bite of steak, spurring himself on." She pointed to a pair of oxfords lying in the corner of a picture of a gleaming yellow Chrysler convertible. One was partially squashed, as if it had just been run over.

"Now, as to the dancers—that was high school. He met Linda, his first wife, at a hop and they got married the day after gradua- tion. People did that back then, back there in Binghamton anyway. Obviously, Ben *needed* to be married. So, the dancers, high school, and Linda. Ben was always trying to make the private into the public. But then, what real artist doesn't try to do two contradictory things? Of course, I don't have to tell the author of the *Diptych* that the trick's to turn the intimate into the cosmic without betraying it. You agree, don't you? A really *good* autobiographical work has to affirm the artist *and* erase him."

"Ben said that?" Harry asked.

Her tight smile made me certain she was about to tell a fib. "Something like it."

In the second gallery, we spent a few minutes in front of a landscape that looked like a Constable on both uppers and downers, bright green pastures and yellow meadows spread out under a huge, livid sky, an über-pastoral marred by bomb craters. Estella was just beginning to explain it to us when Harry recognized a woman standing in a group before another picture.

"Good Lord," he exclaimed. "There's Leda Zeman. I've got to say hello."

And just like that, with a swift, rude "Please excuse me," we were abandoned.

Estella and I watched, fascinated, as he cut the woman out of her flock of art-lovers then, like a good sheep dog, maneuvered her into a corner. I suppose it made a bond, being deserted like that. As Hallinan took Leda Zeman's arm and led her toward the exit, he gave us a shrug: *what-can-I-do-I'm-sure-you understand*. It wasn't yet a year since his marriage broke up. He'd told me how he yearned to pick somebody up on the rebound, or, better still, to *be* picked. And there was Leda Zeman, suddenly at the top of his priority list. On the evidence, for Faulk being married was normal, essential, perhaps obligatory, maybe biblically ordained; but, in any case, the man couldn't function without the guidance, comfort, and companionship a wife. My friend Harry Hallinan was just such another.

Faulk's second wife, Brenda, was a Midwestern hippie afflicted with wanderlust and trendiness. It was she who prompted the big landscapes. The third wife, Olivia, was from a Main Line Quaker family, earned an art history degree from Bryn Mawr, with the customary a minor in French, turned dramatically on her parents and siblings then moved to SoHo. She was, according to her successor, intellectually ambitious and doggedly avant-garde. She met Faulk at a gallery opening, married him two months later, and changed his direction, briefly—thus the deliberately ugly "environmental installations." As everyone knows, most avant-garde art looks obsolete by next Tuesday.

Estella next vouchsafed me an account of her role in the fourth gallery, the amusing imaginary portraits. "It began as a game, a parlor game, just something to distract him. Ben was stuck and miserable so I dreamed it up to give him something to fool with until some real inspiration struck. I'd make up the names and biographies then he'd do the portraits. Oh, we laughed and laughed." She smiled and then fell silent and you could almost hear the unsaid next sentence: "And then he died."

I'll bet they did have fun. Fancy certainly ran free. The portraits vary in style from strict, dry Dürer to sloppy, humid de Kooning. The colors run from hardly any at all (brown paint on a sepia background) to simply arbitrary, to downright psychedelic. Estella was pleased when I asked her about the clever background details.

"We really let ourselves go on those," she said and, for a moment, I thought she might actually chuckle. I'd have liked to see that woman chuckle. "These are from the coat of arms of an extinct Tuscan family. The little cat, tortoise, and ermine are supposed to be allegorical. I found that serpent with a head at both ends in a bestiary; it's called the *Amphisbaena*."

"It seems like it might be allegorical."

"I thought so, too. But I've no idea of what. Do you?"

I recognized the background in one picture. It was the unforgettable sky from El Greco's *View of Toledo*, a popular dorm poster in my day. But the portrait was Roman. Colubra Exactorius, *legatus* of the Fourth Legio, had the distinction of being declared Emperor of Rome in the morning and assassinated before dark. Next came Baron Anmassand von Pappenheim-Stutzig, an eccentric Westphalian nobleman who subsisted solely on chickpeas and the flesh of acorn-fed pigs. He twice attempted to challenge Otto von Bismarck to a duel and wrote a book about the *tödlichste Spinne*, a poisonous spider. The Scotsman Charles Bentwhistle, Lord Lothian, devised a method of making a disgusting wine from the genus *Cirsium*—i.e., the thistle. While exploring the upper reaches of the Blue Nile, His Grace had a fatal run-in with a herd of hippos. Zara Begum had preternaturally long black hair and sang lead for the group Filthy Filthy Lucre. She was pursued by an infatuated Saudi prince and vanished, the rumor being that she was kidnapped and spirited to Riyadh. John Hazel Smith tried selling life insurance in Iowa before finding his métier as a popular televangelist, rapist, and embezzler. Doña Elena Sueno Pretencia y Bruja earned a bad reputation during the reign of Alfonso XII, while Sun Pu'i-cho, a Sui period court poet, wrote one satire too many and was exiled to Goguryeo, now North Korea.

I regret that I have so little feeling for visual art, that I am attracted chiefly by the obvious. Nevertheless, I don't care for what's pretty ("I do it *first*, then they do it *pretty*," the young Picasso is said to have whined to Gertrude Stein; though, later on, in his fame, the complaint changed to, "If I spit, *they will* take my spit and frame it as great art"). Like the refreshingly modest Norman Rockwell, I can grasp the vital distinction between illustration and the real thing, even if I can't find the words to describe it precisely. I can even, on occasions, glimpse the intention behind novelty; still, I don't care for the modernist maxim, "It's art if the artist says it is." Radical relativism seems to me as likely to lead to a dead-end in aesthetics as in ethics.

What is this "obvious" art I like? It must be the predigested, the canonical; in other words, what I think of it is what others have already thought, what I have been taught to think. Confronted with the new—and what's more common these days?—I feel baffled, even resentful. The only difference between me and the rube I heard at the Guggenheim braying that his eight-year-old could do better is that I'm not brave enough to say it out loud. I really do prefer the spontaneous abstracts and imaginative woodcuts Maya did in art class, back when she was still young enough to see with Cézanne's "eyes of the newly born." Of course, there are works that appeal to me immediately, for some private or even subconscious reason. These I suppose I understand—or misconstrue—in my own way. For example, I'm fond of Vermeer's "Girl Asleep" and was shocked to find out the experts say it's an allegory about laziness. It's a wonderful painting that rewards the closest scrutiny. But who can love an allegory about sloth? I always thought just the opposite— that she's fallen asleep because she'd been working so hard at her immaculate Dutch housekeeping.

My teaching stints have taught me that the fear of looking

foolish is an affliction of the Academy, a terrible constraint on free thought. Silence might suggest deep wisdom while speaking up is risky. Better people should wonder if you're an idiot than that you should prove it. In the art world, it seems much the same—except that, instead of silence, anxiety demands that you say something, even something nonsensical: "It's wonderful, a work that vibrates with life but is still wholly penetrated by death." Even that kind of nonsense is preferred to just standing there with your mouth open. In the nineteenth century, nobody would pay ten francs for a Van Gogh; in the twentieth, people are scared of missing the next Vincent. That may be the secret truth of the art market in our time. New is better than good and the new has to be unintelligible— how else could you tell it's new? Ample scope for fraud, for trays of little boxes with old keys in them, reinforcing rods welded to discarded sinks, polyhedrons of rusting iron with heroic titles like *Agamemnon*. As the philistine and the boy proclaiming the emperor naked sound so much alike, I suppose it's safer to mouth clichés, to go along, even extol—albeit with a caveat here and there to hedge your bets.

My anxiety grew as we came to the end of the last gallery, the one which meant the most to my docent. What did I make of Faulk's last works? What could I say about them to his devoted widow? I could say that I liked the imaginary portraits best, which had the virtue of being true. I could say something vapid but safe, such as that they were "craftsmanlike and original"; I could call them "disturbingly interesting" or, alternatively, "interestingly disturbed." I could say that I admired his mastery of so many diverse styles, that would be safe enough. Actually, my only original impression about the portraits was that a game had been played—not just in the last but in all four galleries. Faulk's work metamorphosed with each marriage; somehow I felt certain it wasn't the other way around. But, standing there by his imposing widow, I wasn't about to set foot on perilous terrain. I should be polite, maybe even venture a mumble about muses. It was unthinkable to say anything rude to this intelligent, soignée woman, to speak about creativity and sex. I might just as well say that I felt no emotional connection whatever to anything I'd seen and that I thought her husband's life's-work one of craft, not art, fancy rather than imagination.

I decided to be polite, complimentary, to express my condolences for the loss to her and to Art, and then make my escape. But Estella surprised me.

"Are you free for lunch?"

"Well," I stammered.

"Oh, please say yes. It'd consider it a treat to chat with the author of *The Diptych on Terrestrial Representation*."

Though I was being teased, I couldn't refuse this breathing avatar of the Manhattan cocktail—not the kind concocted of whiskey, vermouth, and bitters, but the one made of culture and money. I said yes.

"Good. But *not* the cafeteria here. I know a nice quiet place nearby. Excellent seafood and the most *perfect* Caesar salad. It's the fresh anchovies." She took me by the arm and laughed. "Ben left me a rich widow and when I sell the place on Long Island—well then, oo la-la. So, lunch is on me."

The restaurant was what one would expect at those lofty Manhattan latitudes: venerable, thickly carpeted, twilit. Estella was greeted warmly and by name. She asked the maître d' if we could have one of the two corner booths.

As we made our way through lunching ladies and deal-making men to the soft leather in the far corner, she whispered, "I've been eating here almost daily since work began on the show. They're very nice."

I resisted a perverse impulse to add, "And you tip so well."

The widow of Ben Faulk turned out to be in a mood for candor, readier to speak than listen. This was lucky for me because I had nothing I wanted to say, though I did have questions.

As soon as we settled in, a cheerful young waitress came to ask about drinks. We both turned down the offer. "You can forget the menus," said Estella. "We'll both have Caesar salads. An iced tea for me and…"

"Make it two."

"Caesar salad's all right?"

"Perfect. With the freshest anchovies."

"The *very* freshest, hardly even deceased." She settled into the soft leather and smiled appreciatively. "Now. Your *book*."

"Yes?"

"It's full of humor, but of a very particular kind. You aren't angry with the world but then you're anything but satisfied with it either. All that dead-pan academic satire about classification just misses being—what?—brittle? You know, I'd have loved to read Ben that passage where you talk about cars. You know, where you write that knowing who *owns* the Buicks and Mercedes-Benzes affects how we classify them. He'd have enjoyed that. And when you say the mistake of the taxonomists is not have read enough poetry—"

"*Good* poetry."

She raised her carefully cultivated eyebrows. "Exactly. Anyway, it's so clever and, again, in such a special way. I wonder how you ever found a publisher."

She was magnificent in her way, not really a type at all but an individual beyond the reach of taxonomy. As for me, I felt like a little boy being teased by a grande dame, then chucked under the chin.

"Ben was impossible with words, you know. He simply couldn't talk about his work; he either got tongue-tied or repeated something he'd read in a review. People thought it was humility or a wish not to pull the veil away from his mystery when the truth is he was simply inarticulate. The visual was his medium, his *only* one." She paused before the next, enormous admission. "He wasn't creative in the usual sense; I mean, he could never *improvise*. Ben's real talent was for completing assignments."

"Assignments?"

"Oh, he gave some to himself, of course; but what I mean is the ones *we* all gave him."

"His wives?"

"I'm sure you noticed. Who wouldn't? The four *phases*. Anyway, it was absolutely useless to interview him though people didn't stop asking and he'd accept, for all the good it did them. Most of the interviews were never printed."

"You remind me of something Socrates said—or Plato said he did. It was at his trial when he was explaining that he was wiser than the poets he because he knew nothing—"

"While they pretended they did?"

"That was the irony. Anyway, he said everybody there—and there were five hundred jurors and probably as many idlers there to enjoy the show—could talk better about their poetry than the poets who wrote it."

"Well," she said, "I guess that does fit Ben, especially when you consider the cataracts of nonsense that have been written about his work. The long piece about the show in last week's *New Yorker* wasn't bad at all, though. Did you see it?"

"Sorry."

That night I re-read the passage from the *Apology*:

> … that showed me in an instant that not by wisdom do poets write poetry, but by a sort of genius and inspiration; they are like diviners or soothsayers who also may say many fine things, but do not understand the meaning of them.

The New Yorker article I read later and it set me to thinking. The "art world"—which is to say, the art market—is tautological. Isn't Faulk's work important chiefly because people who collect important art buy it? Save for the mandarins of art criticism, intrinsic value is elusive to most of us, notional and apt to evaporate. On the other hand, maybe it takes a century or two to know what's good-in-itself. The authorities' taste and education have to be placed in the balance, of course; nevertheless, the market for contemporary work still looks like a casino. If appearance trumps reality in the contemporary art world, that must be because there isn't any reality you could call objective—not yet. So, value lies in the name of the artist, and that name derives its value from who buys the work with the name on it and whether the right people say nice things about it in places like *The New Yorker*... and so the whirligig comes round again.

A Socratic question: Is a work is valuable because it's valued or valued because its valuable? I'd say the former. Supply and demand appear to rule with an iron fist; but, the moment you ask what governs *them*, an abyss opens at your feet. Meanwhile, I wouldn't care to guess how much a Faulk is going to fetch in five years.

Perhaps Estella Gismondi was in a mood to be candid and confided in me because we didn't know one another, because I struck her as an outsider to the world of Midtown galleries, a disinterested stranger whose odd book had amused her. Or maybe it was Harry Hallinan with whom she had intended to have this confessional tête-à-tête but, as he had absconded, she had to make do with me.

"Ben never felt, well, like an im*pos*tor; it wasn't that. You have to know there wasn't anybody more scrupulous. And scrupulous people doubt themselves. Ben just couldn't cope with success. He felt it was wrong, that all his work didn't really amount to anything. Can you imagine how uncomfortable a position he was in, to care enormously about his work and yet to find it impossible to believe it was good, maybe even to take himself seriously?"

I wondered if it was because she'd read my book that she thought I could understand that particular mode of discomfort. "*Did* he take himself seriously?" I asked.

That question provoked an appraising look, maybe the kind she'd have given one of her husband's portraits. Apparently, I passed. "A good question," she allowed then leaned back and took a sip of iced tea. "One night, Ben got a call from the gallery. The owner was bursting. She'd just sold a picture for eighty thousand dollars. When he hung up the phone, Ben said to me, 'Would it be rude to make little of what others make so much of?' That's what he was like, you see. He *couldn't* be an impostor; he was too honest. The dear man had no vanity at all... Anyway, that's the closest I've got to an answer to your question, that Ben worried it would be a shame *not* to take himself seriously when other people did."

"Which means he tried to but couldn't?"

"Yes, I suppose. I never thought of it quite that way. Yes, you're probably right," she concluded, then changed her voice into a pistol. "Do you take your *book* seriously? Your *Diptych*?"

I thought it best to treat the question as rhetorical. I smiled and changed the subject.

"A thrice-divorced artist. How did you come to marry him?"

"That's how we met, actually. Divorce, I mean. It was in our lawyers' waiting room. Same firm, different attorneys—a boy for him and a girl for me. My first husband was a cliché. He traded me in for a newer model." She shrugged. "But Ben, poor baby, was walked out on three times, and he couldn't manage on his own, not the laundry or the cooking, not the bills or the painting, for that matter. He didn't complain, but you could see the devastation—I mean, in his whole body."

"And this pathos moved you?"

"I suppose I saw a cause, a vocation. Maybe I was vulnerable—

but I was a little dazzled, too. His fame." She paused. "I worked at Sotheby's for six years."

"That vocation, did you think of it as becoming Faulk's last muse?"

She looked at me sharply and I knew I was being warned against polluting holy ground with the least scintilla of irony. "I couldn't *know* I'd be the last."

To defend myself I said, "I'm divorced too." Then, for good measure, I added, "And a single parent."

"Really? What's *that* like?"

"Hard. Wonderful."

She nodded with some grace. I guessed she was childless, like Faulk. Maybe Faulk had to be the child. I figured a mother would have asked about Maya.

"Ben had a secret. Well, not exactly a secret, just something he never talked about. It's surprising nobody's ever ferreted it out."

"Something important?"

"Oh, I'd say decisive."

"So, not a secret, but he never spoke of it?"

"Except to me and, if I tell you, you'll figure out why. You're intelligent."

After the splendors of the Renaissance, so they taught me in school, came something called Mannerism. I wrote the term in my notebook as thoughtlessly as I did everything else. Art History 101 seemed to be pretty much a parade of isms. What was Mannerism, exactly? A reaction, a flight to the bizarre and extreme motivated by discouragement, agitation without stamina. Mannerism was sophisticated but eschewed harmony, offered insights without depth. After the generation of geniuses and giants erected their magnificent palaces, what were the next batch of the talented to build? Melancholy to know that, even straining to your utmost, you'll never amount to more than an epigone.

The art of today, ignorant about and confused by it though I am, seems a new Mannerism. After the explosion of creativity and slew of styles—the Impressionists, Post-Impressionists, Fauves, Cubists, Expressionists, Constructivists, Surrealists, Blue Riders, Dadaists, and Action painters—after such eruptions wasn't some sort of neo-Mannerism unavoidable? So far as I know, nobody else has called Faulk a Mannerist, so either I'm wrong or I'm perceptive. I know the former is more likely, but there it is.

Now, a *manner* is quite a different matter. In a masterpiece, a master's manner is sublimated to achieve a great purpose. It's in a great artist's minor works that you see the manner more clearly, the characteristic devices and typical ploys. If you love his work, then you will love these too. What's more Beethovenian than the occasional overtures *King Stephen* and *The Consecration of the House*? If I love *The Rover*, *The Arrow of Gold*, *Chance*, and *The Rescue* it's because I love Conrad and perhaps it's when he doesn't transcend anything that he is quintessentially… *Conradian*.

Faulk's work didn't touch me in this way. Estella must have seen that and perhaps it was another reason she spoke to me so frankly. Because I wouldn't bow down. There was no question of being distracted by expressions of adulation, let alone of my spreading gossip. To me, the art world is as alien as Outer Mongolia.

I suppose it's just possible that she didn't value Faulk's work any more than I did, that it was only the man she loved.

"And the secret that isn't exactly a secret?"

"Miniature golf," Estella declared flatly. Had she not been a woman whose very bearing banished any thought of vulgarity, I would have called her declaration and the grin that followed it wicked. She was tossing caution into a whirlwind, and it fit with the next very next thing she said: "Let's splurge and order dessert. Unless you'd prefer oysters."

We both went for the Black Forest cake and coffee.

I've done my homework.

Miniature golf began in England just before the First World War and had spread to the U.S. by the time the slaughter was getting underway at Verdun. A standardized course was set up in Pinehurst, North Carolina in 1916. Eight years later, a man with the fitting name of Thomas McCulloch Fairbirn concocted a putting surface from cottonseed hulls, sand, oil, and dye. In the diversion-mad Jazz Age, this novelty could hardly fail to catch on. By the time of the Crash, tens of thousands of miniature golf courses had spread over the country. New York City alone had over a hundred and fifty of them—on rooftops (also useful for diving off of). These courses were simple affairs of rolls, banks, and curves and, like the economy, almost all were demolished during the Depression. But in 1938, the Taylor Brothers of Binghamton went into the business and started building new kinds of courses. They introduced obstacles, painted landscapes, huge clown faces, all those fanciful windmills, castles and wishing wells. During the War, the firm flourished through catalogue sales. War was as good for miniature golf as for the aircraft industry. The Taylors contracted with the Defense Department to ship prefabricated courses to Korea and Vietnam for the recreation of the troops.

What really saved Benjamin Faulk from the shoe factory wasn't high art; it was the golf factory. He was hired by the Taylors right out of high school. According to Estella, he started work the day after he wed Linda, his prom date.

"Not long before he died, Ben told me he'd really just been working out things that he learned at Taylor Brothers: invention, materials, color and line, even how to make an installation."

"Was he ashamed of that, too?"

Estella had a delicate way of sighing. "No, I don't think so. He said the work he did in Binghamton was trivial but not meaningless. It made people happy. And it made money. He got married on it. He said he took home more than his father did. He wasn't ashamed about that. On the contrary."

"He only told you about this… at the end?"

She shrugged daintily. "Well, he didn't *know* it was at the end. He was being reflective, not valedictory. But yes. It came up when we were having one of those painful talks about his success, about his being taken eighty thousand dollars' worth of serious. 'In those days, back in Binghamton,' he said, 'you'd think I'd have been pretty humble. But I was terribly proud because I could do whatever was asked of me; but, even more, I was proud of the money I made.'" She paused thoughtfully. "At twenty, he was proud of out-earning his father. But when there was so much more of it, the money humiliated him."

"Art's a racket, then?"

She gave me a tight little smile. All her gestures, I realized, were miniature ones.

"Well, I mean, if we're going to be honest, I guess that's more or less what Ben was thinking. Or worrying about. Anyway, it was the first wife, Linda, who made him move to the city. She wanted out of Binghamton and, as soon as she managed that, she wanted out of the marriage, too."

"And he went on doing what he was told? And he couldn't bear to be alone?"

"At the end, he wasn't alone."

Then Estella Gismondi, Faulk's last and only faithful wife, proudly raised her elegant head and called for the check.

EDITOR'S NOTE

I found this piece in Fein's file for 1975. It was most likely written over the summer of that year. MoMA's Faulk retrospective ran in the autumn of 1974. The artist had unexpectedly died of an aneurysm a year earlier, just before his fifty-eighth birthday.

There are few corrections to the typescript, though it needed more. It seems clear Fein wrote this piece more as a personal record than as something intended for publication. He would not have wanted to violate the confidence of Estella Gismondi, who obviously impressed him.

Benjamin Faulk's reputation declined rather quickly after the apotheosis at the MoMA. His inability to talk about his work, and to promote it, in addition to his not belonging to any school or movement, did not help to secure his fame.

Fein's text is of some interest because of what interested him apart from Faulk's work, his widow, and the art market. For example, it is revealing that Fein should fasten on Faulk's ambivalence about his work and its value. He would have appreciated the irony of Faulk's success provoking doubts about its validity. He would have sympathized with the difficulty Faulk had in taking himself seriously as an artist, with the self-doubt of the "scrupulous".

Fein also seems to have been intrigued by the wellsprings of Faulk's inspiration: the working out of techniques mastered by fabricating miniature golf courses—an apprenticeship in this low craft leading to high art—and the specific direction given that art by each of his wives. Fein had views about sex and creativity but here the matter is discreetly left implicit. Faulk evidently needed muses to give order to his life and also to issue orders for his work. His desire to please women might seem good for them, but bad for him; it may have doomed his marriages. Fein cherished independence of mind and perhaps saw Faulk's yearning to please as both an artistic and a personal failing. In any case, Faulk's work would not have existed—or at the least would not have taken the forms it did—without the marriages. As it had been less than two years since his own marriage broke up, Fein would certainly have reflected on the artist's three divorces.

Fein may have seen a brother in Faulk but also a kind of anti-self. The painter approached the world visually, Fein verbally. For Faulk work was physical, a thing of paint and surfaces; for Fein it was mental, a matter of ideas, phrases and pages. It is notable that the theme of remarriage is echoed in the vignette about the "rebounding" Harry Hallinan rudely rushing off to pursue an old girlfriend. The childless Faulk hastened from one wedding, from one barren marriage, to the next. Fein believed himself ordained to be solitary and regarded his marriage as an aberration. But he also counted it a piece of luck, even as a salvation, as it left him with a daughter and the "hard wonderful" task of raising her.

ON SYSTEMATIC ERROR

"R eally? You don't see *any*thing odd in the passage? Nothing that strikes you as *wrong*? Okay then, I'll read it to you again."

The text for the day was the opening chapter of Freud's *Civilization and Its Discontents*. Some of the students had done at least some of the assigned reading but, in the way of sophomores, none had thought much about it. Freud could be right or wrong but, either way, they might have to reproduce what he said on an examination. What use was there in objecting to any of it—even his calling religion infantile?

In his late work, Freud is preoccupied with religion. *The Future of an Illusion* came out in 1927 and was followed three years later by *Civilization and Its Discontents*. Freud went on chewing at the bone in his final book, *Moses and Monotheism*. Here he rehearses motifs dating from *Totem and Taboo* and reiterated in *Civilization and Its Discontents,* in particular the primal parricide and the superego-formation that sprouts from the sons' remorse. But the first chapter of Freud's most assigned book has a lot more going on in it than an analysis of religion.

Sigmund Freud had about as much religious feeling as a cauliflower; nevertheless, that is where he begins. Since he has had no experience in that line, he takes the word of a friend on the nature of religious feeling. This friend was the writer Romain Rolland who, despite being an atheist, was attracted to Hinduism and became a close friend of Gandhi. Freud had sent him *The Future of an Illusion* and Rolland wrote back to say he agreed with the book's argument but regretted Freud had paid so little attention to the "source of religious sentiments." He described this source as "a sensation of 'eternity,' a feeling as of something limitless, unbounded—as it were 'oceanic'…" It's easy to see why Rolland was attracted to Hinduism. In drawing my students' attention to this passage, I asked if it reminded them of pantheism, monism, Eastern mysticism. They looked at me blankly. So, I told them a joke that was old to me but, I hoped, new to them.

"The Buddha's reincarnated and finds himself on a street corner in Lower Manhattan. He hasn't eaten anything for more than twenty-five hundred years. He looks around, spots a hot dog stand, and marches up to it. Amazingly, the vendor recognizes the Enlightened One. 'Buddha! This is a great honor! Tell me, what can I get you?' The Buddha raises a finger to his lips, considers for a moment, then replies, 'Make me one with everything.'" Only after I repeated the punch line— "Make me one with *everything*"—did they get it.

Freud traces Rolland's "oceanic" feeling of oneness back to infancy when, he alleges, we haven't yet got a proper ego and cannot distinguish between ourselves and anything else—crib, wall, mobile, mother. Still, he isn't persuaded by the claim that this feeling is religious. After all, if being one with everything were the source of religious feeling then there wouldn't be any religions like Western monotheism, which is Freud's preferred model. Western thinking tends to be dualistic: make me *two* with everything. Freud was a non-practicing Jew in a Catholic city, and the Judeo-Christian God is outside of nature and history. "This is why He can be begged for miracles," I observed, "such as an A on an exam for which you haven't studied." Freud maintains that it was "later on" that the oceanic feeling became connected with religion: "The 'oneness with the universe' which constitutes its ideational content sounds like a first attempt at religious consolation …" Freud likes the idea that religious feeling is infantile but prefers an even more "Freudian" source for the psychology behind the universality of what he considered a mass delusion. It is the following passage, where Freud explains his idea, that I read aloud to my students, asking if they didn't hear something wrong in it:

> The derivation of religious needs from the infant's helplessness and the longing for the father aroused by it seems to me incontrovertible, especially since the feeling is not simply prolonged from childhood days, but is permanently sustained by fear of the superior power of Fate. I cannot think of any need in childhood as strong as the need for a father's protection.

"Really? You don't see *any*thing odd in this passage?"

Silence.

"Look, if we had Dr. Freud right here in our classroom, wouldn't you like to ask him if he couldn't think of any infantile need stronger than that for a father's protection? Wouldn't you want to say, 'Come on, Dr. Freud. Think *harder.*'?"

At last, one of the female students did consider that there might be something the matter with what Freud wrote. Infants generally don't long for their fathers, who can't feed them, but their mothers, who can, and to whom they were so recently and intimately attached. No doubt they do need a father's protection but they're hardly aware of it. Milk is quite another matter, and so—as one might have expected Freud of all people to note—is the oral gratification that comes with getting it.

Freud's error is all the more astonishing in that it actually undercuts his assertion that religious feeling originates not in Rolland's pantheistic oneness but in the infantile need for a cosmic parent. The logic of Freud's argument ought to have led him to say that the original deity was a mother not a father, an earth-goddess rather than a sky-god. This might have led him in the direction of James Frazer's *The Golden Bough* and Robert Graves' *The White Goddess*. On top of this, as an aficionado of archaeology, Freud might have adduced ample evidence of early matriarchal religions being displaced by later patriarchal ones. What fun he might have had psychoanalyzing that. He could have pointed to the Israelites' contention with the worshipers of Isis and Astarte, the way the Olympians under a macho Zeus shouldered aside the Minoan/Mycenaean Mother-Goddess, the history of patriarchal Christianity crushing the Old Religion of Northern Europe, burning thousands of "witches"—almost all women—in the process. Freud was a connoisseur and collector of ancient statuettes; he kept a crowd of them on his desk, including plenty of goddesses. He only had to stroll over to the Naturhistorisches Museum to contemplate the 22,000-year-old Venus of Willendorf, dug up in his own country just twenty years earlier.

I offered my students some fanciful mythology. I asked them to suppose that originally men bowed down to the magical female who had the power to create life. Even in the twentieth century there were still primitive tribes who had yet to figure out the facts of life, which, after all, aren't so easily grasped. Spirits did it; walking by a sacred spring did it. I asked them to picture some masculine troglodyte genius—gifted at math, precocious in biology—counting on his thick fingers and then declaring to his astonished buddies that it isn't magical females who bring forth life, but males who plant the seeds. Women were just fields; *they* were husbandmen. Then, in short order came phallic columns, ziggurats, pyramids, and skyscrapers, also primogeniture, burkas, chastity belts, and public stoning (of women) for adultery. And what does a man hand out to his pals when his wife becomes pregnant? Cigars, of course—which aren't *always* just cigars.

Discovering the origins of religious feeling is not the principal point of the first chapter of *Civilization and Its Discontents*. The opening discussion is an artful, Hitchcockian misdirection. Freud is giving an illustration of a principle announced only toward the end of the chapter. This fundamental principle is that, so to speak, psychically nothing ever dies—or practically nothing. Therefore, the infant's feeling of helplessness remains deep inside the adult and is available to be exploited later by priests—or accessed by psychoanalysts. Freud's real point is the stratification of the psyche and to make this clearer, he compares the mind to the recent excavations in Rome:

> Now let us, by a flight of imagination, suppose that Rome is not a human habitation but a psychical entity with a similarly long and copious past—an entity, that is to say, in which nothing that has once come into existence will have passed away and all the earlier phases of development continue to exist alongside the latest one.

Roma Quadrata lies below and before the level of the Septimontium which is beneath and prior to that of the Servian Wall, which is earlier and lower than the Aurelian Wall. In the same way, the limbic system and neocortex did not replace the reptilian complex that preceded them but are built on top of it. Evolution is accretion; we live in a world with both psychiatrists and monkeys in it.

So, the mind, says Freud, is layered and the past persists. There can hardly be a more rudimentary principle of his theory than this. Digging things up was the nineteenth century's great research program; it gave us both archaeology and anthropology. Karl Marx was also an excavator, digging down to the economic "substructure" he was sure determined cultures and propelled history. Nietzsche anticipated Freud in arguing for unconscious purposes, insisting that at the bottom of all our motives lay *das Wille-zur-Macht*. Freud caps this tradition, descending into the abyss, dragging what he finds in the murk up into the light of day. He is like the diver in the Schiller poem he quotes, to a different purpose, at the end of the first chapter of *Civilization and Its Discontents*:

> *...Es freue sich,*
> *Wer da atmet im rosigten Licht!*

What made Freud say *father* when both his logic and his hobby should have led him to say *mother*? Is his error owing to a prejudice against the female sex? Was he, as many feminists contend, a male chauvinist pig who believed women envied his penis, or just a male insufficiently *interested* in females—never mind that most his patients were women? Many feminists of his own time considered Freud a liberator, an enemy of their repression. But things changed after the War. The new, resentful note was loudly heralded by Simone de Beauvoir when she published *The Second Sex* in 1949:

> Freud never showed much concern with the destiny of woman; it is clear that he simply adapted his account from that of the destiny of man, with slight modifications.

And that's just for openers.

Freud said a lot of odd things about women, also about men. But, about the former, he said some *consistent* things to which women might well take exception. In *Civilization and Its Discontents,* he portrays the primal mother as a sex-object for the upright male and declares her descendants enemies of civilization because, instead of playing house, their husbands play at business, culture, war and golf and women resent it. Worse yet, he appears to have a low opinion of the moral capacities of women. In 1925 he wrote:

> ... for women the level of what is ethically normal is different from what it is in men... [they] show less sense of justice than men... they are less ready to submit to the great exigencies of life... they are more often influenced in their judgments by feelings of affection or hostility.

This is drawn from the impressively titled piece, "Some Psychical Consequences of the Anatomical Distinction Between the Sexes," which Freud had *his daughter* read aloud at the Psycho-Analytical Congress in Hamburg. He believed women had a flimsy superego that was not "so inexorable, so impersonal, so independent of its emotional origins as we require it to be in men." To him, as to Piaget and other male psychologists of his generation, it must have seemed axiomatic that the masculine sense of justice constituted the norm, the standard of justice.

In this decade, Freud has been roundly excoriated by feminists for his biology-is-destiny declarations. Yet what have come to be called feminist ethics draw on precisely the same distinctions Freud makes, only with the values transvalued. Empathetic relativism coupled with respect for emotions and interpersonal bonds are *good*, while to be coldly detached, applying only the facts and the law and sternly ruling out of account circumstances, personalities, context and consequences is *bad*. Rigid masculinist ethics of the Kantian variety are liable to be inflexible, inhumane, and, in the end, ruinous. And what is the cause of this difference? Even for the feminists, it is Freud himself who supplies the reason: girls become women by remaining attached to their mothers while boys become men by detaching from theirs.

To me, the evidence is pretty strong that what led Freud to say *father* rather than *mother* at the end of the first chapter of *Civilization and Its Discontents* was a systematic error owing less to misogyny than cultural blinders. Freud grew up in the ferociously paternalistic culture of nineteenth-century Europe. His theories take for granted patriarchal family arrangements and are built on them. He doesn't even hesitate to project them back into prehistory, though he must have known that early humans lived in extended families and kinship groups, not Austrian nuclear families. As for his contention that women inevitably come into conflict with civilization, it is one feminists would surely accept if only he had inserted *male-dominated* before the word *civilization*. It seems likely that it is because Freud's civilization *was* male-dominated that he commits the blunder I find in the first chapter of his most famous book.

Freud usually sounds sure of himself, but we should be fair. Did he really believe that biology is destiny, that the nature of women and men—and even their morality—is determined by their anatomy? Well, one should always take care to read the fine print. Consider, for instance, the final sentence and long accompanying footnote that conclude the fourth chapter of *Civilization and Its Discontents*. These suggest to me that Freud had doubts concerning matters about which he often sounds apodictic. "This may be wrong," he writes about his contention that it is civilization itself and not something in ourselves that denies us happiness, "it is hard to decide." The appended footnote includes admissions that more or less reverse the sexual politics of the rest of the book and even his discipline's capacity to fix gender differences:

> Sex is a biological fact which, although it is of extraordinary importance in mental life, is hard to grasp psychologically. We are accustomed to say that every human being displays both male and female instinctual impulses, needs and attributes; but though anatomy, it is true, can point out the characteristics of maleness and femaleness, psychology cannot. For psychology the contrast between the sexes fades away into one between activity and passivity, in which we far too readily identify activity with maleness and passivity with femaleness…

So, psychology "too readily" asserts that man does while woman is. It sounds to me as if by "psychology" he meant Sigmund Freud, which would be a charming example of Freudian self-doubt and professional humility. I would like to believe it reveals a suspicion of just the sort of error that would lead him to write *father* when he should have written *mother*.

Systematic error is a technical term from experimental science. It is defined by contradistinction; that is, by contrast to random error. Systematic errors are the result of flaws in the design of an experiment or in the experimenter's apparatus. If you repeat the same flawed experiment with the same defective equipment you'll get the identical error every time. If your clock is running slow, for instance, then all time-results will be tardy. Systematic error distorts outcomes the same way every time while random errors do not. Random errors are less dire because they can average out; if it's humid one day it may be dry the next. Systematic errors, though, ensure *consistent* distortions which is why they are difficult to detect. That is, they don't look like errors at all. I found a physics handbook in the library that offers this lapidary advice: *If you suspect that your measurements are biased, you should try to identify the possible sources of systematic error.* Words to live by.

"If you suspect…"? The suspicion of systematic error is, of course, unlikely to come from the person committing it, the experimenter who doesn't know the clock is slow. It is more likely that it will come from a rival. For this criticism, the good scientist should be grateful because good scientists are those who give up their biases the moment they are convincingly demonstrated to them, even if it irks that the demonstration should be made by a competitor. In non-experimental disciplines, I've noticed, the tendency is just the opposite. Historians, philosophers, and anthropologists are more likely to resent an imputation of bias, *especially* if it is accompanied with proof, and clutch their cherished prejudices all the tighter to their breasts, defending them with the ferocity of a mother bear.

I'm not so naïve as to suppose all scientists are disinterested searchers out of truth. Many, being human beings, probably do defend their prejudices—dignified with titles like theory, paradigm, law, certainty—even beyond the point of plausibility. Think of phlogiston, geocentrism, ether, perfectly circular orbits, the miasmal theory of infection, hysteria as a useful diagnosis or bloodletting as an effective therapy. But, in the long run, scientists go with the data because they have to, if they want to *be* scientists. The same can't be said about philosophers because philosophical questions are different from empirical ones. The former can be finally resolved; the latter never are. I think one of the reasons Freud's *Civilization and Its Discontents* is so widely taught is because it is a rare and irresistible hybrid, the philosophical speculations of a scientist. Also, Freud is a kind of epic poet, an elegant stylist who won the 1920 Goethe Prize. Scarcely any of his ideas are not expressed via myth, personification, or metaphor. "Sing, goddess, the mind of Achilles, Peleus' son…"

Systematic error is itself a useful metaphor. In fact, it is so common—once you're on the lookout for it—that it is tempting to regard systematic error as built into the mental lives of human beings. Political conviction can be a source of such errors and this is especially evident in historiography. A Tsarist historian will give an account of the October Revolution entirely different from the one written by an ardent Trotskyite. The unreconstructed Confederate's book about the Civil War won't look much like the one written by a professor of African-American Studies. Ethnocentrism is another source of errors that can be systematic ("God is an Englishman") as are class prejudice ("the rich always arrange things") or patriotism ("American exceptionalism"). In private life, egoism and narcissism do the same ("It's all about *me*"). Religion has been a great source of systematic error and the slaughter that can result from it. Conspiracy theorists are among the most tiresome propagators of systematic error. Such errors can be ridiculous, as in the comedy of humors, but they may also be dangerous and tragic. Systematic error can result in personal misery—for example, I know a woman who falls for the same wrong man over and over again—or genocidal atrocity ("It's all the fault of those damned {fill in the blank}").

The best fable I know concerning systematic error is the story of the sea captain who set out on a voyage from Lisbon to New York but made a half-a-degree error in setting his course and so wound up in Brazil. Now that I think of it, my own worst mistakes are of just this sort; that is, persisting in an incorrect assumption which, taken as a first principle, I fail to question until I'm staring at Rio rather than Manhattan.

Because the questions they deal with cannot be resolved with finality, it comes naturally to philosophers to disagree with one another, both their predecessors and their contemporaries. Many do so by ascribing what amounts to a systematic error to their opponents, especially if they favor a different one. Perhaps the most poignant instance is that of Jean-Jacques Rousseau's critique of Thomas Hobbes.

Writing a century after Hobbes, Rousseau stands the predecessor from whom he took so much on his head. To Hobbes, society is good and nature bad; to Rousseau it's the other way around. Rousseau points to his predecessor's original mistake (the half-a-degree error) that turns into a systematic error tainting all Hobbes says, such as that the government is sovereign rather than the people or that laws are a response to crime rather than its cause. In Rousseau's view, Hobbes' goof is about the state of nature from which, imitating Euclid, he deduces everything else. According to Rousseau, Hobbes' mistake was to judge how people would conduct themselves in the lawless natural state by imagining how seventeenth-century Londoners—corrupted by greed for property, status, by advertising and pornography, and thoroughly accustomed to lying and insincerity—would do so:

> ... this author should have said that since the state of nature is the state in which the concern for our self-preservation is the least prejudicial to that of others, that state was consequently the most appropriate for peace and the best suited for the human race. He says precisely the opposite, because he had wrongly injected into the savage man's concern for self-preservation the need to satisfy a multitude of passions which are the product of society...

Everything Hobbes subsequently deduces about children, Native Americans, international relations, and the causes of war is, for Rousseau, completely wrong because Hobbes' original error became a systematic one. What is ironic is that Rousseau himself commits the same error in reverse, interpreting all the new anthropological evidence available to him in accord with a prejudice in favor of anything he deemed close to nature: children, peasants, Dryden's noble savage. To Rousseau, emotion is natural, thinking artificial, so he elevates the heart over the head, promotes sincerity as the cardinal virtue, adopts the Golden Age theory of history and sees every development since the invention of metallurgy and agriculture as ruinously regressive. Systematic error is, after all, systematic.

As Freud was not only the first analyst but also the first patient, his work is built on an unprecedented sort of autobiography. For me, it isn't his theories and writings that make him a hero; the theories and writings are the reward for undertaking a heroic self-examination, for doing it ruthlessly and imaginatively. But this also means Freud's work is shaped by his social world, above all by the father-dominated family and religion that prevailed at his historico-socio-politico-economic coordinates. No surprise in that. Who is not limited in the same way? What distinguishes culture heroes is that they transcend these coordinates and remain interesting. Freud is almost always interesting, even when he's wrong. In fact, I admire his courage in taking the risk of being wrong. It's a kind of bravery I find rare, especially in universities whose denizens are so afraid of being wrong that they deny themselves many adventures and discoveries. The thing that makes his saying *father* rather than *mother* at the end of Chapter One of *Civilization and Its Discontents* so galling is just that Freud ought to have known better.

I'd like to think that if my students and I really could put the question to him, Freud would strike his forehead, blurt out a Viennese, or even Yiddish, expletive, then excuse himself to dash to his office and begin making corrections—systematic ones.

I found this piece, untitled, in Fein's file for the year 1980. While most of the text is typed and there are several corrections and interpolations, everything after "Because the questions of philosophy cannot be resolved with finality…" is handwritten. It is as though Fein intended to return or add to what he had written but, for some reason, gave up on the project.

During the academic year 1979-1980, Fein served as Visiting Professor at Brandeis University. Among the courses he taught was a two-semester survey of Western philosophy with numerous ancillary readings. Hobbes' *Leviathan* and Rousseau's *Discourse On the Origin of Inequality* appear on the first-semester syllabus. The penultimate assigned reading in the second semester was Freud's *Civilization and Its Discontents*. It seems probable that the essay grew out of the classroom exchange with which it begins.

It is typical of Fein that his subject is not fixed. Is his theme Freud's view of women or the notion of systematic error as a metaphor for human imperfection? Is the essay aimed at contrasting scientists' eagerness to discard their distorting biases with the way philosophers cleave to theirs? Does Fein really mean to argue that systematic error is an ineradicable feature of human thought, one that serves up comedy as well as tragedy? My own view is that this unfinished essay is like many others to be found among Fein's unpublished papers, a kind of riffing, like that of a jazzman who has gotten hold of a tune with possibilities. The musician *plays*—and so does Fein.

This is the only place where Fein writes at any length about Sigmund Freud. He evidently had a high opinion of the psychologist; yet his esteem is peculiar in being independent of whether Freud's theories are true or false. He calls Freud a "culture hero," which is common enough, but also an "epic poet," which is not common at all.

When I showed this piece to Fein's daughter, she recalled an occasion when she and her father were at a party. Their hostess and most of the guests were psychotherapists. Maya remembered that there had been a bristling exchange when one of the therapists said something to provoke her father. Fein retorted with an epigram which she remembered this way: "The difference between Freud and a Freudian is that the latter doesn't know a metaphor from a meatball." According to Maya, on the way home her father told her that he had outraged the man by describing Freud as the greatest epic poet of the twentieth century. "He thought I'd insulted Freud which is funny," he'd said, "since the world is stuffed full of shrinks while there are scarcely any epic poets."

Sidney Fein's indignation at what he considered Freud's gaffe—one which he perhaps only discovered during the course of his own class—is as much a measure of his esteem as his disappointment. That he fastened on and made so much of this Freudian slip is Feinian through and through.

ON CINDERELLA

I WAS eight years old when Walt Disney released his *Cinderella*. That was in 1950. Along with my cousins Ruthie and Hannah, I was taken to see it by Aunt Rachel who claimed to be as enchanted as her daughters. They couldn't stop chattering about this scene or that all the way home. The girls even tried to sing the songs, especially the exasperating "Bibbity Bobbity Boo." As for me, I couldn't work up much enthusiasm for a fantasy I judged to be fashioned exclusively for girls. All the energy belonged to the stepmother, the stepsisters and fairy godmother; even the passive Cinderella is at least in nearly every scene. Men? Cinderella's father struck me as a contemptible, henpecked non-entity while the prince was no more than a prop. At eight, you either identify with a protagonist or you don't. At eight you also don't think about anything behind the camera.

Last month, I took my daughter Maya to see a re-release of what is now touted as Disney's "masterpiece." Maya is almost ten years old and, of course, already knew the story. Among the birthday gifts from her mother a few years back was a deluxe edition of Perrault's fairy tale with Edmund Dulac's illustrations. I wondered if my former wife, who keeps her motives close to her vest, meant something by choosing this particular book. There are themes that might have appealed to her: the absent, sainted mother, an unambiguous warning about second marriages, the fecklessness of fathers. I doubt it would have crossed her mind that our daughter might see *her* in the wicked stepmother.

Maya liked the movie well enough. The fantasy is, after all, satisfying in lots of ways. As for me, I was surprised by how well I remembered the imagery. Still, I didn't give the film much thought. When you take your little girl to a movie you tend to watch it through her eyes.

A few days later, Maya paged through my old copy of *Grimms' Fairy Tales* and happened on "Aschenputtel," the brothers' version of Perrault's story. If I had ever read this I didn't recall it; but when Maya told me that she liked "Aschenputtel" more than both "Cendrillon" and the Disney movie, I studied it with some care.

The Grimm brothers weren't collectors of fairy tales at all. The term "fairy tale," like Perrault's "Cendrillon, ou la petite pantoufle de vair," is a product of aristocratic seventeenth-century France—Versailles, the Sun King, etc. In the early nineteenth century, what the Grimms sought out were *Volksmärchen*, folk tales—gritty, violent, poverty-haunted stories embodying the culture of what subsequent German Romantic nationalists and racists would solemnly christen *Das Deutsche Volk*. Consequently, when Wilhelm and Jacob rewrote some of Perrault's stories, they maintained that they weren't rewriting them at all but drawing on sources older, deeper, and, above all, more Teutonic and therefore more authentic.

According to what I've been able to find out, the key elements of "Cinderella"—the rise of a persecuted heroine, supernatural intervention, the slipper, the grand marriage—go back a long way, long before there was either a Germany or even a France. So it's not easy to be certain whether the Grimms were just recasting Perrault in their own style or not; nevertheless, this is what I am convinced they did. That Maya should prefer their version, which is more sanctimonious and more sadistic than Perrault's, let alone Disney's, a story in which a cruel vindictiveness mars the happy ending and where the father isn't just a wife-dominated non-presence but actively complicit in his daughter's misery, is bound to make me wonder and worry.

"Aschenputtel" begins with a deathbed scene, the mother's parting admonition and promise to Cinderella: remain good and kind and God will protect you. Then comes the second marriage and the horrid step-females. In this version, the sisters are pretty on the outside, ugly on the inside. They promptly appropriate Cindy's clothes and jewelry, dress her in rags, consign her to the kitchen and call her "Ash-fool," which is not just the German equivalent of "Cendrillon" but a traditional insult for a low-status female. Because Cinderella is degraded socially and sartorially, the happy ending and the fancy clothes represent a sort of restoration. In Perrault's version, Cindy gets her name from being forced to sleep in a cold, bare room where she curls up close to the fire for warmth and wakes smeared with ashes. Unlike Perrault, the Grimms have Cindy piously visiting her mother's grave and praying to God to improve her wretched lot.

In the Grimms' version, the father, clearly aware of his daughter's mistreatment, goes off to a fair. The stepsisters ask him to bring back luxuries; Cindy asks for a twig. This she plants on her mother's grave and waters with her tears. It grows into a tree under which she prays three times a day. On these occasions, a white bird (her mother's soul? the Paraclete?) flutters down to comfort her.

The King declares a three-day festival—no *haute* Versailles ball here, perhaps something more Brueghelian—to which all the local maidens are invited so his son can choose a bride. This is also an occasion to etch deeper the stepmother's nastiness. When Cindy begs permission to attend the festival, it's denied because the girl has neither dress nor shoes, a fine example of blaming the robbed for lacking what's been stolen. When Cindy persists, the stepmother tosses a dish of lentils into the ashes, promising to grant her permission if the girl picks them all up fast enough. A brace of doves (sent by her mother in heaven—the godly mother, the good mother, but not a "fairy godmother") lend a talon, so to speak, and Cindy completes the task in no time. The stepmother then throws even more lentils into the fireplace and Cindy collects these just as quickly, but to no avail. The step-things take off for the festival, leaving her to weep.

Poor Cindy repairs to the graveyard to beg for help and this time she gets it. The white bird lays a white gown and silk shoes on her with a warning to leave the festivities by midnight.

The prince dances with her. The clock strikes. She takes off.

The next night the dove dresses Cindy all in silver and the prince dances only with her, but again she escapes before midnight.

On the third night, she's dressed in spun gold with matching footwear.

The prince has ordered the stairway smeared with pitch (something that could never happen in Perrault) and, as Cindy dashes off, one golden slipper gets stuck. The prince declares he'll wed its owner.

There's not much of a search. The next morning the prince shows up to try the shoe on the good-looking stepsisters. Here again we get the distinctive Grimm touch. The stepmother has the elder daughter cut off her toes so the tiny slipper will fit. The prince is taken in, but on the ride back to the castle the heavenly dove flits down and points out to him the blood dripping from the girl's foot. Same business with the other stepsister, except that this time it's her heel that's been sliced off at her mother's direction.

The prince returns, asking to see the third girl in the household. Now here's a key detail: the father tells the prince that, yes, they do keep a *kitchen maid*, omitting to mention that she's his daughter. The prince insists. Cindy quickly cleans herself up and the shoe fits.

The finale is *echt* Grimm:

> When the wedding with the king's son was to be celebrated, the two false sisters came and wanted to get into favor with Cinderella and share her good fortune. When the betrothed couple went to church, the elder was

at the right side and the younger at the left, and the doves pecked out one eye from each of them. Afterwards, as they came back, the elder was at the left, and the younger at the right, and then the doves pecked out the other eye from each. And thus, for their wickedness and falsehood, they were punished with blindness all their days.

Perrault's dénouement is amicable, brief, and not sanguinary at all:

Cinderella, who was no less good than beautiful, gave her two sisters lodgings in the palace, and that very same day matched them with two great lords of the court.

I wonder if there might not be a little Hall-of-Mirrors gag here. Perrault certainly knew what jerks "great lords" can be and perhaps he meant to suggest that, in marrying these awful girls to two of them, they would get what they had coming. In his version, not only is the magic assigned to the secular (or pagan) fairy godmother rather than heavenly doves or a sainted mother, but Cindy conceals her abuse from her father, which mitigates his responsibility so that he appears guilty of inattentiveness rather than cruelty. In the Grimms' version, however, he refers to Cinderella brutally as "my first wife's daughter." Why would Maya prefer *that*?

"Cinderella" is universally popular and there are countless variants. What I've discovered is how ancient the story is. One scholar claims to have traced the story back to the sixth century B.C. In the first century A. D., Strabo recorded the tale of Rhodopis, a Greek slave girl or courtesan, who marries the King of Egypt. In addition to the marrying up, Strabo's version also has the other constant motif of the Cinderella story, the slipper. In this case, an eagle snatches it while the girl is bathing, carries it to Memphis, and drops it literally in Pharaoh's lap. The monarch then searches for the owner of the shoe, finds Rhodopis, bringing matters to their happy conclusion.

In 1634, the Neapolitan Giambattista Basile published the story we know, "Centerentola," in *Lo cunto de li cunti overo lo trattene-*

miento de peccerille or *Il Penamerone*. Basile's got it all: wicked stepmother and stepsisters, persecuted demi-orphan, magic, prince, ball, search, and, of course, slipper. There is one charming touch unique to Basile. He arranges a feast for the shoe-test—all maidens ordered to be present. Here, the slipper comes to life and springs from the prince's hand on to Cinderella's foot.

As a doting retiree, Perrault refined Basile's tale, adding the pumpkin-coach, the fairy godmother, and the slipper of glass— that "*petite pantouffle de vair*" which evidently pleased him so much he made a subtitle of it. A little over a century later, we get the Grimms' Volkified version, the one Maya likes better than Walt Disney's, though I'd have thought Mr. Disney had made his film expressly for her.

Last year the Freudian psychologist Bruno Bettelheim published a book called *The Uses of Enchantment*. It's about the unconscious meanings of fairy tales and has won a great deal of attention and universal praise. I picked up a copy. The subtitle of his chapter on "Cinderella" is candid about the author's idée fixe: "A Story of Sibling Rivalry and Oedipal Conflicts." I have to say that Dr. Bettelheim, like his master, can sometimes be Freudian to a fault. I mean that he occasionally allows theory to harden into ideology and then turns ideology into a Procrustean bed where toes and heels are sliced off to make things fit.

So far as I can discover, Freud himself never wrote about "Cinderella," but he might have been thinking of it in 1910—or accessing it from his own unconscious—when, with characteristic verve and assurance, he wrote the following in *Three Contributions to Sexual Theory*:

> … the shoe or slipper is a symbol for the female genital… selection of the fetish depends on a coprophilic smell-desire which has been lost by repression. Feet and hair are strong-smelling objects which are raised to fetishes after the renouncing of the now unpleasant sensation of

smell. Accordingly, only the filthy and ill-smelling foot is the sexual object in the perversion which corresponds to foot fetishism...

Then he drops this little grenade, like a cherry atop a sundae:

The foot replaces the penis which is so much missed in the woman.

Missed by *whom*, one wonders? According to my sources, Freud didn't get around to proclaiming his theory of penis envy until 1933. This was also the year in which the Nazis burned his books (the feminists would come with their torches later), notwithstanding that their Propaganda Minister owed so much to Freud's nephew Edward Bernays who, in turn, admitted picking up lots of pointers from his uncle during their summer hikes. Told of the fate of his books in Germany, Freud made a famous joke, both prescient and oblivious, and with a touch of the Grimms about it, too. He quipped that the book-burning showed how much civilization had progressed: "In medieval times, they'd have burned me."

I can see how a slipper might be a stand-in for a vagina (the prince possesses the emblem and goes looking for the real thing, which is as delicate as crystal); but then shouldn't it be *his* foot that goes inside the slipper? (I'm thinking of the way Terry Malloy absentmindedly squeezes his hand inside Edie Doyle's immaculate glove in *On the Waterfront*.) As to smells, I don't know. I can certainly picture Cindy smeared with ashes, but it's hard to imagine such a creature *stinking*. In the Grimms' version maybe, certainly not Perrault's.

Charles Perrault came from money, had connections, and was a big shot in his day, leader of the "Moderns" in their famous quarrel with the "Ancients." He was in on the ground floor of the Academy of Sciences and the restoration of the Academy of Painting. He advised Louis XIV on the fountains at Versailles. The luxurious palaces of his stories aren't imaginary. The white turreted Château d'Ussé is said to have inspired "Sleeping Beauty" and looks like it did, too. Perrault elevated the folk tale not just to the fairy tale, but to the world of high fashion—glass slippers and all. The Grimms, on the other hand, lost their father when they were ten and eleven and knew real poverty in their youth. Somehow they made it to the University of Marburg and dedicated themselves to linguistics, lexicography, and folklore. To them, the folk tale was the purest form of culture and the source of German national identity. A century later, Goebbels used their tales to the same end. I suspect the Grimms' penchant for violence and cruelty is connected to their determination to demonstrate this cultural "purity"—crudely understood as having origins that were medieval in the worst sense. A stepmother dances in red hot iron shoes that kill her; a servant is shoved into a barrel studded with nails and rolled down a lane; a frog is hurled against a wall, not kissed. Is it possible to read of Hansel and Gretel stuffing the old lady into that oven without feeling the biting wind of history?

The psychologists aren't wrong about the depths yawning beneath these children's tales; I'm sure they're right in principle. The stories matter, resonate, persist. They may even do more to form conscious-ness than to enact what lies underneath it. But this is only another reason to fret about Maya and "Aschenputtel."

While Bettelheim has plenty to say about "Cinderella," it is mostly the same thing, and not always in the most admirable prose: "'Cinderella,' as we know it, is experienced as a story about the agonies and hopes which form the essential content of sibling rivalry..." The passive voice here ("is experienced") puts me on the alert. Problems with his thesis Bettelheim disposes of with something like cavalier gaiety. For instance, if the point of the story is sibling rivalry, why *step*sisters? The Doctor explains: "... perhaps a device to explain and make acceptable an animosity which one wishes would not exist among siblings." Well, "perhaps" and then again, perhaps not. Also, who is that unidentified "one"? A parent? A Freudian psychologist? It couldn't be the same little being who "experiences the story" because this "one" seems to be an adult who deplores sibling rivalry, not a child enmeshed in it.

To Bettelheim, children respond to "Cinderella" because the story's about being "hopelessly outclassed by [one's] brothers and sisters." Yet everybody can see how superior Cindy is to her stepsisters; moreover, children without siblings of any sort take the story to their hearts no less warmly than those afflicted with brothers and sisters. Bettelheim has an answer ready for this too, and a rather astonishing one: "... this miserable passion"—sibling rivalry, of course—"has only incidentally to do with a child's actual brothers and sisters. The real source of it is the child's feelings about his parents." This seems to me a far more persuasive and fertile thesis and, for a moment, I thought it might even displace sibling rivalry. But it's as if, after writing this sentence, Bettelheim realized he had undercut himself and so he adds: "Even an only child [can] feel that other children have some great advantage over him and this makes him intensely jealous." That is, it's about other kids and jealousy, not parents and neglect. That an only child is likely to feel things quite different from sibling rivalry is a possibility on which Bettelheim does not choose to meditate. He also ignores the fact that Cindy simply isn't the jealous type. In fact, it's her stepsisters who are envious. Nothing daunted, Bettelheim pursues his idea: "Further, he may suffer from the anxious thought that if he did have a sibling, his parents would prefer this other child to him." I have to say that this argument seems to me pretty slack. Notice how "may" is deployed this time as "perhaps" was previously. The sentence feels as misleading as its male pronouns. Bettelheim always writes about "children," as if they were all the same irrespective of age or gender, an abstract class like the "proletariat." He seems not to want to see the story as about *female* feelings, and he is quick to refute the suspicion that it might be: "'Cinderella' is a fairy tale which makes nearly as strong an appeal to boys as to girls"—that "nearly" is an admission not taken up—"since children of both sexes suffer equally from sibling rivalry..." And there we are again, back to the initial postulate. Bettelheim's line of thinking seems to me not only circular but limited. Certainly, sibling rivalry is a theme of the story, but why insist it is the only or even the chief one and that it is for all children or that the one who feels the rivalry most is Cinderella, for that matter? I don't think Maya sees it that way.

The way Bettelheim tosses around "children" reminds me of how undergraduates deploy "society." I've never been sure that there is such a thing as "society"; and, unlike Bettelheim, I'm not interested in "children" in the abstract either. I'm interested in children one at a time, and one little girl in particular.

To be fair, Bettelheim does have more than a single arrow in his quiver of explanations for the appeal of "Cinderella." For instance, he posits that all children believe they are bad and so fear deserved degradation. On this dogmatic ground, he argues that they will be pleased that everybody accepts Cindy's innocence and goodness, as if they themselves had pulled the wool over everyone's eyes. Then there is his assertion that the vileness of the step-relatives makes the child feel better because they're so much worse than she is and fully merit their comeuppance. Still, it seems odd to me that Bettelheim believes any child would identify, even negatively, with the horrid stepsisters. Instead of stating what seems obvious to me—that children enjoy seeing goodness ultimately triumphant and nastiness punished at last—he claims instead that the punishment of the bad relieves the child's guilt for "angry thoughts" directed against his or her own relatives. This is where the second half of Bettelheim's subtitle comes in, the "Oedipal conflicts," de rigueur for the Freudian exegete.

Bettelheim believes "Cinderella" appeals to children because, even if a child actually is treated badly by her family, Cindy's got it ten times worse. In other words, the story offers the solace of comparing down, not up. But Bettelheim is far more concerned with what he calls the child's "dirtiness." He writes a good deal about the "primary narcissism" of the "pre-Oedipal stage" and the "Oedipal disappointments" that bring this placid period of self-love to an abrupt end, leaving the child feeling smutty. The formerly indulgent parents are now critical and demanding—particularly over toilet training, of course—so the child suspects she is not perfect after all but deeply flawed which doesn't prevent her becoming angry with her parents for their discipline and disapproval. This anger proceeds to what Bettelheim calls "dirty wishes," presumably the inadmissible yet Freudianly inevitable desire to liquidate one of them and to marry the other. "Cinderella," he claims, rescues its little fans from the degradation of getting socialized and chided; indeed, it promises exaltation.

If there were more in the story itself to justify such a ferociously doctrinaire reading—if Cinderella expressed more love for her useless father and less for her sainted mother, or if she took an afternoon off from her chores to plot the murder of her stepmother—then what Bettelheim writes would be more persuasive. Given the text, though, his analysis feels willful and overcooked.

In a strangely belated effort to recast the story as conventionally edifying, one that builds character, Bettelheim claims that "… irrespective of the magic help Cinderella receives, the child understands that essentially it is through her own efforts, and because of the person she is, that Cinderella is able to transcend magnificently her degraded life." Here the understanding "child," whom the seventy-three-year-old psychologist perfectly understands, is as vague as "children" is elsewhere. Bettelheim still means *any* child and presumes to know what they make of the story not only with their conscious minds but their subconscious ones as well. This character-is-fate interpretation is uplifting, but ruling the magic out is pretty radical surgery on a fairy tale. I'd have thought it was precisely the sudden intervention of benevolent powers beyond Cinderella's own that would impress a child, giving her hope while also breeding unrealistic expectations, especially among girls who never rid themselves of the fantasy of marrying a prince and living in a white-turreted castle.

The court put Maya in my custody. She visits her mother irregularly. There is no stepmother, no stepsibs, nor are any threatening on the horizon. Does she worry that there might be? Fairy tales suffer from an epidemic of bad stepmothers. Bettelheim never seems to imagine that they might represent actual women and ascribes their prevalence to purely psychological sources. I can think of a simpler explanation. The number of young women dying in childbirth, or immediately thereafter, was high in the Middle Ages. The experiences of Cinderella, Snow White, Hansel and Gretel might have been common—the new mother rejecting another woman's child and, when she had her own, favoring them. It's not exactly unheard-of even today.

This view suggests a psychological interpretation different from Bettelheim's. The remarried father ignores the child who idolizes the absent mother yet feels abandoned by her. I can detect some of this ambivalence in my own daughter. Perhaps that is one reason why she prefers "Aschenputtel," where the mother remains engaged with her child, to "Cendrillon," where she is replaced by an implausible fairy godmother. Since it's not easy to know what's in anybody's unconscious, I see no reason why this should be less likely than what Bettelheim says.

It would be worse if Maya prefers the Grimms' version because the father is complicit in Cinderella's mistreatment. Worse for me. After all, I'm not only her caregiver but her disciplinarian. Still, when I finally asked my daughter to explain her preference I heard none of this. Maya's reasons were straightforward and had to do not with family dynamics, let alone expulsion from some pre-Oedipal Eden, but only logic and ethics.

"If Cinderella has this fairy godmother watching over her, and she can do stuff like turning pumpkins into coaches, why does she let Cinderella get treated so meanly and for so long? Why does she suddenly show up only because there's this *ball?*"

Maya wasn't finished. "And another thing. Why do her spells only last until the twelfth stroke of midnight? And if they only last until midnight, when everything turns back into what it was before, then what about the glass *slipper*? Why doesn't *it* turn back or just disappear? It doesn't make a lot of sense."

She has a point, two in fact. I wondered what she made of the Grimms substitution of heavenly intervention for magic but didn't question Maya on the matter. I just asked if there was anything else.

"Yes," she said emphatically. "The ending. Those wicked stepsisters marrying *lords*? It's ridiculous, you ask me. It's much better that their eyes get pecked out by the doves. They deserve it. That's *fair*."

I asked if she had any problems with "Aschenputtel," apart from the midnight deadline.

"Well," she said, heaving a thoughtful sigh, "if *Mommy* was dead, I don't think I'd visit her grave three times *every* day—I mean especially if I had all these endless *chores* to do."

I asked if she thought the eye-pecking might be just a little cruel.

"Maybe," she allowed thoughtfully, but I could see it was just to placate me. In fact, I suspect the blinding of the stepsisters might be her favorite part. "But I love 'Cinderella' anyway." She paused and looked up at me with a face not altogether innocent. "*Shouldn't* I?"

I told her that people had loved the story of Cinderella for a long time, and not just little girls either.

EDITOR'S NOTE

The personal motive behind Fein's ruminations on "Cinderella" is paternal anxiety.

He and his wife separated in 1974 when their daughter Maya was seven years old. Divorce was granted early in 1976 with Fein as custodial parent.

When I showed her this essay, Maya told me that she has always believed that she was the catalyst, if not the primary cause, of the break-up. She quoted her mother as confessing to her in later years that she did not want a child, though she did like the idea of a sister. After Fein's death in 1984, Maya and her mother did grow closer, perhaps like sisters. But in 1977, the year in which he wrote this piece, Fein was trying to adjust to being the single parent of a nine-year-old daughter.

Less personal, of course, though hardly unrelated to Fein's worries about his new responsibility, is his critique of the recently published and widely celebrated book by Bruno Bettelheim, *The Uses of Enchantment*. Fein was not hostile to psychoanalysis either as a form of therapy or as a tool of literary interpretation. As he says, he believes Bettelheim is correct "in principle." But he was skeptical about the excesses of Freudians and put off by any sort of dogmatism. His essay "On Systematic Error" uses Freud himself as its primary illustration. Nevertheless, even while upbraiding him in that piece, Fein expresses admiration for Freud and accords him deference. Evidently, he felt Bettelheim was owed less of each. Or perhaps it would be more accurate to say that Fein wrote about Freud as a disinterested reader but about Bettelheim as a father or what he called himself in a letter, "a sexless single parent."

What most interested Fein about the Cinderella story was his daughter's response to it—especially to the alternative versions of Perrault and the Grimms. He writes in characteristic improvisa-tional style, sometimes scholarly, more often impressionistic. He notes the peril in German Romanticism and explicitly traces the line from Grimms to Goebbels. He takes Bettelheim to task for showing too much regard for psychoanalytic theory and too little for the narrative. Both concerns are typical of Fein, who mistrusted all theory, political and cultural, from Barthes (see "The Birth of the Author") to de Man, from Freud to Bettelheim. In the same letter in which he calls himself "a sexless single parent" he reports gathering together all the books on child-rearing he and his wife had been given or bought on Maya's birth and tossing them in the trash. He explains in this way: "Maya's entitled to the neurosis nature chose for her."

ON HERESY

HERESY never starts off as heresy; on the contrary, it begins as somebody's idea of orthodoxy. Conversely, orthodoxy itself might be perversely taken as a series of triumphant heresies.

In its first centuries, the Christian Church was preoccupied with fixing what people were supposed to believe and not to believe. Many ecumenical councils were convened and their rulings established right thinking which they called *orthodoxy*, but also wrong thinking, which they called *heresy*. Council after council gathered to proclaim creeds and denounce error. These creeds were matters of life and death, tickets to salvation, but also loyalty tests. This continuous, intense process of inclusion and exclusion consumed enormous intellectual and spiritual energy counted in the sum of which must also be the work of the so-called heresiarchs who were no less zealous or diligent than their opponents.

In a story set during this period, "The Theologians," Jorge Luis Borges interpolates a shrewd and chilling remark: "The heresies we should fear are those which can be confused with orthodoxy." That Borges puts parentheses around this sentence only makes it the more eye-catching; it sounds like a motto for fanatical heretic-hunters.

As the Church insisted that salvation depended on accepting Christianity, it was obliged to define what Christianity meant—and so began the process of ruling in and ruling out. Evidently, there was something about the new faith that provoked all kinds of sects—Apollinarists, Arians, Docetians, Macedonians, Monophysites, Ophites, Antinomians, Christianized Manicheans, and so on and on. Christianity could even breed a kind of religious immorality: the Libertines held that divine predestination made moral restraint pointless and so lived in a kind of perpetual orgy. Other sectarians, believing in the linearity of time concluded that every act is unique. They labored devoutly to perpetrate every conceivable atrocity as a way of purifying the future. A distinction is needed, though. While the Christian *faith* inspired this astonishing efflorescence of strange ideas, the Christian *religion*—the institutional version—required both more and less than faith. A student once asked me to explain the difference between a cult and a religion. I answered him too glibly: "About five hundred years." But part of what goes on in those five centuries is the establishment of orthodoxy.

The word *heresy* derives from *hairesis*, a Greek noun whose meaning floats a little; it can signify the act of taking or selecting, a school or sect, the ability to decide or choose. Organized Christianity narrowed its meaning to something worse than a mistaken decision to something that needed to be consumed by flames both here and in the Hereafter. The theological disputes of the single-numbered centuries were mortal struggles. As every question was of eternal significance, no disagreement was trivial, such as whether Jesus had two natures or only one, if he was the genetic offspring of God or adopted after birth. As the Empire slowly collapsed around them, to the theologians nothing was more urgent than the effort to define and defend the true faith. Pagan philosophy had become a sort of broken vending-machine: fifty cents of virtue in, the candy bar of happiness out. Conditions had changed. Epicureans needed a functioning society to pick up the Garden's trash; Stoics required a stable polity to live the life of civic duty. As Rome crumbled, Augustine proclaimed the hope of happiness in this world vain, while Christianity promised endless happiness beyond this vale of tears and Visigoths and Huns. The new religion's pledge of salvation must have been extraordinarily attractive. Christianity's plasticity was part of its appeal, the obverse of its sponge-like capacity for absorbing pagan feasts and philosophies. Still, one might have thought that Constantine's elevation of his new religion to official status and the summoning of his Council of Nicaea to lay down its orthodoxy might have slowed the hectic theologizing. It didn't. Like mushrooms after three days of rain, heresies continued to pop up all over the place, from sophisticated cities to hermits' huts.

What has made me think of these dusty matters is an article published last year by his brother-in-law after the death of the German heresiologist Rudolf Schattinger. Schattinger was forty-six and a controversial figure in his field when his BMW collided with a bridge abutment. He was famous, or notorious, for his claim to have discovered in the archives of the Council of Chalcedon (451 A.D.) the previously unknown Probatian heresy about which he published a book. Quite a few of his colleagues, pre-eminently the French scholar Guillaume Charconne, accused Schattinger of perpetrating a hoax. Schattinger hardly dispelled the imputation when he published what he claimed was a transcription of the original texts but declined to make the originals available for inspection. His explanation was a promise he had given to the anonymous Turkish bibliophile who owned the Chalcedonian archives and had graciously granted him sole access to them. To Charconne, this excuse was ludicrous; in fact, he published a short article mocking Schattinger—*cet hérétique fabricant des heresies*—comically describing his imaginary Turk as *obèses mais invisible*.

It is no easy matter to distinguish a real heresy from an imaginary one, especially those heresies that resemble orthodoxy. All heresies are acts of imagination; they begin in speculation, what-if deductions. What if we have no free will? What if everyone were damned or saved long before being born? What if Jesus were just an exceptional human being? What if evil were, somehow, good? If heresies should be feared because they lead away from the path to salvation, then an imaginary heresy is no less dangerous than a real one. In fact, the only difference between an imagined heresy and a real one is how many people believe in it.

Heresies are usually named for their founders, but not always. Rudolf Schattinger called the heresy he discovered Probatian, even though there was no Probatius. The archives, he wrote, only described and proscribed the false doctrine but assigned it no designation. He adopted the name from the Latin *probitas*—uprightness, goodness.

According to Schattinger, the Probatians took the position that Christ's redemption of humankind was comprehensive. They accepted Augustine's distinction between the perfection of God and the goodness of all created things: the perfect is immune to corruption while the good is not. They accepted Christ's divine and perfect nature. However, they taught that when Jesus became "consubstantial with humanity" all men, by virtue of his redemptive sacrifice, were sanctified. For the Probatians, this wiping of the slate, this new and pristine goodness was granted not only to Christians but Jews, polytheists, Epicureans, Zoroastrians, Hindus, Buddhists, Neo-Platonists, Skeptics, and animists; it was true of every person and every new generation. The glory of Christ's sacrifice was like sunlight striking impure water. It filled the world and purified every creature. The Probatians rejected Augustine's doctrine that we begin life burdened with the sin of Adam and Eve. In fact, they said it was precisely to cancel that original sin that the crucifixion was endured. Every life begins innocent and good. We are free *of* sin at birth, although not, as the Libertines perversely claimed, free *to* sin. On the contrary. We all begin with an A+, so to speak. The tragedy of our condition is that, as we live our lives, all of us—or nearly all—fall further and further away from God's gift of original goodness, losing points one by one. So, having been endowed by God with the gift of free will along with that of a spotless start, our degradation is entirely on us. The Probatians taught that without free will humans could have remained as innocent as the lion or the barnacle, but also as soulless. They rejected the idea that the Church mediated between God and individuals because they did not accept the goodness of the Church. In fact, the politically perilous logic of the Probatians led them to conclude that, once incarnated into an earthly institution with a hierarchy and grand basilicas, the Church itself ("the body of Christ") itself fell into sin.

One of the more memorable passages in Schattinger's book begins with this question: "Can God be separated from judgment?" He admits that such a disjunction would be all but unthinkable for any Christian—or any monotheist. He acknowledges that judging seems to be one of the essential attributes of what he calls "this singular Deity, the sky-god, the desert-god." Nevertheless, Schattinger claims the Probatians proposed that, having both sanctified us and gifted us with freedom, God refrains from judging us. Our bad grades are, so to speak, recorded automatically. In the same way, they say, His divine omniscience does not imply predestination as a corollary. Schattinger attempts to explain his understanding of the Probatians' view of God's relation to us with a metaphor.

> They seem to have imagined that God observes the activities of human beings as if He were attending a performance of a tragic drama. The audience at such a play knows things are going to turn out badly; after all, it says *The Tragedy of Hamlet, Prince of Denmark* right on the marquee. But does the audience leave? Is the audience bored? Are they not entertained, edified, moved to admiration and pity? The Prince's story is familiar; they read it in high school or college. There is no suspense because everything is happening again, yet also for the first time. (The Probatians entertained the possibilities of a time *both* linear and circular.) Would the audience applaud a bowdlerized version, Ophelia and her wits restored, Claudius spared, a repentant Gertrude entering a convent, a final wedding and the royal line preserved?

On the appearance of his book, Schattinger granted one interview, apparently at the insistence of his publisher.

The man from the *Tübingen Tagblatt*, whose tone hovers between indifference and hostility, began by informing Schattinger that he himself was an atheist. "I thought you ought to know from the outset," the journalist said.

"Fine by me," said Schattinger. "By the way, which God is it you don't believe in?"

The interviewer does not bother to record his reply to this question. But he does include this exchange.

"Tell me, Professor Schattinger—Rudolf, if I may—why is a theologian like a used-car salesman?"

"Some might consider that an offensive riddle, you know. I suppose the answer you have in mind is that ignorance hinders the eloquence of neither."

"More or less."

"Well, I'm not offended as I'm neither a used-car salesman nor a theologian."

"I'm surprised. After all, you hold a professorship in theology. Do you mean to say you have no faith?"

"Let's just say the suspension of disbelief is not the same thing as faith. I am not a theologian but a historian of theology—again, a different thing."

"Yet you've written a good deal about faith."

"Think of it as a job requirement."

"You wrote, for instance, that faith can coexist with doubt."

"I wrote that, for most believers, faith is the opposite of doubt but for a few they are coextensive. I was not writing about myself."

"I see. But would I be wrong to think you prefer the few?"

"It does not concern me."

"Then let's turn to your special subject, which I think is called *heresiology*. Why did you write that the propounders of heresies, the... heresiarchs, are *playful*? It seems an odd word to choose."

"They do seem to me playful, seriously so, like children solemnly arranging blocks or a composer working out a set of variations on a theme of Paganini."

"You mean to say these heresiarchs weren't sincere?"

"Impossible to say. One cannot expect objective certainty about the subjectivity even of the other people on the tram, much less those who lived a couple millennia ago. Anyway, what I meant had nothing to do with the sincerity of men like Messalia, Marcion, or Mani. I only tried to characterize the way they approached the theological issues of the early Church, when things were still rough, up for grabs, mushy. They rang their changes, borrowed wholesale from polytheists and pagan philosophers, appropriated immemorial myths, and declared war to the death over distinctions that make modern people laugh. It was a time when religion mattered infinitely more than physics or mathematics. And truth was determined, like the pope, by voting. Yes, I do find the heresiarchs playful, but playful in dead earnest. A council could turn their notions into orthodoxy or order them bound to a stake. Think of it: a devout man could be burnt alive simply because on one afternoon a rival came up with a more eloquent argument."

"Professor Schattinger, Rudolf, I hope you'll pardon me for bringing up this matter but it is of some interest to our readers. As you know, your critics are not satisfied by your claim that the documents on which you based your book are inaccessible to everyone excepting yourself. Your book has been called a hoax. What do you say to the charge that you invented the Probatian heresy?"

"What can I say except that the Probatian heresy was indeed made up. All such beliefs have to be invented."

"With respect, that's a highly ambiguous answer."

"Haven't you found ambiguity is sometimes a very good thing?"

"Hm. Well, then, let's move on. Do you believe that heresy was and still is destructive to the Church?"

"The Church certainly thought so. It worried about its worldly sway and its supremacy. It was anxious about its unity and power; but I suspect the theological questions were, while serious matters to some, only secondary to others. One must always remember that the so-called heretics were no less Christian than the Bishop of Rome. Indeed, most of them were ordained."

"So it was a case of eliminating the competition?"

"Heresy shouldn't be confused with schism. These heresies were not competing religions, only the blooming of a hundred flowers in one. The Church wielded sharp secateurs. It obviously needed to control the definition of what it meant to be Christian. One must try to imagine the many questions provoked by this new religion to appreciate the variety of answers. What did it mean that Christ was the son of God? Was evil a force in itself or merely the absence of good? Was Satan tolerated by God or were they in an equal battle to win souls? How could God's infinite love, omnipotence, and omniscience be reconciled with the slaughter of a thousand babies? Was sin immanent or contingent? Where did upright pagans spend the after-life?"

"So, playful or not, these answers counted?"

"More than anything. And they continued to matter so long as people accepted that the wrong answers opened the road to eternal damnation and the right ones to everlasting felicity. I realize that this is hardly imaginable for you, but I'm fairly sure it was the case with your ancestors."

"I wouldn't know. May I ask, Professor, what drew you to the study of heresies?"

"In graduate school I found myself at a loss as to what work to do. One morning, my advisor, Professor Rheinach, asked how good my Latin was and, when I said it was passable, he made the suggestion that I study the records of the early ecumenical councils. The notion was practically offhand. I assure you, I felt no vocation. It was also Professor Rheinach who, in his last months, generously arranged with his Turkish friend to grant me access to the Chalcedonian archives. Rheinach himself had not seen them. So, I went to Istanbul to look over those dusty documents. Among them I found references to two previously unknown heresies. Apparently the Council considered them too insignificant to include in their officially published documents. They had bigger fish to fry."

"*Two* heresies? You mean you found another beside the Probatian?"

"Oh, yes. And a most interesting one it is, too."

At the time of his death, Rudolf Schattinger had yet to publish anything at all about this most interesting, second heresy. His enemies were quick to suggest that this was because he had not had sufficient time to dream it up. It was for the sake of the late scholar's reputation that Schattinger's brother-in-law published his article in *Die Bremen Zeitschrift für Theologische Studien.* It begins with this paragraph:

> At the time of his death, Professor Rudolf Schattinger was working on a companion piece to his volume on the Probatian heresy. As with the first, the subject was a heresy which was condemned by the Council of Chalcedon but not mentioned in its official communiqué. The Council, as is well known, was convened to condemn the popular and widespread doctrine of the Monophysites who held that Christ's nature was wholly divine and not human. The Council was chiefly preoccupied with combating the teachings of Eutyches by asserting "the hypostatic union" of Christ's two natures. They promulgated the Chalcedonian Creed—that Christ was "truly God and truly man." With respect to the two minor and localized heresies, the Council took the decision simply to order the relevant religious and secular officials to extir-

pate these doctrines and/or liquidate those who taught them. As Professor Schattinger explained to me, it was in the archives of the Council, to which he was granted exclusive access, that he came across the Council's deliberations on the Probatian heresy, the subject of the book which has provoked so much controversy. But he also found that Council condemned another heresy which he called the Docilian.

Working from Schattinger's notes, the brother-in-law, who I believe is an attorney, provides an account of the Docilian heresy which—whether genuine or fabricated by Schattinger—certainly is interesting.

According to Schattinger, Paulinus Docilis was the young abbot of a monastery near Naissus in the Diocese of Dacia, a mountainous backwater of the Prefecture of Illyricum. Paulinus was said to have been an exceptionally apt student (presumably the source of the cognomen "Docilis"), also notably charitable and humane. Schattinger was evidently taken with Paulinus. The article quotes this note: "Had this man not been condemned as a heretic, he would likely have become a saint. Perhaps he really was a saint."

The Docilian heresy is a paradox in that it opposes the concept of heresy itself, and therefore it is against that of orthodoxy as well. Paulinus set himself against nothing less than the Church's aim of doctrinal conformity. "All purity is partial except for God's," he is said to have preached. In the face of a Church more than willing to annihilate the unorthodox, he argued that it is orthodoxy that creates heresy—rather as Rousseau would later hold that it is law that creates crime.

I can see why the young abbot appealed so much to Schattinger. He cherished the variety and wealth of opinions, refusing to see them as destructively schismatic, deploring the very use of the words *schism* and *heresy*. Paulinus predicted that the Church's endless proscriptions and anathemata would lead it to "take up the sword

474

of Caesar just as the bishops replaced the procurators of Rome." Paulinus' daring is breathtaking: "In our time Pilate would be an archbishop. The Empire gave us the cross; the Church, the stake." The abbot contrasts the broad-mindedness of the Roman Empire to the narrowness of the Roman Church. The former he praises for having "the immense idea of extending citizenship to Celts, Goths, Teutons, Britons, Syrians, Salians, and Jews. They tolerated any cult or mystery so long as it did not disrupt the business, politics, or peace of the Empire." The Romans' persecution of Christians, he went so far as to argue, was out of character, a huge error. Almost facetiously (according to Schattinger's gloss), Paulinus taught that this terrible miscalculation must have been part of God's plan, "for hasn't the great Bishop of Hippo assured us that God invariably contrives to summon good from evil?"

When Constantine convened the first Council of Nicea in 325 A.D. the attending bishops, perhaps still giddy about the Emperor's miraculous conversion, would have perceived the advantages of political legitimacy. They would have been eager to satisfy the Emperor's wish that they fix orthodoxy. I doubt if any considered the drawbacks. The Council of Nicaea consolidated the faith, resolved (apparently) certain Christological and calendar issues, and issued the eponymous Creed that is recited to this day. But Nicea also encouraged self-righteousness and persecution. Certainty is exclusive. "For some believers faith is co-extensive with doubt." Paulinus Docilis, as Schattinger sees him, was the only theologian of his era to point out the terrible consequences of certainty, to understand the inhumane hostility to imagination and variety, to worry about the misbegotten marriage of Church and State.

Paulinus, says Schattinger, went far. He denied that salvation was at stake in theological disputes. He condemned as absurd the idea that God would commit to hellfire any man who believed His son possessed one nature rather than two or be angry with any who diligently sought to follow His son's teachings but could not accept that he was divine. No, said Paulinus in the face of all the councils, bulls, creeds and piles of ashes for which they were responsible, orthodoxy is a public affair and has nothing to do with salvation which is a strictly private matter. According to the Docilians, orthodoxy had become a weapon wielded, often viciously, by prideful and privileged men claiming to have inherited the keys to the Kingdom.

Paulinus upbraided the bishops by recalling a time when pagans, Jews, and Christians mingled freely and even attended one another's rites. This was before the Church became officially sanctioned and thereby set in motion its own degradation. Of course, in its triumph, the Church wanted an official doctrine and to make any other inadmissible. All monopolies are much the same. Once labeled "heretical," no idea could safely be regarded as an amusing or enriching variation, a possibility worth considering, a mere difference of opinion or taste; it was simply *evil*. (Nietzsche ascribed the invention of the word *evil* to the "little bigots" organized Christianity bred in the millions.) The true believers, a "communion" nestled into the warmth of like-minded flocks and obedient to their shepherds, defined themselves as members of a group and saw others in the same way. They were licensed, even obliged, to hate and, at times, even exterminate members of any group outside *their* group. The saved versus the infidels. According to his brother-in-law, Schattinger tells us Paulinus Docilis boldly declared to his superiors that "those you revile as heretics are all Christians" and predicted that the wrong, bloody, and Procrustean task of compelling unity of belief would exhaust itself only when people finally recoiled from it in disgust and so lost their faith.

The article concludes by quoting the last of Schattinger's notes. "So far as I have been able to determine, Paulinus Docilis, like the Probatians, entirely vanished after the Council adjourned on 1 November, 451 A.D."

I found this unexpected—not to say bizarre—essay in Fein's file for 1980. The manuscript is typed and headed with the single word *Heresy*.

It is difficult to know why Fein should have dreamed up a scholar who dreams up heresies. That it is all imaginary I am certain. There was no Rudolf Schattinger, with or without a brother-in-law, no Guillaume Charconne, *Tübingen Tagblatt* or *Bremen Zeitschrift für Theologische Studien*. The heresiarchs may or may not have been playful, but Fein surely was.

During the autumn of 1979, when he was teaching at Brandeis University, Fein devoted a week to discussing Saint Augustine with his students. Perhaps this is what inspired him to write about heresy, but there are other possibilities and none need be excluded. For example, the theme of the pernicious effects of orthodoxy might suggest Fein intended a metaphorical attack on the intellectual constraints of the Academy in and out of which he drifted. Or the piece might be a Jew's mordant commentary on early Christianity, a theory supported by Fein's allusion to Nietzsche's phrase "little bigots" as the originators of the term *evil*. He was acutely aware of having been born in the year of the Wannsee Conference, itself a kind of council aimed at lethal exclusion—aimed, had he been born in the wrong hemisphere, at him. Fein's allusion to Borges' story "The Theologians" points to another kind of inspiration; that is, an urge to write an homage or even to imitate Borges. "Borges' stories are like pistachio nuts," he wrote elsewhere. "None is more than twenty pages long. You have to work hard to get at the delicious meat. But, however small the nut, it's always worth the effort. And then, right away, you want another one." Fein's essay might be a retort to that "shrewd and chilling" parenthetical remark in Borges' "The Theologians" saying, in effect, "The orthodoxy we should fear is that which incinerates heretics."

Was Fein sympathetic to the heresiarchs? He must have known that, had their views been accepted as orthodox, they would have been as keen as any council to persecute dissenters. I do not think Fein is expressing sympathy for heresy generally but that sometime in 1980 he imagined himself into the 5th century. Once there, he invented a pair of heresies of which he could approve and, in the person of the anti-heresy heresiarch Paulinus, a man he could admire.

Paulinus Docilis may be another of those personae Fein "tried on" from time to time, like Philippe Leconte Duparc or Alexander Fernlicht. To the extent that these imaginary thinkers resemble Fein, they are autobiographical, but, as they are also different from their creator, each may be seen as genuine alter egos, "another I." Cicero invented the phrase *alter ego* to refer to one's dearest friend. In the last century, the phrase was turned into a psychiatric term. Fein attached these personae to ideas rather than to plots and so wrote essays rather than stories; it was ideas that gave birth to the characters rather than vice versa.

"On Heresy" has many themes but no resolution. Like many of Fein's unpublished manuscripts it feels improvisatory. He is writing about early Christianity, also faith, the conviction, lack, and loss of it, about intolerance and the hatred that leads some human beings to burn others. In Rudolf Schattinger, Fein imagined a maker of intricate yet edifying hoaxes, perhaps even a "good German." Schattinger comes off rather well in his interview with the atheistic journalist—elusive but humane. The two heresies he devises would then be emblems of a decency the Church was gradually losing (graded down, year by year) as it waned in tolerance and waxed in power. One heresy opposes original sin, the other narrowness and hatred. The first grants each human a clean start; the second embraces freedom of conscience and the variety of opinion it affords.

Fein seems to have regarded the early centuries of the new, still malleable religion as dominated by a kind of faith madness, a wind that blew into the vacuum of dying Antiquity, sweeping up much of it. Faith, he implies, is like nitroglycerine, a dangerous explosive that ought to be handled gingerly. Faith is a passion. Another author revered by Fein, Søren Kierkegaard, says it is the highest passion. But in *Fear and Trembling*, Kierkegaard insists faith is an entirely individual undertaking, that "partnership in these areas is unthinkable." It is not surprising that, in defending his view of faith, Kierkegaard became an enemy of the Established Church as well as Fein's favorite theologian. Faith can lead an Abraham to rise above the morality that lawfully constrains us, above the interests and norms of the community; but congealed into political and bureaucratic power, consolidated into mass delusion, the irrationality of faith can cause people to sink far below the standard of ethics—and often has.

Fein is at pains to keep the question of faith—his, Schattinger's, even Paulinus'—at arm's length, as if it were something too private to bring into the light. So Schattinger distinguishes himself as a "*historian* of theology," one who is intrigued by religious disputes but who watches from the sidelines. Fein was like that, too. When asked if were observant, he replied, "From a safe distance."

ON WONDER

"JUST something I'd like you to see." That was all the explanation I gave my ten-year-old daughter. In the car Maya tried to guess. At first she speculated excitedly: the amusement park? a movie? street fair, hike, zoo? Then she grew suspicious: "Not another one of your *museums*, Daddy!" *My* museums. This was Maya's economical way of expressing disgust and my responsibility for it. Well, I do sometimes make her do things that serve up profit and—dashing my hopes—no delight at all. It's bad enough to tell your child that the Brussels sprouts are good for her; it's downright dishonest to insist that they taste good.

I parked the car a block away so we would have to walk down a side street then turn a corner before Maya saw it.

Just inside the city limits, in the middle of an affluent neighborhood of Victorian houses, I had once stumbled on this park. The wall that bordered it on one side bore a broadside by the guerrilla artist called Fontana Baby.[17] The park itself is an oval of tended grass surrounded by mature copper beeches, a dozen of them. No slides, swings, benches. Just silence, grass, and those twelve patriarchs.

I wanted my daughter to see the beeches. I wanted to look at them again and feel the peace of the park. *Fagus sylvatica purpurea* is my favorite tree and I'd never seen so many perfect specimens in one place. It does you good to look at beeches, instead of reading the newspaper, for instance. Trees are admirable beings. "Except

---

17. For Fontana Baby see Fragment VI, "The Emergence of Craft Typewriters," Felt Collection, New York City.

during the nine months before he draws his first breath, no man manages his affairs as well as a tree does," Shaw wrote.

The bark of copper beeches is smooth and gray. Their trunks grow thick and remind you of fragments of heroic statues. The color of their leaves varies: deep purple, brilliant red, burnished bronze, coppery orange. The dozen beeches in this pocket park are old, uniformly broad, rounded, symmetrical, colossal. Their inviting branches begin a little above head-height for a child of ten. If our distant ancestors were at home swinging through the canopy, then it's a case of ontogeny recapitulating phylogeny. But as we age we give up even the desire to climb trees.

Maya stared at the park, the trees. She halted, arms a little out from her sides, eyes big as they could get in the effort to take it all in. I kept my mouth shut. To see is what I wanted her to do, not listen, except to the quiet.

Maya can be captivated by Disney movies and enthralled by trapeze artists. But neither *Snow White* nor circus performers elicited from her the reaction she had to those centenarian beeches, living things made of real elements. Unlike Disney and Barnum, the trees couldn't care less about entertaining her.

Maya stood still for nearly ten seconds, a perfect emblem of astonished wonder, then gave a yelp and ran toward the nearest trunk and reached for the lowest branch.

In *Theaetetus*, Plato declared that "Philosophy begins in wonder." The Greek word *thauma* does not mean simply a marvel; it also carries a suggestion of puzzle or problem. To Plato the fitting, and perhaps most human, response to wonder is to get rid of it. Wonder, conceived as a hyped-up version of curiosity, is the beginning of inquiry for philosophers who used also to be scientists.

Grown-up scientists love to talk about the wonder they felt as children, wonder at the natural world, like Maya's when confronted by a dozen beeches. The proto-scientists are the kind of kids who asked questions about the life expectancy of a Tyrannosaurus Rex or what goes on inside a black hole. When they grow up they set about looking for answers. They are the enchanted who become disenchanters. In a sense, scientists aim to turn the sublime into the ordinary; and yet I think, for the most devoted scientists, even demystifying the ineffable doesn't do away with wonder. How could it when wonder, and the ambition to probe its causes, is the very thing that keeps their shoulders at the wheel? "I want to know God's thoughts; the rest are details," Einstein admitted.

A scientist's wonder is active. But what of my ten-year-old with her big eyes, open mouth, outstretched arms? Will her wonder be passive, not a spur to further investigation? Have the two cultures got their own species of wonder? Is the passive sort poetic—that is, a feeling sufficient unto itself? Well, maybe.

> There was a child went forth every day,
> And the first object he look'd upon, that object he became,
> And that object became part of him for
> the day or a certain part of the day, or for
> many years or stretching cycles of years.

Whitman's sallying child assimilates indiscriminately, appropriates but doesn't organize a program of research into "the early lilacs" or work out the sociological background of the "old drunkard staggering home from the outhouse." He makes no distinction between the natural and social worlds, outer and inner, artificial and organic, custom or season. All of existence is equally wonderful to him. Unlike the child who grows up and goes forth to conduct field work, whose wonder becomes professionalized, Whitman's child—Whitman himself—cleaves to the unmediated wonder of childhood, gobbling up the world with all five senses, living every day as though it were his first. Whitman concludes his poem by closing the circle but, then reopening it with this tangent:

> ...that child who went forth every day and who now goes
> and will always go forth every day.

What a contrast between Whitman's lines of free and open verse, the democratic vistas of his prosody, and, say, Philip Larkin's regular rhymes and iambs, between Whitman's enchanting new world and Larkin's cramped, class-conscious old one. Larkin's "*Vers de Société*" is about the passing of religious wonder, of childlike faith, of a solitude that is sufficient unto itself. In this disenchanted world, virtues are social, vices personal, and hermits are selfish nutters. Both God and Whitman's wonder are absent. Larkin's opening stanza is unforgettable and clever, yet too jaded to be called humorous:

> *My wife and I have asked a crowd of craps*
> *To come and waste their time and ours: perhaps*
> *You'd care to join us?* In a pig's arse, friend.
> Day comes to an end.
> The gas fire breathes; the trees are darkly swayed.
> And so, *Dear Warlock-Williams: I'm afraid—*

What begins as a refusal of the wonderless social world winds up in resignation to a suburban *soirée* as a wretched substitute, even with gratitude for a night out to escape the self's fiascos and regrets. In place of wonder, we get this anxious, all-too-convincing *faute de mieux*:

> Only the young can be alone freely.
> The time is shorter now for company,
> And sitting by a lamp more often brings
> Not peace, but other things.
> Beyond the light stand failure and remorse
> Whispering *Dear Warlock-Williams: Why, of*
>> *course—*

Like so many things we feel or do not feel or once felt but no longer feel, wonder is a function of perspective. Reckoned from the moment of the Big Bang what could be more marvelous than a bicycle, a bagel, the First Barbary War? *Sub specie aeternitatis* what *isn't* a wonder? But the narrower your focus in space and time, the more things become normal—a bike, a bagel, the slaughter going on somewhere. Not only is the next moment usually indistinguishable from the ones before and after, but the context of all three includes countless facts, beliefs, arrangements—wonders become now commonplace, mere conditions of life, like gravity and summer, telephones, bananas, the two-party system.

One view from the *aeternitatis* perspective is Spinoza's. To him, the wonders of the cosmos are not contingent but unfold with Euclidean logic, in accord with the iron chain of axiom and corollary. Spinoza's is an admirable system. You can't help being impressed by his determination that everything should make perfect sense. In the seventeenth century, I imagine, making sense of matters was much the thing, for Empiricists no less than Rationalists. Yet Spinoza has his own brand of wonder; it is a kind of pantheistic praying. It's as if the beauty of a copper beech might be arrived at by disinterested deduction. I wonder: Can a pantheist love a copper beech—or God?

A few years ago, Thomas Nagel published a seductive article called "The Absurd." It is the obverse of Spinoza's ethics. Professor Nagel proposes a kind of consoling existentialism, one without crisis or angst. This is how it ends:

> If *sub specie aeternitatis* there is no reason to believe that anything matters, then that does not matter either, and we can approach our absurd lives with irony instead of heroism or despair.

Here Nagel sounds a truly contemporary chord. Kierkegaard's faith and Camus' solidarity are put quietly away in the attic, with the rest of the abandoned exercise equipment. But is irony—sovereign balm though it is—really better than heroism or even despair? For that matter, will irony save you from either?

I wonder.

The *Oxford Universal Dictionary* says the etymology of *wonder* is "unknown." (One can only wonder.)

The Anglo-Saxons used different vowels ("wundor") but the meaning's the same.

I learned that the phrase *in the name of wonder* was once used to lend emphasis to the question that followed it, *e.g.*, "In the name of wonder, Sir, has the Great Fire of London gone out yet?"

Wonder can be a noun, a verb, an action, an event, a building, a genius, a feeling. The last is what chiefly interests me, and the *O.U.D.*, never at a loss, explains it this way:

> … the emotion excited by the perception of something novel and unexpected, or inexplicable; astonishment mingled with perplexity or bewildered curiosity.

That covers it, I'd say, everything from Maya's standing still (astonished = to be turned to stone) to Einstein's shaking his marvelous head and giving us his famous dictum: "The eternal mystery of the world is its comprehensibility."

Wonder, then, is something inward provoked by something outward—except for those times when we wonder at the peculiarities of our private thoughts and public behavior. Wonder can be low or lofty, anything from idle speculation ("I wonder who's kissing her now") to the awe we feel watching an impossible over-the-shoulder catch or gazing at a few million stars. When our perspective has narrowed like our prospects and we are, in the worst sense, grown up, our capacity for wonder diminishes. That is, I suppose, what happened to the actor George Sanders. Five years ago, he began his suicide note, "Dear World, I am leaving because I am bored."

Of course, Sanders wasn't *simply* bored. After his death, a colleague reported that fifteen years earlier Sanders had declared an intention to kill himself when he reached sixty-five—which he did, right on time. Depressing enough to hit sixty-five, but you have to add in the four failed marriages (a pair of them to the Gabor sisters), the alcoholic brother's death, the declining career. Nevertheless, Sanders' case cannot be dismissed as purely clinical; his blaming boredom lends it a moral dimension. It's as if Sanders had reached the terminal stage of Kierkegaard's aesthetic life, exhausting all of hedonism's permutations, weighed down by the pointlessness of repetition, feeling his pleasures, empty of any spiritual dimension, had become mechanical. The world had become all-too-intelligible to him: existence *without* wonder. That's how it must be for the deeply cynical. I can picture how, at the end, Sanders' perspective would have contracted to the dimensions of that hotel room in Castelldefels and the little bottle of Nembutal tablets.

There are others whose perspective does not contract, not even to the dimensions of their own disciplines. For that reason they retain, notwithstanding their mental sophistication, a child's wonder. Such people tend themselves to be wonders. How different they are from *les mort d'ennui*. These artists, scientists, and saints also seem to grasp their kinship. I name Einstein and Kafka, contemporaries on the ground floor of modernism. Both never lost touch with the wonder whose evaporation Larkin made poetic, on which Sanders acted. Thus, Einstein:

> The most beautiful thing we can experience is the mysterious. It is the source of all true art and all science. He to whom this emotion is a stranger, who can no longer pause to wonder and stand rapt in awe, is as good as dead: his eyes are closed.

Franz Kafka also understood art and science as proceeding from the same source—wonder, mystery, a person's desire, as he puts it, "to rush beyond the limitations of his own small self."

One afternoon Kafka met his young friend Gustav Janouch in Prague's Franciscan Church of *The Virgin of the Snows*. They spoke about the historic building. The setting must have prompted

Kafka to think of religion, about miracles, or the urge that underpins religion, art, and science. Janouch paid careful attention and recorded what Kafka said.

> Miracles and violence are simply the two extremes of a lack of faith. Men waste their lives in passive expectation of some miraculous directive, which never comes, precisely because our ears are closed to it...

Janouch asked Kafka "What is right?" Kafka pointed to an old woman kneeling in a lady chapel. "Prayer," he said and drew the young man outside before replying at length, a little like Einstein but even more like Kafka:

> Prayer, art, and scientific research are three different flames that leap up from the same hearth... Art and prayer are only hands outstretched in the dark...

"And science?" Janouch asked.

> It is the same begging hand as prayer. Man throws himself into the dark rainbow which spans dying and living, in order to offer existence a home in the cradle of his little ego. That is what science, art, and prayer all do.

Janouch ends his account here. He does not record his reaction; but, if I were Janouch, I would certainly have looked at the tall, doomed, tubercular Kafka with wonder.

Wonder requires open hands, open ears, open everything.

Why not open our eyes and our ears? Why not stretch out a hand in the dark? It's impossible to deny that the world is a terrible place with deadly dinner parties and lethal hotel rooms. But the world also has its little girls and copper beeches. So, it is wonderful.

This piece dates from 1977. I found it, with the archaic word *Wundor* at its head, in Fein's file for that year. The essay is in holograph; Fein never typed it up. His daughter was born in 1967 and George Sanders died in 1972. Professor Thomas Nagel's essay, "The Absurd," appeared in *The Journal of Philosophy*, 68, 20, published on October 21, 1971.

Like many of Fein's unpublished essays, this one feels like an improvisation, a train of thought without tracks. About the many quotations and allusions, it is hard to say if they were deliberately chosen, the result of free association, or if they just reflect what Fein chanced to be reading at the time—like the Larkin poem perhaps. Fein does not always let us know what set him off, but, in this instance, what evidently got him thinking about wonder was taking his daughter to the park with the copper beeches. When I showed the essay to her, Maya told me she remembered the day very well. She also recalled that, at her father's funeral, an old friend told her that sometime in the Sixties, when he had become depressed over the state of the world, her father advised him to "spend five minutes looking at trees for every one spent reading the news."

It may seem surprising that Sidney Fein would express anything other than full agreement with Professor Nagel's celebrated essay and its prescription to take, in the face of an indifferent universe, an attitude of irony. On reflection, though, I think it may be just because, as an ironist himself, Fein understood the limitations of such a stance. Then again, maybe it is only that, in writing in praise of wonder, Fein felt bound to be ironic about irony.

The essay's own irony derives from the contrast it sets up between the world-weary Englishmen Larkin and Sanders versus the deracinated Continental Jews Einstein and Kafka. It is tempting to say that Fein gives his heart to the latter. His admiration for Einstein and Kafka is obvious; he quotes both at length and savors their words. Nevertheless, I think it would be wrong to suppose Fein is without sympathy for Larkin and Sanders. He was not unfamiliar with faithlessness, boredom, or immune to suicidal thoughts. In 1977, he had just turned thirty-five, a dangerous age for some men. He depicts wonder as an exceptional state, seen at its purest in children and diminishing over time. Loss of faith and ennui are two of the perils of middle age. Yet Fein insists wonder is not puerile. Durable wonder like Whitman's requires an openness to the glorious variety of the world, an inward elation provoked by what is outside us, from the starry heavens to twelve copper beeches.

ON TWO SCHOOLDAYS

THE eleventh day of the eleventh month was an official holiday. The schools were closed, yet, for the grown-ups, Armistice Day meant far less than December 7. The day their war began still blazed with infamy. They'd tell you exactly what they were doing on that Sunday morning in 1941. There was no need to press them; they relished talking about where they were, what the weather was like, the people they were with, how they heard the news, what they felt when they did. Adults were far more willing to talk about Pearl Harbor Day than about the war. Perhaps it was good to summon up their anger in its initial purity, to recall the great wave of national unanimity. Imagine, everybody with the same thing on their minds and feeling exactly the same way about it. December 7 was seared into their generation's memory because an immense public happening swamped up all the little private ones; it was a day when, as they liked to say, "everything changed." With respect to the Japanese, what might have been tolerant suspicion or grudging admiration, racial ambivalence or mere mistrust, in an instant precipitated to unalloyed hatred. A straightforward rival might be human but not a sneaky enemy.

At the Gifford Pinchot Elementary School in 1952, each day began with the Pledge, the Lord's Prayer, and a bible reading. On December 7, immediately after she finished with the daily patch of New Testament, Mrs. Roth solemnly reminded us what day it was and said Pearl Harbor Day was a different kind of holiday, not one for celebrating but for reverence and mourning. The year before, there was an assembly just for the boys. The principal made a speech meant to encourage us to embrace the military virtues. The Korean Police Action was well into its second year, and the principal painted a picture of the Asian threat: waves of fanatical Japanese had been replaced by swarms of doped-up Chinese Communists.

In those days, from time to time, bells would ring and we'd be herded into the corridors, ordered to crouch, head to knees. "Retention drills"—that was the euphemism. Thanks to some traitors, Russian planes with atomic bombs could appear at any moment; but, if we were quiet and kept our heads to our knees, we couldn't be vaporized. Despite all this, it was really the memory of the Second World War, not anticipation of a Third, that was everywhere, like the Army-Navy surplus stores. Basements and attics hid German helmets and Lugers, Japanese flags and bayonets. Black-and-white photographs of the youthful dead looked innocently from silver frames on mantelpieces. Except that they wore service caps and crisp uniforms instead of mortarboards and black gowns, they might have been high school graduation pictures.

"What did your father do in the war?" we'd ask each other. One or two fathers would brag, a few might divulge something laconically; but most kept mum. As for us boys, we watched the old war movies and the new ones still coming out. We had toy carbines, army belts and canteens; we played at war across backyard battlefields. With tubes of Duco cement, we assembled Hellcats, Mustangs, Flying Fortresses, Messerschmitts, Zeros, Bettys—planes that became beautiful as soon as they were obsolete. Of all this our parents approved. Starting that very October, we gathered religiously before the new television sets on Sunday afternoons to watch the latest episode of *Victory at Sea*. Here we first saw footage we'd see over and over all our lives—Battleship Row in flames, the *Arizona* exploding, the diminutive Emperor on his white horse, dead Marines rolling in the surf of Peleliu, Japanese soldiers raising their arms and silently yelling "Banzai!," the deadly dogfights, battlewagons lobbing sixteen-inch shells at atolls, kamikazes tumbling through flak and tracers or plowing into carriers ("gunners wanting to live against pilots wanting to die," said the narrator), the desperate, dirty fight for Iwo Jima, the raising of the flag, mothers clutching babies leaping from the cliffs of Saipan, the final cloud of souls billowing up from Hiroshima, the Japanese diplomat on the *Missouri* with his dignified limp and ridiculous top hat.

I knew the iconography of the war, its insignia, uniforms, weaponry. I grasped that island hopping was a lot tougher than it sounded. I thought the war had been won decisively but at a colossal cost, especially to the Japanese who adored their emperor and so presumably didn't mind dying if he thought attacking America was a good idea.

Because they didn't want to talk about it, I sensed that my elders felt deeply about the war, though I wasn't certain what these feelings were, or whether they were the same for men and women, veterans and civilians. You couldn't just ask. Back then, children didn't interrogate adults about their emotions. I suspect many wanted us to think they didn't have any, as if expressing feelings might reveal instability and unsettle the precious post-war young. The grown-ups had seen and felt terrible things; it must have helped to think that they sacrificed and fought so that their children wouldn't have to, wouldn't even know about it, not in the suburbs where every-thing—lawns, cars, teachers, and memories—was supposed to be nice.

But there was one question that had been troubling me. I didn't ask my parents, sure they wouldn't be pleased if I did. School, I figured, was the proper place for intellectual curiosity, not home. And so, on December 7, 1952, thirty years ago, I raised my hand and put my question to the sweet-natured, decorous, equable, sweater-set-favoring Mrs. Roth, the kindly woman who would read stories to us aloud and do all the different voices.

"What is it, Sidney?"

"Mrs. Roth, I was wondering—I was just wondering, well, *why* the Japanese attacked Pearl Harbor."

She was taken aback, literally—a full backwards step toward the blackboard, away from the class. Her motherly face went flushed. Her reply seemed just to burst from her.

"*Why?* Because the Japs are sneaky yellow bastards, *that's* why."

The class went dead silent, as mute as Mr. MacLaughlin, the ex-Marine who lived on Sprague Street and to whom, according to my friend Pete, something bad had happened on Guadalcanal.

• • •

On March 5, 1953, both Sergei Prokofiev and Josef Stalin died, unfortunately in that order. On June 19, the Rosenbergs were electrocuted in Sing Sing. On July 27, the Korean War was indefinitely suspended. A couple of weeks later, the Soviets exploded their first hydrogen bomb. The Nobel Peace Prize for 1953 was awarded to George Marshall, accused of treason that year by Senator Joseph McCarthy who began his second term, also in 1953. Robert Taft, the Majority Leader, meant to restrain McCarthy by relegating him to the chairmanship of the Government Operations Committee. But McCarthy promptly hired Roy Cohn. That same year, McCarthy married Jean Kerr, a researcher in his office, and delivered a televised speech assailing Eisenhower's administration in the same style he had FDR's, Harry Truman's, and the Nobel prizewinner. Public school teachers had to take loyalty oaths, even Quakers of which there were many in Philadelphia. In September 1953, I began the fourth grade.

My teacher, Miss Debecq, was one of those underappreciated, underpaid, unwed women who made the Gifford Pinchot Elementary School so good, despite packed classes and outmoded facilities. Teachers like Miss Debecq kept order, enforced rules strictly and fairly, adhered to high standards; but they also respected our innocence, and we took it for granted that they were caring, dedicated, and humane.

Philadelphia began with Penn's mesopotamian grid then spilled out in every direction. In the 1950s, large parts of the city might as well have been suburbs, like those new subdivisions that seemed expressly built to keep the kids ignorant of where the money came from. The Scouting Movement (*Onward for God and Our Country*) flourished in our neighborhood's many churches and one synagogue. In these patriotic white middle-class enclaves, the sit-coms of the era didn't seem so unrealistically sanitized. These shows were all built around relentlessly stable families and watched by families that thought of themselves as more or less just like them. Father knew best. Mother knew everything. Troubles and plot complications were trivial and resolved in half-an-hour, minus time for commercials. The American Way of Life, brought to you by Procter & Gamble, included indoor plumbing, TV dinners, and big cars with grills fixed in moronic smiles. TV banished all the nightmares, and what was left was the American Dream.

In the fourth grade, we had arithmetic, reading, science, art, music, and a grab-bag called social studies. Miss Debecq was herself inventive and wanted us to be, too. She was particularly fond of our making what she called "booklets". These required construction paper, paste, marking pens, and issues of *Life* magazine from which we could cut out pictures.

For our first social studies unit, we were to study Housing. The idea, Miss Debecq explained very slowly, was for us to learn about people who lived in foreign countries by investigating their dwellings, literally where they lived. Each of us was to choose a country that interested us. Then, consulting such authoritative sources as *The World Book* and *Britannica Junior*, we would make booklets—with lots of pictures—and present them to the whole class. She would be there to *help* us, of course, but really we would be teaching *ourselves* and then *each other*. This way everybody would get the benefit of everybody's work. Now, didn't that sound like a fine idea? Miss Debecq posed this rhetorical question with an audible exclamation point at the end to show that the prospect must be irresistibly enthralling.

The next morning we had to declare our choices. Miss Debecq sat at her desk, fountain pen in hand to record them in her big green grade book. She called on us one by one. My classmates chose European countries mostly—the places their forebears had been delighted to leave behind. There were a few adventurous outliers— Australia, Iceland, Tahiti. These seemed particularly to delight Miss Debecq. ("Oh, that will be so *interesting*, Julie. *Tahiti!*")

When my name came up I said "Russia." This did not please Miss Debecq one bit. "Really, Sidney? *Russia?* The Soviet *Union?*" She was obviously hinting that I still had time to make a better choice. But I just said, "Yep. Russia."

I came home to the news that my mother had received a call from the school principal, Mr. Gibbs, a personage so elevated that I'd only seen him at assemblies. Would she and my father be so good as to come in for a conference? At their earliest convenience. About what? Something to do with your son, Sidney. No, Mr. Gibbs would prefer to discuss the matter in person.

My mother told me about the phone call so calmly that I missed the restrained anxiety. She didn't speculate, let alone accuse. Like Mr. Gibbs, she kept it vague. She had to. Had something happened at school? Not that I know of, I said.

When my father got home, Mother collared him at the door. I heard him say "What?" But he was unnaturally calm, too, only a little less so. He ventured a guess. Had I gotten into a fight during recess? Nope, I said defensively. I'd remember a fight.

On Friday, my father would have to leave work early to meet with Mr. Gibbs. He didn't complain about it but he let me know. Determinedly cheerful, my mother saw me off to school that morning with a wave and a resolute smile. As for me, I was more puzzled than worried—but, of course, I was worried too.

School let out at 3:30 and, instead of going off to play with my friends, I went straight home. My parents were waiting for me in the living room. It felt tense. I could tell they'd been fretting, possibly even arguing.

Even from the way they were sitting on the club chairs I could see that they were troubled. My father's body was rigid as a pharaoh's, my mother's hands never at rest; expressions of some kind of complicated unhappiness screwed up their faces. I looked hard, as children do, for signs of anger at, or disappointment with, me, but I didn't see any. Then I finally caught on. They were *scared*.

Miss Debecq had reported to Mr. Gibbs that one of her pupils had chosen to prepare a report about housing in, of all places, Russia. Mr. Gibbs was sufficiently alarmed to call my parents in for questioning. I don't know exactly what he said to them. I do know what I'd have liked them to say to him.

My mother was first up to bat. "It was about the country you chose for your housing report," she said. That she said it *was* not it *is*, I took as a good sign. Whatever had happened with Mr. Gibbs was over, already in the past. With a forced smile, my father pointed out that there were plenty of *other* countries to research. "And it wouldn't be easy to find pictures of Russian houses, even in *Life* magazine," my mother chimed in. "How about Holland," my father suggested. "They've got very interesting houses there—you know, thin, tall ones, beside canals." "Or one of the African countries," my mother suggested hopefully. "Houses made out of mud and grass."

I dug in my heels. "No," I said. "I want to do Russia." Not to appear merely pig-headed, I appealed to the rules, to fairness. "Miss Debecq said we could *choose*."

They exchanged a tight-mouthed, furtive look. Did they think their little boy had turned into a communist? Were they afraid the G-men would soon be pounding on the door?

"But why? There are so many interesting places. Why does it have to be *Russia?*"

So, I told them. "Russia's always on the news, but in school they never teach us anything about it."

That silenced them. They lowered their eyes. Were they ashamed or exasperated by my obstinacy? Either way, they gave up.

I made my booklet on housing in Russia even though the encyclopedias were out of date and I had to draw most of the pictures. The only thing I remember about my report is that, to keep warm during their ferocious winters, Siberian families curled up on shelves above their tiled stoves.

EDITOR'S NOTE

These recollections are in Fein's file for the year 1982. The manuscript is handwritten on nine pages stapled together. There are only a few corrections. I found the papers clipped to preparation notes for the philosophy course Fein offered at Brandeis University in the spring of that year. I am responsible for the title, as neutral as I could make it.

Fein seldom wrote about his education, let alone his years in the Philadelphia public schools. In his work, he is usually pursuing an idea, picking over an experience, probing some personality or thinker—real or imagined—who has interested him. He seldom indulges in autobiography. He sets his fancy free, conflating essay with fiction, inventing characters to anatomize, and even plots into which to set them. About himself, he tends to be guarded. Even here, behind these recollections of his childhood, Fein is aiming at certain points; and, though he doesn't make them explicit here, I believe he did so in his classroom.

Fein left two clues. In the margin of the story about Pearl Harbor Day he scrawled "Marxist analysis," and, at the end of the story about the housing booklet, he scribbled "Camus' patriotism." Marx

ON TWO SCHOOLDAYS

and Camus both appear on the syllabus for the Brandeis course.

Fein once wrote that teachers, like the prophets, "will grab at anything that comes to hand—a fairy tale, a joke, a chair—sometimes out of inspiration but more often desperation." I admit the following speculations are only that, but they are, so to speak, educational guesses.

What Fein understood by "Marxist analysis" was a close look at the economic "substructure" of cultural changes and historical developments. Any analysis that does not consider economics Marx dismissed as breeding "false consciousness." This, I think, was the pedagogical point of the Pearl Harbor story. For Mrs. Roth and her generation, the significance of the Japanese surprise attack had been fixed by FDR's old-fashioned word "dastardly," and that was enough for them. They neither needed nor wanted to consider that, owing to the U.S. embargo, Japan was down to three month's supply of crude oil by the Fall of 1941. The only available source of fuel was the Dutch East Indies, which the Japanese certainly had the means and intent to conquer. But that would leave them with a thirty-five-hundred-mile supply line vulnerable to only one force, the U.S. Pacific Fleet. But, so what? What did any of that matter on December 7 with the battleships sunk and twenty-four hundred Americans dead?

Why did the Japanese attack, the curious third-grader asked his teacher. Thirty years later, in a class on Marx, I believe Fein recalled his question and the shocking answer he received to demonstrate how the failure to do an economic analysis leaves a void to be filled by something crude and irrational. On December 7, 1952, Fein learned that one of the things that rushes into such a vacuum is racism. And he remembered it.

My impression is that Fein's politics tended to be liberal, but if there were a Skeptical Party, he might have joined it. He was a Democrat, his daughter Maya reports, in roughly the same way he was Jewish, and perhaps for the same reason. It is easy to see why Albert Camus appealed to him. Camus was a serious and imaginative thinker with tastes not so different from Fein's; he was a tough and lucid writer who distrusted ideologies, was personally torn by the Algerian uprising, and who, in the absence of God, chose to stress the self-defining significance of free choices as well as the nebulous but worthy values of decency and solidarity. The book Fein assigned his students was not the usual one, the relatively brief and accessible *Myth of Sisyphus*, but a longer, more complicated and politically charged one, *The Rebel*.

Which of the many sayings of Camus might Fein have been illustrating with the tale of his childish request to find out about Russian housing at the height of the McCarthy era? Did he mean to show his students how even a child's parents could be intimidated by the combination of fear and orthodoxy? Fein's brief note refers to "Camus' patriotism." There are several possibilities, even if one limits the choice to the most familiar ones. For example, Fein might have had in mind this well-known aphorism: "I should like to be able to love my country and still love justice." Impossible to say for sure; however, as an editor willing to risk a liberty, I would suggest another sentence, less bland and tentative, one universally though mistakenly attributed to Camus because he made it famous. In the preface to his *Letters to a German Friend*, published clandestinely during the Occupation, Camus wrote: "To repeat a remark that is not mine, I love my country too much to be a nationalist."

ON HEROIC
APPROPRIATION

I N a double issue of *The Iowa Review* from a few years back [Vol. 12, Nos. 2-3, Spring-Summer 1981] I found a piece called "I, Boudica" by the feminist poet and scholar, Judy Grahn. I imagine the title is a tip of the hat to Robert Graves' *I, Claudius*. For a few decades in the first century, the Roman emperor and the Celtic queen were contemporaries.

What I found striking was Grahn's personal stake in Boudica. Establishing the significance of Boudica, she says, "has been one of the most thrilling acts of my life." There follows a dramatic monologue in verse:

> I am protectress of my horsebound clansmen.
> A red-haired, full robed, bronze-belted swordswoman,
> I am a queen of sacred groves and other old realms
> where astronomers divine from droves of animals
> or flocks of birds, and study the signs in palms;
> a queen of times when men are lovers to the men
> and the women to the women,
> as is our honored pagan custom.

This is a spectacularly romantic image of a heroic warrior queen and self-glorifying lesbian, elite product of a pagan earth-mother culture. Grahn identifies with Boudica. She is not a feminist striving for mere legal equality within mainstream culture but advancing an antithesis to it. As a philologist, Grahn knows Boudica embodies the original meaning of *virtue*, which is not passive womanly chastity but active man-killing potency. She is thrilled by the image of a Celtic Penthesilea, not a Druid Griselda. She wants to appropriate the heroism of Boudica, defying the insults she's endured, encouraging herself in a struggle that is less military than moral, not soldierly but social. This struggle is also sexual. Grahn's orientation makes it axiomatic for her that Boudica was a lesbian. "Considering Celtic customs, it would have been unnatural for Queen Boudica not to be a lesbian," she writes in her recent book.

Another Mother Tongue: Gay Words, Gay Worlds has provoked an etymological controversy, again focused on Boudica. Grahn flips a slur that had long bedeviled her, embracing it as the epithet of a proud queen by arguing that "bulldyke" derives from Boudica's name. Last year, while *Another Mother Tongue* was in the works, an interview with Grahn appeared in John Felstiner's book, *Women Writers of the West-Coast: Speaking of Their Lives and Careers*. Here Grahn states how central Boudica and "bulldyke" are to her, how they have infused her poetry and linguistic research:

> I don't know of an uglier word I've ever been called in my life than 'bulldyke.' I was so haunted by this for many years that I finally decided to take the word by the horns and find out why this strange word is in the vernacular. I've traced it to a Celtic queen who fought against the Romans in A.D. 61 during the reign of Nero and nearly won. The Celts had institutional gay practices, which the Roman authors were horrified by. This queen led a nation which still had gay traditions going on. She had flaming red hair and was a very large woman. The Celtic women warriors were older women who often taught the men arms. It was a totally different sense of fighting than we have any conception of.

> And when she rebelled against the Roman colonists and nearly won, they suppressed her name. Her name was

Boadicea, a word which has come down to us meaning a very militaristic or strong, warrior-like, lesbian-type large female. That's a part of what I'm working on, combining poetry and etymology and my own experiences. There are many other examples besides that one. That's the one that really thrilled me to death when it finally came together.

I don't know if Grahn is right about the origin of "bulldyke" or not. Apparently, a lot of scholars think she isn't. But it seems to me that her point isn't a scholarly but a personal one. She twice calls her discovery "thrilling." I don't imagine many philologists are "thrilled to death" by working out a derivation, though I could be wrong. Anyway, for the poet the upshot seems a simile—"I am *like* Boudica"—or maybe a metaphor—"Boudica, *c'est moi.*"

Physical heroism is self-evident. Military heroes look heroic, at least once the monuments are unveiled. Spiritual and intellectual heroism, on the other hand, have to prove themselves. The kind of hero Kierkegaard calls "tragic" or a "knight of resignation" is of the first sort—visibly heroic. He has to be in order to be mounted on either a stage or a plinth. Kierkegaard jokes (seriously, as usual) that, by contrast, the knight of faith looks like "a tax collector." He too has the self-discipline to give up the world as the tragic hero does; but then he gets it all back, turning the sublime into the commonplace, and so looks as ordinary as an IRS clerk. His heroism is so inward that he is "unintelligible." But the task one takes on in writing about the unintelligible is to make it intelligible. One way is to seize on one sort of heroism and lug it onto the other. The literal meaning of "metaphor" is "to carry over."

Heroes of inwardness need to appropriate the attributes of outward ones to make their heroism visible, intelligible. Socrates does just this during his trial, letting the Athenians know why he won't knuckle under. Kierkegaard does likewise in *Fear and*

Trembling, equating his own trial of faith with Abraham's. But metaphors are duplicitous; they say that two things are the same but also that they aren't. They are suspect because things alike in a way are also unlike. Socrates might just be on an ego-trip, puffing himself up before his fellow citizens; Kierkegaard might be writing the most impudent self-justification ever conceived for dumping your fiancée. It is fitting that Kierkegaard should have titled his master's thesis *The Concept of Irony* and focused it on Socrates. In a sense, "the Danish Socrates" is not only appropriating Abraham but also Socrates, the master appropriator.

Socrates's appropriation of Achilles is historically consequential. It's not just his declaring that, like the son of Thetis, he is honorably abiding by his values at the cost of his life. Socrates revolutionizes the meaning of heroism and virtue—"transvaluing" them, Nietzsche would say. For Achilles' physical virtue Socrates substitutes relentless intellectual inquiry. He converts virtue from military to moral.

The Greeks produced plenty of philosophers before Socrates but none like him. This was an original thinker with an original method, an original personality who exuded a counter-cultural charisma irresistible to young aristocrats like Plato. Classical Athens was New York, Paris, and London rolled up in one—the center of fashion, culture, and commerce. In a city that worshipped riches and equated beauty with truth, Socrates was poor and ugly. With his snub nose, worn-out toga, and bare feet, he was the breathing antithesis of the city's materialism. No wonder he became the first notable non-conformist in history and built his doctrine on the distinction between seeming and being, or that his most devoted pupil called him "a satyr concealing a god." In a direct democracy that ran on speechifying, he openly despised popular opinion, scorned fine rhetoric and those who taught it. It's with just this mockery that Socrates starts off his legal defense, using his favorite distinction to attack the speeches of his prosecutors.

> How you have felt, O men of Athens, at hearing the
> speeches of my accusers, I cannot tell; but I know that
> their persuasive words almost made me forget who I
> was:—such was the effect of them; and yet they have
> hardly spoken a word of truth.

The operant words in this sentence of the *Apology* are *persuasive* and *truth* which Socrates sets against each other. Those eloquent speeches you just heard? Mere pyrotechnics, pure deception. What you're about to hear from me may be plain but it'll be honest. These accusers have got fancy *persuasion* on their side; all I've got is simple *truth*. That this often-imitated gambit is itself a more clever use of rhetoric than anything Meletus or Anytus probably managed just adds another tier to Socrates' layer cake of ironies. Remember, it is Socrates the sarcastic who is claiming sincerity just as later it will be Socrates the awfully smart who proclaims his utter ignorance. And what do *we* think? We think he means it; then that he doesn't mean it; then, no, we think he really *does* mean it…

In the *Apology* Socrates identifies himself with Achilles, for four centuries the Greeks' heroic ideal, a military one, like Grahn's Boudica. Buried in the Greek word for virtue, *arête*, is the name of their war god. But unlike Grahn, who sees her own ideal in the physically dauntless warrior-queen—her size, sexual tastes, and swordswomanship—Socrates displaces Achilles even he appropriates him, altering the meanings of virtue and courage from martial to ethical.

Socrates invokes Achilles just after he disposes of Meletus, child's play for the man who invented cross-examination. The invocation of Achilles is the turning-point where Socrates recasts the trial and we see that he's not interested in winning an acquittal but content to court martyrdom. Only a man resigned to dying could be that *that* provocative, *this* cool. At a stroke, he dismisses the charges of his accusers as pretexts and depoliticizes what was most likely a trial about his associates having overthrown the democracy three times in ten years. In one sentence, he seizes control, asserts his integrity, inflames the jury, and elevates the trial by giving his view of what's behind it, which is

> ... not Meletus, nor yet Anytus, but the envy and detraction of the world, which has been the death of many good men, and will probably be the death of many more; there is no danger of my being the last of them.

Xenophon, who wasn't there, believed his old teacher was grabbing the chance of a glorious exit by committing judicial suicide. Plato, who was there, didn't agree; but, even in his transcript, there's evidence for Xenophon's opinion and Socrates' appropriation of Achilles is a part of it.

It's all about dying nobly: "... a man who is good for anything ought not to calculate the chance of living or dying; he ought only to consider whether in doing anything he is doing right or wrong..." Socrates puts words into his accusers' mouths, suggesting that their aim is to frighten him into abandoning his mission. He is the one honoring the Homeric heroes while they believe "[those] who fell at Troy were not good for much, and the son of Thetis above all, who altogether despised danger in comparison with disgrace..." Then he rehearses what everybody at the trial—everyone in Greece— knows, how Thetis warned Achilles that if he avenged Patroclus he would die soon after. Socrates' point? "I'm standing by my code *as Achilles stood by his.*" He doesn't mention the discrepancy between Achilles' code and his; on the contrary, he reminds the jury of his own military career, that he had fought in three battles for Athens. The effort isn't aimed at distinguishing his values from Achilles' but to show that their heroism is the same: "Achilles stayed at his post before Troy as I did at Potidaea *and I'm doing the same now.*" Only then does the philosopher say what he "conceives and imagines" his post is:

> ... God orders me to fulfill the philosopher's mission

of searching into myself and other men... [if} I were to desert my post through fear of death, or any other fear... that would indeed be strange, and I might justly be arraigned in court for denying the existence of the gods... For this fear of death is indeed the pretense of wisdom, and not real wisdom, being the appearance of knowing the unknown.

The efficiency of Socrates' words is remarkable. Here he works in the atheism charge, his fundamental appearance/reality distinction, and what has irritated his fellow citizens most of all about him—his four decades of demolishing their claims to know something. He'd already related the story of the Delphic oracle (the basis of the claim that his mission is divine) and that he is wiser than everybody else only because he admits he knows nothing whereas everybody else pretends to know what they don't. For example, Socrates supposes that his accusers know that death is an evil to be feared and avoided. But death, he retorts, is a possible good and he would "never fear or avoid a possible good rather than a certain evil." That certain evil would be to abandon his post and not remain steadfastly at it, like Achilles. Socrates' code, unlike Achilles', requires him to be rational, not wrathful. Therefore, as he presents it, not fearing death isn't a matter of reckless valor but applying clear logic.

No one was more ambivalent about Socrates' heroism than Friedrich Nietzsche. The question of whether Socrates was the brilliant and heroic originator of something good or the devil-ishly subtle instigator of corruption and decay is like a running sore in Nietzsche's work. Was Socrates creator or destroyer, hero or buffoon?

When he was still teaching at the University of Basel, Nietzsche delivered a lecture on Socrates. In it, his admiration is for how Socrates did not miss the "splendid opportunity" to dignify his values and mission by dying for them, as Achilles did by avenging Patroclus.

Thus, one must consider his magnificent *Apology*; he speaks before posterity... he wanted death. He had the most splendid opportunity to show his triumph over human fear and weakness and also the dignity of his divine mission. (quoted in Walter A. Kauffman, *Nietzsche: Philosopher, Psychologist, Antichrist*, Princeton: Princeton University Press, Fourth Edition, 1974)

How highly Nietzsche rated the *Apology* is even better conveyed by this memorable remark:

Some ancient writings one reads to understand antiquity: others, however, are such that one studies antiquity in order to be able to read them. To these belongs the *Apology*...

This is Nietzsche at the outset of his career. In general, though he repeatedly changed his mind about Socrates, it's fair to say that between the 1870s and the 1880s he moved from reverence to scorn. The brilliant and heroic philosopher who transforms his culture and exalts philosophy by choosing death before dishonor turns into the demonically subtle agent of a decadent morality and debased culture. In his first book, *The Birth of Tragedy* (1872), Nietzsche extolled the balance between the Apollonian principle and the Dionysian. In his later work, he proclaimed an increasingly hysterical denigration of the former in favor of the latter. When Nietzsche recast the Apollonian/Dionysian dualism as *life-denying* and *life-affirming*, it was clear where he was headed, and when he reformulated it again as *slave* versus *master morality*, he'd arrived. Now Socrates' appropriation of Achilles is not noble but insidious, a betrayal, the subversion of all that is masterful by all that is servile. Well, it's not quite as simple as that. Nietzsche didn't fail to discern Socrates' will-to-power in the aggression and vengefulness underlying his method, how his apparently gentle irony barely conceals a sarcastic humiliation of his opponents. To Nietzsche, even slaves have the will-to-power and what Socrates did is precisely the perversion of that will as practiced by slaves. From a civilizing, rationalizing, moralizing Achilles, Socrates becomes for Nietzsche Achilles' obverse. In *The Twilight of the Idols* (1889), written the year his career ended in syphilitic madness, Nietzsche was still picking at that open wound of Socrates. In a well-known section called "The Problem of Socrates" he writes:

> I want to understand what idiosyncrasy begot that Socratic idea that reason and virtue equal happiness—that most bizarre of all equations which is, moreover, opposed to every instinct of the earlier Greeks... Socrates was the buffoon who got himself taken seriously...

Like those "earlier Greeks," Nietzsche too idealized Homer's Achilles, the self-glorifying and tragic individual, a "master" free of hopes and illusions. In this passage from *The Iliad* Achilles stands over the wounded Lycaon and, preliminary to administering the *coup de grâce*, delivers the sort of speech Nietzsche must have admired:

> See what a man I am also, both strong and comely to
> look on,
> Great was the father who bred me, a goddess the mother
> who bore me;
> Yet over me stand death and overmastering fortune.
> To me a dawn shall come, or a noontide hour, or an
> evening,
> When some man shall deprive me of life in the heat of
> battle,
> Casting at me with a spear or an arrow shot from a
> bowstring.

No hope here of a happy eternity spent putting annoying questions to glorious shades. Nothing about it being better to be a victim than a victimizer. Nietzsche came to regard Socrates' appropriation of Achilles as a cultural disaster. In effect, by proclaiming the advent of his *Übermensch* to the twentieth century, Nietzsche sought to undo

Socrates' appropriation and reverse the "transvaluation of values" that had sapped the vitality of Western civilization he thought Socrates initiated. From Achilles to Socrates was bad... so from Socrates back to Achilles would be good—or, better yet, "beyond good and evil."

If you're among those who think a million bucks wouldn't be too much to lay out for another Socrates, or another Achilles worth a dime, you'll feel differently, more as the young Nietzsche did in that Basel lecture hall. You might even admit that, as Socrates himself says to his old friend Crito, once in a while a philosopher might have to die at his post to keep philosophy from being just overheated Athenian air.

By audaciously appropriating Achilles, Socrates made his own heroism visible or, if you prefer, revealed his pride and provoked his enemies. By contrast, Søren Kierkegaard's appropriation of Abraham is private and indirect; but his concealment turns out also to be an intimate revelation. In *Fear and Trembling*, he gives us a profound and original interpretation of the hero with whom he claims kinship, the prototype of both individuality and faith, Kierkegaard's two great themes. Abraham, of course, is nothing like those swordsfolk, Boudica and Achilles. Like Socrates' or Kierkegaard's, his heroism is inward. Yet he is also a public hero, visible to Jews, Christians, Muslims, sanctified by tradition, swathed in a patina of familiarity. Kierkegaard appropriates Abraham as Socrates does Achilles. The difference is that, while Socrates alters the idea of virtue, he doesn't change the idea of Achilles. Kierkegaard, on the other hand, radically reinterprets what it means to be Abraham, the human reality of his fate, and so introduces a new conception of faith.

The most cryptic of epigraphs must be the one Kierkegaard chose for *Fear and Trembling*. Cryptic really is *le mot juste* because this sentence about a secret message itself conveys an encrypted one.

What Tarquinius Superbus said in the garden with the poppy blooms was understood by the son but not by the messenger.

To end a standoff with the Gabii, Tarquinius, last king of Rome, orders his son to defect to the enemy. The Gabii make the son their chief. Once established, the son dispatches a messenger to find out what his father wants him to do next. Tarquinius takes the man for a stroll around his garden and, while making small talk, casually knocks the heads off poppies with his stick. He then sends the perplexed messenger back to his son who, when told about the poppies, grasps his father's meaning: kill or banish the elite among the Gabii so the Romans can walk in.

What's this got to do with Abraham and the sacrifice of Isaac? To the public, the epigraph is as incomprehensible as the business with the poppies was to the messenger. But *Fear and Trembling* is a work of what Kierkegaard called "indirect communication," and the one in which he is most intimately implicated. The book is a work of brilliant exegesis, full of psychological insight and theological originality. It packs more ideas into one paragraph than most writers manage in several chapters. But it is also a tragic love story, Kierkegaard's own, and the person to whom Kierkegaard was indirectly communicating was Regine Olsen, the woman he claimed to love, wooed, and to whom he became engaged until he broke it off without giving her anything like a good reason. In the tidy society of Copenhagen, it was a scandal.

Kierkegaard's message to Regine is this: I love you still and always will. I didn't dump you. Breaking our engagement was a sacrifice demanded by God, who had other tasks for me. As Abraham had to give up the child he loved best—and loved most of all when he raised the knife—so I had to resign myself to renouncing our union. Or, to put it more crudely, I gave you up to write a book about why I gave you up—and not just this one, but all the others as well.

Who delivers this message? A messenger like the one sent by

Tarquinius; that is, a messenger who doesn't understand the message he is delivering. This is Johannes de silentio, the pseudonym Kierkegaard created to write *Fear and Trembling*. Johannes isn't silent on anything, save for Kierkegaard's broken engagement. He says over and over that he doesn't understand Abraham. The indirect method of the book as a whole depends on Johannes' claim that he doesn't know what Abraham is but does know what Abraham *isn't*: he's not a tragic hero or a dramatic one or a knight of resignation. In short, Kierkegaard is Abraham/Tarquinius, Regine is Isaac/the son, and Johannes is the uncomprehending messenger.

There are two ways to draw a circle. You can just take the chalk and inscribe it on the blackboard. This is what books about faith by people who claim to know all about it do; they communicate directly, or try to. But you can also describe a circle indirectly: just fill in everything that it *isn't* and the circle will be what's left over. This is the method of *Fear and Trembling*: Johannes tells us Abraham isn't a Stoic, Agamemnon, Jephthah, Jeremiah, Brutus, an Oedipal monster, God's executioner, a man driven to despair, a protagonist of a three-act tragicomedy, a lunatic child-murderer, or the dupe in a theological shaggy dog story. Kierkegaard called *Fear and Trembling* a "dialectical lyric," a unique form he devised to describe uniqueness, a kind of musical philosophy or philosophical poetry. Musically, by repetition and variation, it gradually etches into a reader's mind what Kierkegaard thinks Abraham is—what faith and individuality are, along with their price. Though its message isn't only private, meant for Regine alone yet, without the crisis she provoked for Kierkegaard, the book would never have been written. If Kierkegaard had truly intended it to be private, then he wouldn't have published it in October, 1843. He could just have tied the manuscript up with twine and hired a porter to deliver it to Regine. The encrypted message of *Fear and Trembling* is a private one, but Kierkegaard has used Johannes to deliver a message to any reader of any time or place for whom the book *works*, to whom it *speaks*—that is, readers who are sons and not messengers. Such readers wouldn't need to know anything about Regine Olsen, or even Søren Kierkegaard.

Ideally, *Fear and Trembling* should have been written right after Kierkegaard broke off the engagement then blackened his name for two weeks by going around Copenhagen pretending to be a cad before fleeing to Berlin. *Fear and Trembling* wasn't written then, but the two-volumes of *Either/Or* were. The problem of Regine fueled the writing of *Either/Or* with the same sublimated libidinal energy that would later drive the composition of *Fear and Trembling* and then *Repetition*, both completed in a matter of months, during a second retreat to Berlin. It's well to bear in mind that Kierkegaard became the Father of Existentialism because there was no mother.

Either, written in the scintillating prose of the pseudonym Victor Eremita, is about seduction, the one-night stand, Don Juan's *mille e tre*, the uncommitted, unmoored aesthetic life. *Or,* composed in the turgid prose of the dour Judge William, is a tractate on marriage, the domesticated, ethical form of Eros. *Or* is tough to get through while *Either* is hard to put down. In these tomes Kierkegaard plunges into the first two stages of his dialectic "stages on life's way," aesthetic thesis and ethical antithesis. Though *Fear and Trembling* plays virtuoso games with both of these stages, it is devoted to their synthesis, the religious (another reason it's called a *dialectical* lyric, one of the many mocking references to Kierkegaard's *bête noir*, Hegel). Abraham is an ethical man who acts unethically; from the outside he looks like a psychopathological would-be child killer. He's a hero disciplined enough to achieve the "infinite resignation" of Brutus and Socrates, but goes much further, managing something neither of them do, a "movement of the absurd." Abraham gives up but expects to get back. A key theme of *Fear and Trembling* is that faith is "for this world." It is all about getting. Perhaps none of this is in *Either/Or* because Kierkegaard didn't yet believe that he'd really and truly lost Regine.

In formulating Abraham's greatness, Kierkegaard has Johannes write: "… it is great to give up one's desire, but greater to stick to it after having given it up." Abraham's faith is that Isaac will be returned. In other words, God may be "the Absurd" who sets monstrous tests, but, in the end, He's good and loving in *human* terms.

Kierkegaard's belief that "God lodged a veto" against his marriage led him to appropriate Abraham and cast his broken engagement in the mold of the *Akedah*. But there was a second impetus behind *Fear and Trembling*. Regine had a new fiancé, her former tutor, the diplomat Johan Schlegel. Here was a second crisis. A Regine unmarried and pining might yet be reclaimed once the books were written for himself and God; but a Regine wedded to Schlegel was lost for good.

In *Either/Or*, Kierkegaard surveys the crossroads where the aesthetic and ethical divide, but does it at a philosophical distance. It is still his own case he is weighing but he contemplates it, so to speak, in general. In *Fear and Trembling*, the distance vanishes; Kierkegaard is in it up to his neck. Only in imagination was he ever a Don Juan, the Seducer of the *Diary*, or a prospective pillar of bourgeois society. These were thought-experiments, possibilities, roads not, and not to *be*, taken. The analogues to Kierkegaard's situation in *Fear and Trembling* are right up against the bone. While the most significant of these is the appropriation of Abraham, there are others. In fact, they are almost obsessively numerous. But the one which comes nearest to his Kierkegaard's situation in 1843 is the fairy tale about the commoner who falls impossibly in love with a princess.

Kierkegaard placed the story in the "Preamble from the Heart," the lengthy warm-up section that precedes the three "*problemata*" that make up the second half of the book. The three problems are questions morality would answer negatively. Can you justifiably suspend ethics (caring for your son, marrying the woman you promised to)? Is there an absolute duty (to God and/or one's urge to write) that trumps all others obligations? Can you keep matters to yourself (not tell Sarah, Regine, anybody)? Abraham answers yes to all three, and Kierkegaard is saying he did too, that these are what every "knight of faith" must be prepared to do. He lays out the congruity between Abraham and himself formally and passionately. By reiterating comparisons and contrasts, Johannes pounds away at the point that Abraham isn't the ethical hero that organized religion makes of him. Kierkegaard sees no difference between Church and State, as both institutions are agents of socialization. Both want to get us inside morality, not outside of it. The Danish state and the Danish Church insist that God wants us to follow the commandments, not to suspend them. To Kierkegaard, institutional religion misconstrues faith and betrays its heroism, cheapening the one and mitigating the other.

The tale of the commoner and the princess may seem like just another of Kierkegaard's narrative digressions. Though all of them refer to his case, this one has particular immediacy because he is processing the news of Regine's engagement to Schlegel. It begins with this powerful sentence:

> A young lad falls in love with a princess, the content of his whole life is in this love.

What a phrase that is, "the content of his whole life." It is echoed four years later in the title Kierkegaard chose for his devotional discourse, *Purity of Heart Is to Will One Thing*, a book with a dedication that would have been fitting for *Fear and Trembling* as well— to "That Solitary Individual." As Søren the ungratified lover saw himself in Abraham the religious hero, so the single-minded purity of caritas is identical to the erotic love of the lad who loved the princess. The following passage from *Fear and Trembling* describes the knight's resistance to distraction and temptation. It points also to his disregard of worldly prudence, the putting of all his eggs in one basket:

... [T]he knight will... have the strength to concentrate the whole of his life's content and the meaning of reality in a single wish. If a person lacks this concentration, this focus, his soul is disintegrated from the start, and then he will never come to make the movement, he will act prudently in life like those capitalists who invest their capital in every kind of security so as to gain on the one what they lose on the other...

Though the young commoner surrenders the princess, he can hardly give up his love for her, not if it is "the content of his life." The only alternative is sublimation, and Kierkegaard explicitly recapitulates Christianity's appropriation of Platonic love:

His love for the princess would take on for him the expression of an eternal love and would acquire a religious character, be transfigured into a love for the eternal being...

Platonic love is satisfaction without gratification, the reverse not only of what Don Juan's *mille e tre* had to offer but even of Judge William's wedlock. "Everything is possible spiritually speaking, but in the finite world there is much that is not possible"—such as marrying princesses, such as getting Regine back. Spiritually, the commoner can preserve his love for the princess, yet his peace of mind depends on giving the princess up because only "in his infinite resignation he is reconciled with existence." This is Kierkegaard bucking himself up, I think; and his words get more pointed still:

He keeps this love young, and it grows with him in years and beauty. On the other hand, he needs no finite occasion for its growth... He needs none of this erotic titillation of the nerves at the sight of the loved one, etc...

Then he comes to the heart of the matter:

There was a person who also believed he had made the movement, but time went by, the princess did something else, she married, say, a prince, and his soul lost the resilience of resignation.

Such feelings are beneath an aspiring Abraham and cannot be acknowledged (never mind that that's precisely what Kierkegaard is doing); therefore, he addresses this stern reminder to himself:

> ... one who has infinitely resigned is enough unto himself... What the princess does cannot disturb him, it is only lower natures who have the law for their actions in someone else...

What I find humanly touching is that Kierkegaard didn't end the story here, not with this moral, but with a happy ending, as in a real fairy tale. He modifies the story by supposing that the princess also loves the commoner but that her love is no more possible than his. In this case, she too can be admitted into the same exclusive "order of knighthood," giving up her wish yet keeping her love alive, presumably even in bed with her socially acceptable spouse. This sounds like Kierkegaard entertaining the hope that he is the man Regine truly loves, not her new fiancé. He may have been right because Schlegel seems to have been jealous of Kierkegaard even long after his rival was dead. According to an anecdote, Schlegel forbade Regine to read so much as a line of Kierkegaard's writing unless he was present in the room with her. Now *that's* romantic.

Abraham gets Isaac back. Before her engagement to Schlegel, Søren could have hoped to get Regine back too. Now, in 1843, he returns her to himself but only in fantasy:

> These two will then be suited to each other in all eternity, with such a... *harmonia praestabilita* that were some moment to come... which allowed their love its expression in time then they would be in a position to begin

precisely where they would have begun had they been united from the beginning.

Abraham was promised the miracle baby when he was seventy-five and had to wait twenty-five years to get him. Then he is commanded to sacrifice the boy and to contemplate the awful act on a three-day donkey trip. The promised child is almost snatched away in a case of child-murder and pre-emptive genocide, but then returned. So why wouldn't a broken-hearted, Abrahamizing Kierkegaard dream of getting Regine back in *his* old age? It is painful to read this passage about the commoner and the princess picking up where they left off. Kierkegaard had no idea he was going to die just a dozen years later. It's just as he wrote: "Life can only be understood backwards; but it must be lived forwards."

Of course, not everyone who tries to appropriate a hero becomes a world-famous philosopher or even heroic. Because it is an act of surpassing chutzpah, where heroic appropriation fails it looks impudent and pathetic, a tactic of egomania. Heroic appropriation is nothing like hero-worship, which leaves out the pain of actually being a hero. Worship abstracts heroes; appropriation does the very opposite. Certainly, Socrates, Kierkegaard, and Grahn appropriate the glory of their heroes, but this glory has already been established. If it is more their heroes' pain they appropriate that is because their motive lies in their own suffering.

EDITOR'S NOTE

When I accepted to Maya Nunfi Fein's offer to go through her father's posthumous papers and prepare for publication any items I thought suitable, she sent me five heavy-duty cartons containing Fein's files, each designated by calendar year. According to his daughter, placing the papers he had accumulated over twelve months into a dated file was a New Year's Eve ritual for Fein.

ON HEROIC APPROPRIATION

I did not find the essay above in any of these files. A handwritten draft along with a corrected typescript under the title "Heroic Appropriation," all fastened together by a paperclip, were in a separate, smaller box of loose papers. These were not filed because, with a few exceptions, they date from 1984 and Fein died on May 23 of that year. As Judy Grahn's book, *Another Mother Tongue*, was published on January 1, 1984, the text fixes the date of composition between January and May.

The digressive and improvisatory character of the writing here is characteristic of Fein's posthumous papers. Had he prepared the piece for publication, he might have made cuts but this is impossible to know.

It is hard to avoid feeling that Fein did not know where he was going when he began this piece. The essay seems to me the work of a mind in motion rather than a deliberate plan. Perhaps he was amused by Grahn's etymology of "bulldyke," thought more deeply about her celebration of Boudica, then came up with the notion of "heroic appropriation" and was reminded of what Socrates did with Achilles at his trial, which led to recalling Nietzsche's ambivalence about Socrates. Casting about for a third example, perhaps because two were not enough, he fastened on his favorite book by one of his favorite thinkers. Once Fein began to write about *Fear and Trembling*, it seems he found it difficult to keep the focus on his theme, or even to stop, so that this section is nearly as long as the rest of the essay. It appears to me that he was tickled by Grahn and intellectually stimulated by Socrates, but that it is with the case of Kierkegaard that Fein was emotionally engaged.

POSTSCRIPT: AN ESSAY AND A STORY

HOW SERIOUS WAS
SIDNEY FEIN?

S IDNEY Fein's whole intellectual enterprise was a sort of burlesque. He was a trickster, a mocker, a jester at the court of high seriousness. He himself believed in nothing at all, certainly not those putative "doctrines" which it must have pleased him to see tagged with the eponym "Feinian." Sidney Fein was an ironist and, in this sense at least, a true heir to Socrates. But the chief irony, as it turns out, was not Fein's; it was that the seriousness of his world was so high that it couldn't get any of his jokes. Wouldn't get them. Perhaps some or even many of those academics among whom Fein hovered like a black fly in summer did indeed see that he was joking, yet chose to pretend otherwise, preventing the jokes from being released, so to speak, into the sealed air of their offices, lecture halls, the convivial solemnity of their conferences, disciplines, and minds. After all, laughter is both a cause and an effect of levity and these scholars may instinctively have understood that for the good of their livelihoods, no less than for the stability of their solar system, gravity was indispensable.

Let me offer an illustration. If Fein's name has been associated with one idea more than others, it is surely the notion of Critical or Feinian Classification. Even in its simplest form one can see that Critical Classification is really just the demolition of the idea of classification itself, a *reductio ad absurdum* of the whole project. Here is the paragraph from *Diptych on Terrestrial Representation* (1973) where Fein begins to develop his theory.

The strategies of both the classical botanists and the Romantic zoologists are workable but incomplete. The one looks at visible differences and similarities among plants, the other at functional or organic structures over time. The trouble, of course, is that both give excessive credit to their own names, to the phylum, family, genus, species, subspecies, and so forth. The taxonomists really believe, that is, that taxonomy is the method of Nature, that classification forms a sort of one-to-one template with the Creation. The mistake is characteristic of those who have read too little good poetry.

Notice that this is sheer negation. Fein seeks to demolish the work of centuries, to dismiss the patient labors of Cuvier and Agassiz with an epigram. His flippancy would be breathtakingly offensive if one were intended to take it seriously.

Feinian Classification itself is presented with an earnestness that is best understood as mock-heroic, suggesting that the "good poetry" Fein had in mind for the taxonomists is by Alexander Pope.

Whether we choose to classify by visible structure or organico-historical functional evolution, we arrive at the same impasse, namely the paradox that Nature is at once conservative and dynamic. The first method would be roughly adequate were Nature only concerned to uphold the stasis achieved in Genesis on the first Sabbath, while the second earns classification no more authority than a snapshot of a distance runner in action. Moreover, when we adapt either method to those objects that constitute a greater and greater portion of our landscape—that is, all the things we have ourselves made, not excluding methods of classification—the need for a better, a more *critical* method of classification becomes obvious. Two cars are both cars, both may even be Buicks, but let one be a station wagon owned by a suburban family and the other a muscle car owned by an unemployed alcoholic plasterer. Here the class 'Buick' is of no great significance as compared to the vital distinction between the owners and what one may expect from their driving. The objects themselves were not manufactured to be similar but different; the similarity consists more in the fact that "Buick" denotes a complex economic arrangement rather than an actual species of automobile. Even the term *automobile* itself is problematic when one considers the cultural determinants that govern its meaning.

In that last sentence one can hardly fail to notice that Fein is really starting to enjoy himself. And this sense of wallowing in a kind of repressed hilarity becomes more obvious the further he proceeds.

The problem is more vexed than clarified by grammar, where we distinguish between *apple* and *this apple*, *orange* and *this orange*. *Apple* and *orange* do not exist except as classifications, which is to say they do not really exist at all. The most we can say with confidence is *this* apple and *that* orange exist. When we compare apples to oranges, we may observe their differences in appearance, taste, color, structure, provenance, smell, and juice. We may even notice that two oranges, a Navel and a Valencia say, resemble each other more any two varieties of apples, such as Macintoshes and Romes. It is probably this distinction that gives rise to the false abstractions *apple* and *orange*.

All of which is merely Fein playfully doing what the colloquialism says is impossible: "You can't compare apples and oranges."

It makes one's head spin to think how instantaneously Feinian Classification was embraced by philosophers of the number-crunching sort. They are the ones responsible for its cachet and for many drops of that complex and arcane fragrance that perfumes the name of Sidney Fein. "But when we apply the new Feinian Classification, the problem entirely evaporates…" one of the most celebrated said some years ago to absolutely stunning effect in the middle of an incomprehensible conference paper. And so a notion that began as a kind of parlor trick turned overnight into an intellectual fixture. But what, after all, does Fein's idea come down to? Why do I call it a joke, a parlor prank? Well, the idea is neither complex nor original, for all it comes to when rigorously applied is that everything is literally in a class by itself. Fein resurrected William of Ockham's medieval nominalism and played it for what ought to have been laughs.

I repeat: Feinian Classification is the end of classification. A *declas-sification* of knowledge frees the mind from stereotypes, it's true; however, it also thrusts us into a bewildering and anarchic wonderland where nothing is enough like anything else to make sense. One could say also that Feinian Classification is the reappropriation of early childhood, of a stage in our development at which every encounter is a novelty, every object a discovery, every individual unique as the phoenix. Fein's joke returns us to that short-lived ontological moment when all play is work and all work play, when every object is a toy and each human or animal a playmate.

This return to the childish, though hardly the pin in the pinwheel of Fein's comic method, still conveys something of his general *modus operandi*. For example, consider the chapter titled "Devouring the Mother" in *Want, Desire, and Need* (1977). Here Fein lays out with deadpan earnestness his reductionist theory of "The Ambivalence of Conscience" in terms of "post-infantile orality." The joke here also consists in reducing adult perplexities and anxieties to the knee-high perspective of a three-year-old. He begins unobjection-ably enough: "Moral dilemmas always take the form of a conflict between two goods and two bads, never between one good and one bad." Why is conscience felt to "bite?" he then asks. It is hardly to show erudition that he cites "agenbite of inwit"; rather, he does it as a parody of the polymaths' love of alluding to other fields, above all literature, the *lingua franca* of the properly educated. All right, so why *does* conscience "bite"? Simply because, Fein says, our original moral dilemma and the pattern for all subsequent ones is established when we are weaned—unless, he adds, weaning should occur *after* toilet training, which is another joke. He reasons thus: it is good to suck the mother's breast, to "devour" as much of her as one can; and yet the demand *not* to do so—and thus to please the mother and save her from the pain of one's suddenly erupting teeth—is also good. Sooner or later, the child *is* weaned, of course, but at the price of turning the repressed dental aggression against itself. Only later on, after we have submitted to the laminations of language and culture, do we speak of "the voice of conscience" though, says Fein with his Buster Keaton face, we really ought to speak of "the canines and bicuspids of conscience." This send-up of Freudian analysis and Kantian logic has turned out to be surprisingly popular with Freudians and Kantians. Perhaps one shouldn't be surprised, for it was the distinguishing knack of Sidney Fein precisely to be taken most seriously by those of whom he was most making fun.

For what better illustration could one ask than Fein's political views, out of which no less than half-a-dozen doctoral dissertations have already been teased? The extended monograph Fein coyly titled *Aristocratic Democracy* (1983) is not only his last book but one of his subtlest satires. This political treatise is often referred to as Fein's "most unexpected production," a rather foolish description given that Fein seldom took up the same subject twice, was bound to get to politics sooner or later, and, in any case, had no particular field of expertise from which to make "unexpected" forays. Nowadays, "Fein Studies" threatens to become a minor field.

But from irony to cases. Why should I want to call *Aristocratic Democracy* a satire? Satire must have an object—what then is Fein's? His target, as usual, is multiple. For example, Fein's core argument that democracy works best when the many choose "aristocrats" to lead them is at once an attack on political hacks who like to make a virtue of their mediocrity and on those plutocrats—or their trust-funded offspring—who despise the common good, are ignorant or cynical about power, and whose civic responsibility extends about as far as the next charity ball. Once again, Fein in his politics returns to the world of childhood. Here is one of his most characteristic passages:

> Aristocracy and democracy are more than apparent opposites; they are paradoxically conjoined in our natures. Boys and girls—the gender really does not matter, only the age—are instinctively democratic but nevertheless inclined to be hierarchical, even sacral, in their view of power. Thus, all children hate bullies—i.e., tyrants—and yet will quite happily submit themselves to the most distinguished of their number not only without complaint but with the devotion of cultists. Like all good democrats, they enjoy voting and yet are satisfied to be influenced by a due regard for those whose excellence they seek to emulate. They believe in the sovereignty of law—indeed, no humans so relish rules as children—and yet, being children, they esteem the rule-giver even above the rules. Nevertheless, and this is a vital point, children never exempt the nobles among them from the rules. Nor will the nobles seek such exemption. Such an eventuality would mean the dissolution of the children's polity as it would of any other society that wished to see itself as democratic.

Fein includes also sophisticated parodies of certain political opinions, as in the following send-up of one brand of conservatism:

> Just what should be democratic in a democracy? Or, more to the point, what institutions should *not* be

democratic? Taking democracy in its purest sense of "rule of the many," no one could seriously deny that scarcely anything in a democracy apart from the government (or, let us say, *portions* of the government) should be democratic. Thus, armies, engineering firms, universities, printing plants, farms, merchant ships, orchestras, and hospitals for the criminally insane are all run pretty much by the same principles under democracies as they are under monarchies or military juntas—albeit with certain easily imagined exceptions that may all be traced back to the nature of governmental authority.

Fein's parody of political philosophers becomes more obvious still in the metaphor-ridden parts of the book, such as in the following unintelligible python of a sentence, which reads as if badly translated from the German:

When one weighs up such will-of-the-wisps as a "general will" or a "vox populi" whose structural referents are occulted, blurred, and subject to such varieties of interpretation as to support endless and fruitless debate, whose collective and discursive qualities are such as to require a more or less interminable archaeological expedition across a rough landscape that is all the while undulating even as the demographers attempt to map out its strata, then one begins to feel that the sheer mathematics of a democratic society will, in effect, yield only an unreckonable stack of figures whose sum must amount to less than its discrete and irreducible surds.

Fein's argument reaches its bathetic crescendo in his concluding contrast of the "democratic aristocrat" with the "aristocratic democrat." The more he insists on his distinctions, the less of a difference there is. Distinctions without differences: this is Fein's way of poking fun at what frequently passes for political debate, what passed for it in his day as in our own.

> The democratic aristocrat is fully cognizant of his or her
> excellence and, while willing to subordinate that excel-
> lence to the good of the mediocre, he or she will not
> readily submit to the will of the mediocre. The aristo-
> cratic democrat, on the other hand, achieves excellence
> precisely through and not in spite of such a subordination,
> while raising the tone of the average by means of his or her
> articulation of its views and interests... etc., etc.

One can only guess how Fein would have chuckled when he read
the puffs from one ex-presidents and three senators his publisher
obtained for the dust jacket of *Aristocratic Democracy*. Fein is not,
as one says, "our universal genius." He is more like our universal
solvent.

Dissolution is the governing purpose of Fein's oeuvre, though he
accomplishes it as quietly as rain falling on limestone. In keeping
with his one-shot-only treatment of topics and genres, Sidney Fein,
so far as we know, composed only a single poem. While it has no
title, I believe we may confidently fill this blank with the word *poetry*
itself. Unlike the other works I have cited, this double decilinear is
not at all well known. It is to be found on page 37 of Volume IV,
no. 2 of a defunct literary journal called *Lethe*. Forgetfulness may
be the fate of all writing, and will surely be the fate of these verses.
But, before oblivion overtakes us all, here is the Collected Poetry
of Sidney Fein, that subtle underminer of forms, that unobtrusive
hoister with windy petards.

> People who write poems talk to themselves.
> The lyric ego is naked nerve.
> Do you read poems and never write them?
> You're rare as an unambitious actor.
> Is *this* the beat that launched a thousand ships?
> *This* rode in triumph through Persepolis?

Poetry is fine, of course—but poets?
I feel, cries the poet, or so you think.
All these lines contain just ten syllables.
People who write themselves talk to poems.
Raw nerves, sticky lips—hard people, poets.
Eloquence does not become a raw nerve.
People write themselves who talk to poems.
Some poets gargle behind sticky lips.
People who love paradoxes are hard.
People who talk to themselves aren't real poets.
Hard people suffer their paradoxes.
Can these lines be rearranged to make sense?
Has sense be rearranged to make these lines?
People who write talk poems to themselves.

How serious was Sidney Fein? Well, serious enough, I suppose. It is with his voice as he says it is with the voice of the people, a matter for archaeology. He too cut his teeth on the soft breast of traditions by which he was nourished and which he loves, yet found himself doomed to harm. Fein felt both the pain and glory of his critically classified uniqueness, that spiritual privilege and personal tragedy. In his last work, the commencement address he delivered on the occasion of receiving an honorary doctorate of humane letters and which he chose to call "We Who Are About To Die," a text made up of virtually nothing but allusions as if in penance for his originality, Fein himself offers up a summary of his life's work, its seriousness, its mockery, and above all its child's vision of the world:

It was the artist Cézanne who prayed "to see with the eye of the newlyborn." And so Cézanne did. And so he may teach all of us to see. It is the same newlyborn eye that forever sees the Emperor marching through the town in his imperial nakedness. Who knows whether we may not behold much the same scene should we, in the fullness of time, be transported to some other life where, newly-born all over again, we shall at last see without these dark, bespattered spectacles.

FEIN ON
MEANINGLESSNESS

"YOU won't forget to phone tonight, will you?" That was the last thing Jane said to me before I left. She stood bravely in the doorway, blocking and filling it, as pregnant as pregnant can be. I am ashamed to admit that all I could think was, "My God, what the hell happened to her ankles?"

My flight took off late and was stacked up for forty-five minutes at the other end so I landed just in time for rush hour and didn't arrive at Fred and Sylvie's until seven. Battered and ravenous, I badly needed alcohol and comfort food; I wanted to be petted, ministered to as if I was just back from turning the tide at Gettysburg.

Fred buzzed me through without even asking who it was. I could have been a burglar or a rapist, but I couldn't really imagine myself being a rapist or a burglar. It was hard enough imagining myself an assistant professor and I'd been one of those for four years.

Fred opened the door. "Hi. Bring a suit?"

Not only was this not a welcoming embrace, it wasn't even a question. Fred himself was sporting quite a fancy suit, a double-breasted job that hung in an unmistakably not-off-the-rack fashion.

"A blue one," I said.

He opened the door wide. "Blue'll do."

The Soffers' apartment had been redecorated since my last visit two years earlier when Jane and I had come for a weekend. Dark maroon and whites, half a dozen good antiques, a new beige rug and camel-backed sofa. Fred was prospering.

Shapely, petite, energetic, Sylvie Soffer burst from the bedroom in a knockout of a cocktail dress and spike heels. "Hi there, sweetie. About time," she said then turned her bare back on us. "One of you can hook me up." Sylvie seemed to have lost some weight since I saw her last and her hair looked a shade lighter, but it may only have been the black dress. Hating myself, I looked at her ankles.

Fred took my bag into the spare room, which featured a large computer with all the cybernetic trimmings, and tossed it on the sofa-bed that used to be in the living room. "Your bathroom's in there. Remember? Okay. Chop-chop, bub. Into that blue suit. We're running late. Don't want to miss the hors d'oeuvres."

On the way down in the elevator, Sylvie asked how Jane was doing with only a month left to go. "No problems, I hope?"

"Baby kicks like a Rockette."

"Never mind the baby," said Fred with a smirk. "How about the book. Books are harder to make, Sylvie."

"For *men*," she snapped and whacked him playfully with her sequined handbag. "Wham, bam, thank you, ma'am."

"Really, Jane's just fine," I said. "We got through morning sickness okay. Her biggest worry's whether she'll have striations above the bikini line. As to the book, I figure it'll take me maybe two, at most three days here, once I find what I hope to, and maybe a month or so to finish up. Then I sit back and wait for the verdict."

"*Pater et auctor.* Very nice. And then associate professor?"

"We'll see," I said superstitiously.

By now we were out of the elevator and into the lobby. While Fred went outside to flag down a taxi, Sylvie explained that we were off to the Harmons, one of whose investment funds Fred was managing. "Terrific couple, hugely philanthropic. And wait till you see the art! I mean the place is *encrusted*. You'll love it."

I wondered how Sylvie knew I'd love it.

Inside the cab, Fred gave more Harmon details. "Oh, they're more than just a meal ticket, though God knows they're certainly that. Delia and Well know pretty much everybody."

I was surprised to hear my old friend speak this way. When we were undergraduates together Fred and I had seen the world more or less in the same terms and were not reticent when it came to judging it harshly. Neither of us would have been capable of pronouncing a sentence like "The Harmons know practically every-body" in an admiring tone. But Fred had done as his father ordered, picked up a quick MBA and jumped feet first into finance, while I went on to grad school. "Jesus, do I envy you," he had said on graduation day. So Fred immersed himself in the real world, while I thought about reality. Maybe if you're deep enough into reality, you never need to think about what's real at all, but if you're not, you can't help doing so. Was the grass really greener over here? No doubt about it, Fred and Sylvie were climbing. I began to consider my hosts in a new light, by the tastefully indirect illumination of their new recessed light fixtures, so to speak. I recalled the best couplet from the doggerel I had written for their wedding toast.

> They grow prudent, they grow prudent.
> They shall dress less like some graduate student.

"I think there'll be a little surprise for you tonight," said Fred putting his finger beside his nose in a way that made me feel about five years old.

Sylvie giggled.

The brownstone was lit from the outside as though for an old-fashioned Hollywood premiere. Grauman's Chinese. As we drew within half a block of the place our cab joined a queue. The line curved so I could see magnificently arrayed couples alighting from taxis and limousines. I thought guiltily of Jane in our low-ceilinged one-bedroom apartment, the bookcases made of boards and cinder blocks, the stained wall-to-wall. Why hadn't we grown prudent?

Was it possible the baby would take after my mother-in-law? And what if I didn't get tenure?

Finish the Fein book, get tenure. Get tenure, buy a house. Buy a house, become a pillar of society. Finish the Fein book, or else.

I had worked hard for three summers revamping my doctoral dissertation, *Things Said in Jest: The Phenomenology of Self in the Texts of Sidney Fein*. I thought I had a deal with a university press. In fact, I believed I was about finished when my editor suddenly insisted on more than the three hundred pages I had submitted. It wasn't enough to plumb the chasms of the *Diptych on Terrestrial Representation*, catalogue the intricacies and unexpectedly revolutionary implications of Feinian Classification, anatomize the frisky, yet penetrating psychological analyses of *Want, Desire, and Need*, trace the peregrinations of Fein's occasional essays, and wind up by marching boldly through the partisan minefield of Fein's last book, *Aristocratic Democracy*. The editor was blunt about the shortcomings of my revision and what he wanted to make the book longer as well as better.

> Let's try for something a little more than just dumping the excess documentary apparatus and gouging out the review of the critical literature. Sure, it's obligatory in a thesis but lethal in a real book. Plus, you're a few bricks shy of a load. You've got to give us at least one chapter on the unpublished work, or I'm afraid it's no deal. I'm sure you know word is Fein was working on some interesting stuff at the end. For Heaven's sake give us at least one piece of the Feinian field that's not forever somebody else's. Understand?

So I badly needed to get into Fein's papers. As my editor was perfectly well aware, these papers had been deposited two months earlier in the library of Columbia University where Fein had been a student. I got right on the phone to the Special Collections folks. Yes, they had the Fein papers. There was even a preliminary catalogue. I called Fred. New York hotels cost an arm, a leg, another arm. Sure, I could stay. Long as I needed. Only too glad. Would Jane be coming too?

"Fred here's my favorite Fred since Fred Astaire," said Delia Harmon, taking my friend by the arm.

"You mean since Flintstone," quipped Wellington Harmon, slowly enfolding Sylvie in the crook of his left arm while putting out his right hand into which my own vanished. Wellington Harmon was as big as his name.

Fred had already done the introductions.

"I loved my Ancient Philosophy course at Bennington," said Delia. "The professor was so, you know, brilliant."

I didn't know what to say to this. Fred saved me with a well-worn one-liner whose impertinence nobody noticed.

"Well, Delia, you know what they say. No idea so stupid that some Greek philosopher didn't believe it."

Then it was Sylvie's turn to tease me. "*You* don't believe stupid ideas, do you?"

I shrugged. "I'm not Greek."

Everyone laughed and I began to feel a little better.

I felt better still when Fred took me over to the bar and I got a dram of Laphroaig in me. There was a short ton of shrimp just a hoe's-length away.

Fred pointed to the walls. "So what do you think of their collection?" he asked as if he owned it.

"Well, there's certainly a lot of it."

"Too much, you think? Too cluttered?"

"Not particularly. All they need is six or seven more walls."

"Wouldn't that cut down the size of the rooms?"

"Well then maybe a Quonset hut out back, or a domed stadium."

Actually, it was hard to see the walls at all. Paintings and queer installations, fanciful mobiles and metallic statues leapt at you from every direction. In between, beneath, around, and in front of them the youthful rich wore their money as vaingloriously as Renaissance merchants, mingling, looking over each other's shoulders. My blue suit made a poor showing.

"All by living artists, you know. That's a point of honor for Well and Delia, to collect only living artists. More of a gamble, invest-ment-wise, you see. More of a challenge to one's discernment."

"What if one of them dies?"

"They sell. Nine times out of ten for a tidy profit. Mortality's awfully good for prices, artwise."

Fred asked so I told him more about the Fein book. Though I'd have preferred not to, one thing led to the other and I began to whine about tenure, the idée fixe of my kind, but he already knew all about that and wasn't interested.

"Tell me about Jane."

I was embarrassed that he had to ask. Fred had dated Jane before I did and I suppose that might still be a sore point. That was why I felt relieved when Jane said she didn't feel up to making the trip.

"She's doing fine. Doctor says everything's ship-shape."

"The amnio?"

"Clean as a whistle. No Elephant Man."

"You weren't worried about leaving her then, I mean in the last month?"

"Nope. Doctor said it'll be a good three weeks yet."

"Really? Pick a name for the little schmitzik yet?"

I made a face. "Jane wants to call him Bernard after her grandfa-ther but I keep imagining this little kid being called Bernie. I mean, *Bernie*? Bernie's an old guy who smells like cigars."

"So what's *your* choice? Søren, Immanuel—Sidney, Junior?"

"I was always partial to Alexander, actually. Or maybe something Asian."

"Asiatic? I like that. Mao. Sukarno. You know, if I could ever talk Sylvie into giving up her job and her figure I'd like to have about half-a-dozen ankle-biters."

"You'd better get started then. Tick tock."

"Not with a guest in the house, pal."

"I'm a heavy sleeper."

Fred chuckled then turned around and began ticking off celebrities for me. I'd only heard of about half of them.

"Now, you see that woman over there?"

"Which?"

"The long luscious one with the red hair and the incredible heinie, there on the left of the psychedelic garbage can."

The woman was wearing an off-the-shoulder emerald green dress, a tight one.

"Yes?"

"Well, bud, that's Maya Nunfi Fein."

"Maya *Fein*? You mean the daughter?"

"Told you I had a surprise for you. Admit it. If I'd let you, you'd have wanted to stay home, right? Sylvie knows her from work. Want me to introduce you? Maybe you could get an interview on the spot."

I felt panicky not only because this woman happened to be Sidney Fein's only child but because she was so redheaded, so florid, so lovely. I felt the same catatonia I did back in dancing class when we were ordered to ask the girls to do the box step. I'd wanted to ask Marjorie Krasker—who didn't?—but I couldn't get my knees to bend. Beauty doesn't always attract. Just as often it's frightening and makes you feel small, ugly, inadequate. Maya's was the sort of beauty that, the spectacular curves notwithstanding, is not at all soft, the type that makes you look ruefully at your fingernails.

"Don't really feel up to it," I admitted.

Fred smiled indulgently. "Suit yourself. You know, if you'll excuse my saying so—"

Cowardice made me irritable. "That's a phrase I can't stand. *If you'll excuse my saying so.*"

"Really?"

"Always makes me think of a pitcher winding up for a bean ball."

Fred chuckled. "I was only going to remark on how married you are. I mean that as a compliment."

We got back from the party after midnight, too late to phone Jane. I read myself to sleep with a musty copy of *Remains of the Page*, the book I'd been reading on the plane, a bizarre, anonymous novella I'd found in a corner of a used book shop.[18]

In the morning I took the subway uptown. I had phoned the library for an appointment and they couldn't have been sweeter. "The Fein papers? No problem, Professor. When can we look forward to seeing you?"

The man at the desk directed me to the office of Ms. Gloor, a pleasant middle-aged woman with a vague, fixed smile, impossible to tell what was prompting it. She rose from her desk as soon as I tapped on her open door. I introduced myself. "Oh, yes," she said, "we're all ready for you." She took me to a tiny windowless room with nothing in it but a wooden table and three plastic chairs. "You won't be disturbed here. Now just settle in and I'll have one of the work-studies bring the papers." She paused by the door and added, "Only two boxes," as though it were her fault there weren't more.

---

18. This obscure novella was written by a member of the Typewriter Underground. See "First Notes on the rise of the Typewriter Underground," Felt Collection, New York City.

"Oh, excuse me. I'm sorry but I'll need a copy of the catalogue too."

"Of course. Don't worry. I'll make sure it's right on top."

The catalogue was lightly annotated, only a single page divided into two columns headed *Box One, Box Two*. The first cardboard file contained thirty or forty pounds of correspondence and various rough drafts, interesting no doubt, but not suited to my purpose. The second file, by far the lighter of the two, was the one I was interested in because the catalogue claimed it held, along with dozens of false starts and fragments, the manuscript of an uncompleted book, most probably the one Fein was supposed to have been working on when he died. The title the catalogue assigned the manuscript was intriguing, like all of Fein's titles. *The Possibilities of Meaninglessness.* Forty-two holograph pages.

Just the thing to make them break out the champagne at the Press. And it looked like I was going to get first crack at it. The only trouble was that the forty-two holograph pages weren't in the box. Puzzled, I headed back to Ms. Gloor's office.

"Oh, that's right. I'm terribly sorry. I should have mentioned it," she explained, looking more apologetic than ever. "You see, the catalogue's complete but the collection isn't. We prepared the list but the lawyer supplied the boxes. Sorry. I'm not putting this very well. What I meant to say is that there are certain items the executrix chose not to hand over to the Library."

"But what's missing is the very thing I want," I whined.

The good woman offered up her unfocused smile. "Oh dear." I could see how she yearned to be helpful. Her voice rose at the end as if imploring me to succeed. "Perhaps you could contact the lawyer, or maybe go straight to the executrix?"

I knew, but I asked anyway. "And the executrix is—?"

"That would be Fein's daughter."

I found a pay phone outside the library and called Sylvie at Lincoln Center, where she manages interns and volunteers. She gave me Maya Fein's number and a warning.

"Look, Maya's a very unusual woman. Impulsive, probing, sort of unpredictable. If you want something from her, I think you'd better be prepared for her to make it a personal matter."

"A *personal* matter?"

"Maybe I'm wrong."

"Sylvie, have you ever talked to her about her father?"

"No, I can't remember his ever coming up. I mean we sent a sympathy card, of course—she's a big donor—but that's about it. She's what people call a piece of work."

"And a redhead, huh?"

"Yep. A redhead."

Maya Fein's line was busy from noon to quarter past one. I dialed the operator. "The receiver's off the hook, sir." I kept at it. I phoned about a dozen times from a little student restaurant where I had the sort of lunch I'm used to. Then, at last, I got an answer.

"What?" The voice was rushed, prickly.

"Ms. Fein?"

"Who else?"

With over an hour to think about what I was going to say I ended up saying everything at once.

She sounded suspicious. "Hey, you're not by any chance the jerk who wrote that article in *San Jose Studies*, are you? The one about whether my father was *serious* or not?"

"No." I knew the article and had actually thought it daring, perceptive, and, in an odd way, sympathetic to Fein. I had cited it in my book.

There was some noise in the background. It sounded like banging and there was a muffled voice.

"Look," she said, "come over here right away and we'll talk about it. Okay?"

"Fine," I said.

"What?"

I laughed. "I said fine, Ms. Fein."

The banging grew louder and her voice became suddenly tense.

"*Right* away," she insisted and gave me the address. "Got that? And take a cab."

"Okay."

Maya Nunfi Fein lived in a grand old building on the upper East Side. I thought I knew a lot about her father, but I had never asked myself whether he was rich or not. Philosophers and scholars require secure incomes, but affluence is rare. It was only later that I learned about the family trust generated by the ladies garment business. Maya Fein was an heiress in every sense. A big donor.

I nodded at the doorman and pushed the button under "1905, M. N. Fein." The speaker crackled. "Hurry!" I heard, then the buzzer went off. I took the elevator to the nineteenth floor. Feeling a little jumpy, I tried to concentrate on Jane and the baby and the book rather than why Maya Fein was in such a hurry to see me.

Even before the elevator door opened I could hear his baritone. "You fucking bitch I'll…" He was battering at the door, using the flat of his hand to maximize volume.

I stuck one foot out of the elevator and stopped, perplexed. Maya Fein knew I was on the way up. She wanted me there; she had said to hurry. This was apparently a damsel-in-distress situation, and not just any damsel but the daughter of Sidney Fein. My duty, as both man and tenure candidate, was clear. On the other hand, why hadn't she called the police? This fellow was clearly out of control, hopped up. He was even wearing a black leather jacket.

I've never been one of those "sticks and stones" types. Though I take a liberal view of speech-acts, to me violent language is every bit as shocking as violent action and I respond to both with a powerful urge to turn tail.

I hesitated but then matters were taken more or less out of my hands.

He spotted me spotting him.

"Hey, dickhead. What're *you* looking at?"

I said something that still astonishes me. I don't know whether it was inspiration or some childish idea that the elevator door could be safely shut in half a second. The thing I said was, "I'm looking at an asshole."

He was down the hall in what seemed three bounds.

I released the door and fell back into the elevator but I had forgotten the polite timing mechanism. The door stayed open. I looked around. A moment before he would have been on me I ripped the little fire extinguisher out of its glass case. My fingers found the release all by themselves, the little dears, and as his face came around the edge of the elevator the extinguisher blew some sort of foam into it with a noise like a protracted belch.

His swearing rose several decibels as he fell sideways, knees up against his chest, hands fumbling at his face. He announced several plans for my immediate future.

In the middle of all this, Maya Fein appeared on the scene, red hair down and peignoir open over a nightgown the color of honey.

"Here," she said to me. "Let's throw the bastard in."

She meant into the elevator.

Still clutching my weapon, I worked my way gingerly around the man, who was rolling this way and that, rubbing his eyes, swearing. Maya and I pushed him into the elevator. "There," she said with a sigh, nonchalantly pushing the down button, dusting off her hands.

I stood there, astonished and heaving.

"You're here about my father's papers, right?"

I nodded, still trying to catch my breath. "Won't he just come back?"

Maya smiled. "I certainly *hope* so. But never mind about *him*. Come inside and we'll talk. Cup of coffee? You're not one of those *decaf* people, by any chance?"

Maya Fein's apartment was spacious and elegant, like the pictures in the brochures for five-star hotels.

As we walked through the door, she said, "Absence lessens ordinary passions and augments great ones, just as the wind blows out a candle but makes a fire blaze."

"Excuse me?"

"La Rochefoucauld. You married?"

Without stopping for an answer, she headed straight into the kitchen so that I had to call after her. "Yes."

"Well then, which is it with you—candle or blaze? With that guy, it's a goddamned conflagration."

It occurred to me that Sylvie Soffer knew whereof she spoke.

Maya came back with two mugs of fragrant coffee. "Excuse the way I look," she said. "I was just getting out of bed when that lunatic turned up. A girl doesn't feel comfortable getting dressed when somebody's trying to bash in her door. You don't mind, do you?"

"Mind?"

She pointed down her body all the way to her bare feet.

"No, not at all."

And, to tell the truth, I didn't.

"What'll you do if he, you know, comes back?"

"Sufficient unto the day is the evil thereof."

"Don't you think it might be prudent to—"

"Prudence is what I pay lawyers to have for me," she said in the offhand way the rich refer to being rich. "So, tell me now, what do you want from me?"

"I'm a scholar, a student of your father's work."

"He'd have been delighted to meet you. You know, when I was little my father was all the time locking himself off in his study to write. I resented it. I once asked him who he was writing to and he said—" here she made her voice go low— "he said, 'I hope for the graduate students of the next century.' No offense, but you look a little old for a graduate student and, unless I slept even later than usual, it's still this century."

"No, I'm a professor. But I did do my doctoral dissertation on your father."

"No shit?"

"And now I'm turning it into a book, a full-scale study of his work."

She smirked. "You *like* the idea of writing a book about someone else's books?"

I shrugged.

Maya Fein stalked across the oriental carpet and plumped down in a velvet wingchair. "Tell me. What's your wife like?"

I might have said many things about Jane but all that came out was, "She's pregnant."

"Pregnant?" Her eyes grew wide with interest. "Was it *planned*?"

"Yes. We thought—"

"Call me old-fashioned, but I've always believed there's something a little cold-blooded about planned parenthood. I mean the phrase *is* decidedly clinical. It sounds like an antiseptic oxymoron. Personally, I've always felt accidental."

She did look a bit like an accident waiting to happen. But I felt it would be a spectacular smash-up and, besides, the coffee tasted wonderful. It had been two years since I had drunk such strong coffee. I knew I'd pay for it later.

"Do you really think life ought to be planned out, that it *can* be? Or was that your wife's idea?"

"Well," I said, "of *course* people make plans."

She shook her head. "Not *people*. You. Has *your* life been planned out? Did you plan to marry your wife and write about my father? I'll bet you didn't plan on throwing Brian into an elevator this afternoon."

"Well, naturally life's full of chance events. I mean the margin of choice is limited by a number of factors, but within those parameters—"

She scoffed. "Pardon me, but do you always talk like that?"

What could I say?

She put down her mug and got to her feet. "Look, pardon me for a couple of minutes. What with Brian showing up at the crack of noon and all, I haven't even been to the bathroom yet."

I'm pretty sure I didn't actually blush.

"My father—that's Sidney Fein to you—used to call it the only reliably contemplative part of a person's day."

"And what are you going to contemplate?" I dared to ask.

She snickered pertly. "*You*, of course." She looked pleased with herself. "The planned parent within premeditated parameters."

I glanced around the room which, now that I really looked at it, did not strike me as the room of a young single woman. Antique oriental. Heavy mahogany furniture. A wall of books, probably her father's. I pulled out a hardbound copy of *The Magic Mountain* and checked the flyleaf. "To My Daughter on Her 16th Birthday. May you learn at least as much as Hans and make better use of it. *Facilis descensus Averni*. With love from Dad." More portentous than warm-hearted. The descent of Avernus is easy. It made me wonder what it might have been like to have Sidney Fein for a father—or Maya Fein for a daughter.

I heard the flush and quickly resumed my perch on the sofa.

She came back in brushing her hair but still barefoot, still showing off those ankles.

"There," she said, "that's much better. Now, tell me what you intend to say about my father."

I laughed. "Well, that's rather a big question. Naturally, I'm profoundly interested in his work, the variety of forms in which he wrote, his insights into so many areas of life and thought. I want my book to be a comprehensive study. A full-scale appreciation."

"A twenty-one-gun salute, eh? Then you think it makes sense, my father's work?"

"It does to a lot of people; it certainly does to me."

She laughed the way grownups laugh when a child lisps out something particularly foolish.

"Well, you'd *have* to say that, wouldn't you? I mean, if I've got it right, my father's work is your gravy train. You're what they call a *Feinian*, aren't you?"

I drew myself up. "Maybe we could talk about some of the papers you kept back from the library."

"You want to know *why* I kept them back?"

"Sentimental attachment?"

"That's one way of putting it, I suppose. Tell me, does your wife read my father's books too?"

"No, Jane isn't interested in philosophy."

"Good for her. My father used to say it wasn't a fit subject for women."

"Really? Why?"

"Because women embody whatever meaning life has, so they don't need to think about it."

Then why did he want you to learn as much as Hans Castorp, I would have liked to ask, but then I realized she was just teasing me. I had never come across any restrictive view of women in Fein's work.

Then came three heavy but not necessarily homicidal knocks at the door.

Maya fetched a sigh. "That'll be Brian again. Excuse me." She got up, then stopped. "It might be a good idea for you to go into the bedroom. Just in case."

"You're going to let him in?"

She flashed a wicked smile. "Maybe."

I did go into the bedroom. It was heavily draped and the drapes were dark red so that the room seemed sunk into a placental sea. The bed was disheveled and big. The sheets were pale pink. I could only make out their voices, not their words. No shouting, at least. A few minutes later, Maya came into the bedroom.

"I decided to send him away," she said and sat down on the bed. "Come here." She patted the pink sheets, as you might for a cocker spaniel.

"I don't think—"

"You know, I saw you at the party last night. The Harmons'. You were checking me out. Why? Because I'm Fein's daughter or for some other reason?"

"Maybe we could get back to—"

"Imagine what it would be like. All of a sudden like this. After all, I *am* Fein's daughter. Once-in-a-lifetime opportunity. A chance event, totally unplanned, exceeding normal parameters. It would be almost like merging with your subject, in a sense, wouldn't it?"

"What—"

She reached out and grabbed my hand. "Anyway, it's the best way to get what you want. And you *did* save me from an abusive boyfriend, didn't you? So, you're my St. George, my very own Perseus. I mean, it's the least I can do."

"I don't—"

"Oh, such qualms!" She did something with one hand and the peignoir fell behind her. Then, in an unforgettable, ineffable motion, she slipped the honey-colored nightgown over her head. All that red hair fell over her face.

I allowed myself to be gently pulled down beside her.

She put her lips to my ear, kissed it, whispered, "You want that last book, the one he was just starting, don't you?"

"That's the one," I confessed.

"It's necessary to choose between loving women and understanding them. Chamfort. So which is it going to be, Professor?"

With the last of my resistance melting, I objected, "Without any understanding, love's just meaningless."

"Bingo!" she exclaimed, throwing her arms around my neck. "Now, let's see how many unplanned orgasms you can manage."

When I woke up, Maya was standing by the bed fully dressed and holding a manila envelope.

"Hi there, Professor."

"Umm?"

"I've been out, sleepyhead."

I yawned. "Out?"

"Just to the corner copy shop."

"Copy shop?"

She waved the folder in front of me. "Forty-two pages of precious paternal holograph. The master's very own handwriting. It's what you wanted, isn't it? All right, then. Time to get up and go. Time to fulfill that plan of yours."

Maya Fein handed over the envelope then more or less threw me out.

Dinner was a trial but I evaded Fred and Sylvie's questions and went to bed early. I was too upset even to look at Fein's manuscript that night, though, between his daughter, the caffeine, and my troubled mind, it was a sleepless one.

I flew home the next morning. I read the manuscript on the plane, which was fitting because in a plane you really aren't anywhere at all. The disorienting sensation of being outside time and place didn't vanish when I landed. I was exhausted and slouched back to my low ceilings and enceinte, ankleless wife.

I'm still deciding what I'm going to do with the manuscript, whether or not to include an account of it in my book, what to say of it if I do.

How serious *was* Sidney Fein? "Well," concludes the author of the article of that title, the one that may or may not have affronted his daughter, "serious enough."

Here, then, is a sampling of Fein's final ruminations that concern the meaning of meaning, the meaning of no-meaning, to secure which may have cost me my own confidence in the meaning of my life.

FROM THE POSSIBILITIES OF MEANINGLESSNESS
unfinished manuscript by Sidney Fein

How does the artist bear himself with relation to the meaning of his or her material? Or, to put it a little differently, how does an artist choose a subject? I would propose that the successful artist can only adopt material that is already his or hers in the sense of being conformable with that particular artist's characteristic vision, form, and style. The subject of *War and Peace* is precisely Tolstoyan, as that of *Pride and Prejudice* is Austenian and *The Trial* Kafkaesque. The greater the artist, the truer this principle will be. The inchoate, the messy and botched can be traced to some incommensurability between artist and subject. Even a gifted artist will appear bathetic when he is working on the wrong subject. After *The Great Gatsby*, Fitzgerald tried to write a medieval romance with a hero modeled on Hemingway. Nathanael West's crypto-Joycean *The Dream Life of Balso Snell* is a failure, but two years later he discovered the Susan Chester letters that led him to write the distinctively Westian *Miss Lonelyhearts*. In art, the eponymous adjective defines the work even as the work does the adjective. When Thomas Mann gets his hands around the neck of a proper subject—a child prodigy, for example, or a self-divided artist—he wrings it until it is unmistakably Mann-like. So, too, for Chekhov and his world-weary doctors, or Salinger and spiritually precocious toddlers.

There is no dearth of subjects in the world. All the same, virtually all artists experience terrible periods when they feel there is no vein for them to mine, when the white canvas or blank sheet of paper swells up like Moby Dick before an un-harpooned Ahab. Out of concern, their friends may offer subject after subject, hand them plots, drive them to picturesque prospects. This is useless since the true artist has to work from the inside out. Anything that is not his own is meaningless to him. She must find her proper food and, if she does not, suffer from indigestion. Given all this, we may suppose that it is only partially the case that artists select their subjects; it is no less true that their subjects choose them.

The choice of the artist by a subject has been very little analyzed because people suppose there is nothing analyzable about it. Surely, they say, inspiration is indefinable. We should be content to say that Picasso was "inspired" by the bombing of Guernica or that the death of Manon Gropius compelled Berg to write his *Violin*

Concerto. But I suppose there must be a movement anterior even to such inspiration: first a Picasso must *want to* paint; a Berg must *need* to compose.

To say that art's first principle should be the desire of the artist to be an artist threatens to involve us in an infinite regression. Nevertheless, if we insist on looking for the irreducible meaning of a work of art, I think we will find it in the inner compulsion of the artist to *make*, all other motives being accidental, forced, ancillary to a desire that may be anything from devoutly spiritual to childishly vain or crudely careerist.

Art, then, is what the artist produces when he or she finds the right material out of which to fashion meaning. Without that material, with nothing but *the urge to make*, the artist is in despair, lost on a featureless plain, clogged with coagulated yearning. Without *his or her* subject, the world, overflowing with subjects, will feel meaningless.

• • •

After a couple world wars, meaning can no longer be convincingly grounded as either transcendental or eternal. Radical skepticism and solipsism are two responses to conditions in the second half of the twentieth century. The radical skeptic suspends judgment indefinitely and thus his condition turns Eleatic. The skeptic is a sort of fetishist who rejects fetishes. The solipsist accords exclusive deference to the self and its impressions and so becomes terminally hermetic. Nevertheless, this exaggerated respect for the self cannot be justified, even in the eyes of the solipsist. It is no better than a circular argument. Both types look at "meaning" from the outside, so to speak, and find it a mirage. I would prefer to submit the concept of meaning to an analysis from within. I do so on the hypothesis that there simply is not so much as a yard of soil outside on which to stand. If there were such an "outside," Archimedes could have moved the earth. But even then, where would he have moved it *to*?

• • •

Let me be frank. Nobody can do without meaning, not even those ferocious philosophers who undertake the most corrosive deconstructions. Even they understand the meaning of a red light, a handshake, the offer in a woman's eyes, the blue jeans on their students, the words of Nietzsche's *Genealogy of Morals*, the significance of a bad review. *This* means *that*, they will have to admit. But in stating that A means B they merely define A in terms of B. A and B are clear, while *to mean*, the essential relation, escapes them and so they are reduced to claiming that the relation is simply one of equivalence. But our sense of what it means *to mean* is precisely that the relation should *not* be one of equivalence. One dime is equivalent to another dime, but it does not *mean* that dime. No system is airtight. Some gas always escapes.

• • •

Take the case of a man hiking through the woods. He comes on a stream and in this stream he finds a stone shaped precisely like the Venus de Milo. Will he say that his find is meaningless? Form suggests significance, or at least the perception of form demands that we search for a meaning. Formlessness is just what we dismiss. Noise is formless, music formed. We *hear* noise while to music we *listen*. Form makes us pay attention. But is it not fair to say that it is the quality of our attention that makes all the difference? For example, I can imagine an acousticist for whom noise is music because he understands its form, out of what elements it is constructed. He does not merely hear; rather, he *listens* and so to him the noise has meaning. In effect, the noise is music in so far as music is meaningful noise, as in the Biblical phrase "make a joyful noise unto the Lord." Geologists see the form in rocks, meteorologists in clouds. Meaning is often the consequence of expertise, the highest type of attentiveness. That expertise which is generally shared constitutes a common culture—in language, literary references, street signs, in-jokes, hit songs, table manners, etc. But we all also possess individual expertises, thus the existence of private meanings, images and dreams we personally find meaningful but whose meaning we cannot convey to others. By definition, what is *privately* meaningful must be *generally* meaningless. Private meaning accomplishes nothing for the group, which can only resent or reject it. However, if somebody's private meaning promises to make life easier or longer, the group bows before it. Why else would the ignorant respect scientists, scorn artists, and sleep in on the Sabbath?

·   ·   ·

A critic remarks of a certain poet that "he finds meaning in everything." This is deemed a special virtue, but the verb is telling. Common parlance has it that one discovers meaning more or less as Columbus did the New World, by chance. And this may be true, so far as it goes. Only one change is needed, that the New World should exist *because* Columbus found it, and found it only by dint of sailing blindly into the Western sea, the "limitless inane." For centuries we have been beguiled by the Platonic paradigms, those invisible perfections, and by the Platonic opinion that all knowledge is recollection. But now the pendulum swings. The solidity of reality evaporates under our microscopes, dissolves in our cloud chambers, melts under the totality of our critique. Plato still triumphs, of course, but in how different a way! Modern physics is a thin tissue of pure ideas.

·   ·   ·

Like a man who observes a woman at a party, like a woman who knows she is being observed, the observer and the observed cannot escape their effects on one another. Therefore, meaning, like breathing, is two things, not one.

·   ·   ·

Meaning is inseparable from context. If a man should say to me,

"I went outside and turned the corner around," I would have a hard time making out his meaning. However, if I were aware that the gentleman happened to be German I might grasp his point quite easily. A grander example. The Gospels go to Greece and Jesus becomes the Logos, to Denmark and he becomes the chief of a warrior band, to the Ivory Coast and he becomes a shaman. Is it only the flexible genius of Christianity that is at work in these transformations? No, I reckon there is more. The context must already be there to allow such meanings, including the universal questions to which Christianity offers itself as an answer.

Most spiritual questions are primitive and often enough so are the answers. Orthodoxy is constructed of old answers to old questions. An entirely new question, on the other hand, and an utterly unprecedented answer will necessarily appear meaningless. *Credo quia absurdum* said the pre-orthodox Tertullian to his shocked, pagan friends. Even today, nearly a century since the early works of Stravinsky and Picasso came into the world, much of the general population regards the one as incomprehensible cacophony and the other as childish daubing. All that is lacking is familiarity. Perhaps meaning is domesticated meaninglessness.

• • •

Objective meaning is certainly an illusion, though, as a quality, objectivity is routinely ascribed to facts. Nevertheless, let us agree for the sake of argument that facts are indeed objectively true—that is, not subject to disagreement, provable. However, while facts may be objective, no fact is meaningful. A bunch of fellows got together in a building in Philadelphia during the summer of 1776. A fact, but the meaning of that fact is not a fact in the sense that it too is objective; that is, not subject to disagreement, or provable. Kierkegaard was right to say that truth is subjective. Meaningful truth is. We may put the matter this way: what is objective is not meaningful and what is meaningful is not objective. Meaning emerges against a background of meaninglessness as a crow does against a milky sky.

What then is meaninglessness? Meaninglessness is the blank paper on which I am writing these ruminations—my last, if my frail heart is prophetic.

• • •

Meaning comes into the world with consciousness, just as silt comes into the sea through rivers; indeed, the role and consequence of consciousness is precisely the muddying of waters through the construction of meanings. Consciousness is unclean and, according to Genesis, came into the world with two siblings, sin and death.

For consciousness to believe the proposition "Everything is meaningless" is no more possible than for a locomotive to renounce its tracks. Nevertheless, we do have an idea of meaninglessness, as we do of train wrecks. Whenever I have this idea it is *ipso facto* a bad day. But where could the conception of meaninglessness come from except my desire that it *not* be so? Meaninglessness is like an empty pitcher we hasten to fill, if only with our deep anxiety to fill up vacancy and annihilate annihilation. It is against this conception of meaninglessness that we butt our busy heads. You might even say that, in this sense, our heads were made for butting.

In other words, meaninglessness becomes a profoundly meaningful idea as soon as we ask whether it has a *significance*. No one is exempt from anguish, certainly not the faithful. In fact, nobody can be completely human without at least the *threat* of experiencing this sensation of meaninglessness, however it may be beyond one's power to bear.

• • •

I say, then, that meaninglessness is itself no threat to our humanity but rather its guarantor; it may be as much of the ground of being as we shall ever discover. What really threatens our humanity is not the apprehension of meaninglessness but indifference to it. This is a religious idea. To conclude, then, consider the following tale which is told of Rabbi Menachem Mendel of Kotzk:

A Hasid came to the rabbi. "Rabbi," he complained, "I keep brooding and brooding and don't seem to be able to stop."

"What do you brood about?" asked the rabbi.

"I keep brooding about whether there really is a judgment and a judge."

"What does it matter to you!"

"Rabbi! If there is no judgment and no judge, then what does all creation mean?"

"What does that matter to you!"

"Rabbi! If there is no judgment and no judge, then what do the words of the Torah mean!"

"What does that matter to you?"

"Rabbi! 'What does it matter to *me*?' What does the rabbi think? What *else* could matter to me!"

"Well, if it matters to you as much as all that," said the rabbi of Kotzk, "then you are a good Jew after all."